THE TAROT READER

Also available by Finley Turner

The Engagement Party

THE TAROT READER

A NOVEL

FINLEY TURNER

NEW YORK

Books should be disposed of and recycled according to local requirements. All paper materials used are FSC compliant.

This is a work of fiction. All of the names, characters, organizations, places and events portrayed in this novel are either products of the author's imagination or are used fictitiously. Any resemblance to real or actual events, locales, or persons, living or dead, is entirely coincidental.

Published in the United States by Crooked Lane Books, an imprint of The Quick Brown Fox & Company LLC.

Crooked Lane Books and its logo are trademarks of The Quick Brown Fox & Company LLC.

Library of Congress Catalog-in-Publication data available upon request.

ISBN (hardcover): 979-8-89242-307-6
ISBN (paperback): 979-8-89242-315-1
ISBN (ebook): 979-8-89242-308-3

Cover design by Danna Steele

Printed in the United States.

www.crookedlanebooks.com

Crooked Lane Books
34 West 27th St., 10th Floor
New York, NY 10001

First Edition: October 2025

The authorized representative in the EU for product safety and compliance is eucomply OÜPärnu mnt 139b-14, 11317 Tallinn, Estonia, hello@eucompliancepartner.com, +33757690241

10 9 8 7 6 5 4 3 2 1

To Roman and Ellie

CHAPTER 1

Jade

WITH THE LIGHTS dimmed in the room, all I could see was the glimmer of each sitter's eyes as they sat eagerly at the table. There was a shimmer there—hope, mostly, but also fear.

We sat in a circle, palms pressed firmly into the glossy wood, waiting.

"Beloved spirits, we seek your guidance," I said. "We ask that you commune with us and move among us."

Wind whipped into the windows, causing the thick, old glass to creak against the windowpanes. The sitters—what we called those who sat with us for readings and séances—tensed in their seats. Some shifted their shoulders back, eager and confident, while others curled them inward, as if it could protect them from forces they couldn't see.

The wind snapped against the windows again. "Ah, someone has joined us," I said softly. "Welcome."

The older woman directly across from me whimpered, and the other sitters glanced at her but quickly returned their focus to their hands on the table.

I tilted my head back, speaking into the air above the table. "If you are with us, please give us a sign to indicate your willingness to communicate."

We sat in silence, waiting for a signal. After a moment, the man to my left sighed and shifted in his seat.

"Give us a sign," I urged again, trying to keep the frustration out of my voice.

The sitters flinched at a thump behind the wall, and the woman who had whimpered earlier silently cried.

I raised my hands, hovering them higher above the table. "This space is protected, and we command that if you have ill intentions, you must leave this instant."

Wind lashed against the window once more, and although it remained closed, a cold breeze curled through the room. I shivered, anticipating what was to come. Another thump, harder now, and a painting rattled against the wall and came loose. Its thick frame smashed into the floor, the impact vibrating against our feet, yet the glass remained unbroken.

With a low voice I said, "We recognize your presence. Who do you wish to speak to?"

As I'd instructed each sitter before the séance, they lifted their palms off the table, raising them a few inches to the ceiling. I said their names one by one as their hands hovered.

"Stacey Carter," I said. Her hands trembled as she raised them. There was only silence, and after a few moments, I motioned for her to lower her hands.

"Dylan Carter." He raised his palms with confidence. His wedding band cut into the thick flesh of his ring finger, the gold gleaming against the candlelight.

A knock against the wall behind me made us all jump, followed by scratching, like fingernails burrowing into the walls, trying to get in. The timing of it didn't make sense, and my heartbeat quickened.

"Buddy?" Dylan whimpered, and his wife gripped his hand. They were desperate to make contact with the spirit of their teenage son, who had passed in a car accident one year prior. Dylan raised his hands off the table again, slipping his right hand out from his wife's despite her tight grasp on it.

I gulped, my cheeks flushed. "If you wish to commune with Dylan Carter, please make the same noise." My voice was commanding and confident, but my throat tightened with uneasiness. Something was wrong.

About twenty seconds passed, only our breath and the patter of rain on the window audible in the dark room. The muscles in my throat loosened, relief coming over me. "I'm sorry, Dylan. The spirits did not react to your call." I motioned for him to lower his hands.

One tear trickled down his cheek and into his beard. He wiped it away before resting his hands on the table.

"Catherine Belaforte," I said. She raised her palms, pushing through hesitation made clear by her rapid breathing. She closed her eyes. I could tell she truly believed, more so than the others.

A floorboard creaked at the doorway, followed by silence. The sitters' eyes darted around the room, checking to see there was no one there. Seconds later it creaked again, closer to the table that sat in the middle of the dark room. The tension in the room built. Something was coming.

"Catherine Belaforte," I said again, louder this time. Immediately, the floorboard creaked once more, right behind Catherine's seat.

She gasped at the noise near her, her eyes searching the dim room for the source. Catherine was an older woman, made older in appearance by the grief of her father's recent death. As she searched the darkness, the wrinkles around her narrowed eyes deepened.

"Do you wish to speak to Catherine?" I said into the darkness. The candle flickered as another breeze disrupted the room's stillness.

Wind gusted again outside. The curtains, which were partially open, snapped themselves back, exposing the brutality of the storm outside. The sitters' heads whipped to the window, their chairs creaking as they twisted to look.

Lightning struck, outlining the shape of a human figure. But there was something deeply irregular about it. The torso was too lanky, the rib cage too narrow. The figure was utterly still in the brief flash of the lightning. Dylan Carter's chair smacked against the floor as he jumped to his feet.

"Did you see that?" His voice was half accusatory, half excited. Mumbles of nervous affirmation bubbled around the room.

"Yes," I confirmed. "It's a strong spirit. It's rare to see such a stark physical manifestation. Catherine, this spirit is here for you. Your connection must be strong to have allowed us to witness this."

Catherine smiled, the whites of her wet teeth shining against the candlelight as tears streamed down her face. Lightning flashed again, and the sitters looked eagerly out the window, desperate for a sight of something from the beyond. But there was nothing.

I gasped, drawing their attention to me. "I'm sorry." I put my hand to my face, pinching the bridge of my nose. "Something is happening." A low humming noise began, a deep buzz that sounded half human and half mechanical. "I feel unwell," I said.

Concern flashed across the sitters' faces, and a mix of something else—something I was familiar with. It was the look of someone silently demanding *Don't do this. Don't take this away from me.*

"I'm okay." I answered their silent question. "I just need a moment." I swayed slightly, almost indiscernibly, back and forth.

"Darling girl," I said, but the voice was not my own. It was deep and gruff but laced with immense longing.

"Daddy?" Catherine exclaimed with a tight voice, so small, like she'd regressed back into childhood. "I love you."

The energy drained from my body so violently that my head slammed into the table. As though from a great distance, I could hear the worried gasps of the sitters. The two sitters to each side of me reached out, their hands pressed firmly into my back, trying to rouse me.

When I picked my head up, Catherine Belaforte took a sharp inhale. "Jesus, Ms. Ravencroft. You're bleeding."

I brought my hands to my face, feeling the warm, syrupy trickle of liquid coming from my nose.

"You fainted," Stacey Carter said. "You must have hit your nose."

"I'm so sorry. This sometimes happens when the spirits are too eager to speak through me. I'm too weak to continue."

"You called me *darling girl*. Nobody has ever called me that except for my father."

The Carters were whispering back and forth. "Why did *she* get to talk to him?"

Catherine spoke again. "It's a miracle, Jade. Truly a miracle."

* * *

I waved goodbye to the sitters as they exited the shop. The Carters lingered behind, clearly unhappy they couldn't communicate with their son but still in awe of the appearance of Catherine's father.

"Can we come back again? We were so close to speaking to him," Stacey Carter asked as she handed me her payment.

The promise of returning clients sent a thrill through me, as did the feel of the growing wad of money in my pocket. "Absolutely. I can still sense him waiting to speak with you. We just need to do some special preparations. I can do a private session for you two, and with an added ritual it will only be fifty extra dollars."

"Perfect," they said in unison.

Catherine approached as the Carters left. The wide smile she wore wiped years off her, and she stood taller. "Thank you so much. I finally was able to say goodbye. I never had the chance."

She startled me by gripping me tightly in a hug, and I couldn't help but smile. That was one of my favorite parts of my job—the sense of closure and relief that I could give sitters.

When they were all out of sight, I locked the door and blew out the candles in the front room. I made my way back to the séance room and opened the giant wooden armoire, pushing on the back of it and ducking through into the adjoining room.

My sister Stevie sat surrounded by gadgets, props, and a box of Cheez-Its. She was leaning back in her chair, tossing snacks into her mouth with one hand.

"No more smoking before séances," I grumbled, snatching a rod out of her hand and tossing it on the ground. Fishing wire dangled from it, with a dull, rusty hook on the end. She pulled back, making sure I couldn't snatch the snacks out of her hands.

"I didn't smoke!" she squeaked. She looked at me with wide, red eyes and pressed her lips together to stifle a laugh. Her hair was soaking wet and limp down her shoulders.

I rolled my eyes. There was nobody in the world who could annoy me more than her, but a laugh still built in my chest. "Yeah, okay. It reeks in here."

"I just did a little baking," she said with faux innocence. She stood and picked the rod off the floor, wrapping the fishing wire around the metal pole. "Want a brownie?" Her eyes were so narrowed that I couldn't see her irises. A high-pitched giggle escaped, and she tried to disguise it by clearing her throat.

"You idiot. Get it together." I ripped off my wig, tossed it on the table, and furiously scratched my scalp. "I can't stand this thing," I grumbled, frustrated by the lingering itch.

"That's what you get for buying a wig from a Halloween store," Stevie said.

"You have no idea how hard it is to talk normally with a blood capsule shoved up your nose." I pointed to the wig. "And trust me, when I have the money, I'm buying one of those five-hundred-dollar real virgin hair wigs."

Stevie waved her fingers in the air and put on an accent. "Ah yes, the hair and soul of a virgin to fuel your mystical powers."

"What accent was that supposed to be?"

"Russian, obviously."

"Well, it sounded Jamaican."

"Whatever. Nice incantation, by the way. I think I heard it on an episode of *Charmed*."

I grabbed a towel off the chair and tossed it to her, but her reaction speed was so slow it hit her in the face. She left it there for a moment before pulling it off.

"Thanks," she said. "I didn't realize it was going to rain."

"Clearly," I laughed. I'd bought her a black rain jacket months ago for situations like this, but she'd obviously forgotten. "You messed up a lot tonight. They bought it all, but it really screwed with me."

"My performance was immaculate. What did I screw up so badly?"

"You picked the wrong cutout, for one," I said, thinking of the eerily long-limbed figure outside the window during the séance. The sight of it had scared me at first. I'd expected to see the cutout we typically used for older spirits—slightly hunched shoulders, a bit wider and shorter.

"No I didn't," she said. She shoved a fistful of Cheez-Its in her mouth.

"Yes, you did. It was supposed to be for Catherine's father. You picked the creepy one." I pointed at the cardboard cutout that leaned against the wall with the four other variations we'd created. Rain still clung to the lamination of the one Stevie had mistakenly used tonight.

"Yeah, I guess it does look kind of demonic. But everything else went great, so you're welcome." She towel-dried her hair feverishly, reminding me of a wet dog shaking itself off.

I began to correct her, thinking of my panic as the fake spirits had thumped against the wall when I called on Dylan Carter. In our research leading up to the séance, we'd found much more information about Catherine Belaforte's family than on the Carters. We'd catered the entire night to her, and if the Carters had been more forceful, I would have had to wing it. I'd done it successfully before, but I would much rather feel in control during a séance than have to rely on my nonexistent theater experience.

To be fair, Stevie whacking at the wall at the wrong time had ended up guaranteeing the Carters' return. The poor souls believed it was a matter of which spirit was the strongest, when really it had been Stevie's timing error.

I dug into my pocket and pulled out the wad of cash from tonight. After charging fifty dollars for each sitter, we'd made two hundred fifty dollars, which was decent enough. I plucked out seventy-five bucks and handed it to Stevie.

"Sah-weet," she chirped. "Look at us, sis. Making the family proud."

My stomach dropped when she said it, but I tucked the cash back into my pocket, ready for tonight to be over.

* * *

Harry Houdini once said there are three types of mediums: the deluded, the psychotics, and the criminals. I was the latter. I came from a long line of criminals. We didn't break into people's houses or rip purses from women's arms as they walked down the streets. People came to us, and we only took what they gave. We were mediums.

Well, we acted like we were. If there really was such a thing, I owed them my greatest apologies. I was a fraud. A trickster. But I never went out of my way to hurt people. Hurt people came to me, seeking solace in the realms beyond ours, and I tried to give that to them.

A part of me didn't feel bad about what we did for a living. People were glued to their televisions from the second they got home from work until they went to bed, and what were they doing? They were watching people pretend.

There was a reason it was called con artistry. It was a performance that required you to not only be the actress but also the stagehand, the set designer, and the director. It was a one-woman show, and I was the artist. I had my sister, but most of the time she was too stoned to help.

Neither of us had gone to college and I didn't even make it through high school, so it wasn't like we were set up for a great future. My younger sister, freshly twenty-one, bartended at a bar across town, and I ran our witchy little shop with her occasional help. Now I found myself juggling the roles of sister, mother, and businesswoman, all at the age of twenty-five. Scammed out of enjoying my twenties by my own parents.

When you looked at the row of cafés and shops on this street, it was clear we didn't belong. Expensive cars sat parked outside storefronts, shaded by rows of perfect trees whose colors were shifting as autumn approached. A boutique down the street sold candles for forty dollars each, and an hour of talk therapy next door would cost you one hundred dollars an hour, even with insurance.

We had been grandfathered into the expensive property by my parents, who signed the lease agreement right before shit went south for them. Luckily, I'd been able to take over the lease.

All around us were crisp signs and seating dotted between manicured plants. Then there was us, with our chipping off-white paint and the stark black-and-white sign my sister had painted above the plum-colored door. When I'd asked her to come up with a logo for us, she'd been so excited she'd worked on it for days. There had been torn sheets of paper covering the floors and furniture with her early ideas. Then came the paint, which I was still finding specks of in our kitchen two years later.

Now, above our front door in delicate black lines, there was a crescent moon cupping a crystal ball, all surrounded by tiny stars.

Everyone had known who we were as soon as we hung the sign. We were mediums. Or palm readers, psychics, tarot readers. Whatever someone wanted us to be when they walked through the door. But they would never know the type of people we actually were. The type of family we came from. My sister and I were never going to be as bad as our parents. They'd crossed the line, and we were trying to distance ourselves from that life.

We were not thieves. We were scavengers.

CHAPTER 2

Jade

IT WAS EARLY morning, my favorite time of day. It was mostly because my sister slept until noon every day, fighting for her life in a cannabis-induced lucid dream, and it was my one moment of peace and quiet.

I pushed open the bedroom window and reveled in the crisp, chilly air. It cut through the stale smell of sleep and last night's incense that clung to every piece of fabric in my bedroom. It was the end of September, and although fall was creeping in, the summer sun was still fighting for dominance. I longed for autumn, for overcast skies and chilled winds—the type of weather that always put people in a spooky mood, which was good for business. A cold front was coming soon, according to the news, and I looked forward to the additional clients it would bring.

I was about to tuck my head back inside when a voice shouted, "Hey!" to my left. It startled me, and I bumped the back of my head into the windowsill.

"Son of a bitch," I hissed, my hand gripping the back of my head. I stuck my head farther out, looking for the source of the voice.

"Hi." The man waved enthusiastically. He had the energy of a golden retriever, and I couldn't help but smile.

"Hey, Daniel." I let go of the growing knot on the back of my head and waved.

"They delivered one of your packages to my door again. Want me to bring it over?"

"That'd be great. Meet you down there."

I carefully removed myself from the window and tugged on a pair of jeans, then smoothed my hair in the mirror and wiped the remnants of sleep from my eyes. I'd been so tired last night that I'd washed my face with minimal effort, and traces of my eyeliner remained. I'd found clients took me far more seriously when I wore smoky eye makeup, which was ironic, because in most areas of life, the more makeup women wore, the less people took us seriously.

I took my cup of coffee downstairs and poured Daniel one. We'd been friends for two years, ever since we'd moved into the building. Daniel was a psychologist and had taken over his father's practice when he retired. He had a swanky apartment above it, and I envied his lifestyle, but not the student debt he had from years of schooling.

I opened my door and there he was, package in hand, smile plastered wide across his face. I could see why his patients would open up to him with his harmless, comforting energy. I'd once told him his aura was indigo, the aura of someone empathetic and caring. I didn't actually see auras, but that's what I felt about him, and it clearly pleased him to hear it. So what was the harm?

"Trade?" I held out the mug, and he took it gratefully as he swapped the package for the steaming black coffee.

"You're amazing. You have no idea how much I needed this. I stayed up way too late preparing for this conference I have next week. I'm beat."

"Same," I said. I took a sip of coffee and told him about last night's séance.

"You don't look tired. Must be blessed with something I don't have." He ran his fingers through his wavy, caramel-brown hair, which still showed remnants of a rough night's sleep.

I let out a playful scoff, and he blushed.

Phyllis, the neighbor to my right, scowled at us while watering her plants, and I gave a perfunctory wave. She was an old, irate woman, easily set off by any noise or inconvenience, especially if it was caused by me. She shook her head and stomped inside, her hose left limp on her front porch.

"Wow, she really loves you." Daniel laughed, and I scoffed again. He rocked on the balls of his feet. He was too polite to ask to come inside for coffee. I'd invited him in a few times, and he'd always stared around in wonder at all the occult knickknacks. "I guess I'll go get ready for the day. First client at ten."

"The one with the yellow Hummer?" He nodded. "I hope his wife signed those divorce papers. For her sake."

His eyes widened. "How did you know that?"

I waved my hand at the sign above our door: *Ravencroft Psychic Parlor and Shoppe*. Our last name wasn't actually Ravencroft. Legally, we were Crawfords, but in an attempt to distance myself from my parents, we'd leaned into the over-the-top occult aesthetic and adopted it for the shop and ourselves. It had been Stevie's invention, and she'd proudly put up a portrait of Edgar Allan Poe with a stuffed raven next to it.

His eyes glistened with awe. "You're amazing."

"Okay, yes, I'm a psychic, but you leave your office window open sometimes, and I can't help but overhear. He's an enthusiastic crier."

His face was beet red now. "I really need to stop leaving it open. That's a HIPAA violation to end all violations. Let's keep that between us?"

I ran my fingers along my closed lips and threw away an imaginary key. "Wow, our first secret together."

He grinned. "I guess our jobs are one and the same, huh? Keepers of secrets." He took a sip of his coffee but didn't finish it. It was his trick—albeit a transparent one. If he took my mug back to his place, he had an excuse to knock on my door again. I waited for the question I knew was coming.

"Mind if I finish this in my office? I'll bring it back later."

"I know you will." I smiled, leaning my shoulder against the column of the porch.

He raised his mug in cheers. "Have a good one, Jade."

"Always do, Daniel." I grinned as he turned to walk away with a little shuffle before hitting his stride. He was so easy and carefree, despite listening to other people's problems and dark secrets all day long.

I did the same, for much less money of course, and it wore me down a bit more every day.

* * *

I closed the front door behind me and sat at our kitchenette table. The apartment was a tiny area above the shop, and the only thing that separated the two spaces was a crimson velvet curtain in front of the stairs. It unfortunately absorbed the smell of anything we cooked. And more unfortunately, last night Stevie had cooked fish.

Every single morning, I read the obituaries. In their grief, people often divulged bits of information they might normally not. Grief was my cruel right-hand man as I raked in money off people's suffering. It was wrong to use it to my advantage, but more often than not, I could see a weight lifted off clients' shoulders as I comforted them with messages from their deceased loved ones. It wasn't entirely ethical, but I'd always believed it could be healing if people let it.

Often the grieving would wander in on their own, but sometimes it wasn't so organic. I studied the people around me, and when you were armed with enough information, it wasn't so hard to gently lure them in. Nothing was ever forced. I thought of my mother, who'd taught me everything she knew.

All it takes is a little coaxing, Jade. Like a bowl of milk set outside your front door. Eventually the stray cats will come.

I shook away the thought and scanned the remaining obituaries. There weren't many today.

"Rosalyn Harborough, age 81, passed away on September 21 after a long battle with kidney failure. In her honor, a service will be held October 1 at noon at the Moravian Church, followed by a bake sale. All proceeds will go to the National Kidney Foundation."

For a moment I saw the obituary through my parents' eyes. October 1 at noon. That meant the entire family would be at the church for at least an hour, followed by more time at the bake sale. Their house would be empty. The perfect time to strike. But not for me. I would not be like them.

When I was done, I turned on the TV, and it shuddered awake. I changed the channel to the news and shuffled around with a duster while I listened.

The deep robotic voices of news anchors drifted through the room. I was karate-chopping the throw pillows on the sofa, trying to make them look a little less like they were from the 1990s, which they were, when a news segment began.

"We're interrupting this segment with breaking news. City council member Thomas Nichols has been reported missing. He was last seen on Thursday morning, jogging around Salem Lake. If you have any information concerning his whereabouts, please contact local law enforcement."

The screen showed a headshot of a man in his late forties. I felt sorry for his family but was quickly distracted by the clock: almost eleven. I had a standing appointment with a client every Monday morning. Daniel didn't realize it, but Cheryl always came in to see me before attending therapy.

I needed to make the shop look more mystical. Right now it was a grungy mess. The harsh light of day sucked out the magic, revealing the crooked nails holding up the velvet curtains and the incense ash stains I could never seem to get out of the rug under my tarot table.

I moved on autopilot, doing my routine the same way I did it each day. Windows shut, curtains closed. Incense and candles lit. A nature sounds playlist playing. And of course, I had to get myself ready. Jeans and a white T-shirt didn't exactly scream *I see dead people.*

I ran up the stairs, two at a time, and pulled on a black maxi skirt and a dark-red blouse. I tugged on my wavy black wig, then quickly put on earrings and a smattering of bracelets.

The wig was ridiculous in the daylight, but it looked better in the dim lighting of a reading. My natural hair was already dark—a flat, lifeless brown—but sitters always responded better to the stark black wig. My real hair was close enough in color that nobody ever noticed when I was out during the day. Maybe they assumed I transformed for sessions, like a bat transforming into a vampire, just with a bad wig on.

I slid on the moonstone ring that had been given to my grandmother by a sitter who was especially moved after a session in which my grandmother manifested the spirit of her dead cat. In reality, it had been my grandmother's cat that she had locked in the bathroom for the session and was yowling to be let out. On my grandmother's stealthy cue, my grandfather let the cat out. As my grandmother blew out the only candle in the room, the black cat skulked in, camouflaged by the darkness, and rubbed enthusiastically against the sitter's leg. The woman had been so happy afterward that she'd slipped the ring right off her finger and shoved it into my grandmother's open palm.

The final and most important step was a thick gold ring with an emblem of Saint Agabus, the patron saint of divination and fortune tellers. It had been handed down by the women in my family, the emblem toeing the line between our facade of traditional Catholic beliefs and dabbling in the occult.

My family was technically Catholic, but in the same way french fries are technically vegetables. I remembered asking my grandfather if we were real Catholics after a sixth-grade classmate said I shouldn't wear my cross necklace.

"Yes," he'd said. "But we're not practicing."

I hadn't understood what that meant. Was talking to God something that took practice? Why wouldn't God listen even if we were bad at it? "Why aren't we practicing?"

"There's no need to practice when you've perfected it." His laughter had boomed around the room, and the other adults had joined in. I'd stomped off, thinking they were laughing at my ignorance. The next day at school, I'd told the classmate we were perfect Catholics and she must be bad at it if she still needed to practice.

I studied my appearance in the mirror. It was three minutes until eleven, and Cheryl always got here exactly on time. She'd smoke a cigarette outside the front door, inhaling furiously all the way down to the filter, savoring every last second.

I hastily swiped on eyeliner and mascara and slung open my bedroom door, rushing toward the stairs. At the same time Stevie shuffled out of her bedroom, rubbing the sleep from her eyes.

"Whoa," I said, almost knocking us both down the slim, creaky staircase. "Nice to see you've risen from your slumber, sleeping beauty."

"Cheryl?"

"Yep," I said, halfway down the stairs.

"My window was open. It reeks of cigarettes in there now." Our bedrooms both faced the street, and nestled in between was our shared bathroom.

"That sounds like a you problem," I shouted up the stairs, and Stevie mumbled a string of obscenities back at me as she hobbled to the shower.

You gotta love sisters.

I opened the front door as the clock struck eleven, and Cheryl pushed her way in before I could even say hello. She shuffled to her seat at my table, where my deck of tarot cards sat patiently waiting next to a fluttering purple candle.

"I desperately need someone to talk to," Cheryl said breathily.

She always did. She was the type of person who was always on the brink of a meltdown. Most of the time, her issues were of her own making, but she always cast her blame elsewhere.

"I can sense that, Cheryl," I said calmly as I sat down. Obviously, I could. Anyone within a block could smell the anxiety seeping from her along with the stench of cigarettes. "Let's begin."

CHAPTER 3

Jade

"PLEASE PLACE YOUR hands on the table, close your eyes, and take a deep breath."

She inhaled quickly, and her eyelids twitched as she pressed them together. I knew she wanted to rush me along and get the answers she was seeking, but I had a process. To get people to truly believe, you had to lean into the performance. There was no spiritualism without the ritual, just as there was no entertainment without the performance. People didn't come to me, or other mediums, just for answers but also to be swept away by an experience.

She opened her eyes, and I picked up my cards. "Place the stack of cards between your palms, and ask your question."

"Will my son break up with his girlfriend and get married to a good woman?"

I swallowed my annoyance. I couldn't remember how many times I'd told her she could ask only one specific question per reading or else I'd have to charge more. It was all fine in the end, because she always tipped me half the cost of the session. She was also responsible for a steady stream of business for me, as she told every single person in her bowling league about me.

"Awaken the cards," I instructed.

She shuffled and handed them back to me. I split the cards into three stacks, placing two fingers on each as I silently encouraged the cards to speak to Cheryl. Or at least that's what she thought I was doing. I flipped over one card from each stack, my crimson-painted fingernails lingering for a moment before moving on to the next.

"Major arcana represent forces outside of our control. These are the most important. Minor arcana represent day-to-day truths we may be able to change, if we're willing."

"Yes," she said impatiently. "And what do they say?"

"The first card is the World." A nude woman danced above the earth, surrounded by a wreath and four intently watching creatures. "It signifies a relationship that provides deep fulfillment and gratitude."

She smiled smugly, thinking the gratitude was directed toward her. Cheryl's fatal flaw was believing every positive reading was a reflection of her goodness and every negative reading a curse put on her by someone else.

"My insights are telling me your son will indeed get married to a good woman."

Cheryl leaned back in her chair. "Thank goodness. This girl he's with is no good. He just needs to be patient and wait for the right one."

The second card, the Six of Cups, was reversed. Right side up, it meant familiarity, healing, and happy memories—something Cheryl believed she gave her son. "The Six of Cups is reversed." I tapped the card, where a boy in a medieval village was surrounded by six flower-filled cups, one of which he was handing to a girl. "This means there will be independence and a shift forward, such as leaving home."

"He's going to leave me?" She leaned forward. "Who will it be? How long until he meets her?"

I pointed to the third card: the Hierophant. A pope sat benevolently on his throne, staring back at me. "He's already met her. The Hierophant signals a meaningful step in a relationship, often in some form of commitment. Oh." I closed my eyes. "I'm seeing a ring," I said, suddenly feeling inspired to grant her a vision, free of charge. This was how you kept your regulars—the freebies.

"A ring!" she exclaimed. "So it must be soon. Oh, fantastic. He just needs to redirect his attention to the right woman."

"The ring . . ." I paused, opening my eyes and peering into the middle distance. "The ring is not in a jewelry box." I tilted my chin down, as though I were struggling to maintain my grasp on the vision. "The ring is on a finger. He will be married soon."

She blanched at my words. "To *her*?" she asked. I nodded. "How could he propose without asking me first?"

I'd been holding on to this piece of information since Friday night when Stevie returned home from work. Being a bartender at the most popular bar in town made Stevie a wealth of knowledge. The drunker people got, the more they shouted their conversations to each other, right in front of the bartender, who they assumed either couldn't hear them over the music or didn't care.

What they didn't know was that I paid her to care. For every piece of information she brought me, I paid her a small bonus. The amount depended on the value of the secret and whether it was related to any of my clients. For what she'd overheard on Friday night, I'd paid her fifty dollars, triple the amount she usually got. She'd held it up to the light, pretending to check the money for signs it was counterfeit. "Well, howdy doody," she'd said as she'd tucked it into her pocket.

"Keep your gigantic ears open, Stevie," I'd said as she walked away. She'd laughed and raised one middle finger as she'd skipped up to her bedroom.

"The Hierophant and the World are major arcana, meaning you cannot change them. However, the Six of Cups is minor. Although I don't believe you can come between your son and his fiancée, it's in your power to improve things. Instead of pushing him away to where his independence means a complete separation from you, you can encourage a healthy distance between you while he builds his new family."

"Distance?" she guffawed.

"I know what you need." I opened a drawer to my right and rifled through it. Each drawer was filled with some sort of occult bric-a-brac: crystals, candles, feathers, and even tiny little bones for divination. "This is black tourmaline. It will protect you from negative energy and draw love toward you and your family."

She took it with a shaking hand and sniffled a thank-you. "Isn't there a spell you can put on them to make them break up? Some sort of curse?" She had an inky black stream of tears and makeup running down her cheek. I handed her a tissue, but she just gripped it angrily in her fist.

"I'm sorry, but I don't work with dark magic." A handful of sitters had asked for more sinister services like this, but I never agreed. Even if it wasn't real, a small, superstitious part of me didn't want to toe that dangerous line. Perhaps magic wasn't real, but maybe karma was, and I didn't want that stacking against me.

She rummaged through her purse and pulled a wad of cash out. "Please," she said as she slammed it on the table. My eyes widened at the amount. A hundred-dollar bill. Three twenties. Two tens.

"I'm sorry, Cheryl," I murmured. "I'm not that type of psychic."

She shoved the bills back into her purse. "I'm sorry. I'm so embarrassed."

As she continued to cry and vent her frustrations about her son's choice of partner, I leaned back in my chair and listened intently. These were the moments that kept away the moral panic. For every sitter that left our shop, they'd at least gotten one thing:

Someone to keep their secrets.

CHAPTER

4

Jade

THERE WAS NOTHING I hated more than bills. I knew when they were coming each month, and yet somehow the sight of them in the mailbox still struck me like a swinging fist.

The thick stack of white envelopes in my hand glared back at me against the afternoon sunlight, and I winced, barely noticing as Daniel popped up beside me. More than half the time, he conveniently decided to check his mail at the same time I did. The sight of him was welcome, but I couldn't keep the sinking feeling out of my gut as I said hello.

"Hey!" he said cheerfully as he unlocked his mailbox. He drew out an academic journal and playfully thumbed through it as if it were the most interesting thing in the world. He wore a tight T-shirt and gym shorts, and somehow he made the light sheen of sweat around his hairline look regal.

"Gone for a jog?" I asked.

"Yep, I usually do a loop around Salem Lake if my day ends early. Shame about all that construction."

My eyebrows rose at the mention of Salem Lake after seeing the councilman's missing-person report. I was about to mention it when he fumbled with his mail, dropping it at his feet.

He bent forward to pick it up, and the primal part of my brain appreciated the ripple of muscles along his back. He popped back up, but his smile dropped as he read the vicious red stamp plastered against the envelope in my hand. *LATE NOTICE.*

"Ouch. Sorry." He winced. "I know what will help with that."

"What, a trash bag full of cash?"

"That would definitely help, but unfortunately I lost mine. If I find it, it's yours." He cleared his throat. "I made some breakfast—more than I could ever eat. We call it the Egg Thing. You want some?"

"The *Egg Thing*?"

"It's a breakfast casserole. Want to try it?"

"You made breakfast at four PM?" I asked as my stomach growled.

He laughed. "Breakfast food should be eaten at all times. Come on."

I followed him into his building, looking around as he flipped on the lights. The bottom floor was his private practice, where he and two other psychologists saw their patients. On the right, there was a short hallway with three offices, a white noise machine perched dutifully outside each door.

I pointed at his door: Dr. Daniel Lachman. "I hope you have the biggest office."

He grinned. "Corner office. Want to see?"

I nodded, and he pushed open the door. The room was bigger than I expected. There were two large windows on the exterior walls, allowing golden rays of light to spill onto the carpet. Each window had a curtain rod in the middle, giving his patients privacy while the upper half remained open.

There was a small desk in the corner and a seating arrangement nestled against the windows. A stack of folders rested on the desk, each labeled with an individual's name—patients. I didn't recognize the name of the folder on top, but the one below rang a bell.

Ian Stellman. The high school teacher who had just gotten placed on paid leave. There were whispers around town about him and why he'd gotten in trouble, but nothing had been confirmed. There was a rumor he'd been caught with liquor in his desk, but another deemed him a pervert.

One well-worn leather armchair faced a plush couch that was long enough to allow his patients to decide how much space they needed. The cushions closest to him were worn and frayed, and I smiled at the thought of him making his patients so comfortable.

I took a seat in the indent, and he sat across from me. "What's your biggest concern about the bills?" His voice was casual. Disarming, even.

"That I won't be able to pay them."

"Not knowing what's inside those envelopes is making things worse, don't you think? A lot of the time, anxiety comes from the unknown. Why don't you open one of them and see what's inside? Pick the one you think will be the worst."

I clutched the late notice in my hand.

"What are you feeling?"

"Like I'm going to crap my pants."

A bark of a laugh surprised me, and despite the clench of nerves in my gut, I smiled back at him.

"Open it up when you're ready. Should I go run out for some adult diapers?"

"I think I can manage." Why was I blushing? Usually he was the one with flushed cheeks. His skin was perfectly clear, though, as he grinned back at me with confidence.

I took a deep breath and slid my pointer finger under the envelope flap, savoring the aggressive, jagged tear along the rental company's return address. I slid the paper out and was surprised to see that alongside the usual rent statement, there was a letter.

I read aloud, my voice wavering. "'We are writing to inform you that your monthly rent payment will increase by ten percent beginning next month. Due to increasing costs of insurance . . .'"

A single tear tumbled down my cheek. Daniel sprung to his feet and sat on the couch next to me. Even through the panic building in my chest, I couldn't help but notice the warmth of his knee against mine. He took the stack of bills from me and placed them out of my line of sight.

"I know it might seem stupid to cry over five hundred dollars, but we were barely making rent as it is. Last month after bills, we only had a hundred dollars left for food for the entire month." I furiously rubbed the tears from my cheeks. "We're so screwed."

"I'm sorry. I shouldn't have pushed you to open it in front of me. I invaded your privacy."

"No, you didn't. If I'd opened it at home, you would have heard me scream at them on the phone anyway."

He smiled softly and stood. "Food's the best medicine. Come on." He took the pile of bills in one hand and extended the other to me. I took it, lingering in the comfort of it for a moment before letting go. As he walked away, he rubbed his thumb along his pointer finger, as though he was trying to keep the feeling of my hand there.

* * *

"Behold," Daniel said. "The Egg Thing."

Despite my flurry of emotions only minutes ago, a smile broke across my face. A giant casserole sat on his stove, the steam drifting up lazily toward the vent light. The kitchen smelled of cheesy eggs and sausage, making my stomach grumble again. "Looks great," I said quietly but sincerely.

He took two plates out of the cabinet, scooped perfectly tidy squares of casserole onto them, and handed one to me. "Why don't you take this home?"

I grinned at him as I took the plate.

"What?" he asked incredulously.

"I know what you're doing."

"What, giving you perfectly cooked, delicious food?"

"You do this with coffee mugs too. So we have an excuse to see each other when we give it back." I leaned against the kitchen island and took a bite. He was right—it was delicious.

"I have no idea what you're talking about," he said with a mischievous grin.

"Thank you for the food. And the free therapy." We said our goodbyes, and minutes later I was sitting at our kitchen table, about to take the last bite, when Stevie entered. "What the hell? Where's mine?"

I shoved the last bite in my mouth. "Daniel."

"Ohhh, lover boy makes you food now?" She was rooting around our nearly empty pantry and pulled out a crumpled cardboard box. "Great, a single granola bar. And it's been expired for two months."

"Vintage. Yum." I tried to match her playful energy but failed.

My phone rang and I picked it up, only to be met with a robotic voice. I nearly dropped it when my stomach flipped at the greeting: "This is a call from Forsyth Correctional Center, from inmate—"

I hung up, my heart racing. *No, no, no. I do* not *need this.* I sat back down at the table, staring at the bills on the table. *Why was he calling?*

"All right, what's wrong with you?" Stevie asked.

I sighed. "Our rent's going up."

She turned around, riffling through the fridge. She asked with her back to me, "Okay, by fifty bucks again? No need to get your panties in a wad."

"Five hundred." I turned the bill toward her as she turned around to face me.

"Shit. Panties tightly wadded."

"Very tightly. We have to come up with a plan. How many extra shifts can you pick up?"

"Nobody ever wants to work the Monday lunch shift. I could take that, but the tips are terrible, since there's no one there."

"Okay, let your boss know today. If anyone complains about being tired or not feeling good, convince them to give up their shifts. The only other thing I can think to cut is our cell phone plan."

"Whoa, whoa, reel it in. We can't just *not* have phones. Do you expect me to send faxes or something?"

"If we break the contract, we'll save over a hundred dollars a month, and that bill is actually coming up in a few days. I read all about it, and you can still use your phone like normal if you're connected to WiFi. And we'll still have the shop's landline. So no. No faxes."

"Oh, that's not so bad."

"Great, I'll call and cancel today. That just leaves the first installment of your tuition payment plan. It's not for another two months, but it's four hundred, so just keep that in mind."

Stevie winced. "Sorry." It was a sore spot for her. She often claimed the cost would be too much of a burden, but I wanted her to have more opportunities than I did. As much as I loved her help in the shop, she deserved better.

"I told you to stop saying sorry about that, Stevie." I took the rent letter and folded it up. "I'm going to get in touch with some clients I haven't seen in a while and see if they're interested in a reading."

"Cold-calling? When has that ever worked?"

"It always works when you tell them you had a vision."

"You're going to lie? I mean, I know we're always *sort of* lying, but only when they come to us."

"It is what it is," I said, trying to convince myself as much as her. "Wear your low-cut top tonight. See if that gets you more tips."

She scoffed and pointed to her chest. "Have you seen these things? We'll be rich in no time."

I feigned a laugh, and eventually Stevie took her pitiful, expired granola bar into the living room. As I listened to the drone of morning news, I asked myself the same question Stevie had.

Was I willing to blatantly lie? It didn't seem like I had a choice. I had no other talents. After all, lying was in my blood.

CHAPTER

5

Jade

STEVIE AND I were walking slowly back from the coffee shop, each of us holding a giant bag of coffee beans that the shop owner had heavily discounted for us. The weather was growing cooler, and I reveled in the lack of sweat dripping down my back. Stevie seemed to be appreciating it too as she bent over and picked up a fallen amber leaf.

"First one." She smiled even as she struggled to get a grip on the bag of coffee beans. Our mom had always saved the first of the season when we were kids, and it had become a tradition for Stevie to carry on.

We passed a narrow, damp alleyway between a flower shop and Laundromat, and a gust of cool air pushed its way through. A little white dog sat next to a trash can, its legs turned brown from dirt.

"Hey there, little lady," Stevie cooed, dropping her bag of beans and sticking her hand out for the dog to sniff. It stood, tail wagging, then lunged, snapping at her hand and snarling. "Shit," she said, stumbling back. "Screw you too."

"Watch out for Cujo," I cackled.

"Shut up," she grumbled. She picked up her bag of beans. "Jerk," she said under her breath, and I wasn't sure whether she was talking to me or the dog.

After my laughter had ceased, Stevie asked, "So what's the deal with you and Daniel?"

"What do you mean?"

"He's obviously in love with you."

I blew air out of my mouth in a huff. "There's a difference between being nice and flirting, Stevie."

"Right," she said with a slow drawl.

On the final block to our apartment, Stevie came to a halt. "Lookee here, a reward and everything," she said, pointing at a missing-pet poster for a raggedy white lapdog: *Missing dog: Angel. $100 reward for her safe return.*

White tabs at the bottom of the page had the owner's number. Only two had been torn off.

"Looks like Cujo," I teased. "Are you scared?"

"I think it is. And no, I'm not scared of that little rat. You're so annoying." Stevie ripped off a tab. "Are you thinking what I'm thinking?"

"That a hundred bucks wouldn't cover the hospital bill when that thing takes a finger off?" I walked up our stoop and fished my keys out of my back pocket. We huffed up the stairs and dropped the coffee on the kitchen counter.

"Aren't you going to ask me what my idea is?" Stevie asked.

"Enlighten me."

"We call in the tip for the dog. Easy hundred bucks."

I groaned as I shoved the bags into the pantry. It didn't sound worth the effort.

"*But,*" she exclaimed, "we submit it as a vision, you plug the shop. Boom, one hundred dollars and free advertising."

I whipped around, one eyebrow raised. I nodded slightly, then more enthusiastically as I thought it through. "Grab the shop phone."

"Hell yeah," she said breathily as she skittered across the floor, bringing back the landline. "It's ringing."

I put the phone to my ear, my heart racing.

An older man answered. "Hello?"

"Hello. My name is Jade Ravencroft, and I was calling about the missing-dog poster."

"Angel? Have you found her?"

"Well, in a way. I'm a psychic—I own Ravencroft Psychic Parlor and Shoppe in the West End. I had a vision last night and I believe it was about your sweet little dog."

Stevie rolled her eyes at my description of the dog and waggled two fingers above her skull like devil horns.

"Okay . . ." he hesitated. "What did you see?"

"I saw a small white dog, its legs covered in dirt. She was lying down in an alleyway next to a trash can. In the vision, I smelled roses and fresh laundry."

"I'm afraid that's not very helpful, young lady."

I gritted my teeth. *I'm getting there.* "There's an alleyway between Francie's Florals and the Laundromat on Second Street. I believe you'll find her there if you go soon."

"I'll have my grandson drive there now. I'll send him with one hundred dollars, and if he finds Angel, he'll bring it to your shop. I sure do hope you're right." His voice was pinched with excitement.

"I do too," I said, right before the line died.

An hour later, I was reading tarot for a young girl and her mother, painting the brightest, most hopeful picture I could with every card I pulled. The front door chimed, and I half listened as Stevie greeted the newcomer.

"How can I help you?" she asked, a hint of a smile in her voice. A man spoke but was interrupted by an intense bout of yipping.

Angel. Our plan had worked.

"Sorry about her. Here's the hundred my grandpa promised. Thank you for finding her."

Stevie must have extended her hand to the man, because the growling intensified and Stevie gasped.

"So y'all are really psychic, huh?" the man asked.

"My sister is. Jade."

"Well, I'll be damned. I'll tell everyone about you. Thanks again. Hey, you wanna get a drink some time?"

Without hesitation, Stevie responded in a flat voice, "No. But thank you."

Poor guy. No chance in hell.

The bell chimed, and Stevie's shadow passed by the crack in the velvet curtain. She'd really pulled through today. It was a harmless scam—if you could even call it a scam. Something to be proud of.

I returned the girls' cards to the deck and shuffled. I smiled at the mother. "All right, is it your turn now?"

The mother nodded enthusiastically, and the show began all over again.

* * *

"Efforts to find beloved councilman Thomas Nichols have intensified. He was last seen September twentieth after going for his daily jog around Salem Lake. After a sweep of the lake, a damaged cell phone was found, which family has confirmed belonged to Nichols. Authorities are escalating search efforts due to concerns of foul play and encourage potential search volunteers to contact local law enforcement. The family is now offering a reward of two thousand dollars for information."

I clicked the power button, unwilling to listen to any more reports about the missing councilman. He was clearly an important member of the community—he'd garnered favor by investing heavily in public education, parks, and assistance programs for those financially struggling. While he did deserve his accolades, it irked me that he was being given so much airtime—nearly every news segment began by discussing him—when other missing people seemed to be forgotten before the investigation even began. Sure, I hoped they found him, but what the hell was I supposed to do about it?

Aside from the one hundred dollars for finding the dog, seventy dollars was all I'd made today so far. The closer we got to Halloween, the more clients we typically got, but that was hardly the case today. It was nearly nine and I was fed up, almost ready to call it quits after only reading one palm and two tarot sessions. They hadn't even tipped.

I rolled up the bills from the night and hopped precariously up on the kitchen counter. For the past few years, I'd hidden our cash in an empty can of chicken noodle soup and shoved it to the back of the highest shelf in the cabinet.

We had barely enough to pay for a grocery run, and at this rate we'd never make enough for rent. Maybe the first month, but what about after that? I thought of the missing dog again and how easy it'd been. How harmless. The missing councilman's family was also calling for information, and with a far heftier reward than for the dog. But I had no idea where he was and quite frankly didn't want to know.

How wrong would it be to call, make up some random location for where he was, and hope for the best?

It's wrong, Jade. His family is suffering. You're thinking like a vulture. Like a Crawford.

Minutes passed and I paced the room, my decision changing with each turn of my heel. If I submitted a tip, worst case, I'd be wrong. Best case, I was the genius psychic who everyone would be begging to give them readings.

I lifted the landline from its cradle gently, like any moment it might explode. Was this a bad idea?

Yes. Don't do this.

I paced from the kitchen to the living room, biting my nails as I turned and took the same manic path again and again. I paused, taking a long, deep breath. I felt something inside me crack and give way, and despite how repulsed I was with myself, I was even more disgusted by the surge of adrenaline. Of excitement.

Do it. Do it now.

Readying myself to take the leap, I exhaled and gripped the phone hard in my hand as I dialed the police.

* * *

"Winston-Salem Police Department. How may I direct your call?"

"Uh, hi. Hello. I would like to submit a tip about the missing councilman. Thomas Nichols."

The phone clicked, and tinny hold music began playing. Only ten seconds later, a deep voice answered the phone. "Sergeant Whicks. Who am I speaking to?"

"Hi. My name is Jade Ravencroft." I introduced myself with my working name. I didn't want them to make the connection between me and my parents. "I wanted to submit a tip about Thomas Nichols."

A brief moment of silence. "This is being recorded. Is that okay with you?"

"Yes."

"All right, let's hear it."

Why hadn't I thought of what was I going to say? Oh God, this was a terrible idea. Not only was it morally wrong, but so many things could go wrong. Could I get fined for this? Arrested, even? I opened my mouth, still not knowing what was going to come out. "There's a waste management facility being built about two miles away from Salem Lake. I think he's there." Heat flushed my cheeks. I couldn't believe I was doing this.

"And why do you believe that?"

"Well . . ." I paused. *Here we go, brace yourself.* "I'm a psychic. I have a shop in the West End. Ravencroft Psychic Parlor and Shoppe." The real truth behind my tip was that last week Stevie had complained about the construction noise while we walked around the lake, lamenting the blanket of trees that had been gutted from the ground and would soon be replaced by cement buildings and mounds of waste. It wasn't magic. It was just the first place that came to mind.

Another pause. I could have sworn I heard a sigh in the background. "All right, Jade. Thanks for the information. This is a solid lead." His voice dripped with sarcasm, and I wanted to reach through the phone and shove a middle finger in his face. "Bye-bye now." *Click.*

Mortification swept over me. I was proudly a psychic to anyone with spare cash in their wallets, but claiming it to someone official like a police officer was one of the most embarrassing things I'd ever done. I knew they thought I was batshit crazy. And maybe they were right. What kind of sane person would do what I just did?

I poured myself a glass of water, my mouth dry as bone. His reaction was justified, I reminded myself. I couldn't be angry about a rightful reaction. Psychics weren't real. Only scammers and frauds, I told myself. Just like my parents.

"Wow," a voice said behind me.

Every muscle in my body tensed as I jumped. "Jesus, Stevie. You scared the shit out of me."

"My bad. What the hell was that?" She pointed at the phone. Her purse was slung across her shoulder, and she wore her typical work uniform: tight black jeans and an even tighter low-cut black top. It was clear why she was a favorite with some of the frequent male drinkers.

The flush in my cheeks was spreading across my body, and I was beginning to sweat. "Well, our vision about the missing dog went so well, I just figured I could try it with this missing-person case."

"Yeah, but the difference is you knew where the dog was, but not this missing guy." She paused, feigning suspicion. "Or do you know?"

"I know it's stupid. But what's the harm? If it works, we become filthy rich." I pinched the bridge of my nose and tried to shake off the embarrassment. If it didn't come to anything, only Stevie and I would know about the failure.

"Seems kind of fucked-up. But whatever works for you, sis." She laughed as she plopped her keys carelessly into her bag.

"Late shift?" I asked, already knowing the answer.

"Yep, I'll be home around one." Stevie turned, distracted by the fact that she was likely running late, like she always was. "Catch you on the flip side, Madame Ravencroft."

Within seconds, she was gone and I was left to sit with my embarrassment. Regret was already sinking in, and I was about to pick up the phone to call the police back. Could I claim it was a mistake without getting charged for wasting police time? I could say I had another vision—one that contradicted my tip. But then that'd just be another lie.

I took another sip of water. A loud knock on the front door made me jostle my glass, spilling a small stream of water down the front of my shirt. The cops were already here, handcuffs waiting, I thought.

I walked over to the living room window, which I'd opened as the sun set, reveling in the hint of crispness in the air as fall approached. I stuck my head out the window and peered down. Daniel was gazing up at me, his head tilted as far back as it could go. His hair glowed like fire under the orange streetlamps.

"Tired of me yet?" he called up, smiling.

"How could I ever tire of you, Daniel?"

"Want to watch a movie tomorrow?" He was shouting up at me, and two women at the outdoor bar seating across the street scowled at him. God only knew our perpetually angry neighbor Phyllis already had her phone in hand to call the police.

"Depends on what the marquee says," I shouted back.

"Well, not to brag, but I just got Hulu, so the sky's the limit."

"Oh, so you're a billionaire, huh?" I laughed. "Your place tomorrow at eight?"

His smile broadened, and he gave a dorky thumbs-up before shuffling back to his apartment. I peeked out farther and watched the windows brighten as he turned on more lights.

I wondered what it was like to live in a vibrant, bright space. Our shop was so dim, and the dark and mystical energy was sometimes comforting, but more often than not I found it claustrophobic.

CHAPTER

6

Jade

THE NEXT MORNING the shop's landline rang, and a silly part of me hoped it would be our rental company, apologizing for the error they sent us. Instead, I was greeted with a familiar yet unexpected voice.

"Jade?"

My mouth hung slightly open, no air passing between my dry lips. My grandmother. A part of me yearned to speak with her after years of her forcing distance between us, but I also harbored anger toward her for completely abandoning us. I knew she loved Stevie and me, but she'd been so jaded by my father's actions that she'd withdrawn herself entirely from the family and was now living a happy life at a senior living facility in Florida.

"Jade? Are you there?" My grandmother's voice was low and raspy from years of smoking. It enveloped me like a blanket fresh out of the dryer, the warmth of it draping across my body, because underneath the rasp, she sounded a bit like Mom.

"Grandma?" I was shocked by the croak of my voice.

"It's so good to hear your voice, sweetie. I don't have long, but I have something to tell you."

"All right. Are you okay?" Her voice trembled, and a tense shiver rose in my body to match it.

"I'm fine, I promise. Listen—" Someone in the background urged her to wrap up the call, and I knew well enough that she stared daggers at them, because they quickly stopped. Grandma's eyes—just like my mother's had been—were a piercing green, almost unnaturally so, sharp pieces of polished jade behind thick, black eyelashes. I'd always wondered if that's why they'd chosen my name. "Your father is out of prison."

Blood rushed to my head, thrumming in my ears. "When? How? He was supposed to be there for seven years."

"He got out about a week ago—on good behavior. Ironically."

"Have you heard from him yet?"

"Yeah, you wouldn't believe it. The little shit sent me an email. An email for an eighty-five-year-old woman, are you kidding me? All it said was 'I'm out.' So I checked with the prison, and sure enough, *poof*. He's gone."

She kept ranting, growing increasingly angry about my dad's ambiguity, but I could hardly hear what she was saying. There were too many noises all at once—the sound of the cars outside, people beginning their workday in a rush, the heat failing to keep up and spitting out stale cold air. My mouth was hanging open, my tongue dry against the back of my teeth. I couldn't say anything. What was I supposed to say?

"Just be safe, sweetie," she whispered in warning, like she was worried he was listening.

"What do you mean?"

She sighed. "If he could do what he did to his wife, he's capable of anything. Remember that."

How could I ever forget what he did? I wanted to bite back, anger flushing my cheeks. Did she think that in the years since she'd abandoned us, I'd somehow forgotten my father was the reason I was motherless? Screw that, *parentless*?

An authoritative voice approached, likely a staff member at Grandma's senior living facility, urging her off the phone. "I have to go. Be safe."

Click. Again she was gone.

* * *

My family came from a long line of liars, thieves, and scammers. Every woman in my family was born with The Gift. We told others, and sometimes ourselves, that The Gift was the power to foresee the future, to commune with the dead. In reality, the gift was not a gift at all. It was a curse. The curse of a flimsy spine and a willingness to do wrong even at the slightest pressure from others.

On the surface, the women were the manipulators, lying to their clients and stealing from strangers. We stole information and in my parents' case, even others' belongings, but the women weren't the root of the problem. It had always been the men.

The story goes that it all began when my great-great-grandfather William Crawford took his wife, Mary, to a presentation on spiritualism in 1849. He was amazed as the crowd threw money on the stage in the hopes of having their fortune read or being hypnotized by a greasy man with a waxed mustache. That night, long after Mary had fallen asleep, he snuck out to the inn where he suspected the performer was staying. He plied him with drinks, and when he was drunk enough, he wrung his secrets out of him like a wet rag.

"How do you do it? Is any of it real?"

"The crowd's emotions are real," the performer said. "That's all that matters to them."

When the performer slumped over at the table, William fished a thick, palm-sized notebook out of his pocket. Every page was covered in what appeared to be gibberish. Each night for the next month, he spent hours by candlelight attempting to decode the notebook. It stumped him, night after night, as he tried to decipher the list of names and symbols.

> *Cora Mary Hofer . . . Mother Minnie Allory ○ . . . Father Horace Allory ✝. Blind in one eye . . . operation did not restore sight . . . Grandmother Mary Elizabeth Scott ✝ Died from a disease she could not shake . . . Grandfather Clifton ○ running around. This disturbs Minnie . . . Fr. of Father Herman Wegner ✝ . . . Son is John Wegner ♡ . . . Fr.'s mother was named Wilharber . . .*

Each page was riddled with nonsensical tidbits of information such as this, with names and symbols neatly drawn. Tabs on the side divided the notebook by state, city, and county.

Day by day, name by name, William deciphered our city's section. After asking around about the names in the list, he finally cracked the code of the symbols. The first name in the list was the performer's target—the one he would draw up onstage. A circle next to a name meant the person was alive, while a cross indicated they'd passed. A heart was the target's love interest, and information about friends, abbreviated "Fr.," was also noted.

The performer noted small, seemingly useless details about a target's circle of people, like a relative's blindness resulting from a failed surgery. With this, he would feign sudden blindness onstage, conjuring feelings of darkness and fear as he convinced the target he was communing with her late blind father.

The performer dated his entries, and William discovered he arrived to town two days early for each performance every single time. With that time, he would visit the local cemetery, writing down names and dates of death. He would then go to pubs and inns, scribbling down pieces of overheard conversations. He created a web of relationships and secrets owned by the town and then deployed it during his shows to convince the audience of his occult powers.

My great-great-grandfather became obsessed, creating his own notebook filled with webs of information. William wasn't even a religious man, much less one to believe in spirits and mystical powers, but the draw of the money was too tempting to resist, and so was his ego. As time went by, he became more and more hesitant to admit he hadn't come up with his complex system. It was stolen, his entire identity shifting to match the performer he'd left drunk at the inn that night. His skills grew, and each member of the family continued in his wake. That's all there was in the Crawford family.

Spies, not spirits.

* * *

I stood with the phone in my hand, heart racing. I had to tell Stevie about Dad, but it was the last thing I wanted to do. She waffled back and forth between being angry with him for what he'd done and missing him, and I wasn't sure which way she would swing when I told her the news. I wouldn't know how to react if she had even a shred of desire to rekindle their relationship.

When I finally worked up the courage, I went downstairs and found her puttering around the shop, which was miserably empty.

"Stevie," I said. "I have some news."

She spun around. "Are you pregnant?" she gasped. "An immaculate conception will really draw in the customers."

I ignored the playful jab about my desolate dating life. My palms were clammy, but I had to bite the bullet and tell her. If I wanted her to be safe, she needed to know. "Grandma called to tell me Dad's out of prison."

Her face reddened, but she didn't speak. I couldn't tell what she was thinking.

"He got out on good behavior, supposedly. Him escaping through some underground tunnel seems more likely, if you ask me."

She sighed, and I waited nervously for her to speak. "Only he could weasel his way out of a seven-year sentence and make it two," she said, picking nervously at her cuticles. "Do you think he'll try to come back to the apartment?" she asked.

My heart dropped. It wasn't something I'd thought of before, but it made sense. He probably still thought the lease was in his name.

"No chance in hell he'll get in, even if he wanted to," I said. "I had all the locks changed after he went to prison, even on the windows. Dad is the most conniving man we have ever known. If he wants to find a free place to stay, there are plenty of people he could sink his fangs into."

"Nice of grandma to crawl out of her hole to deliver the good news," Stevie grumbled. "So helpful."

I glanced furtively at Stevie as she rearranged items in the shop, checking to see if she was all right. "I'm fine," she said. "Stop looking at me like that."

"Like what?"

"Like I'm a little girl."

Despite her claims that she was okay, her movements were jerky and clumsy. I winced as she nearly knocked over a bowl of crystals.

"You good?" I asked, and she just sighed. The bell above the shop's door chimed, and a middle-aged woman stepped in, her nervous energy palpable. She nearly collided with the shelves of candles and herbs for sale, but didn't seem to notice.

"I'm here for a reading," she said flatly. Underneath her eyes were deep circles ringed with smudged, unwashed eye makeup. She wore clean, well-tailored clothes that were at odds with her disheveled face and hair.

Stevie gave me a look that said *Good luck with this one* and scurried out of the room without a word, closing the velvet curtain behind her.

Great, I thought. *A cold reading. My favorite.*

Unlike a hot reading, where you could set yourself up for success with already-acquired information, a cold reading required intense focus on your sitter and split-second thinking, with guesses about the person based off throwaway comments they made or small physical details. If you'd had a sleepless night or were distracted, forget about it.

"I can help you. I'm Jade. What's your name?" I spoke to her in the soft, low voice I used when I worked.

"I need to know if he was unfaithful," she demanded, ignoring my introduction.

I got this exact same question at least once a week. I took a deep breath, my mind racing to come up with a game plan. "I see," I cooed, and motioned her to my table. Once she was seated, I asked, "May I see your hands?" I extended my hands to her, and she flinched.

Domestic abuse? I wondered, taking mental notes.

She hesitated, her eyes wary. Finally, she gave me her hands. I gripped them, holding my breath at the shock of her thin, frail fingers. Her wedding ring was so loose that it nearly slid off in my hand.

She hasn't been eating. She's been worried about this for a while.

I gently unfurled her hands and asked her to close her eyes, but they widened in resistance.

"It's okay. It's only for a moment."

Finally, she closed her eyes. Her eyelids twitched furiously, the fine muscles around her eyes unable to relax. My eyes darted around her face and body, searching for details. Her two thumbnails had been chewed so low they were bright red, while the nails of her pointer and middle fingers were stained yellow. I could picture her standing in a window with the same distant look on her eyes, the nicotine of her cigarette seeping into her fingernails while she anxiously gnawed on her thumb.

What was I going to tell her? My mind was going blank. Something about her energy was leeching into me, a feverish desperation. I closed my eyes, trying to focus.

When I opened them, I flinched at the sight of her staring right at me. She sat there unblinking, her chin tilted down so she was looking up at me through her brows.

I cleared my throat, trying to shake off the goose bumps that crept up my forearm that was still linked to her. *Go with something vague. Clearly something is eating her alive.* "I don't believe he's being fully honest with you."

Her shoulders crumpled inward as she sighed—a look I knew too well. She'd known the answer all along and didn't want to believe it. It wasn't a lie, after all. Nobody was ever fully honest. If a client was desperate enough to come to me and question their partner's loyalty, something was clearly wrong, and I wanted to push them to finally do something about it.

"This line here is your marriage line." I pointed to the small line at the base of her pinkie. "See how it's forked? This is telling us your relationship is in peril. The fork is quite large, which means the split may be permanent if you can't work through it."

I was shocked at the low laugh that came from her. She wasn't smiling. "I couldn't even find him if I wanted to work through it." She said it so low it was barely audible.

"And do you see how it forks downward? This may indicate your partner will face a devastating illness or injury. You must reconcile your differences quickly, before it's too late." That was a risky line, but I had a fifty-fifty chance of being right, and it always struck a chord.

She snatched her hand away from me and slapped a ten-dollar bill on the table, her palm making a resounding *whack* against the wood and sending a trail of crystals skittering onto the floor.

"This is all a crock of shit. I don't know why I even came." There was fury behind the declaration, but it was clear she didn't believe it herself by the fact that she just stood there as though she were waiting for me to prove her wrong.

Behind me, the velvet curtain whipped open, revealing Stevie in the doorway. One hand was on her hip and the other extended to the side, holding on to something. Even though I couldn't see what it was, I knew. We kept a baseball bat at the back doorway, ready to chase off drunken sitters or creeps. We'd never had to use it, but Stevie lovingly referred to it as Rambo, and part of me knew she would swing if she needed to.

"Do I need to walk you out, ma'am?" Stevie asked.

"I can manage," she snapped back. The bell chimed as she slung the door open and marched outside, disappearing around the corner.

"What's up her ass?" Stevie grumbled.

"Another disloyal husband."

"Surprise, surprise," was all she said as she scooped up a handful of crystals and placed them on the table.

"You gonna do the medium app before your shift?" I asked.

"Ugh. I'll do an hour, but I'll try a live stream this time and see if I earn more. You?"

"Tomorrow."

"Just yell if that woman comes back. I'll show her how we do things." She raised the bat to her shoulders and geared up for a swing.

"I don't think Rambo's services will be needed today," I said as Stevie set it down. "Hey, I won't ask again, I promise, but you sure you're all right? About the Dad stuff?"

She sighed. "Yes. I promise. You ask again and you know what happens." She pointed to the baseball bat, and I held up a pinkie finger in promise.

She made her way up the stairs as I tidied up my reading table, lining up the crystals and stacking my tarot cards in a neat pile. I shuddered as I thought of the woman staring up at me through her brows. I felt sorry for her and whatever she was going through, but at the same time, the criminal Crawford part of my brain hoped her desperation would bring her back for another reading and another chance to empty her wallet.

CHAPTER

7

Stevie

When I picked up Dad from prison a week ago, I'd told him I never wanted to see him again. I should have known he'd never listen.

"After this, please don't call anymore. Don't write letters, don't send pigeons. This is it, okay? This is goodbye," I'd said to him in the passenger seat of my borrowed car after driving him to meet a friend.

As I exited the pharmacy, I immediately knew he hadn't listened.

There was a man standing across the street facing away from me, and the familiarity of his beige Carhartt jacket set my teeth on edge. It was similar to the one my dad had always worn. No, I corrected myself, that was the exact jacket he always wore. I studied him, waiting for him to raise his right hand to take a drag off his cigarette.

Yes, there it was. The cigarette burn on the right forearm where one night he'd fallen asleep on the front porch after drinking too much. I vividly remembered looking out the window to see the cigarette tilted so far back in his hand that it was burning a slow but steady hole in his jacket. I'd rushed outside, only eight years old, to slip it out of his hand and brush away the ash. I was trying to wake him when Jade startled me from an open window.

"Just leave him out there."

"But he'll freeze," I'd whimpered.

"That's his problem," she'd said as she snapped the window shut and retreated back into our shared bedroom.

There was no doubt in my mind it was him. I stormed up to him and tapped him on the shoulder. "Are you following me?"

He turned his head as he exhaled a plume of smoke. "Not necessarily."

"I told you to leave us alone."

"I'm just keeping an eye on my girls." He took another drag. "Heard you got into college."

The fact that he'd said it as a flat, emotionless statement without a hint of congratulations was like a punch to the gut. "Who told you that?"

"Doesn't matter."

I clenched my jaw. "Doesn't matter because I probably won't be going anyway. Even with my scholarship, tuition is too high."

"Scholarship? I'll be damned." The comment almost sounded judgmental. Two police cars drove by, and my dad shot them a nasty look. "Seems like they're everywhere these days."

"Probably because of the Nichols case. The councilman's gone missing."

"Screw that family. People always get what's coming to them," he said.

"Yeah, that's how you ended up in prison, right?"

"Don't be a smart-ass. You know I'm nothing like them. God-awful people."

I paused, debating whether to ask what I'd been wondering about since hearing the news of the councilman's death. "Did you have anything to do with the councilman going missing?"

"Now why in the hell would you ask me a question like that?"

"I'm just asking."

"No, Stevie. I had nothing to do with that."

"It's just, after everything with—"

He cut me off. "Don't put your nose where it doesn't belong," he said, his voice so low and stern that I recoiled.

"It's too late for that advice."

"What do you mean?"

"Jade submitted a bogus psychic vision about him to the tip line."

The color drained from Dad's face. He took a step toward me, and I resisted the urge to step backward. He aimed his finger at my face. "You and your sister need to keep your mouths shut. Whatever is going on with that man is none of your business. Stay out of it." He turned on his heel and flicked his cigarette into the street. It sparked as it hit the ground, then faded as it rolled into a puddle.

As he walked down the street, I held my breath until he turned the corner. After all this time, a small part of me had hoped he'd changed. But clearly, I was wrong.

CHAPTER

8

Jade

I WAS LEANING BACK in my chair, idly filing my nails, when the front door chimed. There was a fleeting spike of panic as I thought of the reading earlier today—the look in that woman's eyes had given me the creeps, and I half expected to see her standing in the shop doorway staring up at me through bony brows.

"Welcome," I said, turning on my mystical facade and flinging my nail file under the table. "I'm Jade. How can I help you?"

I guessed her to be about seventy years old based on the shock of white hair that framed her face in a layered bob.

"What can I do for you today? We have a Halloween sale right now: Amber and tourmaline are half off." She looked at me blankly, prompting me to add, "Orange and black stones for Halloween. It's silly, I know."

She nodded, but dove into her purpose for being here. "I'm Lisa Doyle. I've had a lot of trouble in my house for the past two months, with no explanation for it. You're my last resort."

A spark of excitement budded in my chest. I motioned to a sitting area in the corner, and she took a seat in a tattered armchair. "Well, Lisa, I'm glad you're here. What kind of trouble are you having?"

"Two months ago we bought a new house in Buena Vista."

I made a mental note of the neighborhood. Even the smaller homes were worth over three hundred thousand dollars, maybe even half a million. I studied her a bit harder now as she continued, clocking the diamond ring on her right hand and the sharp crease of her slacks.

"The house seemed perfect when we toured it, even for the first week or so, but as soon as we began renovating, everything started going wrong. The lights were constantly going off, and five electricians all said nothing was wrong. Then things started going missing and turning up in odd places."

"You must feel so unsettled."

"That's not the worst of it. I don't even want to say it." Her eyes were watering, and a confusing wave of sympathy and delight coursed through me. There were so many possibilities here.

"It's all right," I soothed. "Take your time."

"Dots of black mold started appearing. Every morning when we woke, it had grown. By the time we got an inspector out, it was nearly six feet long. And the shape of it . . ." She shivered. "It's in the shape of a person."

The hair on my arms inched upward, the gooseflesh almost painful. An idea took hold, and I took a deep breath, debating whether or not she was a good target. The sensible, moral side of me—the one that was shrinking right before my eyes—bit back. *Target? Really, Jade? Stop thinking like your father.*

I reached forward and gently clasped her right hand in mine, squeezing lightly before wrenching my hand away, gasping as if her skin had singed mine.

"What? What's wrong?"

I shook the imaginary pain out of my hand. "Sometimes I'm especially sensitive to physical touch. Spiritual information can be transferred that way. I think my intuition was right. When you walked into the shop, I felt a dark energy coming from your right hand. It doesn't belong with the rest of your aura. May I try again?"

I winced as soon as her skin touched mine. In reality, it was pleasant. Her skin was soft and warm, her nails well manicured. But it wasn't soothing touch I was after. It was her ring. Her beautiful gold ring, a large diamond nestling between two smaller, glimmering diamonds.

"Where did you get that? Something is terribly wrong with it."

"My husband gave it to me for our anniversary about six months ago. He got it from an antique jeweler while we were in Prague celebrating."

"This ring is the root of your problems with your new home. It needs to be cleansed."

To my surprise, she wiggled the ring off her hand and handed it to me. "Do whatever you need to do. Please."

My mouth grew dry as the filthy Crawford side of my conscience stepped up to the plate, ready to take a swing. "Cleansing an object this severely polluted will take time. I'll need a few days, maybe a week."

Her eyebrows grew closer together, and her lips pressed into a tight line. "I'm not sure if I'm comfortable leaving it here."

Of course you're not. You can sense the seediness in me that I'm losing control over. I don't want to be this person. But the money . . . I swallowed the guilt down.

"Of course. I understand it means a lot to you, but interrupting the cleansing will set us back, or even worsen the problem. The spirit might sense our progress and become angry."

"Can't you just come to the house and cleanse that instead?" she asked. My parents had done many house cleansings, but the process was complex and theatrical, like a séance, but without any of the comfort of a room rigged with tricks and props.

"I don't typically do house cleansings, I'm sorry. Here." I took out my gold hoops and handed them to her. "Twenty-four-karat gold. Keep them as collateral until we're finished."

She took my earrings and gingerly slipped them into her purse, not knowing they were three-dollar pieces of junk from Amazon.

"It will be fifty dollars up front, and depending on the extent of the cleansing, the final installment could be anywhere from another fifty to one hundred dollars."

With a sigh, she pulled out her wallet and handed me a perfectly folded stack of bills. I rubbed my fingers against it, so slightly that she couldn't see, relishing in the feel of it.

"Leave me your number, and I'll call you with updates about the ring. Does that sound okay?"

"Yes. Thank you so much for helping me."

"You're in good hands."

She smiled, and the relief on her face nearly made me hand the ring back to her and cancel the whole thing. But I bit it back and waved as she walked out the door, a new lightness to her step as she made her way home.

* * *

The diamond ring in my hand glistened in the setting autumn sun as I stood in front of the pawnshop, waiting to be buzzed in.

The door finally clicked open, allowing me into a vestibule where we had to do this same song and dance over again. Mr. Pulaski had been robbed enough times that he wasn't messing around anymore, made clear by the security cameras and loaded shotgun that rested behind his cash register.

The last door lock clicked, and I let myself in. "Hi, Mr. Pulaski."

"Jade, hello. My favorite treasure hunter. Has Stevie found any more lost jewelry at the bar? That David Yurman bracelet sold within the day."

"No, but I have something better." I slung my tote bag onto his scuffed glass counter and pulled out Lisa's ring. "There's a catch. I need a duplicate."

"Why?"

"I'm a lady of mystery, Mr. Pulaski. I need an exact replica, but gold plated and cubic zirconia. Make the plate finish thick. I can't have it wearing down."

He shouted into the back room, "*Kochanie!*" His wife stepped out from behind a half-open door. One eye was still covered with a magnifying lens that was secured by a headband. Her one enormously magnified eye blinked happily back at me.

"Mrs. Pulaski! How's the family?"

"Chris is Chris, you know? Always manages to land on his feet. Adam . . . well, that's for another time. What do you have for me?"

I handed her the ring, and she clicked her tongue in approval. "I need an exact replica of this, but it needs to be affordable. And then I'll sell this one to you."

Mrs. Pulaski said something to her husband in Polish, the harsh consonants a mystery to me. Though she was American and had learned Polish for him, you'd never tell by her accent and the quick cadence of their conversation. At first I'd found their shared tongue romantic, but I'd soon realized it was so they could have stealthy negotiations right out in the open.

"I can do it. Two hundred for the replica. How does that sound?"

"Depends on how much you can give me for the real one."

They spoke back and forth in Polish before Mr. Pulaski said, "One thousand five hundred."

Mrs. Pulaski picked at a cuticle. Her husband stepped ever so slightly ahead of her, as if he were ready to catch a bullet.

I shook my head. "This is vintage, 1910." I picked a year at random. "From Prague." At least that part was true.

More low and quick Polish. In English, Mr. Pulaski lobbed back, "One thousand six hundred. Final offer."

"How about we do seventeen hundred. Homecoming is soon, and there'll be plenty more drunk college girls losing their jewelry at Stevie's bar. Sound good?"

Mr. Pulaski stuck his hand out. "Deal."

"Pleasure doing business with you." And it really was—I'd grown fond of them over the last few months of treasure hunting, as Mr. Pulaski called it.

"I can have this replica done in about a week. I'll call you."

"You're the best." I turned on my heel and waved as I let myself out, taking a deep breath as I entered the crisp fall afternoon. A trepidatious hope loomed like a half-bloomed seed in my chest.

Then my celebratory breath hitched as I caught a glimpse of the last person I wanted to see.

* * *

"Lisa!" I sputtered.

Her eyes were narrowed as she greeted me. "Jade, hello." Her tone was flat and pinched.

"Lovely weather for a walk," I said just as a gust of wind blew my hair into my mouth.

She shrugged. "Some might say. I need to ask you something."

Dread crept in on me. She was connecting the dots and was going to ask me why the hell I was standing in front of a pawnshop the same day she'd given me her beloved ring.

A blur of movement across the street caught my eye, but I ignored it and stepped to the side, trying to get the pawnshop out of her line of sight. She shuffled to the side just as I'd hoped. "What is it?"

She sighed. "I know you said you don't do house cleansings, but I want to ask you to make an exception. My husband and I have been feeling terribly ill. We can hardly breathe, and there's this thick mental fog over both of us. Would you be willing to stop by and take a look? Maybe you can tell if it's . . . spiritual or not."

This poor woman had come to me in good faith, albeit a naive and desperate faith, and I'd immediately betrayed her. We were all born our own person, but the behaviors instilled in us by our parents were sometimes impossible to break, constantly echoing in our heads at the worst possible moment. And right now that echo was all I could hear. This was a chance to even the scales and improve her life, even if the comfort it would provide was all placebo.

My thoughts were interrupted by the sight of more movement across the street. You rarely saw people in the alleyways between buildings, except for business owners tossing out trash at lightning speed. But this person was standing still, and I could swear they were staring right at me, a trail of cigarette smoke billowing upward. The only problem was that it was too cloudy, making the alleyway unnaturally dark for this time of day, so I couldn't see their face.

"Jade? What do you think?" Lisa prompted.

I swallowed, my throat dry as I remembered how wrong my parents' house cleansings had sometimes gone. "I can't do a full cleansing, I'm sorry."

Our parents had done a handful of home cleansings when they were at the peak of their popularity, and most of them had gone well. One, however, stuck in my mind.

The Irvines had moved from New Orleans to North Carolina in the early 2000s and had come to my parents for help soon after moving in, claiming their house was haunted by a malevolent spirit. My parents hadn't had a babysitter that night, or pretty much ever, so we'd tagged along. Because what's a more appropriate place for children than a home possessed by a poltergeist?

The Irvine house had been riddled with mysterious happenings, from freshly purchased food rotting within a day to waking up to all the mugs, plates, and bowls stacked high to the ceiling. The Irvines had never stopped for a moment to think of the real-world causes to these strange events or the fact that their son was not the little choirboy they thought he was.

After watching *The Exorcist* one night at a sleepover, little Johnny Irvine had started waking up in the middle of the night to do anything he could to convince his parents their house was haunted. All he wanted to do was to move back to New Orleans, where his grandparents and best friends lived, but rather than express that, he decided to scare the living hell out of his parents and waste hundreds of their dollars on my parents' so-called spiritual extermination services.

Luckily for my parents, Johnny's mother and father didn't figure that out for quite some time. What they did figure out was that my parents had stolen from them. During the cleansing, as they walked room to room to sage the air and murmur their pseudospiritual platitudes, my father pilfered the Irvines' things and stuffed them in mine and Stevie's pockets. He thought he'd stolen just enough to make decent money but not enough to be noticed. He took jewelry, but never the nicest piece in the jewelry box. He took prescription pills, but never the entire bottle—just a skim off the top.

He thought that since the Irvines had been stupid enough to ask him and Mom to cleanse their house, they'd be stupid enough not to notice. It was actually their son who noticed first. He had been peeking out in curiosity from behind corners like the creepy little ghost he pretended to be, and only at the end of the cleansing did he tell his parents Dad had stuffed our pockets with their things.

The disappointment on Lisa's face put a pit in my stomach, so I resigned to meeting her halfway. "How about I stop by and sage the house for you? I can do it in three days, if that works."

Her shoulders slumped with relief, and she pressed her hands together in prayer. "Oh, thank the Lord."

Guilt crashed into the spark of joy from her relief, the two swarming around each other like oil and water. Something good could come of this. Even if I knew it was all bullshit, I could make her feel more at peace in her own home.

"And the ring?" she asked anxiously as she rubbed the indent on her finger where it used to rest. "Do you think you'll be able to . . . fix it?"

"Yes, of course, but I'll need some time with it. Since it's antique, there are multiple people's energies attached to it. I want to do a thorough job."

"Of course. Take your time. I trust you."

Trust. The word rattled around in my head as we said our goodbyes, Lisa whispering a sincere and gentle "Thank you" in my ear before pulling away.

I resisted the urge to get away from the pawnshop as quickly as possible. I should be sprinting back inside and telling the Pulaskis I needed the ring back. Screw the plan, screw the money.

Are you really going to lie to yourself? You enjoyed it just a little. Admit it.

Maybe a small part of me did. But that spark of endorphins was so easily dampened by the guilt that it was hardly worth it. How had Mom and Dad done this so often without the guilt eating them alive?

"You have to do whatever it takes to provide for your family," Dad had said.

Bullshit. Sure, some of the money had gone toward bills, but most of it had gone toward booze and tools to help him scam more people, whether it was information on clients or props for séances. He'd spent two thousand dollars on the high-tech sound system in the séance room—the one that made clients hear spirits in surround sound—and my parents had only been able to use it once before my dad was arrested. Before he got Mom killed. After we were financially stable, we were done with all this.

I finally made it back to our shop, my heart pounding as I wrenched open the door. "Stevie!" I shouted out as I ran up the stairs to our apartment, tossing my bag haphazardly on the coatrack and flinging my shoes off as I went.

I didn't hear her typical response of *What?!* from anywhere in the small apartment. "You'll never believe what just happened," I said loudly, trying to tempt her out of hiding. I was desperate to tell her about the pawnshop, and a part of me wanted her to convince me that what I'd done was okay—that it was just a part of survival when we didn't know anything else.

And tell her about Daniel too—God, I want to sit on her floor and giggle like a little schoolgirl at the thought of our movie night tonight, even though she would convince me it wasn't *just* a movie night. It was a date night. A first date. Why did I suddenly feel like I was going to throw up?

A door shut downstairs, followed by a creaking floorboard. There was no chime, so it wasn't the front door. It had to have been the door to the séance room or our prop room, which we had no need for this week. I skittered back down the stairs, but the shop was empty.

"Stevie?" I called out meekly, opening the door to the séance room and peering in. It was empty and dark, just as expected.

Stevie didn't have work until much later tonight, and she hadn't mentioned any errands, but it was clear now she wasn't home.

A tingle of anxiety crept over me as I checked the locks on the doors and windows. I was suddenly overly aware of the fact that our father could be out of prison at this very moment, walking around in the same world as Stevie without me there to protect her.

Maybe my warning to him when we'd last spoken had been enough. He knew I didn't want anything to do with him.

I just wasn't sure if the same was true of Stevie.

* * *

I sat listlessly at the tarot table, shuffling the cards as I observed people on the street strolling by with shopping bags and to-go coffees. A group of students clad in Wake Forest gear walked by, and I immediately tensed as I thought about the looming first tuition payment for Stevie. I chewed on the inside of my cheek, watching another person walk by without even glancing at the shop.

I split the deck in two and bridged them together, watching the cards flip and fold into one another in a satisfying, mesmerizing stack when I stopped, sending the remaining cards in my left hand shooting across the table.

Two men in suits approached from the right, walking past the wide shop window while turning their heads to look inside. Seconds later the bell above the door gave a tinny chime.

"Are you Jade Ravencroft?" the larger of the two men asked me. I stiffened as he flashed his detective badge. His foreboding height drowned out the light coming in from the window, and I suddenly wanted him out.

It wasn't a great start that they didn't even greet me with a *hello* or a *how are you*, but I took a breath and reassured myself that I didn't do anything wrong. At least legally.

Not true, a voice chimed in my head as I thought of the ring I'd pawned. My heart quickened in my chest, and my dry tongue felt too big for my mouth.

Don't think about the ring. Stop thinking about the damn ring. My anxious brain was telling me that yes, magic was real and telepathy was absolutely a skill detectives had and, oh God, I was going to prison. How ironic that as soon as my father got out of prison, I'd take his place, as though the scales of justice demanded the flesh of at least one Crawford.

The shorter detective spoke next in a high-pitched voice, as though he had a glob of peanut butter stuck in his throat from a hasty lunch. "My name is Detective McCade, and this is Detective Woolridge. We'd like to ask you some questions. This will all be confidential, of course."

"Okay," I said. I stood and started to drag the chair I was sitting in over to the chairs to join them, but every muscle in my body was tensed and primed to toss it straight at them and flee out the door. Instead, I placed it directly across from them and sat, crossing my legs at my ankles like a good little girl.

"We'd like to talk to you about the . . ." He fumbled. *Oh God, they found Lisa's ring at the pawnshop.* Finally, in disbelief, he said, "The vision you called in regarding Councilman Nichols."

Relief flooded through me, but a portion of guilt still squeezed tight in my throat. When I spoke, it was audible. "Oh, yes. It's terrible what happened to him, so I wanted to help."

"What *happened* to him? What do you mean by that?" The larger detective, Detective Woolridge, leaned forward, pressing his elbows against his knees, fanning out the muscles in his arms like a damn silverback gorilla. How did these two even get paired up? Did the little one ride around on his back?

"Well, I mean that he's missing."

"Did something happen to Mr. Nichols that you're keeping to yourself?"

"What? No. That's not what I meant at all. This entire situation is awful. That's all I meant. I don't know anything about the missing-person case aside from what I saw in my vision."

Woolridge grunted but didn't speak. Detective McCade chimed in his slightly aggravating voice, "That's what we came to ask you about today—this vision of yours. Can you start by telling us more about it?" His tone had taken a turn—it was a bit more pointed.

I straightened my back and explained how my visions arrived as flashes of images.

McCade was scribbling in his little spiral bound notebook, but Woolridge was still leaning forward with his pectoral muscles flexing menacingly at me. "Flashes of images," Woolridge said, clearly amused. "Sounds a lot like a memory to me."

"And what do you see in these images?" McCade asked, not giving me a chance to ask Woolridge what he meant by that.

He clearly thought I had far more to do with this than just some vision.

I had to tread carefully with this question. If you were thinking in black and white, I was lying about having a psychic vision. But I wasn't lying about an image popping into my head of the construction site by the lake, but that was only because I'd been annoyed by the noise the last time Stevie and I had gone on a walk there.

"First, I saw Salem Lake. I thought it was a memory. But then I saw the nearby construction site, and it was like I was a bird, looking down from above. I remember getting dizzy, like I sometimes do, and then I saw Councilman Nichols' face. I didn't realize what it was about until I saw the news."

The buttons across Woolridge's chest held on for dear life as he flexed harder, his gaze growing even more shrewd. "You said you saw the news segment, had your vision, and called right after. About what time was the news segment?"

Why would that even matter? "I guess it was sometime in the morning of the twenty-fourth, I think."

"Hmm. That's odd," Woolridge said. "McCade, check your notebook. What time did Miss Ravencroft call the station?"

McCade flipped back in his notebook, bending the papers as he went. Looked like Woolridge made him a little nervous too. McCade rubbed his brow like he was disappointed, like I'd failed some secret test. "Nine fifteen PM."

Shit.

"That's not right after the morning segment, in my opinion." Woolridge gave a huff of a laugh, sending the smell of garlic across the room. Why hadn't I thought to get my story straight, maybe write down everything I'd done and said so far?

My patience was wearing thin. "The story was on throughout the day. It can be hard to keep track of the time."

"Right." Woolridge shrugged his dumb giant shoulders. Every action, every word was condescending.

The silence in the room was stifling, and it was becoming clear that at least Woolridge found my tip suspicious. "Have you found any more information about the councilman?" I asked.

"We're not at liberty to say just yet," McCade said.

"Well, I hope he's found safe and sound."

"But only if he's found exactly where you said he'd be," Woolridge said low and fast.

"Excuse me?"

McCade glared at him before he stuck his hand out to me. His palms were dry and rough against my clammy, nervous skin. "Thank you for your time."

Detective Woolridge didn't bother shaking my hand and was already walking to the door. He looked up at the shop's sign above the doorframe. "Nice speaking with you, Madame Ravencroft," he said with disdain.

"You too, Detective Woodruff," I said back, a wide, insincere smile on my face. He let out a nearly silent huff, the kind that tilts your chin up and back. I took pleasure in the fact that it doubled his chin, when he clearly cared enough about his appearance to spend hours in the gym.

They glanced at each other and walked out of the shop. My heart raced with pride in myself for jabbing back at him—making him feel he was insignificant enough that not even his name was worth remembering. When they were out of view of the shop window and I sat, my heart rate slowed, regret and embarrassment twisting their fists around my heart.

Why did I say that? What is wrong with me?

The detectives hadn't actively accused me of anything, but Woolridge had made it more than clear he held no respect for me nor my profession. The last thing I needed was to sharpen that derision into action, his dislike for me driving him to pin something on me.

I lowered my forehead on the tarot table, where my cards lay scattered. As I sat there with my eyes closed, I wished I'd never submitted the tip at all.

CHAPTER 9

Jade

After getting ready to see Daniel, I paused in my bedroom doorway before turning around to spritz perfume on the nape of my neck. Even though Stevie was probably at work by now, I could practically feel her laughing at me.

Oh, you're trying to impress someone, huh?

I wasn't sure, to be honest. I'd always found him cute, but in the kind of way you'd find a puppy cute. Goofy. Harmless. But there had been a shift in something after he'd comforted me about the bills. He'd been gentle but not patronizing. Helpful but not insistent.

He's a therapist, I told myself. *That's his job. It doesn't mean anything.*

My heart thumped wildly as I locked up the shop and walked next door. His practice was dim, and a ray of golden light peeked out from Daniel's half-open office door. Thinking he was inside, I poked the door with one finger and stepped inside, but it was empty.

I paused at the sight of the patient files on top of his desk, the names of patients clearly labeled in thick black Sharpie. Behind the desk were three enormous filing cabinets, each drawer stuffed with patient information. So much information that I could use against my clients.

Against? I barked at myself.

Daniel's footsteps creaked above me. These buildings were old, and every footstep made the building groan like it was in pain. I bit down on the desire to riffle through the files and stepped back out into the lobby, making sure to leave the office door cracked open as much as it was before.

"I'm here," I said as I opened his apartment door, and was greeted with the buttery smell of popcorn. Everything was tidy, with hardwood floors and shining appliances. Soft golden lamps dotted the living room that connected to the kitchen, reflecting off the clean, white walls. It was so different from our place, with its heavy crimsons and suffocating velvets. His apartment was like breathing cool night air after being stuck inside a smoky bar.

"I'm glad you could make it," Daniel said as he ushered me inside. I smiled at him in agreement. "You pick the movie. I'll pick the drinks." He opened the fridge and plucked out two bottles of beer.

I scrolled the endless catalog of streamable movies and picked a horror movie at random. He raised his eyebrows at my choice. "Gotta get in the Halloween spirit," I said.

"Aren't you always in the Halloween spirit?" He grinned, popping the top off a beer and handing it to me.

I took a small sip. "You got me there."

My eyes followed Daniel's hand as he wiped the condensation from the bottle onto his button-up shirt, which was untucked and slightly wrinkled from his workday.

"How was your day?" I asked. "Anything interesting?" Another nervous sip.

"My last two patients of the day were tough, but they're still pretty new. Some people take time to open up." He tilted his head and raised an eyebrow, clearly a playful jab.

I smiled. "I have no idea what you're talking about."

Daniel took the popcorn into the living room and I followed, excitement fluttering in my stomach as I joined him on the couch. I was relieved he hadn't asked me about my day. If he had, would I have told him about the tip? No, I decided. It was best I didn't.

The movie began and Daniel kept a respectable distance, the bowl of popcorn in between us. Another hour passed, and Daniel paused the movie and returned with two more beers. The television lit up the right side of his face, casting blue-toned shadows along his jawline.

I took a sip, already feeling the tingle of a buzz in my limbs. He leaned back into the sofa, and without thinking, I put the bowl of popcorn on the coffee table and shifted closer to him.

He glanced at me out of the corner of his eye as my knee rested against his thigh, a whisper of denim against denim. Goose bumps ran up my forearm, both from the chill of his air conditioning and the electric tension that was building in the room. Or maybe I was imagining it. I'd been too busy the past few years for anything vaguely romantic, and I'd nearly forgotten this feeling, much less what to do. Every single skill I used for reading people was out the window.

Stop overthinking it.

Still, all I could focus on was the heat against my knee, such an innocent part of my body, but distracting nonetheless. I inched closer to him, my left thigh pressed softly against his. He looked at me in surprise, then a brief smile fluttered across his face.

The movie was drawing to an end, and my head buzzed pleasantly with the two beers. "Did you like it?" he asked as the credits rolled.

I nodded, unwilling to admit that I couldn't remember a single detail of the plot. My eyes flitted to his lips, which were full, the skin smooth and inviting. He leaned a bit closer, the anticipation amplifying. I almost reached out for his face, eager for the heat of his skin against my palm. He was so close.

Until he wasn't. He reached for the remote and paused the movie on the rolling credits.

I stood, embarrassed. "I'd better get going."

"Let me walk you down." He opened the door for me and followed me downstairs. The light from his office sliced through the room, setting the front door aglow.

I turned to him, halfway through thanking him, and almost took in a sharp breath. He was closer to me than I'd thought. His hands were in his front pockets and my eyes drifted down his arms, taking in the way the dim light cast shadows across the divots of his muscles.

"Maybe next time I can take you out to dinner?" he said.

"That'd be nice," I half whispered. I couldn't stop looking at his lips, which were parted in a smile.

"Good. Want me to walk you home?"

"It's a long journey, but I'm sure I can manage."

I waved goodbye and tried to keep a straight face as I walked home. I closed the front door behind me and let a wide, wild smile spread across my face. It was a pure, joyous emotion that I hadn't felt for entirely too long.

CHAPTER 10

Jade

IT WAS NEARLY two in the morning and I'd given up on sleep. My blankets lay in a chaotic wad at my feet. A dull thud drew my attention, but I brushed it off. The apartment and shop were in an old building, built around 1920, and the bones of the structure groaned night and day, especially as the weather turned colder and the pipes ached with the chill.

I kicked away my blankets and drew my knees into my chest, rocking side to side in an attempt to alleviate the backache I'd given myself from tossing and turning. I was only twenty-five, but all the time I spent hunched over tarot cards and séance tables had aged my spine by decades.

Another sound, louder this time. It was a ghostly metallic groan, like the building was wrenched with pain. The sound ceased, just to climax with a crash.

I jumped out of bed, my body moving me into action, then freezing as my fear took over. I had no idea what the sound was or where it was coming from. The sound echoed out again and Stevie joined me in the upstairs foyer, crossing her arms across her body. Her hair was mussed and her eyes crusted with sleep. She was shaking, and her skinny legs were riddled with goose bumps.

"What was that?" she whispered.

"I don't know. Go back in your room," I told her as I took one step down and tried my best to peer around the twist of the stairs. But I couldn't see anything. I took a breath, as if I could expel the adrenaline coursing through me, and stepped farther down. Stevie, of course, hadn't followed my instructions and was close at my heels.

It felt like it took an hour to reach the bottom of the stairs. We usually left the velvet curtain that separated the apartment from the shop open at night—it was mostly for keeping drunk people from wandering up into our apartment to find a bathroom more than it was for adding any security—but for some reason I'd left it closed tonight.

Or had I?

The sickly metallic sound was nearly constant now, and the thump that sounded like fists was percussive and insistent. My stomach lurched as I pictured the front door. It was an ancient steel door covered in layers of paint from all its previous tenants. *Someone is breaking in,* I realized in the same moment that Stevie said it aloud.

"Stay here. I'll check."

This time, Stevie followed my directions. I took three steps forward and raised my hand to the velvet curtain, my fingers nearly vibrating with each quick, shallow breath I took.

The noise paused for a moment, and I peeled the curtain back an inch to peer out. There was nothing to see—only the gray wash of night over the shop's already-dark colors, the rich amethyst and ruby hues becoming dull and flat.

I opened the curtain all the way and moved forward, glancing back to make sure Stevie stayed put. She was still there, now with something in her hand. A baseball bat. Her trusty Rambo. The sight of her with it was somehow both laughable and intimidating—her pale skin nearly fluorescent in the moonlight that streamed in the long, skinny window in the stairwell, the baseball bat wider than even the thickest part of her bicep.

In the darkness, I was able to see through the front windows that there wasn't a soul in sight. The word *soul* echoed in my head, and I felt foolish for wondering if the sound wasn't from a person at all but from a spirit. A soul so furious with our career of spiritual contempt that it had finally come for justice.

Stevie shrieked as the noise began again in one long shuddering screech. I flipped on the light. Why hadn't I done that in the first place? I always mocked the beautiful but utterly stupid characters in the horror movies Stevie liked to watch, laughing at the way they froze in fear, forgetting they could just turn on the lights or call the cops. And here I was in the middle of the night doing exactly what they did. Flailing in the face of fear.

I turned around to say just that to Stevie when my stomach dropped. A blob of gray mottled the corner of the ceiling, about three feet wide. I stood in utter defeat as a steady stream of drops released itself from the gray cloud in the ceiling, the plaster becoming pudding-like and bulbous against what I imagined was a hidden stream of water above it.

"No," I groaned as I inspected the damage. Dread was heavy in my gut. "How do we turn the water off?"

"I have no idea." Stevie made her way to my side, the bat limp in her hand. "Shit."

Here it was—the rug being pulled out from underneath me. Divine retribution for my wrongs.

Stevie set the bat down and moved into action, pulling shelves away from the water. Because it was just our luck, a display of tarot cards and books on spiritualism were directly below the water, all of them soggy and expanding like sponges. That was at least two hundred dollars down the drain.

"It's the first freeze of fall. The old pipes must have finally given up." Stevie was panting with the effort of rearranging the shop, trying to save it from the barrage of moisture.

"*Give up*," I scoffed. "Right about now, I'd love to do the same."

* * *

It was four in the morning when Stevie and I finally went to bed. We'd spent two hours arranging every bucket, bowl, and Tupperware container we owned to catch the water dripping from the ceiling. As I lay in bed afterward, I became convinced that it was revenge for stealing Lisa's ring and that somehow her moldy decaying ghost had transferred itself into our building.

After a measly three hours of sleep, I called a plumber, who now stood in front of us. He stared up at the water damage, his slight paunch peeking out from his untucked polo shirt. He turned around to face us, a look of dismay on his face. "Well, how do I say this? The culprit seems to be"—he paused, a blush forming on his cheeks—"lady products."

"Pardon?" I asked, which only made him blush deeper.

"You know. Um, hygiene products."

I glared at Stevie, whom I'd lectured at least a dozen times already when the toilets would back up, but she was avoiding my eyes. Our rental agreement clearly stated that if the leak was caused by regular wear and tear, it'd be covered. If it was caused by the renter's negligence or improper use, we'd be responsible for the entire bill. I could throttle her, but it'd have to wait until the plumber left.

"These pipes haven't had any maintenance since they were installed, so it was only a matter of time before something took them out." His Southern accent was thick, and the slightly slowed cadence was lulling me into a false sense of calm. "Looks like they were the originals from—"

"The 1920s," Stevie said in unison with him. "Yeah, unfortunately, that's what we thought."

The plumber smiled at her, impressed by a woman he assumed to be very knowledgeable in his field. That wasn't the case, but Stevie had that effect on men, much to her dismay.

"I hate to break it to you, ladies," he said, "but this is going to cost a pretty penny."

"How pretty?" Stevie asked. She crossed her arms in front of her, pressing her breasts together so that her cleavage was in full view. Despite my frustration with her, I bit back a laugh and tried to cover it by clearing my throat. She glared at me, then faced him again with a hesitant smile. Her gaze darted to his hand, and I clocked his ringless left hand just as she did.

Mom had always taught us that if someone was blinded enough by good looks and charm, you could get plenty of extras out of them if you faked a little interest in them.

"Usually this repair would run for about two thousand. Not only do the pipes need replacing, but the ceiling needs work. You'll have to call someone else for that—I can refer you. The innards of the building are spotted with mold, so this leak seems to have been going on for some time."

The innards. The phrase set my stomach on edge as I imagined the building as a carcass on the side of the road, riddled with decay.

"Two thousand?" Stevie and I said in unison. The only difference in delivery was that mine was barked out in disbelief and anger whereas hers was pitiful. Her damsel-in-distress act was really gearing up.

"There's no way we can afford that. I'm so sorry for wasting your time," Stevie said. Her bottom lip stuck out slightly, and her chin quivered. Even though the flirting was an act, I knew she was genuinely upset, and I wouldn't have been surprised if she burst into tears. Honestly, I could have too, but I knew if I did, neither of us would be able to get a hold of ourselves.

He looked between the two of us, noting our red eyes and dark circles from lack of sleep. And likely noting the shabbiness of the shop, which was painfully evident with the curtains drawn back and the overhead lights turned on.

"All right. Let me call my boss and see if there's anything we can do for you ladies."

As soon as he stepped out the front door, I whispered to Stevie, "Nice boob maneuver. I bet he'll take a solid four dollars off for those things."

Stevie rolled her eyes. "These are worth *at least* fifteen each."

We did our best to rearrange our products after shifting everything away from the brigade of buckets, which were already half full with murky water. Stevie dragged in extra velvet fabric that we'd used to cordon off the tarot table for private readings and I fetched the staple gun without her even asking, both of us working in tandem like we always had.

Moments later the plumber walked back in, phone still in hand. "We can do it for a thousand; how about that?"

"Hmm," I said. "How about eight fifty if we display your business cards at checkout?"

We waited, holding our breath, while he and his boss negotiated. Finally, he said, "We've got a deal."

He was clearly proud of himself, eager for Stevie's approval. "Thank you so much," she said. "We appreciate it." She climbed up on a chair, staple gun in one hand and a bolt of fabric in the other.

"You need help with that?" he asked, his eyes roving over a sliver of Stevie's midriff as she reached up to the ceiling. Her ass was directly in his line of sight, and it was clear he would linger the entire day if it meant the view stayed the same.

"We got this. Thanks." Stevie winked at him, but I could see the annoyance set tight in her jaw.

He let us know he'd be back with a crew later in the day. As soon as he left, Stevie and I got to work on our hastily crafted partitions. While we cordoned off the water damage, we debated if we should close the shop entirely until the work was completed, but Stevie shot it down.

"Are you kidding? We need the money. We'll just cover it up and pretend it never happened."

She was right. We needed every penny we could earn. Bills were piling up, and we were going to have to make a sacrifice soon to be able to keep our head above water. I just didn't know what that sacrifice would be.

CHAPTER

11

Jade

I STARED AT THE patchwork of bath towels and kitchen rags splayed out in a chaotic mess on the floor. They had turned our water off, so all that was left while we waited for the plumber to return was preventing damage from the water that pooled on the floor, leaving the shop soggy. A mildewy smell had already taken over and I'd resorted to propping the front door wide open, leaving me feeling vulnerable.

I was gripping the phone, arguing with my pride as my thumb hovered over the keypad. I didn't want to ask for a handout, but after the catastrophe with the ceiling, I was desperate. I typed in her number and gritted my teeth, not knowing how she would react to me calling.

I shifted on my feet as the phone rang, then stiffened as I heard her gruff voice. "Grandma, hi. It's Jade."

"Oh, hello, sweetie. Is something wrong?" she asked in a panic.

"Well, yes, but don't worry, it's not about Dad." I knew, based off her final warning to be careful, with Dad being out of prison, that she would immediately assume he'd shown up and wreaked havoc. Something *was* wrong, but luckily it didn't involve him.

"All right then, what's the problem?"

I cleared my throat. She wasn't the softest of women—the type to always talk about hard work and bootstraps. When my mother had died—her *daughter*—her advice had been to "buck up, buttercup. Time heals all wounds." Not necessarily incorrect advice, but all I'd really wanted was consoling and commiserating. "Our ceiling caved in last night, and the cost is wiping out our bank account. I wanted to reach out to ask for help. I never do this, but—"

She cut me off. "You need some money? Of course, honey. I'll put it in the mail today."

My heart jumped with hope and joy from finally hearing gentleness in her voice. "Thank you so much. You know I hate handouts; I just didn't know what else to do."

"Not a handout, honey. Just a little help. All right, doll, gotta go. It's pickleball day, and I'm about to rip Glenda a new one."

I didn't know what pickleball was, but I did know Glenda was in grave danger. I wished her luck, and we said our goodbyes.

"Hello, Jade," a voice said behind me, causing my breath to hitch. I hadn't even heard the bell above the door chime. I spun on my heel.

My stomach immediately dropped. "Lisa, hello! Sorry, I didn't hear you." In the chaos, I'd forgotten about her ring, which was still sitting in the back of the Pulaskis' pawnshop, ready to be replicated and sold. I pushed away the makeshift curtains and motioned to the ceiling. "Sorry the shop is a mess. What are you doing here?"

The color drained from Lisa's face, and she took a wavering step back. A strangled mew escaped her throat and tears sprang into her eyes.

"Lisa?" She made the sign of the cross as she stared up at the ceiling. "What's wrong?"

"Jade . . . oh Lord. I'm so sorry. Look what I've done. Oh no . . ." She trickled off, her fist now clenched tight around the gold cross pendant she'd pulled out from under her blouse.

"Lisa, it's all right. There's nothing to be worried about. It's just—" I was going to say *a water leak* when she interrupted me.

"A curse."

Oh. I hadn't even been thinking of her mold-ridden house as she'd stared up at the shop's ceiling, but now it was obvious. She thought that by my taking the ring, whatever was haunting her house had transferred itself to me and my own home. My gut reaction was to grip her by the shoulders, look her in the eye, and sternly tell her *It's mold, Lisa. Mold!*

But then the deeply instilled Crawford business ethic, or literally the opposite of ethics, kicked in and I realized what an opportunity I had sitting in front of me. Not only did I have the potential income from her ring, but now I had what she thought was proof she had some sort of serious supernatural infestation—one so strong it had crawled on its occult tendrils all the way from the nicest neighborhood in the city into my shabby psychic parlor. In her eyes, it was undeniable now that she needed every service I could offer her. At whatever cost.

"The cleansing of the ring has proven harder than I initially believed." I stepped toward her, but instead of letting the curtain fall closed, I draped it behind a nearby shelf, showing her the full damage the water had caused. Or in her mind, the curse.

The ceiling had quickly degraded to a murky brown-and-black paste. Clumps of it had fallen onto the mosaic of towels I'd laid on the floor. The water spot was now nearly as long as a grown adult—exactly how she'd described the moldy spot on her own ceiling. Where I saw hundreds of dollars' worth of damage, she saw spiritual infection.

"The ring needs further cleansing. I was just about to call you with an update."

"So it's not working?" Lisa asked in a pitiful whisper.

"Not yet. But it will. I have a few tricks left up my sleeve." *Tricks.* That was all I had. She just didn't know it was literal. I waited for her to concede as she blinked back at me, but the steely resolve that overtook her previously anxious face took me by surprise.

"How about you give me the ring back? I can drive it as far away as possible and throw it out the car window. Or off a cliff. Anything." Her eyes were wide, nearly vibrating with a sudden anger. Was the anger at the ring or at me? "Just give it back. I'll still pay you. Give me the ring."

I tried to swallow the lump in my throat. I couldn't think of anything to say. There was no finesse left in me, no more smooth words nor charm. She was growing more frustrated and she stuck her hand out, palm up and open in demand.

"You must not disturb a cleansing," Stevie said from the doorway, making me jump. She was dressed in black, likely on her way to a shift at the bar, but with her dark hair and bloodshot eyes rimmed with black makeup, she looked like more of an expert on the occult than I did. "If you interrupt the cleansing of a cursed object, the spirit will grow stronger. Then it won't even need an object anymore. It would only need a person."

Lisa closed her hand into a fist and snatched it away. "Fine," she murmured. "Do whatever you need to do."

"We'll get you your life back, Lisa. I promise."

* * *

I stood in the Pulaski Pawn Shop vestibule, growing colder by the second as the wind blew through the cracks in the external door. It was unseasonably chilly again today, the clouds thick and menacing overhead as they blotted out any hint of sunshine.

I buzzed a second time and followed it up with an impatient series of knocks on the glass doors, wondering where the hell Mr. and Mrs. Pulaski were. I'd never seen the shop open but empty. Even if there were no customers, there was always some sort of under-the-table business going on inside. After all, the Pulaskis lived in the apartment above the shop and could pop downstairs at any hour.

A minute or two later, Mr. Pulaski emerged from the back room and rushed to buzz me. "So sorry, Jade! My apologies," he said breathlessly as I entered and shook off the lingering chill.

"No problem. You all right, Mr. Pulaski? You don't look all that well."

His skin was clammy, and his usually coiffed silver-and-black hair was plastered against his forehead. He brushed it back and released a huff of breath. "Busy day, but feeling great. You know I always look great too." He patted his belly, and the signet ring on his pinkie glinted against the fluorescent light. He always poked fun at his appearance, but today's joke lacked the usual smile.

He had sweat building in his armpits, darkening his gray polo shirt to a deep charcoal where his arms met his chest. He pushed back his shoulders under my gaze, and I could swear that despite his forced confidence, he was squirming a bit. "You sure?"

"Yes, yes, what is it you need today?" He waved his hands in front of him, then leaned against the glass countertop.

"I just wanted to check on the status of the ring I brought in. Has it sold?"

"Hmm, the ring? The ring . . ." Mr. Pulaski tapped his fingers along the glass, and with each tap, my patience wore thinner.

"Oh, come on, Mr. Pulaski. Don't act like you forgot about the ring I brought you yesterday. The vintage gold diamond ring from Prague?"

"Prague, ah yes. It hasn't sold yet." He pushed off the counter and crossed his arms against his chest, then immediately unwrapped them to unlatch the display case under the counter and bent down to fiddle with his merchandise.

I crouched to meet his eyes through the glass case, not letting him off the hook yet. If he was uncomfortable, he had to know I was ten times more uncomfortable with the weight of this scheme on my shoulders. "How is that possible? That David Yurman bracelet sold in one day—you reminded me yourself. This is five times more valuable."

"Yes, that's part of the problem. Something that expensive narrows the market to a select few buyers."

"How narrow?"

"There are only three interested."

I groaned. My family had worked with the Pulaskis enough to know the cadence of these types of sales. Mr. Pulaski straightened, avoiding my gaze once more. Unfortunately for him, I had grown up with a younger sister who challenged me nearly every day as to who could be the most annoying.

I stood and leaned against the counter. "Is there another problem you're not telling me about?"

There was a rustling in the back room, and a burst of movement made the curtain separating the shop from the back room swish slightly in response. I wondered if Mrs. Pulaski was in the back eavesdropping. I wouldn't fault her for it—I would have done the same. Floorboards creaked above me, and I eyed Mr. Pulaski as he shifted on his feet.

"Are the boys here?" I asked. They had two sons a bit older than me, and I wanted to be nowhere near them. They had none of the gentle charm of their parents and had gotten involved with the wrong people, so their parents had kicked them out years ago.

"No," he said quickly, then cleared his throat. "Anyway, a sale like this can be off-putting. One of the prospects will likely back out today. I'm waiting for confirmation."

"Off-putting how? They buy stuff like this all the time."

"Not necessarily. They buy plenty of stolen jewelry, but none so easily identifiable. Half-a-carat solitaires from Jared's, or a tennis bracelet from Kay's. A custom vintage ring from Prague—with an inscription, nonetheless—is like waving a red cloth in front of a bull. There are so many levels of provenance here that can point authorities right back to us. And to you."

What the hell is provenance? I didn't bother asking. "Okay," I said, dragging out the word. My body was practically vibrating with anxiety, and I shifted my weight back and forth so I wouldn't let out a frustrated roar. "Fine. Call me about the final three prospects, okay? We're down to the wire with this one. The owner is starting to ask questions, and it's only been a day."

"The replica's nearly done, so let that soothe you, please. I'm doing my best." Despite his soft tone, he was sweating even more than he had been earlier. The intensified scrambling in the back room made me think Mrs. Pulaski was in a state of panic as well, but I tried not to let the energy in the shop get my blood pressure rising even more than it already was.

"All right, Mr. Pulaski. I'm sorry for coming on so strong. You know how it is with a rushed timeline."

"Of course. I'll be in touch as soon as I hear anything."

"Thank you," I said, feeling less hopeful than ever. When I exited the pawnshop, the wind was whipping even harder and it had begun to rain.

CHAPTER

12

Jade

When I opened the front door to Daniel's practice, he must have heard the door creak open, because he shouted, "Be down in one second!" from his upstairs apartment. His footsteps were shuffling back and forth, and I smiled, picturing him putting on deodorant or peeling off a tiny square of tissue from where he'd nicked himself shaving. He'd asked me to join him for drinks with friends, and I was relieved we weren't going to dinner alone just yet. This could bridge the gap. Ease me back into dating.

I studied the lobby waiting room, wandering over to the bookshelf where there was a collection of psychology textbooks alongside children's books and magazines for patients. Daniel didn't take children as patients, but one of his coworkers did, judging by the paper cutouts of Disney and *Sesame Street* characters pasted all over their office door.

Daniel's phone rang upstairs. "Ugh, sorry! Make that two seconds," he yelled down at me, clearly flustered. Daniel's low voice reverberated through the walls as he spoke on the phone. It was clear he was trying to rush them off, but whoever was on the other end was either stubborn or clueless enough not to notice.

Daniel's office door was cracked open as usual, and my eyes zeroed in on his filing cabinet. The greedy, dishonest part of my mind salivated at all that private information I could harness.

I took a step toward the door, then one back. *That would be wrong,* I chastised myself. Daniel trusted me enough to be in his space without being supervised, and he'd never done anything to deserve dishonesty.

Footsteps crept around the bend of the L-shaped staircase, and Daniel peeked his head out. "I'm so sorry. It's my mom. I'll be just another minute. Feel free to come up and grab a drink."

"I'll give you your privacy," I said, waving him away with a smile.

The part of my brain that was raised on deceit whispered to me: *Get rid of him. Take the opportunity.*

I stepped forward again, listening to Daniel talk to his mother upstairs. I had no time to lose. I inched open the door and scanned the labels on the folders. Many of them were the same ones I'd seen the first time I'd been in his office.

There were about six patient files on the desk, but if I took all of them, it would be too obvious. I could probably get away with taking half. I picked a few at random and shoved the files in my tote bag. I could no longer hear Daniel speaking to his mother, just his footsteps. I knew the office door would creak, so I opened it as little as I possibly could, shoving my tote bag out through the crack first, then sucking in my belly as I slipped my body through.

I wasn't even two steps into the lobby when Daniel started walking down the stairs, already apologizing for the holdup. "I'm so sorry. She hardly ever calls, but when she does, she tells you every single thing that's happened in her life, all the way down to what she's eaten. It can go on for hours if you're not pushy enough."

I laughed, but a tiny voice in the back of my brain wanted to tell him to be more grateful that he still had a mother to talk to. I would have given anything for my mom to be able to call and tell me what she'd eaten. I'd even listen to her tell me about her bowel movements—I just wanted to hear her voice. But all that wasn't really something you should say to someone you just started casually dating, so I kept my mouth shut.

"You ready?" he asked, holding his hand out. I looked at his hand, then back up at his face, blushing. I'd never had a man want to hold my hand in public before and my palms were already growing sweaty at the thought, even though I *liked* the thought of it. A look of self-conscious worry was creeping over his face, but when I reached out to grab his hand, it disappeared. All he wanted was connection and I wanted that too, but I'd just stolen from him. What kind of a person was I?

It's not stealing if you're going to give it back, I argued with myself. It was true—I was going to take notes and put the files back—but I'd started our relationship on a horrible foundation of my own making.

I didn't know how I was going to make it through the night with the two opposing parts of me going to battle over what I'd done. I would have to do what I always did and pretend everything was fine and I'd done nothing wrong. It was the Crawford way.

"I'm ready," I said with a smile. "Let's go."

* * *

After returning home, I pored over the files with a frantic energy, and I was nearly crawling out of my skin with the need to talk about them by the time Stevie returned to the apartment.

"What's this all about?" Stevie asked me as I ushered her over to the couch, one hand firmly on her back. She reached for the television remote, but I scooted it out of the way with my other hand, sending it skittering across the coffee table and onto the floor. She studied me with wide, red eyes before muttering, "Okay, weirdo."

Once she was seated, I reached behind the TV and grabbed the patient files, tossing them in front of her on the coffee table. I tapped them feverishly. "Open it."

"How much coffee have you had today? Any crack?"

"I've had three cups of coffee. No crack. How much pot have you smoked?" I jabbed, half serious, half joking.

She blinked at me, her red eyes so irritated and dry that I could have sworn I heard her lids stick together when she blinked. "Not enough, apparently. What is this? You want me to read your poems about Daniel's ample backside?"

"Just open it."

She obliged, cautiously flipping the cover back. Her eyes drifted back and forth as she read before they snapped back up to me. "Who are these people? This is really . . . this is extremely personal information."

"Extremely *useful* information," I corrected.

She turned the page, reading on. Her eyes sobered, the redness remaining but any hint of a smile leaving. "Just because it's useful doesn't mean it should be used. Where did you get this?"

"I—" My voice croaked, self-consciousness seeping in as my confidence waned. For a split second, I wished my parents were on the couch instead of Stevie. They would have been proud of me, I thought bitterly. But was that what I really wanted?

"Is this from Daniel's office?" She closed the notebook and stood, moving away from it as if it were poison. I remained silent, weighing my words. She studied me, watching as I chewed on the inside of my lip. "Jesus Christ, Jade. It is, isn't it?"

"Yes."

She blew out a huff of air and raked her fingers through her hair. She paced the floor. "Do you have any idea how illegal this is? Do you want to end up like Dad?"

"Don't do that. You don't even know what I'm trying to do with these."

"Don't do what? Bring you back into reality? There are other ways to earn money, Jade. I could get you a job at the bar."

"I don't want to serve watered-down drinks to college kids and perverts, Stevie."

She balked at me, blood rushing to her cheeks. "Wow. Real nice. I work just as hard as you, if not harder and without *stealing*, so why don't you shove—"

"Wait, listen," I interrupted. "I brought you in here because I have an idea."

"Oh, goodie. Would you like to steal from the Make-A-Wish Foundation next? Kidnap a blind person's guide dog?"

"No. Just listen. We can help these people, Stevie. We can seek them out, get them to come into the shop. These are some seriously fucked-up people. Maybe they just need a little guidance."

"They're already getting guidance. From a professional—Daniel."

I kept my voice calm despite her increased frustration. "A lot of these people are grieving—really struggling. You know I'm right when I say we can bring them comfort. Just take a look at the files yourself."

She scoffed but began thumbing through them anyway, clearly uninterested in taking part. She paused on the last file, her eyes narrowing. "This guy. Ian Stellman. Have you heard of him?"

"Yes, he's the teacher that got suspended with pay after a girl came forward about him hitting on her. He's the one who drives the yellow Hummer and scream-cries during his sessions. Didn't they hire him while you were in school?"

Stevie nodded, and her face flushed. "Yeah, my junior year. A string of other students came forward after the first student, and a lot of their stories were worse."

"This file is one of his victims. She was the second to come forward."

Stevie flipped the page, anger glistening in her eyes. When she spoke, her voice was high and tight. "He assaulted her *in the classroom*? What a sick freak."

"I know." I took the Stellman file off the table and flipped through the pages. "There are tons of references to a Tom in Stellman's appointments. Who do you think that is?"

"No idea. The Stellmans have connections everywhere, so it could be anyone," Stevie said.

I read from the file. "'He shouldn't have gotten involved.' That's from their appointment a few days ago. Involved in what?"

Stevie shrugged, but I could tell her energy was ramping like mine as she too felt potential connections coming together. There was something big here.

"Tom, Thomas . . . You don't think there's any way . . ." I half whispered.

"You think Tom is Thomas Nichols?"

"Only in the appointment after the councilman went missing does he ever start saying this Tom person shouldn't have gotten involved. If he's talking about the councilman, maybe whatever Nichols got him involved in is why he's missing. And maybe Stellman is responsible."

"If we could get proof of that, the cops would leave you alone. They clearly think your vision is suspicious."

"We need him to confess."

"And how are we going to do that? He's sitting pretty in his house with his paid leave. He has no reason to change that."

"We convince him to come to the shop. He clearly feels some sort of guilt. We can use that in our favor. I'll do a reading and record it."

"How are we supposed to get him here?" Stevie asked as she sat on the couch. "It's almost impossible if someone hasn't already shown interest."

"We need to find out where he goes and what he does first. Then we can lure him in."

Stevie rubbed at her red eyes and sat on the couch. Her knees bobbed up and down, full of nervous energy. "He's come to the bar a few times since he was put on paid leave. Same drink. Same seat at the bar. Predictable—the best type of person for a hot reading."

"Stevie." I flopped down on the couch next to her. My head was spinning. "This is perfect. You can call me when he comes in so I can lure him back here."

"No need. I'm gonna do it."

I winced, my stomach immediately in knots at the thought of her alone with him, even for a moment. "Absolutely not. I don't want you involved in this."

"You've already involved me by showing me this. And come on, what better bait than a former student? A young one at that."

I glared at her. "You want to be pervert bait?"

"Come on. Think of those girls. He ruined their lives."

"I have to be there to make sure nothing goes wrong." My mind was racing as I pictured all the things that could go wrong and how powerless I would be to protect her, even if I was there.

"You know that makes no sense. You'll blow your own cover. Please, just let me help."

"Fine," I finally said. She was never as eager to be on the acting end of our schemes. Always the stagehand, scurrying behind the walls to make the magic happen. But now, with her skin flushed and eyes wild with excitement, she was ready to step out onto the stage. The change was startling.

I stuck out my hand for a handshake, and she shook it firmly with a clammy hand. She laughed in disbelief as she stared down at the patient files spread across the coffee table. "We're going to get ourselves killed one day."

CHAPTER

13

Jade

"JADE!"

I pulled my right ear out from my headphones, music still streaming in from the left side. I waited to hear my name again, but nothing. I peered out the window into the street. The pavement glistened in the sun after an early-morning shower, and a few people trickled in and out of the buildings along the street. I was dreading starting the day. I'd had a fitful night of sleep after my conversation with Stevie. I couldn't stop trying to connect the dots between the councilman and Ian Stellman, but I was coming up short.

I'd nearly slid the headphones back on when I heard Stevie yell urgently, "Jade!"

"What?" I shouted back, a little annoyed, a little curious. I hadn't even heard Stevie leave her room this morning.

"Come here!" she yelled.

My annoyance rose. She'd been like that ever since she learned to talk—never an explanation behind her demand. Just a simple, direct order. She was always thankful after, but the vague way she asked for things grated on my nerves.

"Get the fuck in here!" she yelled again. I guessed her small allotment of patience had worn out.

I tossed my phone to the side of my bed and hopped down, sliding my feet into my slippers. They were ridiculous, frilly little things—lavender fur with white stars and crescent moons—that Stevie had gifted me last Christmas.

When I found my sister, she was standing wide-eyed in front of the television, wrapped in a fleece robe. She gnawed on a fingernail while the other hand gripped the remote in a vise. I couldn't tell whether she was terrified or thrilled.

"What is it, Your Highness? Did you smoke too much and watch *Hereditary* again?" But when I looked at the TV, it wasn't a horror movie. It was the news. Along the bottom of the screen, the ticker said, "Breaking news: Body of councilman found."

A commercial began, and Stevie looked at me wide-eyed. "The anchors said the same thing earlier but mentioned a local business helping. You don't think . . ."

"There's no way."

The news returned, and Stevie clicked the volume button multiple times until the anchor's voice rose to an almost unbearable volume.

"Geez, Stevie, turn it down. I won't be able to listen if—" I stopped talking.

"We're back with a tragic update. Beloved councilman Thomas Nichols has been found dead. His disappearance on September twentieth rattled the community, who now mourn the loss of an incredible community figure. His body was found at the construction site for a future waste management facility approximately two miles from Salem Lake. Police made this discovery after a local psychic, Jade Ravencroft, called the hotline to report a psychic vision regarding his location. We will provide updates as we receive new information."

The woman set her stack of papers on her desk. Her co-anchor said, "A truly troubling story, Anna. What a magnificent gift this Jade Ravencroft has." It seemed like he truly believed I had a psychic gift. Like I'd done some good for the community.

The anchorwoman let out a tiny, almost imperceptible scoff.

Stevie muted the TV when they moved to their next story. She stared at me, expecting me to say something, but I gaped back at her. I didn't even know what to say, but I should say *something*. Anything. I opened my mouth, but only a tiny croak came out.

When I finally spoke, she did too. "What the fuck?"

* * *

My vision was right. Oh my God, I was right.

My guess, I corrected. I'd made a wild, desperate guess and I'd somehow gotten it right.

"So are you, like, actually psychic or something?" Stevie erupted into a fit of laughter and held her stomach with one hand. Her laugh had always been infectious, and I couldn't help but join in. "Oh God," she said, "I'm gonna pee."

"It never ceases to amaze me how this family always finds a way to claw ourselves out of our little holes," Stevie finally said after she caught her breath.

"The holes we dig for ourselves, you mean."

"I guess," she sighed. "It's not like we dug this hole, though. Mom and Dad dug it for us."

"Dad did," I said a bit too severely. She was still smiling, but her eyes made it clear I'd been too harsh. "Sorry. Well, that old bastard would be seething with jealousy over this trick."

Our dad had always used the word *trick*. Never *scam*. A trick had an air of innocence, which was exactly the opposite of the crap he'd been getting up to before he was sentenced.

"Wait, wait, wait. How much was the reward again?" Stevie asked.

I cleared my throat, desperate to get back to the levity we'd had right after the news announcement. "Two thousand dollars."

She was laughing again now, tears of pure exhilaration brimming against her lower lashes. "I hope this doesn't make them think you did it."

Although it was clearly a joke, the words wiped the smile off my face. When I'd submitted the vision to the police, I'd only been thinking of the potential money I could be rewarded. Wooldridge had been a jerk, but there wasn't any reason for him to think I actually killed the councilman. In my greed, I hadn't for a second thought of how it might make me look if my tip was right.

Like a murderer.

* * *

Soon the phone began to ring nonstop, and Stevie answered what she could downstairs while I tackled the emails and direct messages on social media. The repairmen were scheduled to begin work soon, and Stevie was downstairs collecting the soiled towels and full buckets of murky water before they arrived.

"Um, Jade," Stevie said behind me as I answered an email from a journalist asking to arrange an interview. "You won't believe who's here to repair the ceiling."

My stomach dropped as I pictured our dad downstairs, waiting at the door with a toolbox and a shit-eating grin on his face. "Dad?"

"What?" Stevie said. "God, no. It's Adam."

I rolled my eyes and groaned. This wasn't anywhere near as bad as our dad being downstairs, but it was still going to be miserable. Adam was the older brother of my toxic ex-boyfriend Chris Pulaski, who I'd wasted two years of my life on after meeting them at his parents' pawnshop. He'd shamelessly dumped me after Mom died, complaining that in my grief, I'd given up on myself. It had only added salt to the already-deep wound, but now, two years later, I was glad to be rid of him and desperate to never see him or his brother again.

I braced myself as I walked downstairs with Stevie. There Adam stood with two other workers, readying materials to fix the gaping hole in the shop ceiling. One of the men was clearly the boss, as he barked orders at Adam, who gritted his teeth in annoyance. He was just as petulant as his brother, only he threw his tantrums silently, and somehow that was more frightening.

"Adam," I said, not bothering to say hello. "I didn't realize you were doing construction work."

"Yep," was all he said, and he turned on his heel to fetch something from their van.

"Isn't he a ray of sunshine?" Stevie murmured. The three men eventually began their repair, and Stevie and I did our best to cordon off their work with shoddy velvet drapes and strategically placed bookshelves. Despite all our hard work, the harsh clanging of tools disturbed the carefully curated ambience in the shop.

The incessant ringing of the shop phone added to the onslaught of noise, and I gritted my teeth in panic as Cheryl entered the shop with no appointment. She'd come in for a last-minute reading to ease her anxiety about her son, but as our reading began, it became clear the day wasn't going to slow down in the slightest.

I flipped over a card for her. "The Four of Wands. Cheryl, how lovely. This card signifies celebration and unification within a family. Have you made progress with your son?" The phone rang again the moment she started speaking, and I winced. "One second." I waited a beat for Stevie to answer, but after two more rings, I leapt up from the tarot table, picked up the phone, then quickly slammed it back down.

"I listened to your advice, and I decided to change my mindset. For the sake of my family, I'll be throwing them an engagement party."

The phone rang again, and I hustled over and hung it up with a slam, then took it off the hook so nobody else could call. Where the hell was Stevie? She'd taken a phone call after Cheryl arrived, but now she was nowhere in sight.

"That's fantastic. Things are looking up for you and your family. You deserve it." I wasn't sure if I fully meant that—she was actually kind of a terrible person at her core. But people could change, I reminded myself, and everyone deserved a second chance.

Well, most people. I thought of my dad and wondered how long it would take him to relapse back into his typical behavior, if he hadn't already. A year? A week?

The front door chime made us both jump in our seats. Below the OPEN sign, I'd flipped around a placard that said READING IN PROGRESS.

We'd gotten the sign because we realized people wandered in more often when they knew a reading was going on: moths drawn to the spectacle. They'd pretend to wander around, smelling candles and herbs, but really they were eavesdropping on the reading. More often than not, if someone wandered in during a reading, they ended up getting one themselves.

We'd added the little curtained-off area after Stevie started working at the bar. She'd returned home after her first night rambling about how much more people would drink and how much longer they'd stay if you put them in what she called the "very intoxicated people" section. So we'd recreated that in the shop with some cheap velvet cloth we'd nail-gunned to the ceiling.

I peeled back the velvet curtain and secured it with a gold cord, apologizing to Cheryl for the interruption. I had begun to stand to let whoever it was know I'd help them momentarily when to my relief, Stevie's footsteps approached the newcomer, clicking the shop phone back onto the receiver as she passed it. She was wearing her typical psychic shop uniform—a long black dress, black Doc Martens, and a black lacy shawl draped across her shoulders. She joked that when she was working at the shop, she might as well dress as her namesake, Stevie Nicks.

When I peeked out farther, I took in a sharp, startled breath. It wasn't just one person. It was a crowd, each person holding their weapon of choice, whether it be a microphone, camera, or pen and paper. A few taller men stood behind them, pointing cameras right at Stevie. Reporters.

I crept out of the cordoned-off area and motioned for Cheryl to stay put. The wide windows next to the front door revealed even more people, some of them pressing their hands to the glass, trying to peer in.

I smoothed my skirt down and fussed with my hair before walking to the door. This was it. Our time to shine.

"Welcome," I said in my Madame Ravencroft voice, "to the Ravencroft Psychic Parlor and Shoppe."

* * *

As soon I uttered half of the word *welcome*, the reporters flooded in, elbowing each other and jostling for the best position.

Despite the fact that there wasn't an inch left uncovered by the journalists, there were still three of them left out in the cold. One of them propped open the door, and they peered in jealously.

"Are you Jade Ravencroft?" a woman asked, pointing her recorder at me, and I nodded. She was on her own, no camerap-erson in tow behind her. I took her in—her crisp white button-up, black slacks, and black boots with a slight heel. She had a confident air about her, like she had all the time in the world, making her stand out from the others, who had the chaotic energy of hungry dogs circling around one bowl.

A man in a bright-blue windbreaker with a news channel logo reached around her and shoved a bulbous microphone in my face, nearly bumping my chin. The woman with the recorder gave him a withering look but stood her ground even as their elbows jousted.

"Tell us about your vision of Councilman Nichols," the man barked at me.

Another reporter from the doorway shouted, "Who did you get the information from?"

I cleared my throat. "My information came from a vision." The crowd murmured, some in mocking disbelief but others mere inches away from being convinced. "I'm a psychic."

God, what have I done? This was exactly what I'd wanted, yet it was too public. Too vulnerable.

"There's no such thing as psychics," a reporter shouted from the middle of the crowd. I clenched my jaw. His polo said Star News—the local channel that was infamous for poor reporting and even poorer journalistic integrity.

"Perhaps there's no scientific proof, but humans throughout time have been given spiritual gifts. I'm one of many women in my family with such a gift."

The Star News reporter scoffed. I glanced over at Stevie, who was openly snarling, and I prayed none of the cameras were pointed at her to witness it. "Would you be willing to prove that you have a gift by hosting a public séance?"

I blanched. The concept had never crossed my mind, despite the many celebrity psychics that were on TV or performed in flashy shows in Las Vegas. If I said no, it would be an immediate red flag. So I gave a smile and agreed to the only option. "Absolutely. Stay behind, and we'll set up the details."

The reporter flashed his teeth in a wide, wolfish smile, and all my muscles clenched as I thought of all the things that could go wrong in a public séance. And clearly, he was thinking the same thing. "This should be good," he laughed to the cameraman next to him.

I startled at the loud voice right behind me. "Everything Jade says is true. She's been given an incredible gift. She reunited me with my son."

Approving chatter rippled through the packed room of journalists, who were already spinning their tales into a tidy TV-worthy segment.

"Cheryl." I clasped one hand against my chest. "I'm so sorry about all this."

The steadfast reporter with the recorder turned to her. "Ma'am, can you elaborate?"

Cheryl stepped forward to the nearest microphone. Had she applied lipstick? "My son and I have had a rocky road lately. I didn't approve of the woman he fell in love with, but Jade helped me come to my senses when she had a vision he was going to propose. And she was right." More hushed whispers among the crowd. Cheryl continued, "She helped me realize my faults, and now I'm happy to say I'm throwing my son and future daughter-in-law an engagement party. And of course Jade will be invited, because without her, the party wouldn't be happening at all."

A strange mixture of pride and embarrassment washed over me, and I worked hard to keep my face placid and calm. Cheryl was singing my praises exactly how I hoped all my clients would, but I was fighting the tiny urge to correct her. I could tell them I was more like a therapist, albeit an unlicensed one. And uneducated. And tack on unethical to my résumé too.

But I had to go along with it. This was my career. My livelihood. Over the next hour, reporters asked more questions, and I sweated my way through my answers. Eventually, I politely asked them to leave and call to arrange further interviews. I wanted to keep an air of mystery, and I couldn't let them think my entire day was empty. Despite my request, two reporters lingered.

The reporter who'd challenged me to host a public séance stayed behind to arrange the details. He approached me with a business card.

"This is the owner of the community theater," the reporter said, shoving the card into my hand. "He's already agreed to host you."

I clenched the card, trying to keep the annoyance off my face. He'd clearly come to ambush me, thinking he could prove some point by having me publicly fail. He had no idea how wrong he was going to be.

"Maybe you're the psychic," I said with a smile, "since you and"—I looked down at the card—"Mr. Melville both knew I would accept the offer."

The reporter laughed stiffly, and for the next ten minutes we created a rough plan for the event. It would be held in just five days, and anyone who was interested would be able to anonymously enter themselves for a chance either to participate as a sitter or as an audience member. My head spun, but Stevie nodded to me, silently communicating she'd take care of the logistics.

One final reporter remained, and despite the fact that I'd asked them all to leave, it didn't bother me. Something about her made me want to prove myself to her.

"If they see you lingering, they'll storm back in and I'll never be able to get rid of them." I smiled as I tidied up the shelves that some of the reporters had bumped into. Someone had carelessly toppled over a row of chakra candles, leaving a rainbow-colored mess on the floor. I picked up a flattened and disfigured red root chakra candle and sighed. Ironic, considering the meaning—feeling rooted and secure in life.

"I'll pay for that," the reporter said. "I'm Maria Prescott, by the way. I'm with the *Charlotte Observer*."

"Nice to meet you. And thank you, but don't worry about it." I tossed the candle in the trash.

"Have you ever had that many people in the shop at one time?" She set her recorder on the shelf next to her with a little notepad on top. I wondered if it was still on.

"Can't say I have. Well, maybe when my sister had a party last year. It was for my birthday, but she somehow forgot to invite anyone I actually knew."

Maria chuckled. "Stevie, right? Is she gifted like you?" There was a slight pause before *gifted* but no hint of sarcasm. It was clear she didn't believe in psychics but wasn't trying to make an enemy. Our jobs had a lot in common, I assumed. Poking and prodding, weaving a story with what you learn. I only hoped for her sake that she made more money than me.

"No. It's usually just one sibling. And only ever girls."

She nodded but said nothing. The urge to fill the silence itched away at me, but I had no idea what to say. I'd run out of my usual lines and my head was blank.

The phone rang—my saving grace. Her eyes followed me and she leaned into the shelf, making herself comfortable for the long haul. I raised my voice over the overstimulating ringing. "It was nice meeting you. I better get this."

She pulled a card out of her back pocket. "Let's set up some time to talk. I'm writing a piece about the councilman, and I would love to pick your brain. Everyone's curious as to who you really are."

Who I really am? It was an odd compliment, shrouded in what felt like a vague threat.

"Sure."

She left the card on the shelf next to a bin of bundled sage and tapped it with her palm. "Good luck with the crowd."

I picked up the phone and was surprised to hear Daniel's voice. I tried to keep a straight face, because Maria was lingering. He spoke quickly. "It's Daniel, but pretend this is an important call. Maybe she'll finally leave."

"This sounds like a complex issue. Let me consult the cards," I said, trying to keep the smile out of my voice. I glanced at Maria, who waved and left the shop. "Oh thank God, I thought she was never going to leave."

"I figured. I was watching the news, and when I heard your name, I rushed over to your place, but there was a wall of reporters. I saw you through the window, and you looked cornered."

"It felt that way too. Today has been insane. The shop's a mess from the stampede of people."

"My office is a mess too, but that's my own fault. I can't seem to find anything lately. Seems like I'd lose my head if it weren't attached."

My chest burned as I held my breath. Had he noticed the missing files? Was he testing my reaction or about to ask about them?

To my relief, he excitedly began talking about my tip to the hotline, asking me to tell the story from the beginning. Even though I'd told the story a thousand times today to journalists,

I was excited to tell him. He congratulated me as if it were a truly amazing feat, and I ate up the praise despite knowing it was all a fluke.

I hung up and tidied the shop, still smiling. I glanced out the window as a car went by and paused, shivering as I wondered if Daniel seeing me through the window was sheer one-off luck or if watching me through the window was a habit. If he could watch me that easily, then anyone could.

CHAPTER

14

Stevie

LATER THAT AFTERNOON, the shop had finally grown quiet. Jade and I sighed in relief as we sat in the shop, alternating between giggling delirium and panic over the news frenzy. We were in the middle of a fit of nervous laughter when the shop bell chimed and two detectives stepped in, immediately wiping the smiles off our faces.

"Hello, ladies," the smaller detective said. He turned to me and said, "I'm Detective McCade. This is Detective Woolridge."

"What are we laughing about?" said Woolridge. I already disliked him and the way he stood with his preposterously muscular legs wide apart, hands resting on his belt as if he needed quick access to his gun.

Jade ignored his question. "How can I help you?"

"I'm sure you saw the news about the councilman. We wanted to ask you a few more questions," McCade said.

"Okay. Stevie, could you go look for the clear quartz clusters in the back to restock the shelves?" Jade asked. I paused, feeling like a child waiting for a hall pass in school. The detectives didn't say anything, so I rose to my feet and went to fetch the crystals. Rather than returning to the shop and standing under the brutal stare of the detectives, I stood at the closed velvet curtain and eavesdropped.

"Yes," Jade finally said. "I saw the news about the councilman passing away. It's awful."

"He didn't pass away. He was murdered," Woolridge corrected.

My pulse quickened at the word. *Murdered.* I'd known they suspected foul play, but I was hoping it was just an accident or a case of a man packing a bag and never wanting to be found. I thought back to my dad's face, crowned by acrid cigarette smokc. *Don't put your nose where it doesn't belong.* Was he lying and he knew more than he'd let on? Had it been a threat rather than advice?

"I was trying to be respectful," Jade said. "*Passed away* is a little more palatable than *murdered.*"

"Nothing about this is palatable, Miss Ravencroft."

Jade didn't speak, but I could picture her face with her bottom jaw tilted slightly forward. She always did that when she was angry, resting the tip of her tongue between her teeth like a cork to keep her true thoughts from spilling out.

"We wanted to ask you about your relationship to the councilman," said McCade.

"I had no relationship with him. I've never even met him."

"Has your sister?"

"No, I don't think so."

"What about other members of his family? Any friends?" McCade asked, making stomach acid rise in my throat. There was no way they could know about our plan for Stellman, was there?

“Don’t know anything about them.”

Woolridge cleared his throat, interrupting McCade before he could ask another question. “Can you see any political enemies in these little visions of yours?”

“Um,” Jade faltered. “No, I told you everything I saw.”

Is that who they were thinking did this—some political adversary? There was complete silence from the detectives, not even a scratch of pen on paper.

“That’s all I have for now. Thank you for your time,” McCade finally said. “Not too long before reporters will be knocking down your door.”

Jade laughed. “They were here this morning. It was a nightmare.”

“A nightmare that’ll benefit you, I’m sure,” Woolridge said under his breath in that liminal volume one uses when they really want someone to hear them but can pretend they didn’t if called out.

“Has the Nichols family been in touch with you?” McCade asked.

“No,” Jade said.

The question made me realize I had no idea how the reward worked. I’d daydreamed of the family showing up to the shop with an oversized check, eyes full of grateful tears as journalists snapped pictures.

“I’m sure they’ll be in touch soon. I’d imagine they’re eager to speak with you.”

The detectives said their goodbyes, and I waited before slinking back out into the shop. Jade had her arms folded on the tarot table, her forehead pressing into them.

“You okay?” I asked.

She snapped her head up with a startled breath. “What? Yeah, I’m fine. Did you find the crystals?”

"Yep." She could clearly see the large box in my hand. She was just filling the silence.

"Did you hear any of that?" She motioned to where the detectives had been standing.

"No," I lied. "What did they say?" I wanted to see if she'd bring up their questions about me knowing the councilman, or if she'd do what she usually did and try to shield me from the truth.

"They just asked if the Nichols family had been in touch with me yet about the reward money."

There it is, I thought. *Typical Jade, trying and failing to shield me from the worst of it.* "Oh yeah, I hadn't thought about that. When do we get the money?"

"I have no idea. They said the family would 'be in touch' about the money and the police might also 'be in touch' with us about the investigation again."

"That's a lot of touching," I said, eliciting a small chuckle from her. "I guess I didn't think they would want to talk to you more than once."

Jade shrugged. "I figured they might, but I didn't think they would be such assholes about it."

"They ask anything else?"

A moment ticked by. "Nope." She covered the lie with a weak smile. I knew she was trying to protect me. That's what family was supposed to do. I nodded, waiting for her to tell the truth, to believe that I was strong enough for it. But she never did.

CHAPTER 15

Jade

I FLOPPED ONTO THE couch, sighing as I hit the soft cushions. After the reporters left, only one group of local college kids had come in around happy hour. Those tended to be the most fun but most exhausting. It was easier to swindle a few extra dollars out of sitters who had been drinking, especially if you knew they weren't taking it seriously. That was a pattern I'd discovered long ago: It was easiest to get money out of those who took it the least seriously and those who took it the most seriously. Everyone in between was more of a challenge.

Other than that, not a single customer had entered the shop.

"Wow," Stevie had said as she flipped the shop's sign around, making sure it was flipped to OPEN. Unfortunately, it was. "Would have thought we'd be swarmed. I guess our grand plan was a bust."

"The reporters and detectives probably scared them off," I'd said, my arms crossed like a surly toddler.

I grabbed the bottle of red wine Stevie had left on the coffee table for me and poured myself a glass. She always left a treat in some form before her late-night shifts, whether it was chocolate or a glass of wine, and I was eternally grateful after my long day that it was the latter.

Tonight I was doing a shift on the medium app, and I had to be "on." It was a hit-or-miss side hustle, but there had been a noticeable uptick in the past few years with peoples' growing anxieties around the violence in the world—seemingly one disaster after another. Widespread trauma and panic always brought more people to psychic mediums as people sought out comfort and answers by any means possible. My dad used to always brim with excitement when something horrible happened on the news, but all I felt was dread.

I grabbed the phone off the side table and opened the TarotTalk app. I typed in my credentials and jumped at the near-immediate *ping* that notified me a caller had connected. Sitting up from my slumped position on the couch, I took a deep breath, getting myself into character. I pressed connect. "This is Madame Ravencroft. What answer are you seeking?" My opening line always made me cringe, but if I didn't say it, I'd be fired.

The caller spoke frantically, as if she'd had too much coffee. "Um, so I was wondering if I'm going to get the job I applied for last week?"

Boring. These types of questions were easy money but so, *so* boring. "Let's ask the cards." I picked up a dingy stack of tarot cards—not my beautiful, gilded stack I used for in-person sessions—and thumbed the side of the stack, making the satisfying noise that always gave sitters hope.

"I see," I said, well aware of the tension building on the call.

"What? What do you see?"

"The Ten of Pentacles. Ah, and the Wheel of Fortune."

"Like the show?"

I stifled a laugh. "No. The Wheel of Fortune indicates a change in fortune. And the Ten of Pentacles represents wealth gained through hard work."

The caller squeaked a little on the other end. I'd done these calls so many times, with this exact question asked, that I knew exactly what cards to tell them I saw.

"This is amazing," she said. "I knew it. I killed the interview. Thank you so much!"

For every minute she stayed on the call, she paid twenty-five cents. Of that, I earned half. A measly 12.5 cents a minute. However, if I got past the ten-minute mark, that rate doubled.

"One more card for you before you go." I paused. "Oh my."

"What is it?" she asked hesitantly. I felt a little bit bad about that, but I wasn't going to fully kill her spark.

"The Eight of Cups," I said somberly.

"The what?"

"The Eight of Cups can mean many things, but in my experience, it's a warning. The orientation of the card can change the meaning. Yours is upright. Here it's a warning to be smart with your financial decisions. Does this new job provide better pay?"

"Yes, the pay is better. But I'll have to move to Raleigh, so it'll be expensive."

"If they offer you the job, you need to negotiate that. Be brave and stand up for yourself," I advised. As much as I wanted peoples' money, I wanted to offer real advice. Make a real difference.

"You're right. My current job just hired this new guy, and they're already paying him more than me. And he has no experience!"

"This is something you must work on. One more card. Are you ready?"

"Yes."

This time I actually plucked a card from the deck at random. I flipped it over and tossed it on the couch next to me.

Shit.

"Well? What did you pull?"

"Your final card is the Seven of Swords."

"Swords don't sound good. Or are they? Like I'm a warrior or something?"

"An upright Seven of Swords can mean there will be deceit in your life. You may have an enemy posing as a friend, perhaps at your current job or the new one."

"Shit. I bet it's Susan."

"Tell me about Susan." I took a sip of my wine, satisfied I'd kept her on the line this long. We'd reached the ten minute mark, and my cut was doubling.

"Susan works at this new company. We've been friends since middle school and have always had a little bit of friendly competition going on, but sometimes she takes it too far. She's on the hiring committee and said she'd put in a good word for me. Do you think she's full of it?"

"I can't be sure, but it's best to be wary of competition. Remember to stand up for yourself. Show courage."

"Courage. Okay. I can do that."

When we said our goodbyes, I took a few more calls, then decided the next was my last. A caller clicked in and I accepted, only to be met with heavy breathing.

Great, I thought. *Another creep thinking this is a sex line. Or worse, knowing it isn't and using it like one anyway.*

"Madame Ravencroft. What is the answer you're seeking?"

The breathing grew faster, as did the grinding of my teeth. "If you don't have a question, you'll be disconnected," I grumbled. Their heavy breathing continued.

Actually, I decided, *if you're going to be a weirdo, you can pay me for it.* I set the phone next to me on speakerphone and turned the TV on, muted. I was changing the channel when a sound stopped me in my tracks, my fingers digging into the rubbery buttons.

"Jade," the voice on the other end croaked. I stared at the phone, trying to convince myself it was my imagination. It was late. I'd had a glass of wine.

I picked up the phone. "This is Madame Ravencroft speaking."

More breathing, so raspy I could almost feel the wet heat on my ear. "Hello, Jade."

The hair on my arms stood on end, and I hung up as fast as I could, not caring that the app might penalize me for it. Who the hell was that, and what would they get out of pranking me, especially when they literally had to pay for it? Even more concerning was the fact that they'd been able to reach me out of the dozens of other psychics on the app. I wondered how long they'd been calling and hanging up, trying to be connected to me.

Downstairs, the clunky old grandfather clock in the corner ticked to midnight, making me jump. I let out a stuttering breath and forced myself to go to my bedroom.

Forget about it. It's just a prank.

But as I lay in bed trying to sleep, the minutes then hours ticking by, I couldn't get it out of my head.

CHAPTER 16

Jade

I STOOD IN LINE at Salem College's financial assistance department, staring down at the college T-shirt I'd splurged on for Stevie. We'd never officially celebrated her acceptance because she pushed it off every time I tried, claiming she was too busy. But I knew it was because she was self-conscious that she'd be one of the oldest students on campus at twenty-one.

The person in front of me stepped aside, and the employee greeted me. I pulled out the piece of mail detailing Stevie's tuition payment plan. I needed to get Stevie's monthly tuition payments down, and I'd come in person so I could pull on their heartstrings if I needed to.

The woman smiled as she looked up Stevie in the system, making small talk as she typed and clicked. "You must be so proud of your sister."

"So proud. She'll be the first in our family to go to college." Her smile dropped and mine followed. "Is something wrong?" I asked.

"That's strange. She's not in the system."

"That can't be right. Can you look again?"

"Let me call admissions. One second." She dialed the extension and spelled out Stevie's name to the person on the other line. The conversation was quick, and the women grimaced as she relayed the news. "It seems like your sister called in last week and opted out of enrollment."

My heart sank. Last week was when we received the rent notice. She must have done it that day without telling me. Tears welled in my eyes and the woman panicked, trying and failing to soothe me. The employee sent me off with a handful of tissues and a look of pity on her face. I walked to the car in the pouring rain, not knowing whether to be angry at Stevie or sad for her, but I cried nonetheless.

By the time I'd reached the shop, the rain had soaked through my clothes and a tooth-rattling shiver had settled in that I knew would linger for hours. I walked past a customer talking to Stevie, and they both glanced at me in surprise when I tossed my bag behind the curtain to the stairs with a squelchy, wet *plop*.

"One second," Stevie said to the young woman who was now holding two bundles of sage up to her nose, so much that they were practically inside her nostrils. "You look like hot garbage," Stevie whispered. She pulled me behind the curtain as the front bell chimed and the sound of chatter filled the shop.

"Thanks, Stevie. Love the support." I rubbed the heels of my hands under my eyes, wiping away droplets of rain from my face.

Stevie grimaced. "That made it way worse." She pointed to the mirror on the wall by the stairs, and I glanced over to see black makeup smudged along my under-eyes. "What's your deal?"

The front bell chimed again, and the sound of murmuring voices hummed like a hive of bees, ratcheting up my anxiety. Now wasn't the time to ask her. "We can talk about it later. You should probably go back out there."

"Yeah, I know, and you should probably get yourself together because it's about to get *a lot* busier out there. Go upstairs and fix that"—she motioned to my face with waggling fingers—"and then read the paper on the kitchen table. Then check the shop's social media."

"What are you talking—"

Stevie turned my shoulders to face the stairs and gave a violent slap on my butt. "Go on. Up, up!"

I picked up my drenched tote bag and dragged it behind me up the stairs, the pathetic thud with each step driving home my failure to make Stevie feel secure. Had I really created such an unstable environment that she felt the only way to keep us afloat was to give up something she'd worked so hard for?

Stevie greeted the waiting customers with a bombastic, cheerful voice I'd never heard come from her. A pleasant murmur greeted her back, and I welcomed the warm feeling of hope budding in my chest.

In the bathroom, I toweled the rainwater out of my hair and wiped the smudged mascara from my face. Before I made my way downstairs, I remembered Stevie's order to check the shop's social media. I picked up my phone, mindlessly making a cup of tea while I tapped into the news article we'd been tagged in. "Local Psychic Helps Find Missing Councilman," read the headline.

My heartbeat surged in my chest, the shiver I'd had before becoming a near-violent shake. I needed to sit before my legs gave out. I sat and continued reading, my breathing audible even over the sound of the boiling kettle on the stove.

"Local psychic Jade Ravencroft of Ravencroft Psychic Parlor and Shoppe has helped authorities find the body of beloved councilman Thomas Nichols, who went missing on September 20. After receiving a tip from Ms. Ravencroft, police were able to discover the location of the councilman, who was unfortunately found deceased. 'When she called in with a vision of where the councilman was, we immediately took her seriously and sent officers out to the construction site to initiate a search,' Chief Officer Blanton states."

I scoffed at the blatant lie, remembering how they'd blown me off and treated me with nothing but suspicion and derision. I skimmed the article, knowing I'd be rereading this at least ten more times, if not framing it on the wall. It continued, "This is not the first time Ravencroft has successfully predicted the location of a missing loved one. Mr. Neville, a 90-year-old veteran, raved about Ravencroft's talent after she called him to report the location of his missing dog, Angel. 'She has a gift from God,' Neville states."

My eyes welled with tears. This was an enormous victory for the shop, and there was no telling how many people would read this and pay us a visit—hell, there was evidence of it right now downstairs. I pulled up our social media pages, reeling at the number of comments and new followers we'd gained. The story had gone viral on multiple platforms.

My stack of bracelets jingled as I raced down the stairs. I enjoyed this new weightless, hopeful feeling in my body. For once, I thought triumphantly, people were taking us seriously. When I peeled the curtain back, I nearly gasped at how crowded the shop was. Everyone's heads whipped to me, and I plastered on a serene smile despite the fact that my heart was racing, my mouth nearly salivating at the thought of how much money we were about to make. I'd be able to convince Stevie to call the college and explain. I needed to get her back on that admissions list.

Stevie mouthed *Say something!*

"Welcome, everyone! I know many of you are just browsing, but if you're interested in a reading, please join me at the tarot table." I took my seat in the alcove, appreciating that Stevie had already lit candles and arranged everything I would need. I reminded myself to thank her later for picking up my slack. I didn't do that enough.

To my surprise, as soon as my thighs touched the seat, eight people had organized themselves in a tidy line. I made panicked eye contact with Stevie, who asked the patrons for privacy and encouraged them to continue browsing, promising she'd remember the order in which they'd lined up.

A new sitter took their spot across from me, and I released the rope around the velvet curtain, wrapping us in a cocoon of privacy, or at least the illusion of it. That was what this was all about—the illusion. The reading sped by, and it was clear they just wanted to lay eyes on the newly famous town psychic. A trail of new clients came, one after the other, and I eagerly smiled back at them, ready to put on a show.

* * *

Between clients, my heart thumped with excitement at our spurt of success but also the desperation to take a second to talk to Stevie about everything.

"It seems like most of them just want to interview you about the murder," Stevie whispered. "Did that one lady actually ask you if you killed him yourself?"

I nodded, holding back a nervous laugh. It had shocked me at first, but the woman had clearly been half kidding. I was about to ask Stevie about revoking her college acceptance when a woman entered the shop and tentatively approached us. Stevie busied herself with tidying the shelves. I ushered the woman into the alcove and she sat in her seat, her hands twisting with anxiety in her lap.

"Here," I offered, plucking a crystal from on top of the drawers next to me and handing it to her. "Amethyst. For your nerves."

She gave a timid smile as she took it and thanked me. "This is my birthstone," she said quietly.

"I know," I said. Her eyes widened, unaware she'd set me up for an easy home run.

She did much of the same for the rest of the appointment, dropping hints about her mother's failing memory. When I asked about her dementia and if they could afford to hire someone for part-time in-home care, she nearly began to cry.

"I can barely afford to feed her as it is, much less hire someone," she said with a warbled, tearful voice.

For the remainder of the reading, I stretched the true meaning of the cards to comfort her. By the end of the reading, she was openly crying, and I handed her a box of tissues. "These sessions can feel worse before they feel better. You've been brave." To my surprise, my voice cracked, and I fought against the tightness in my throat as I thought of my own mother, knowing I'd never have the chance to watch her grow old.

She dug through her purse with a shaking hand and put a ten-dollar bill on the table, inching it toward me. I pushed it back. "This first session is on me, and take the crystal. You deserve it."

Her chin quivered. "Thank you. The paper was right. You really do have a gift."

"I hope to see you again soon. Best of luck with your mother's care."

As she left the shop, I let out a deep exhale, relishing in the brief moment of silence in the space, which promptly died as the phone rang upstairs.

"Can you man the shop for a second?" I asked Stevie. She gave a thumbs-up as she straightened a line of prayer candles.

I answered the phone with a distracted "Hello?"

"Is this Jade Ravencroft? Er, Madame Ravencroft?" asked a voice on the other end of the line.

"Yes, this is Jade," I answered.

"Greetings. My name's Max, and I would like to extend an invitation for you to have a booth at the upcoming renaissance fair. I understand we rejected your previous application—um, for the last two years, sorry about that—and are reaching out to correct our mistake and extend our deepest apologies. And additional apologies for the last-minute invitation."

My cheeks flushed at the mention of their previous rejections, calling them mistakes when they clearly weren't. "I accept your apology, and of course, we'd love to have a booth."

"Glorious!" he exclaimed. He had the theatrical lilt to his voice of someone who'd spent hundreds of hours playing Dungeons & Dragons and took his role as Dungeon Master very seriously. "As a show of apology for our mistake, we would like to waive the one-hundred-dollar deposit required to reserve a booth."

I held back the overpowering need to pump my fist into the air and instead took a deep breath and said, "That's so kind of you. I look forward to it."

"Tremendous. Sometime tomorrow, I will drop by your shop to deliver our booth guideline booklet, and I can answer any questions you may have."

We ended the conversation, and I finally let out the overjoyed expletives I'd been holding in, startling Stevie. This was a goal we'd never accomplished, nor had my parents. I relished in the comforting serenity washing over me and wondered if we'd finally made it.

* * *

Stevie

Jade had just wrapped up with the last client of the day, and the relief I felt when she flipped the sign on the door to CLOSED was instantaneous. Today had been a complete clusterfuck, albeit a profitable one.

I was counting the cash in the register when I glanced up at Jade, who was studying me as she tidied her tarot table. She did that all the time, so although it annoyed me to be so profoundly *seen*, I let it slide. "Are you ready for Lisa's smudging? We're leaving at, what, quarter till eight?"

Jade didn't answer, and when I looked up from the register, her face was flushed, eyes glassy.

"You good?"

"I know about college, Stevie." Her voice warbled as she said it, and dread washed over me. I knew she was going to find out eventually.

I sighed. "I've decided I don't want to go."

"I don't believe that. It's about the tuition, isn't it?"

"We can't afford it, Jade. Please just be realistic about that."

Her shoulders sagged, and I knew some part of her agreed with me. "There's so many other things we could sacrifice. Just not that, please. And the shop seems like it might really take off. You saw how crazy today was."

"I don't know," I said quietly. It was true—I didn't know what to do. I'd called the college in a panic and hadn't thought it through, but I knew the payments were too high and our credit was too bad for student loans. It was the hard choice but the right one.

She hugged me. "You have to go, Stevie. You're more than all this."

It was then that I felt something crack open inside me, a deep sadness and longing for an average life. For parents who were dependable and asked me when I'd be home after a party or ordered me to clean my room. I wanted normalcy. Jade was trying so hard to give that to me. She'd been the one to push me to apply, even years after graduating high school and with me not doing anything with myself.

But Jade was far from average and certainly far from normal. She'd gotten us wrapped up into such a big lie, and now I didn't see how we were going to get out.

CHAPTER 17

Jade

IT WAS JUST before eight as we stood on the sidewalk outside of Lisa's home, our jaws slack.

"Wow," Stevie said with both amazement and trepidation. All we needed to do was a quick smudging, a prayer, and boom—we'd earned one hundred dollars in under an hour. We would put on our best performance and give Lisa some relief and peace in her home.

Stevie and I walked up the cobblestone path to her front porch, where plump crimson and mustard mums sat by the door, unaware that they were only a slab of brick and drywall away from a supposed haunting. Lisa answered the door, and as she ushered us in, I studied her home. She'd lit scented candles, a failing attempt to cover a sour, musky smell, and their flames danced in the air as we passed by.

A hefty wooden cross was the center point on a wall of photographs by the stairs. It cast a shadow against the wall that danced with the flames, the cross's black shadow becoming bloated and slanted on the wall, covering a photograph. It was Lisa and her husband standing next to a priest shrouded in a long white cassock.

Lisa approached my side. "Roger's father was a priest at the Episcopal church. He died almost ten years ago, but Roger still goes to church every Sunday. That's why he didn't want to be in the house when you came. I hope you understand."

"Of course. We want you both to be comfortable. If you're ready for us to begin, could you please crack the windows? This will allow the sage to encourage any spirits trapped to exit the house for good." In reality, it was because sage always gave me a headache and I didn't have the energy to fight the dull ache in my skull that would inevitably plague me. Lisa began obediently.

Much to my dismay, the bundle of sage in Stevie's hand kept going out. This was supposed to be a quick and easy job, but clearly the universe had other ideas. Stevie took the lighter out of her jeans pocket, flicking the spark wheel with her thumb. Each time, a single spark sprung forth and died.

"You were supposed to bring a new lighter," I hissed at her under my breath.

"I thought I did," Stevie grumbled.

"Clearly not. This wouldn't have happened if you didn't smoke so much."

Stevie glared up at me, a mixture of annoyance and apology in her eyes. I softened my face and apologized for being on edge. At least I could tell by her clear eyes that she hadn't smoked tonight. She was reliable on that front—you ask her for something, and she would do her best to deliver, even if she complained about it along the way.

"I'll check my bag," I said. I walked into the kitchen and rummaged through it, snatching a white lighter. I grimaced at the bad omen, thinking of all the musicians my father had told me about in the "27 Club" who had died with a white lighter nearby. Why couldn't he have told us normal bedtime stories?

I set my bag down and glanced at the window in the kitchen, which was one of the last ones still closed. I walked over and cracked it open, not even having to bother with the broken lock.

A chill blew in through the crack and I shivered, something catching my attention outside. My heart dropped down into my gut. In the darkness of the night, I could have sworn I'd seen the distinct outline of a human standing in the trees.

Swallowing was a struggle, but I stepped closer and peered outside. Two enormous magnolia trees stood guard a few feet from the window, providing privacy to Lisa's home. Or cover for someone to lurk in.

There was nobody there. Had I even seen someone? Maybe I was a little too good at creating a spooky atmosphere.

Stevie called for me in the living room. Lisa stood by her side with her arms crossed in front of her, braced against the chill flowing in through the cracked windows.

I smiled, my cheeks twitching from the effort. Despite what I told myself, all I could think about was the shadow outside, knowing that with the blinds drawn back and the lights on inside, we were in full view for anyone to see and we would be none the wiser.

I shook the thought away and lit the bundle of sage, placing it in a ceramic dish on the coffee table.

"Before we smudge your house, we'd like to begin with a prayer." Lisa's face softened, comforted by the idea. I'd known by Lisa's cross necklace that she'd be more comforted by a familiar prayer rather than any New Age incantation I could make up, so I'd assigned Stevie with the task of brushing up on her Lord's Prayer so she could lead it.

Stevie nodded at me, ready to begin. We took our seats around the coffee table. "Let's join hands and close our eyes," Stevie said. Lisa extended her hands to us, which were clammy and cold, and closed her eyes.

There was a beat of silence, and I opened my eyes to see Stevie mouthing *What's my line?* I rolled my eyes at her poor memory but also felt that childish enjoyment of watching your sibling squirm under pressure. I pursed my lips and bobbed my head as if to say *You got this.*

"Our Father," Stevie began. *Good start,* I thought. "Who art in heaven. Hollow be thy name." *Okay, maybe not.* I stifled a laugh. Stevie's eyes grew wider as she continued, panic mounting. "Thy kingdom come, thy will be done. On earth and . . . also in heaven."

Lisa's eyes were still closed, but I could tell by the crinkle around her eyes that she'd noticed the mistakes.

"Give us this day our daily bread," I joined in, as did Lisa, putting Stevie out of her misery. Stevie mumbled quietly through the rest of the Lord's Prayer but proclaimed the last word of each sentence enthusiastically.

As we prayed, I studied Lisa's face, wondering if she would ever realize we were frauds. It could be years later that it finally happened. We had to give her *something*, and relief was good enough. My sleep at night depended on it.

The sage smoke lazily billowed up toward the black splotch on the ceiling. Lisa was right. It really did look like the outline of a corpse. I cleared my throat and said, "Let's begin." I stood and they followed suit.

"We cleanse this space. Be gone, any negative energy. Be gone any ill will," I intoned as we walked with Stevie, who waved the sage in all directions around the living room.

We were passing the gallery of hanging photographs when the front door swung open, banging against the wall. Lisa shrieked and moved behind me. A gust of wind blew in, sputtering out half the candles. The room was barely illuminated now, and shadows danced wildly against the ceiling.

"What the—" I bit my tongue, trying to maintain my professionalism, but my heart was beating like a drum in my ears, drowning out the noise of Lisa taking quick, desperate breaths behind me. The door ricocheted from the initial impact against the doorstop and banged against the wall once more. I raced toward it and shut it, trying to maintain a facade of calm despite the flush of my skin and panicked sweat in my underarms.

"Some spirits react violently to cleansings. But the door opening is proof we forced the spirit out and slammed the door behind it. Your house is safe now." My words calmed her breathing. "I always recommend taking a few days away from the house to let the energy settle. Do you have anyone you can stay with?"

"Yes, my sister. I already packed a bag. Just in case." Lisa sprang from her seat and rushed upstairs, returning only moments later with two leather duffels. "I'm ready to leave," she announced as she took her purse off the hook and rifled through it for her wallet. "Here's the remainder of the fee. Let me walk you out."

She handed me the bills and cautiously opened the front door, peeking left and right before waving us out. She locked the door behind us and, without another word, she was in her car and backing out of the driveway.

"What's wrong with you? You're shaking," Stevie asked.

"It's nothing. The door freaked me out. I thought I saw—"

"Oh yeah, that was my bad. I don't think I pushed it closed when I saged the doorway." She chuckled. "It kind of worked, though, right? You saved it, as always."

When I didn't respond, she studied me more closely. "Wait, you said you thought you saw something?"

Lisa's taillights glowed red as she drove down the street, away from her false haunting.

"Never mind. It was nothing."

CHAPTER

18

Jade

When we arrived back at the shop, Stevie and I wordlessly trudged up to our beds, where we fell asleep almost instantly. It was probably four in the morning when I shifted in my sleep at the sound of a creak.

Just the wind blowing against the windows, I assured myself sleepily. I had begun drifting away again when there was an undeniable click of the doorknob and the groan of hinges opening. Sleep fogged my mind and I told myself it was just a dream, but as my eyes darted to the door, it was clear I was wrong.

The door was cracked open, exposing the pitch-black landing outside my door. My stomach clenched in fear as the door opened farther, groaning like it was mortally wounded.

I tried to sit up, but my muscles refused to move. In the opposite corner of the room, there was a tall black shadow. It was too tall to be a human. My heart raced, and a low groan emerged from my throat as I struggled to move. I'd finally done it. Spirits were real, and I'd antagonized them enough that one had finally come for me.

The shadow approached, but there were no footsteps, just a lazy drag before each creak.

I screamed as it lurched across the room, coming right at me. I shot up out of the bed, throwing the covers off me. My sheets were drenched in sweat, and I panted as I searched the room for any evidence of my dream.

Not a dream, a night terror. They were so rare that in the moment, my brain never registered what was happening and my body reacted as though it were staring death straight in the eye.

I turned on my bedside light. The room was empty, as expected. My breath slowed, and I was desperate for a sip of water. I rose to my feet and froze.

My bedroom door was cracked open half an inch. Had I left it like that? I'd been so tired, I couldn't remember. It was just a coincidence, I told myself as I walked to the bathroom and stuck my mouth under the running water.

I didn't want to sleep alone. I shuffled to Stevie's door and cracked it open, not wanting to strike fear in her the way my night terror just had. I hobbled toward her bed and reached a hand out, expecting it to meet her warm, sleeping body.

All I felt was cold sheets. Disappointment and confusion washed over me. Where was she? I needed her. She was the only one who would understand.

I shuffled back to my room, fighting the pathetic, childish tears that were building. I threw my comforter over my sweaty sheets and curled up on top, leaving my bedside light on as I stared at my door, fighting sleep until it eventually won.

* * *

"Stevie," I said to the sleeping lump under the blankets the next morning.

Stevie wiggled under the blankets and groaned. "Go away."

I poked her back, desperate to talk about my nightmare last night. I hadn't had true sleep paralysis since the week Mom died. I thought I'd healed enough, but something in me was cracking open with every bad decision I made.

"What?" Stevie rolled over onto her back, her eyes wide with annoyance.

"I had the dream again. The thing in the corner."

She rubbed her eyes. "Shit. Sorry."

Stevie could be an asshole, but she always knew when to apologize. "I came to your room after, maybe around four. But you weren't here."

"I was outside smoking," Stevie said, fidgeting with a fistful of blankets. "I couldn't sleep either."

I let out a huff of air. "I don't feel great about Lisa's ring. I think that's why I had the dream. I feel like I'm turning into Dad, or like I'm the puppet and he's pulling all the strings, even though we have no idea where he is." Stevie balled up the fabric in her hand, not meeting my eye. "Stevie? We don't have any idea where Dad is, right?" I put extra weight on the final word, trying to provoke her into looking at me.

She took a deep breath, and when she finally looked up, she was a perfect picture of composure. I was growing too paranoid from lack of sleep and the whirlwind surrounding us. Stevie was the only person I truly trusted—now was not the time to second-guess that.

"Of course I don't know where he's staying. His drunk ass probably doesn't either." She laughed, but it was hollow.

"I'm going to make some coffee. Feel free to join me if you want."

She thanked me, and I closed her door behind me. As I was doing so, I heard a long exhale, like she'd been holding it until I left the room.

I stepped outside to grab the mail, and my heart leapt when I saw an envelope in my grandmother's scratchy handwriting. I tore open the envelope and peeled open the letter.

"Dear Jade," it said. "I'm glad we're finally back in touch. I know you are in a hard time and want to help. But remember, too much help can be a hindrance. Keep working hard and trust that success will come. Love, Grandma."

There was a single bill folded into the letter, and I peeled it out. Fifty dollars. That was it. I should be grateful for anything, but from her reaction on the phone, I'd thought she'd understood the severity of our money problems. I wasn't sure what I'd been expecting, but it wasn't this. I shoved the money in my pocket and went back into the shop, where I wadded up the letter and threw it in the trash.

In the shop, I turned on music to drown out my racing thoughts as I packed boxes for the fair tomorrow night. The front door chimed, and my heartbeat escalated with excitement. "Welcome! Be with you in one second," I said as I finished wrapping an amethyst cluster in bubble wrap.

"I have to say, I'm impressed with how far you've come," a deep voice rumbled near the front door. The familiar tone of it made my gut clench—the last time I heard it was nearly two years ago when he dumped me over the phone, just a week after my mother's funeral.

I turned around to see my ex-boyfriend Chris leaning against the front door, his arms crossed in front of him. He was bigger than I remembered, more similar in size now to his brother, and his unfamiliar burliness made my body react with both frustration and fear. He was blocking potential customers from coming in, but also me from getting out.

"What are you doing here?" I asked, embarrassed by the tinny sound of my voice.

"I stopped by to check out the famous Ravencroft psychic. Smart to get rid of the Crawford name after everything. Last time I saw you, your parents were still training you to be a thief. Looks like it paid off."

"They weren't training me to be a thief. They were training me to read tarot. Which is exactly what I'm doing. Also, we never would have dated if your family hadn't started working with my dad, so you really don't need to be coming at me with that tone."

"Aw, come on now, Jade. Don't be embarrassed. It's just how we were raised."

"If you're not going to buy anything, you should leave. I told you I never wanted to speak to you again two years ago, but it sounds like your listening skills are still subpar."

"So are your repair skills, apparently," he said, ignoring my barb about our failed relationship. He pointed up at the half-fixed ceiling and all the materials the repairmen had left in piles on the floor. Frustratingly, they didn't work on weekends unless I agreed to pay double. "That looks like shit."

"Tell that to your brother."

"Excuse me?" He raised one eyebrow. Chris had the uncanny knack of turning a polite phrase into something vaguely frightening.

"Never mind," I said quietly.

"How'd you pull off the Nichols tip?" he asked. I silently straightened items, only to move them again. He stepped farther into the shop. "Come on, Jade. Just tell me."

"It was a psychic vision. Simple as that. You know how that works just as well as I do."

"No, I actually don't. There's a certain honesty in the type of work my family did with your dad. Stealing without playing with people's minds. You, on the other hand, are some sort of mental terrorist, giving people hope where there is none."

"Careful on your high horse; you might fall and break your neck." I turned, begging the burn in my cheeks to dissipate. He laughed casually, only enraging me more.

There was a timid, muffled knock on the front door, but Chris didn't move. I stomped toward him. "If you block my customers, you owe me money. Get out of the way."

I tried to push him aside, but he didn't move an inch. He looked down at me with a satisfied smile, and I recoiled from the memories his woody cologne conjured up. He was the intense, toxic fling almost every woman had and winced every time she remembered. But the brief pleasant moments were unfortunately just as vivid, seared into my mind by all my senses. "Move," I ordered, shoving pointlessly once more.

He backed away from the door, and we were both greeted by the panicked face of a pale, thin man in a fedora.

"Who the hell is this guy?" Chris asked, staring through the window at the pamphlet the man was holding. It must be Max, the renaissance fair worker who'd called yesterday. This was the worst timing imaginable. Chris had always been the jealous type, eager to flip the switch into a rage at the slightest, most insignificant provocation. I ignored Chris and opened the front door.

"Um, hello. I'm Max." He looked between me and Chris, his chin tilting up as he looked at Chris's imposing frame. "I have your booth guidelines here," he said, struggling to avoid Chris's glare.

I reached out to take the booklet, but Chris snatched it from his hands. He handed the booklet to me and crossed his arms across his chest. "All right, now get the fuck out."

Max stood wild-eyed for a moment before turning and running as fast as he could down the street, his arms stiff down his sides. I yelled after him to wait, embarrassed by Chris's outburst and wanting to apologize, but he kept running.

"What's wrong with you? He works for the fair. I just got invited last minute, and your little hissy fit could make them change their mind."

He shrugged. "I didn't like his face."

I rolled up the booklet, pointing it at his chest. "Get out. Now. And this time, try listening: Do not contact me again." I opened the front door and held my breath, waiting to see if he'd listen or continue standing there, domineering my space.

My breath hitched as he stepped closer. "Have fun at the fair, Jade. See you around."

I clenched my jaw to keep from spitting venom back at him. He never listened—whether out of sheer laziness or spite, I didn't know. I slammed the door shut, watching through the glass window as he sauntered slowly down the street, a freshly lit cigarette leaving a toxic trail behind him.

CHAPTER

19

Jade

LATER THAT AFTERNOON I was wrapping up with Eloise, a new client who was nearly eighty and needed help walking to her car. As I shut her car door, I spotted another elderly woman, but one who was much less kind and much more vindictive.

Phyllis had lived in the upstairs apartment in the building next door for almost thirty years—something she happily bragged about to anyone who would listen. Her family had run an antique shop on the bottom floor for nearly eighty years, and apparently each person who lived in that apartment had been more miserable than the next.

I waved to Phyllis as Eloise drove off, nearly sideswiping a shiny black Volvo. Phyllis was midconversation with someone I couldn't see from this angle, and like every conversation with Phyllis, it looked to be one filled with gossip and self-righteous anger. She ignored my wave and instead pointed aggressively at me with a long, furious finger.

A head peeked out from behind the column of Phyllis's stoop, and my stomach dropped. I resisted the urge to roll my eyes and instead gave another fruitless wave to the increasingly annoying reporter, Maria. Since we last spoke in person, she'd called at least twenty times, always at the most inconvenient moments. Maria's lips spread slowly to the side in a menacing grin as if to say *I've got you now.*

I had no idea what they could possibly be talking about, but I knew it was definitely about me. Phyllis had had a vendetta against my family from the moment my parents leased the building. It had started with complaints about lack of upkeep, then progressed to threats to call the police about loud arguments and Dad stumbling home from the bar, occasionally misnavigating and passing out on her front stoop. After he went to jail, Phyllis had been forced to come up with brand-new complaints, and she'd wasted little time.

For a moment I pictured her short, frail frame scurrying through the dark rooms of the shop, looking for evidence of the crimes she was always accusing us of. Her building had the exact same layout as ours, so she would know which dark corner to dip into to remain unseen. I shivered at the thought, as well as Phyllis's growing scowl as she and Maria stared at me.

I needed to hear what they were saying. I acted like I was walking into our shop, but at the last minute I skirted around the side into the alley between Phyllis's and our shops, where I could hear their conversation plain as day.

"Those girls and their shop have always been a nuisance," Phyllis said. "People go in and out at all hours, not to mention the utter ridiculousness of what they're peddling."

"Which is?" Maria asked.

"They're peddling malarkey," she spat out, and I withheld a laugh. "The older one, Jade, spews vague nonsense, and those desperate people eat up every crumb."

"There's nothing illegal about that, necessarily. Plenty of institutions have commercialized hope." I was surprised at Maria's defense of me, but more than likely she was trying to get a reaction out of Phyllis to get more information.

"She's got criminal blood in her. I wouldn't be surprised if their shop is a front for something."

"What do you mean by 'criminal blood'?"

"Her father's a jailbird," Phyllis stage-whispered. "Some argument gone wrong."

A hand gripped my shoulder from behind, and I gasped loud enough to interrupt Phyllis's gossip. Their conversation halted, then picked back up, but when I turned around to a large, looming figure, I lacked the focus to follow any of it.

* * *

Chris stood in front of me, his ominous frame blocking the narrow alleyway. My pulse quickened, fully aware I was trapped in the space between him and a locked chain-link fence. But he wouldn't hurt me, right? Sure, he had a temper and had lashed out at me, but he'd never hit me. *But I could tell he wanted to.*

"Is your memory so bad that you forgot I told you to fuck off just this morning?"

Infuriatingly, he smiled. "Oh, I remember. I just came by to apologize and offer my help."

"I don't need your help. With anything." I tried to sidestep away from him, but he backed up and kept me trapped between the two buildings.

"My brother got me a gig at the renaissance fair setting up equipment," he said proudly.

My stomach dropped. Having a booth at the fair was a huge deal for the shop, and I didn't want them dampening it.

"Look, I'm trying to smooth things over. I wanted to offer you a ride. Figured you still don't have a car."

I snarled at the dig. "Like I said, I don't need your help and definitely don't want to keep running into you."

I pushed my way past him onto the sidewalk, grateful to be in a more open space but regretting that Phyllis and Maria were going to be privy to what was likely about to turn into an argument.

Chris grabbed my bicep to stop me. His grip was just tight enough to dance between discomfort and pain. "You know I can make you more money if you just let me help you. My brother and I could sell that ring faster than Dad and you know it," he said, his voice raised in annoyance. Panic mounted at the thought of him sneaking into his parents' pawnshop to take Lisa's ring just to spite me. Phyllis and Maria were now unabashedly eavesdropping.

"I don't want any help from you," I said in a harsh whisper as I jerked away my arm, "especially if you'd be selling it to the type of people you and your brother work with. I don't want ties to any of y'alls little friends."

"Well, that's too damn bad, because they'll all be at the fair. That's who we'll be working with."

Shit. "I'll be sure not to stop by and say hi. You do the same."

I stomped back into the shop but was stopped by Stevie in the doorway. Was the entire street eavesdropping on everyone? This was a nightmare.

"How much did you hear?" I asked her flatly, annoyance bubbling over.

"Enough." Her glib tone set me more on edge. "Seems like Daniel heard too."

"What?" I whipped my head around, but he was nowhere in sight. I pushed past her and she followed, closing the door behind her. "What do you mean?"

"He had a weird look on his face. He looked pissed—I didn't know his face could even look like that."

"I'm sure it's nothing," I said unconvincingly, already debating whether I should go seek Daniel out and nip this in the bud or just leave it. "I meant to tell you that Grandma sent us money."

"Really? Thank God."

"It was only fifty bucks. She wrote a letter basically saying too much help would make me lazy. Safe to say I don't think she's too keen on rekindling our relationship."

Stevie rolled her eyes. "Typical."

"It is what it is. We have more important things to do than talk shit about an eighty-five-year-old woman. Have you packed the boxes for the fair like I asked?"

"I got two done," she said proudly.

"Just two? What the hell have you been doing all day?"

"I just woke up," she said incredulously.

"It's one in the afternoon," I grumbled back. She gave me a look of confusion, as if that was supposed to mean anything to her. "Let's just get it done."

"Aye-aye, Captain."

I ignored the ache in my arm from Chris's grip as I continued loading boxes, all the while trying not to think about the Pulaski brothers and all their friends being at the fair tomorrow.

* * *

That night, Daniel walked into the shop but loitered near the front door. His hands were tucked into his jeans with his shoulders raised up to his ears, which was an unusual posture for him. He was typically so laid-back and open, but everything about him now was shut off.

"Hey," I greeted him tentatively. "Everything all right?"

"Yeah, why do you ask?" His tone was verging on manic.

"You don't seem good, no offense. You look great, though, as always," I tacked on with a smile, not wanting to hurt his feelings.

"Who was that man you were talking to today? The one you shooed off?"

I froze, remembering Stevie recounting the angry look on his face. I wished I could read his face right now, but it was obscured by the shadows in the dim shop. "Oh, that was just an old friend. Not a friend anymore, actually; just an old asshole, really."

"Right. I see." He picked lint off his T-shirt, although there was none in sight.

The lack of questioning was a familiar tactic from my work, and dammit, it was working. I wanted to shout at him to spit out what he was really thinking.

"Follow me, I need to sit." I took a seat at my tarot table and motioned for him to do the same. I was relieved when he stepped forward, the light on his face showing me he wasn't quite as angry as he sounded. "He's someone I used to date. I hadn't seen him in years until this morning, when he stopped by for the first time. This afternoon was the second and hopefully final time."

His shoulders relaxed at my explanation. The Daniel I knew was back. "What did he want?"

"I have no idea. But I think the news article had something to do with it. He's greedy, and it's probably his dream to be a trophy husband someday. He's barking up the wrong tree, though." I motioned to the shop and the velvet curtain around us that was hanging on by an old staple.

"Need me to kick his ass?" Daniel asked.

I laughed, partly at his goofy smile and partly at the idea of him trying to beat up Chris, who easily had sixty pounds and three inches on him. "I'll call you up if I need that, but I shouldn't be seeing any more of him." It was a small lie, as I knew fully well the chances were high I'd run into him at the fair tomorrow.

He picked up my stack of gilded tarot cards and shuffled them once, impressively well, and flipped the top card around. It was the Ace of Wands. "How do you know what any of these mean?"

"It's just like anything else. You study and practice, and eventually you know it like the palm of your own hand."

"Well, I've only looked at the palm of my hand maybe fifty times in my life," he said with a laugh.

"You should look at it more. It can teach you a lot about yourself. And even if you don't believe in it, it forces you to self-reflect." His hand rested on the table, and I reached out to grab it, gently flipping his palm upward. His finger grazed along the base of my wrist. "Well, I can tell straightaway you have air hands."

His eyebrows rose, and I could tell he was holding back a smile. It was cute he was trying to take this seriously when I knew his logical brain told him this was horseshit.

"That means you have square palms and long, delicate fingers. It shows an analytical mind, intellectual curiosity, and luckily for your patients, fantastic communication skills."

He grinned, taking in the compliments. "What else?"

"There are five lines to focus on: the life, heart, head, fate, and sun lines. Where do you want to start?"

"I'm a shrink, so let's go with head."

I smiled up at him. "The head line stretches from under your pointer fingers downward." I lightly touched the outskirts of his palm, dragging my thumb horizontally downward across the sensitive skin. His fingers twitched and his chest rose with a sharp intake of breath. "Your head line, not surprisingly, is clear, long, and flat, meaning you're clear thinking. You don't often act impulsively." I said the last word breathlessly as his knee met mine under the table.

"And the heart line?" His voice was lower than usual. He leaned forward with his free elbow on the table, the wood creaking below the weight of his upper body.

"The heart line is sometimes called the love line." My voice came out warbled with nerves. I cleared my throat. "It's right above your head line but sweeps across in a curve." I brushed my thumb across, but this time his fingers didn't twitch. Any shyness from his face was gone as he looked back at me, his gaze hot on my face.

I didn't break eye contact as I said, "Yours curves up to the middle finger. You're a passionate person who's focused on what you desire." I paused, noting the quick rise and fall of his chest. He nodded almost imperceptibly. "You go after what you want when you want it," I said slowly, my voice a near whisper.

Our eyes were locked on each other's as his hand turned over, gripping firmly but gently onto my wrist. There was a beat between us—I wasn't sure if it was seconds or minutes—the air in the room sparkling with an electric charge.

He stood, bumping against the table as he reached for my face with both hands, cupping my jawline on both sides as his lips met mine. I stood to meet him, but he pushed me back into my seat, leaning over me as the kiss deepened. I could smell the lingering scent of his cologne he'd likely sprayed this morning, a salty-sweet scent like eating dessert on the beach, the water spraying across your face as the wind picks up.

And for a moment I forgot about it all—the bills, the sudden fame, the investigation. Maybe for tonight, just for tonight, it was okay to forget.

CHAPTER 20

Jade

AT THE RENAISSANCE Fair, the air was thick with fog and a slight chill, providing the perfect ambience for a successful night. "Okay, here's the plan," I said to Stevie, who itched at her wavy black wig with an emerald silk wrap looped around the crown of her head. "I do all the readings. You collect the money and sell items. Do not—*do not*—do any readings. Got it?"

She agreed and flipped the long, synthetic waves behind her bare shoulders. Although I'd never say it out loud for fear of inflating her ego, she'd never looked more beautiful than tonight with her dark-green eyes rimmed with smudged black eyeliner. "You should dye your hair this color," I said, which was as far as I was willing to go with the compliment.

"I look like a goth who got abducted by pirates," she grumbled, fiddling with her corset. "How much longer till I can take this thing off?"

"A few hours. Gates open in twenty minutes, so go practice smiling or something." I pinned up one side of our velvet curtains. They were worn from overuse, but as the sun set, the rich purple velvet would look luxurious in the dim lighting instead of cheap and frayed.

"Look who it is, the Crawfords finally crawling their way onto the fairgrounds."

It was my ex, Chris, with his brother Adam in tow. Uneasiness made me queasy but I stood tall, not wanting it to show.

"Chris. Adam," I said flatly.

"You need any help setting up?" Chris asked. Next to him, Adam's stance was wide, his hands clasped low in front of his belt buckle as he stared at me with sharp, black eyes. His clothes were rumpled like he'd rolled out of bed.

"We're good, Chris. Thanks," Stevie answered for me. Stevie's mouth was twisted into a pucker, and I could tell she was eager to get rid of them. Clearly she wasn't enjoying Adam's looming presence either.

"How's the ceiling?" Adam asked with a sneer.

"It's fine. Would be better if y'all could work on the weekends," I said.

Chris looked between us, clearly confused. He said to Adam, "You got on Ray's crew? He told me he didn't have work for me last week."

Adam shrugged. "He needed extra help, I guess."

Chris told Adam, "Go meet with Mark; he'll tell you what you're doing tonight." Adam left without a word.

"Sorry," Chris said. His apology was unprecedented, and I scanned my memory, sure I'd never heard that word come out of his mouth. "He's been having a hard time since his friend died."

"I heard about that. He died in prison, right?" Stevie asked. I winced at her bluntness, wishing sometimes she'd soften the edges, even if it was the truth.

Chris nodded and stood in silence, clearly wanting to say something, but I'd grown tired of his presence long ago. "We better get back to work."

"See you around," he said, and left the booth after lingering for a moment longer.

"What's up with him?" Stevie asked, to which I just shrugged.

As the fair's opening approached, Stevie and I put the finishing touches on our booth—straightening our hand-painted shop sign, polishing the crystal ball, and setting out tarot cards. Stevie had bought a children's cash register at a garage sale, painting the blinding blues and reds jet black with metallic gold trim. Somehow she'd pulled it off, and I gave her a proud nod as she organized the change in the plastic slots.

As I straightened out a row of crystals and candles, I sensed someone standing in front of our booth. I jumped at the sight of Max silently standing at our table. He was wearing a long navy robe with the hood up, the hems decorated with sparkling silver. His face was painted a shade lighter than it already was, and his lips looked frostbitten with a light-blue lipstick.

"Oh, hi, Max. Nice costume," I said.

He smiled, flipping his hood down. "Thank you. I'm a frost mage."

"Of course," I said confidently, although I was as clueless as Stevie, who stood smiling dumbly beside me. "I wanted to say sorry for the way that customer acted at the shop yesterday."

"Oh, I thought he was your boyfriend," he said with a glint of hope in his eyes.

"Nope. Just a rude customer who didn't even buy anything."

"Apology accepted. I don't tolerate bullying, which is why I calmly walked away." I smiled at his rewriting of events. "I stopped by to see if you needed anything and to let you know the gates are opening in a few minutes. I get to blow the horn this year." He beamed.

"Amazing. Congratulations," Stevie said, clearly amused by this man but also weirdly fascinated. She was always collecting the oddest groups of friends, none of them having anything in common except knowing Stevie. With a flourish of his cape, Max walked away. Moments later, the horn bellowed and excitement and carousel music filled the air.

"Never thought he'd be the one to get everyone horny," Stevie joked.

"Real mature," I laughed as we got to work, excitement brimming so much that I couldn't stop smiling.

* * *

As fairgoers filtered in, we garnered an immediate line, and my panic grew as it became clear that not only did the sitters want a full, in-depth reading, they also wanted to try to slip in questions and comments about the Nichols case.

"I think the wife did it," one teenage girl said. "She just seemed emotionless on the news. Total weirdo."

I fended off the comments, always looping them back in with a cheap guess about their life or prediction about love or money. Within the hour, however, my patience was growing thin while my panic continued to mount. The line wrapped across the two booths to our left, and the businesses next to us had come over to ask us to speed things up since our line was blocking their booths. A pair of cops stood behind the line, hands on their belts and eyes sharp as they watched the crowd. It was completely normal to have police at these events, but the fact that they'd been standing directly across from our booth made me nervous. At least it wasn't Woolridge.

"Stevie," I whispered so the group of young women in the front of the line didn't hear. "While I read these girls, make a sign that says five-minute limit. Reduce the price from ten dollars to five."

She rushed to the back of the tented booth, and the unpleasant sound of frantic markers scraping against poster board made my skin crawl. When Stevie stapled the sign to the side of the booth, half the line groaned in frustration at the time limit, while the others simply saw the slash in price and smiled.

The change served us well, and by the second hour, my throat was dry and my bladder full. "I know I said not to do readings," I said to Stevie, "but I really need to use the bathroom. If people give you a hard time about the pause in readings, just shut them up with a pendulum reading, okay? Need reminders on how those go?"

"Nope, pretty self-explanatory. Yes-or-no questions only, swing, swing, blah-blah-blah."

"Pretty much." I gathered my skirt in my hand and whispered good luck to Stevie as I weaved through the line of waiting customers. The owner of the leatherworking booth to our left shot me a nasty look, since our line was still blocking his booth, only making me walk faster.

The sun had finally set, but the entire fairground was alight with sparkling lights from the booths and rides. There had once been two separate events for the renaissance fair and the fall carnival, but eventually they'd been combined and attendance had skyrocketed.

I walked past the line for the haunted house, shuffling past a mangy clown who reached out for me with a sinister giggle. I slapped his hand away and kept walking. I hated haunted houses. I hated clowns even more.

The restrooms were thankfully tidy, no longer a row of foul porta-potties but instead a building with actual stalls and sinks. As I washed my hands, two drunk women in the stalls chatted with slurred words, their buckled pirate shoes turned inward as they used the bathroom.

"My hot therapist is here," one of them said as I dried my hands.

"The one you hooked up with, then fired you, or the new one in the West End?"

I froze, wishing the woman next to me would turn her faucet off so I could hear better. The only therapist office I knew of in the West End was Daniel's. To be fair, he was hot, and there was nothing wrong with his patients thinking so, but I couldn't ignore the jealousy creeping in.

The woman giggled. "The new one. But God, I'd fire him if it meant he'd hook up with me."

"With your track record, it's only a matter of time."

I tossed my paper towel in the trash, missing, but stomping off anyway. I'd invited Daniel to visit our booth tonight, and he'd said he was busy with a conference and couldn't come. I'd romanticized the whole thing, imagining us walking through the fair arm in arm, and the disappointment at his rejection had been brief but intense.

Maybe he was here to surprise me, I tried to reason with myself, feeling hope buoy up in my chest. I shot it down quickly. The women were drunk enough to be slurring, so they were probably mistaken or were talking about someone else. *Get a grip.*

The clogged, crowded pathways of the fair slowed my pace as I dodged swaying fairgoers who cluelessly sloshed beer from their steins and chalices. I took a different route back so I'd avoid the haunted house, but to my dismay, an enormously tall man with a black-beaked plague doctor mask stood to the side, his head turning as each person passed him, eliciting squeals and shrieks.

Annoyed by the haunted house actors wandering so far out of their area, I crossed over to the other side, keeping him in my vision as the crowds meandered between him and me. As I walked back to our booth, I picked up my pace, noticing all too well that his eyes stayed on me the entire way back.

CHAPTER

21

Jade

WHEN THE FAIR was over and the guests were long gone, Stevie and I loaded boxes into the car that Stevie's coworker had loaned her for the night. It had been a successful night and the pouch I'd brought for cash was pleasantly full. I tossed it on the center console, satisfied with our hard work.

Despite the chill in the air, sweat built under my wig until I finally ripped it off, throwing it into the back seat with a grunt. Stevie followed suit, then viciously unlaced her corset. She sighed in relief and twisted her back. She turned to me to say something, then froze, her eyes not meeting mine.

"What are you looking at?" I asked as I unlaced my own corset.

"Creeper, six o'clock," she said, a combination of annoyance and fear in her voice.

I turned to look, my stomach dropping at the sight of the plague doctor from earlier. The only people left on the fairgrounds were vendors and employees who were packing up and long out of character. Masks had been removed, face paint was smeared, and sneakers were being put on in the place of wedged boots. Except for one person. The man from earlier still wore his all-black outfit, a hat sitting atop a long leather beak mask that didn't move an inch as he stood there, not speaking to anyone.

"Am I crazy or is he watching us?" Stevie asked.

"You're not crazy. He was being a creep earlier too." I scowled at him, letting him know I wasn't bothered by his gaze, although that was a lie. My hands shook as I raised my arms to slam the trunk closed, only to notice we'd forgotten our sign at the booth.

"Shit, can you go grab the sign?" I asked. Stevie hesitated as she glanced at the statue-still man then back at me, opening her mouth to protest. "Go all the way around the left where the jewelry booth was and you won't have to walk near him. I'll watch him."

She hurried off, and I leaned back against the car. I folded my arms across my chest and stared right at him. He was so still that I wondered if he was a mannequin for a costume display.

A group of men walked by, visibly drunk. My stomach dropped as the masked man's head turned and steadily followed them as they neared me. Two of them were still dressed in their haunted house costumes, with fake blood dripping down various parts of their body.

"Psychic lady!" one of them yelled, pulling my eyes away from the plague doctor.

I gave them an unenthusiastic smile, hoping they'd get the point and keep moving. Within seconds, I was surrounded by a group of five men, all about mine or Stevie's age. The smell of stale beer breath wafted into my face.

I could no longer see the man in the plague doctor mask over their heads and I shifted on my feet, desperate to keep an eye on him to quell my anxiety. I needed to know he wasn't following Stevie.

"You looking for someone?" the man in the front asked with a crooked smile.

"Nope," I lied. "I'm on my way out." I fiddled in my skirt pockets, looking for my keys.

"You know, I'm psychic too," a tall man said from the back of the group.

"Yeah? That's nice. You should apply for a booth next year." I was smiling to keep this from escalating any further, but I wanted to tell them to fuck off.

"Oh yeah, I see you in my future. All over it," he said with a low, slurred voice.

"You sure you're not just hallucinating?"

"What, you can't see me in your future? The things I'm doin' to you?"

"Not interested in seeing that now or ever."

"Can't change fate, psychic lady." His friends laughed, and although they stood still, the space between us seemed to close. "Chris and Adam say hi. Ya know, Chris told us you were a good time. I wanna see if he's right."

"I bet Adam wants to find out too," another one said, and they all howled with laughter.

"You guys can go ahead and fuck off now," Stevie said, pushing her way through the group.

I matched my tone with hers. "You heard her. Fuck off."

As if on cue, a loud pop sounded in the emptying parking lot, causing everyone nearby to stoop down. With one eye squinted, one of the men said, "Dude, is that your car?"

The leader of their feral little pack shot up, his eyes locking on his car, whose alarm was now blaring in a panicked staccato beep. A lazy stream of smoke billowed out from under the hood, and when the owner ran to it, the others followed.

"What the fuck, man!" the owner howled as he lifted the hood. Thick smoke blasted him in the face. "Did you leave it running this entire time?"

Stevie and I burst into a fit of laughter, but there was a nervous edge to it—the kind that two people share when they realize they've barely avoided danger.

The men hopped in a nearby truck, their bickering fading as they sped through the lot. Stevie and I were now among the few left here. The carousel had been entirely disassembled at this point, and booth tents lay collapsed on the ground. The few remaining employees were loading equipment onto the backs of trailers.

The row of light posts began to turn off, a heavy click starting at the end of the row far away from us. The approaching dark unsettled me, and the few remaining employees picked up their pace. It was funny that the older you got, the less willing you were to admit that darkness was still unnerving—the unknown of it allowing your mind to conjure up what you feared the most.

"Come on," I said, slamming the trunk shut and opening the driver door. "Let's get out of here."

"Gladly." Stevie slid into the passenger seat, shutting the door just to reopen it and yank her long skirt into her lap.

There was a blur of movement to my left, a shadow barely visible in the now-darkened fairgrounds. It was getting closer, and I desperately tried to convince myself it was just a worker passing by as I twisted the keys in the ignition.

My fingers dug into the steering wheel as the engine sputtered. I turned the key and the engine faltered again. I glanced out the window in panic. The shadow wasn't an employee. It was the masked plague doctor, and he was coming straight to my rolled-down window. I pressed the button to roll it up, but it was useless without the engine running.

"Piece-of-shit car," I growled, twisting the keys again.

Stevie let out a fearful groan as the man approached. "Twist it harder!" she shouted as I gave it another try.

"What the fuck do you think I'm doing?" I snapped back through gritted teeth.

Adrenaline coursed through me as one gloved hand gripped the lip of the window. I leaned away from it as a low voice asked, "Do you need any help?" The mask distorted his voice, sending a chill up my spine.

"No!" I shouted as I turned the keys with every ounce of hope I had. Panic surged as he reached his hand inside.

Tears stung my eyes as the engine roared to life. I struggled with the gearshift—I hadn't driven a manual car since I got my permit at fifteen. The man's hand reached in, grabbing the puffed white sleeve of my blouse. "You're going to need help if you keep digging around."

I panicked, my hand meeting his to try to rip it off. My fingernails dug uselessly into the leather gloves. "Get off me!"

Stevie put her hand on top of mine on the gearshift, yanked it back, and yelled, "Go!"

My blouse tore as the man held on for as long as possible, the car pulling away into the lot.

I sped out of the fairgrounds, holding my breath until we reached the highway. Only then did I let it out, my breath escalating so severely that I pulled onto the side of the road. Stevie and I sat silently in the idling car as we tried to collect ourselves. Wordlessly, I started the car moving again and drove us home, my knuckles clenched around the steering wheel.

* * *

Our street was packed with cars and late-night revelers strolling the streets. Many of them were still in their costumes from the fair, and I scanned the road nervously looking for the plague doctor. The halo of gold from the streetlights was suffocated by a heavy fog and it was clear a storm was building, the clouds overhead straining to hold in rain.

There wasn't a single parking spot on our street, so we circled around multiple times in complete silence. Stevie wiped away the dried tears under her eyes and reassembled her facade of courage, despite her breath still stuttering with each inhale like a child after a heavy bout of tears.

"Thank you for defending me against those guys," I said quietly.

"No problem. Never trust a group of drunk men," she said in a low voice.

I reached out to squeeze her arm before pulling into a spot, and we dragged ourselves out of the car with our skirts balled in our hands. "Let's just leave the stuff in the car for tonight," I grumbled. I locked the car, and we began walking the block to our shop.

The lights in our shop were off, but the space in front of Daniel's building was illuminated. A part of me wanted to bang on the door, begging for Daniel to house us just for the night.

The conversation I'd overheard earlier about the hot West End therapist popped into my mind. The other two doctors in Daniel's practice were approaching their seventies, so I doubted the women had been talking about them. I'd have to ask him about it later, but in a joking way to cover up the hint of jealousy that was stirring inside me.

"You remember when you said Daniel gave you the creeps yesterday when I was talking to Chris?" I asked Stevie, who nodded. "Were you joking?"

She hesitated. A group of drinkers at the bar across from our shop squealed as a new group arrived, causing Stevie and me to flinch. "Well, yes and no. I don't think he's creepy at all—I like him. It was just weird, the way he was looking at you."

"Looking at me how?"

"Well, he was standing across the street just . . . staring. He looked pissed, and he hardly moved the entire time you were talking to Chris. Like, barely even blinked."

It was an unsettling thought—being watched by someone without knowing—and this would make the second occurrence of Daniel doing just that. I thought of the plague doctor at the fair who'd watched us with such intent stillness. Paranoia stirred, wanting to make connections, but I pushed them away. For both Daniel and me, our jobs were about listening and observing. We couldn't necessarily help it when that drifted over into our personal lives.

"Thanks for explaining," I mumbled as we approached our shop. I got my keys out of my skirt pocket, struggling with them in the dark. I wrestled the door open and flipped a light on inside the shop. Stevie trailed behind me, then her footsteps stopped.

"Um, Jade . . ." she said in a high, tight voice.

"Yeah?" I drew back the curtain to the stairwell, flipping another light on.

"Come here." Her voice was even higher now, and it cracked. Tears were brewing.

I rushed over, my entire body clenching with fear as I followed her pointed finger. It was a tarot card, stabbed into the door with a small pocketknife. The tarot card was frayed at the edges, a clear sign of heavy use.

"A Ten of Swords," Stevie whispered.

On the card, a figure lay dead on the ground, ten long swords protruding from their back. It meant only one thing.

A disaster was on the horizon—the lowest point in our lives. As much as we tried, tragedy was unavoidable, and it was coming for us.

CHAPTER 22

Jade

THE NEXT MORNING was Monday, which thankfully meant the repairmen had returned to finish their work. Nervousness had built over the thought of having to be around Adam again.

"Excuse me," I said, interrupting one of the new workers. "Will Adam be working today?"

The man looked at me, confused. "Who?"

I explained who Adam was and what he looked like, but the man gave a disinterested shrug. I couldn't blame anyone for not remembering him, since he barely spoke at all. The crew worked tirelessly in our shop as Stevie and I tried to go about our normal business, but with every thump of a hammer or chime of the door, we flinched, waiting for another bad omen.

Ignorant to our restlessness, there had been a steady increase in the amount of customers and clients stopping by the shop, all of them shamelessly nosy and eager to meet the woman who was psychically talented enough to find the body of a dead man but not quite talented enough to save him.

"Good God." Stevie's voice was muffled behind one hand clasped over her face as she stared at one of the repairmen, who was bent over, digging through his toolbox. The farther he bent over, the more his pants slipped down his backside. I was greeting a small group of college students when both the students and I followed her glance.

"Damn, dude," one of the male students said under his breath to another.

"I've never seen a butt crack go up that high," one of the young women said in what sounded like appreciative awe.

The sight of it briefly broke me out of a vicious internal cycle I was in, debating what I should do about Lisa and her ring. We'd earned a decent amount of money at the fair, but it had immediately disappeared when I'd paid our water and heating bills. We desperately needed Lisa's ring to sell, but still, the guilt of the act was eating away at me. Each night my sleep grew worse as I lay in bed wondering how I'd let myself take it this far. If the ring sold and the Nichols family finally gave us the reward money for my tip, maybe, *just maybe*, we could make it work.

Now, as the plumber's exposed butt crack stared back at me—oh, it just *winked* at me when he shifted his weight—I had an idea. The scales of justice were too far outweighed right now, and even though I was on a high, the scales would have to tip in the opposite direction sometime soon. And they wouldn't just tip, they were going to crash, according to the tarot card stabbed into our door last night.

The students debated for over five minutes on who would get a tarot reading, only for them to all chicken out and dash out of the shop in a fit of nervous giggles.

"Stevie," I whispered. "*Psssst.*" I waved her over.

"How about that strip tease? He really knows how to put on a show."

"I don't feel right about how far we've gone with Lisa. She's given us way too much money."

"Isn't that the goal?"

"Yes, but I always need to *help* the person too. Even if it's a placebo. If I don't give them something in return, it's just stealing."

"Okay, Saint Jade. Where are you going with this?"

"Lisa and her husband are staying with family for the next few nights. We're going to break in and finish the work on their ceiling."

"We?" She waved her finger between the two of us. "*We* don't think this is such a good idea. Break in? You do remember how Dad ended up in jail, right?"

I winced at the blatant omission of the real question: *Don't you remember why Mom's dead?*

"That was different. Can you call it breaking in if it's to do something nice? To leave the house in a better state than it was before?"

The wheels in Stevie's brain were beginning to spin. I could tell I was getting her on board.

"Okay," she said, "but even so, neither of us know how to fix a moldy ceiling, and we can't exactly afford the chemicals and whatever else they use."

"We just need a temporary fix. They won't notice if we borrow some of their paint," I said, eyeing the enormous bucket of paint for the ceiling.

"You're insane."

"Stevie, please. I have to help her." *I have to help myself feel better,* I added internally.

"Fine." The ferocity of her glare surprised me, but before I could tell her this would all be worth it, she stormed out of the room, leaving me staring up at the gaping hole in the shop ceiling.

* * *

Stevie

Jade and I sat parked in the street across from Lisa's house. All the windows were dark, just like most of the other houses on the street. The only difference was that all of Lisa's neighbors hadn't fled their house due to some supposed haunting. They were just enjoying the type of deep sleep that only came with the guaranteed comfort and safety this neighborhood could offer.

We climbed out of the car and gathered the tools we'd borrowed from the repairmen, who had left all their materials in the shop overnight.

"Follow me," Jade said, and I trailed behind her. Instead of going to the front door, she went to the side of the house and approached the kitchen window.

"What are you doing?" I whispered.

"Getting us inside." She fumbled around for a place to grip the window and began, but failed, to push the window up. "I saw the lock on this one was broken when we were here," Jade said proudly. She was struggling in the dark to find a place to grip. Even with the moon shining brightly, the line of enormous magnolia trees behind us towered overhead, blocking out any light.

I got out my phone and aimed my flashlight at the window, panicking all the while that a neighbor would see it and call the cops. Jade slid the window up and I shivered, eager to be inside. Jade climbed in first and I followed, closing the window behind me. The silence in the house was so loud and unsettling that we stood rigid for a moment before moving farther.

I reached out for the light switch, but Jade grabbed my wrist. "Don't turn any lights on. Just one flashlight."

I nodded. Even in the dark, the moldy blotch on the ceiling was visible, and it was clear to see that it had grown since we'd last been here, the black dots bloating like a body left in the water.

Jade set her paint down and surveyed the room. "Help me move some of this furniture." We shifted the couch and side tables out of the way, and Jade said excitedly, "Time for a little makeup." I could tell she was eager to do this, more to clear her own conscience than to better Lisa's life. Eventually, the mold would come back and Lisa would likely realize what had been done.

"Oh crap, I forgot the drop cloth. Be right back," I said. Once I'd crawled out of the kitchen window into the cool night air, I sucked in a deep breath. It was stuffy and humid in the house from the air being turned off, and the idea that we'd been inhaling tiny mold spores for the past ten minutes had convinced me I couldn't breathe.

And in my stupid little mind, the cure for that would be a joint. I pulled an Altoids tin out of my back pocket, enjoying the comforting sound of my lighter rattling around inside. I was standing in the pitch-black shadows of the magnolia trees as I lit the joint, and I stood there for a moment admiring the blooms, wondering how long the trees had taken to grow.

Far down the street, two headlights appeared, so I rushed to the car and hastily stubbed the joint out and put it back in the

Altoids tin. The last thing I wanted was a charge for possession on top of breaking and entering.

But we're doing something nice! I'd tell the officers with red eyes. *Kind of!*

I got in the car and peeked over the dashboard. As the headlights approached, it became clear it wasn't a police car. That would have made me sigh with relief if it weren't for the fact that they came to a stop about a hundred feet from me and idled in the middle of the road.

What were they doing? Had they seen me or what house I'd come from? My mind raced and the two small puffs I'd taken had given me a fuzzy head, but now it was cut through with anxiety. *Stop being paranoid.* But hadn't my childhood with my parents been a good indicator that I *should* be paranoid? That people sometimes *are* out to get you?

The truck began moving again and was now close enough that I could see two men, both wearing baseball caps, which cast shadows over everything but their mouths. One took a long drag from his cigarette, making the end cast an amber glow on the scruffy five o'clock shadow along his jaw.

My stomach churned as they neared me. *Please drive by, please, please,* I begged as I ducked down behind the dash. All that I could see was the slow, steady approach of the headlights. The truck rumbled, and from the vibration of the engine, I could tell they were idling right beside me.

I needed to lock the doors, but it was such an old car that there was no way to lock it other than by manually pulling up the lock on each door. I yanked the driver's side lock, but it was jammed firmly in place.

I peeked over the dash again just as two men opened their car doors and stepped out. My heart pounded as I crawled into the back seat and crouched down, hoping they hadn't seen me. If they were eyeing this car to steal it, hopefully they'd take one look at the piece of junk and move along.

One of the men rapped on the window, and unable to control my fear, I let out a yelp. I was certain the man was going to lurch inside and drag me out. Or worse, he would come inside with me.

"Can you step out of the car, please?" one of the men said.

"Rather not," was all I could think to say. My voice was flippant, trying to play it cool, but my heart was racing.

"You live in this neighborhood, ma'am?" I didn't answer, and he yanked the car door open.

"You can't open my door," I shouted. "That's breaking and entering." The irony of the accusation wasn't lost on me, even as my pulse raced.

"Ma'am, I asked if you lived here."

The fear coursing through my body kept me from speaking.

"I asked you—"

"No, I don't live here. I'm visiting a friend," I finally spat out.

"Who's your friend?"

"No offense, but I don't think that's any of your business."

"Is that so?"

I nodded petulantly. "For all I know, you could follow me back to their house. You seem like the type—hanging out in the street, following women into their cars."

He winced like I'd slapped him in the face. "That's literally the opposite of what I'm doing. We're with the neighborhood watch."

"That's nice. Maybe you should get back to the *watching* part instead of the *breaking into people's cars* part."

"Without proof you're visiting a resident, you need to leave, or we'll call the police." He took a step back and motioned to his friend.

I set my jaw in defiance. "I didn't realize I needed a permission slip to visit friends. Sorry, my daddy forgot to sign it."

His friend approached, and I pushed myself even farther back into the seat. The man had his phone at the ready, and on the screen were three glaring numbers: 911. I watched in terror as his thumb hovered over the green circle at the bottom of the screen, ready to connect.

* * *

Jade

While waiting on Stevie to return, I pulled three value-sized boxes of baking soda out of my bag, along with three plastic bowls and essential oils. I set the bowls around the room, filling them with baking soda doused in peppermint oil to soak up the paint smell. If Lisa walked in here and it smelled like a hardware store, she would know we were trying to pull the wool over her eyes.

When I was done, I went around to each window on the sides of the house and cracked them just enough to let fresh air in but not enough to be visible from the street.

I was bent over stirring the paint with a wooden stick when I paused. I'd thought I'd heard a man's voice outside. I knelt on the floor between the sofa and the wall and crawled over to the front window. With a shaking hand, I pulled back the curtain less than half an inch and peered out. Two men were standing in front of our car, the driver's door gaping open. I flinched as I heard Stevie arguing with them.

I had to do something. But what? Distract? Pretend I was Lisa and don her bathrobe so I could go outside and curse at them for making too much noise? No, they could be neighbors, and they'd know even in the dark I wasn't Lisa. I'd have to distract.

I crept to the cracked kitchen window and crawled through it. I crouched behind a gardenia bush, peeking over to get a better view of the street. One of the men was showing his phone screen to Stevie, his voice verging on shouting. I nearly sprinted forward as Stevie stepped out, clenching the drop cloth to her chest, and my heart ached at the sight, the memories surfacing of her cowering as a child with her stuffed animals gripped to her in the same way. The man put his phone in his pocket, clearly appeased by her cooperation.

Stevie and the men exchanged more words and my entire body shook, my mind conjuring up all realms of possible conversations, and each was worse than the next.

On instinct, I picked up a landscaping rock and inched forward to another bush, closer to the street. I raised the rock behind me, ready to launch it into one of the cars down the road in a last-ditch effort to distract the men. They were still speaking, but it was so low now that there was no chance I'd make out a single word. Stevie stood stock-still in the street, and I knew by her posture, even in the dark, that she was petrified.

Stevie pulled out her own phone and held it up to them. Whatever was on her screen appeased the men, and they walked to their truck, leaving Stevie standing in the street. I peeked out from behind the bush and hissed out, "Pssst!"

Stevie took two shambling steps, then caught her stride. When she reached me, I dragged her to the open kitchen window.

"What was that? Who were those men?" I blurted out.

"Neighborhood watch." Her response was flat and distant, her mind elsewhere. She didn't elaborate.

"What did they say?"

"They were asking why I was here," she said. "They were about to call the cops, so I lied and said we were surprising a friend by painting their nursery while they were in the hospital."

"And they bought it?"

"Only when I showed them this." She pulled out her phone and showed me a picture of a freshly born baby, held by a woman in a hospital gown.

"Who the hell is that?"

"My friend just had a baby last week. It was the only thing I could think of in the moment."

"You're a genius," I said with a laugh, but she didn't laugh with me. "You handled that better than I could have," I said, and reached out to loop my arm through hers, but she yanked it away. I studied her face. "What's wrong?"

"They almost called the cops on me, Jade. What would have happened to me if they did?"

"It turned out fine, though."

"Just barely. I'm sick of *just barely* being fine," she said.

"Can you please just come inside with me and help me finish this?"

She sighed. "I'm really tired of all this."

"I know. I'm sorry." This time she let me loop my arm into hers. I ushered her back into the house, where for the next four hours we scraped and sanded away Lisa's moldy ceiling and slapped on two new coats of paint. It was just past three in the morning by the time we finished, and we drove back in silence, not even the radio playing.

When we got back to the apartment, Stevie rushed in ahead of me, not bothering to even turn on lights as she hurried upstairs and slammed the door to her room.

CHAPTER

23

Stevie

A GROUP OF SIX stood across from me in the dim theater lobby. It was the day of the public séance, something we'd never done before and was make-or-break for our business. That's how everything felt these days—a dance too close to the edge, each decision made out of desperation and a sad inkling of hope that we'd come out of this okay. The only thing comforting us was the fact that the Pulaskis had called us this morning to let us know Lisa's ring had sold. It filled the glaring hole in our wallet just enough for comfort, and if the Nichols gave us our reward money, we would be able to afford the rent increase and things would finally settle down. The feeling of hope was strange, lingering in my periphery in a way I wasn't used to.

The sitters had arrived ahead of the crowd as requested, but my eyes still darted around, waiting for the small audience we were allowing to watch to show up too early and ruin everything. I studied the sitters and knew Jade was doing the same. To select who was here tonight, I'd created two automated raffles on our website: one to select the sitters and the other the audience. We'd advertised both as being completely random and anonymous through a raffle software, but in reality the contact data they'd entered into the form went straight into our inbox, where we'd secretly weeded out over one hundred applicants that we thought would be too difficult to read or would be too disruptive based on their online presence or any previous knowledge of them. One of the audience applicants had been Maria, eager to drum up drama for a story, and Jade had deleted her name from the list with a smug, satisfied smile.

"If you'll follow me," Jade said to the sitters, "I have a room for you all to place your coats and belongings. It's necessary to separate ourselves from material objects that may hold a distracting energy."

A woman in a neon-pink jacket spoke up. "I'm not leaving my stuff with anyone. No way." A few of the other sitters murmured in agreement.

"I understand and knew you might feel that way, so I'll be locking the door and giving one of you the key for safekeeping until the séance is over. Morgan, would you do the honors?"

Morgan's chest puffed up with pride as she became the de facto leader of the group of sitters, and she nodded, all her suspicions out the window. Her social media had been rampant with New Age ideology and digital flyers for workshops she led on Reiki and acupuncture. It had been easy to plan ahead, knowing she'd eagerly accept leadership.

Little did the sitters know that if you twisted the handle and lifted it as hard as you could to the right, the latch would give, and voilà—you had full access to the sitters' personal belongings.

And as Jade took them back to deposit their items for safekeeping, they had no idea I'd follow behind three minutes later to avail myself of that access.

I entered the back room and closed the door behind me. I bounced on the balls of my feet and tried to shake off the heady mix of adrenaline and anxiety that was making me breathe so quickly the room was starting to spin.

Jade's voice through the wall was a soothing drone, but despite that, my heart raced. I didn't have much time, and the choreography today was tight. There wasn't a second to spare. The sitters' bags and coats lay across the chairs and tables in the small office, and I knew what I had to do. I started with the purses first. We women carry a snapshot of our lives in our bags without realizing it: medications, cosmetics, not to mention the glorious trove of information on cell phones. I zipped open a small black purse and took out the phone with shaking hands. I needed to move quickly.

Shit. It had a passcode. I put it back in the bag and rifled through the compartments. Bingo—a prescription bottle for warfarin. I was clueless about its purpose, and adrenaline pumped as I pulled out my phone to look it up. I was lucky the theater had open WiFi; otherwise we would have been screwed, both for looking up small details like this and for communicating during the séance. The search results told me the prescription was an anticoagulant, a medication to stop blood clots. Jade could do something with that. I texted her the information, along with the patient's name on the bottle: Emily Benson.

I had only five more minutes to gather information for Jade before the sitters and the small audience were seated. The following items I found had potential as well, including a gold

Alcoholics Anonymous chip for ninety days sober and a funeral program that helpfully listed one of the sitters as the son of the deceased along with the Bible verse he'd read at the service.

With just three minutes left before Jade was to begin, I returned the sitters' belongings exactly as they were and walked to the lobby. Jade would have just two minutes before the séance began to read and digest the information I'd texted her.

* * *

Jade

After the sitters draped their coats and bags over whatever surface they could find in the back room, they followed me onto the stage, where I'd placed a circular table with a black tablecloth along with five creaky metal fold-out chairs provided by the theater. It was five o'clock now, Stevie's cue to let the audience of thirty into the lobby, where she was waiting with a guest list, our appointment book, and a display of items for sale.

As the sitters took their seats, Andrew, a middle-aged man, said nervously, "You can hear the people waiting in the lobby from here." The group chuckled, an air of anxious excitement palpable.

"Before we let the audience into the theater," I said after they'd all been seated, "we're going to center ourselves. It's crucial that we maintain focus as a group; otherwise I may begin to pick up on energy from the audience."

They nodded eagerly, ready to do anything to convince the spirits to ignore the crowd and gift them with something spectacular—some sort of proof that we continued on after death. Some sort of hope that their existence wasn't just a blip in history.

I led them through a series of statements, affirming that they had no ill will and were open to receiving whatever was channeled through me. The final step was one I didn't always do but added a certain amount of physical drama that heightened sitters' reception to my performance.

I stood and lit the same bundle of sage I'd used at Lisa's, and a plume of smoke drifted upward and trailed behind me as I circled the table. Their heads twisted to watch as I circled around once, then twice, in complete silence.

"Looks like what I used to smoke in college," the oldest man in the group joked, but Morgan, taking her duty as key holder very seriously, shushed him. He shifted in his seat as he rolled his eyes.

Once I was done, I placed the sage on a glass tray in the middle of the table alongside a thick white candle, which I lit with a flourish. "I'll be letting in the audience now. Please remember to maintain focus." I walked up the aisle to the double doors, knowing Stevie was standing guard on the other side. There was a small alcove next to the doors that was completely shadowed in darkness, and I stepped into it, pulling out my phone. I sighed in relief as I saw that Stevie had found useful information on the sitters and this wouldn't be a cold reading. I digested it as quickly as I could, repeating the details in my head as I opened the doors.

Blood clot. Dead dad. Alcoholic.

It was a brutal reduction of three complex people into a single useful fact, but it had to be done for this to work. I shoved my phone in my pants pocket and rapped on the door, letting Stevie know I was coming. I swung the doors open and greeted the small crowd with a smile. "Welcome to the séance."

The crowd filtered in, and Stevie guided them to the front four rows in the middle section of the theater. She was just a shadow as she slipped out of the room.

I began as I usually did, asking the attendees to raise their palms upward, showing their willingness to communicate with the spirits. *Ease them in,* I reminded myself, pushing away the adrenaline surging through me.

Brenda would be first. After a few moments of silence, I let my eyes roll back into my head and swayed. "I'm dizzy. Seeing double." I began to tremble, letting my jaw chatter. "I can't stop shaking." I closed my eyes as I shivered, holding on to the edge of the table as though I would fall out of my chair. I took a sharp inhale and regained my composure.

"Brenda," I said, and she stared back at me, not saying a word. Based on her age—I guessed close to sixty—the chances were low that her grandparents were still alive. "Your grandparents are proud of you."

Her eyebrows rose. "Proud of me?"

"'Ninety,' they keep saying. Ninety . . . there is some significance to this number."

"Yesterday I was ninety days sober. I got my gold chip." Her smile was proud, rightfully so.

"Congratulations. Your grandparents were with you while you detoxed, and yesterday when you received your chip."

"I highly doubt that. My grandparents didn't speak to me for years before they died." She leaned back in her chair and crossed her arms across her chest.

I fought against the urge to tense at the volleyed information. I nodded as though I already knew this. The lie came easily. "They distanced themselves from you because of your addiction. They didn't want to enable you," I said, trying to drum up the language they used in AA. My dad had gone to two measly meetings, but he constantly mocked the terminology they used. "They worried the relationship would become codependent."

Her mouth was slightly agape, her cheeks flushed. "Well," she stuttered, "that makes so much sense. I thought they hated me. Thank you."

A wave of small smiles and wide eyes moved through the theater, and I took a calming breath. *This is going to go well,* I told myself. *Off to a good start.*

I bid her grandparents goodbye, thanking them for the closure their imaginary pride conjured in Brenda. I had the sitters recenter themselves, then I winced, drawing in a hiss.

"Are you okay?" Andrew asked next to me.

"Yes, sorry. My blood." I clutched at my heart.

"Your blood?" asked Emily, the target of my next trick.

I moved my hands to my legs, gripping at them. "It's as though my blood is stopping. There's a terrible pain in my legs. I need to stand." I rose halfway from the table, then flopped back into my seat, the sitters on either side of me gripping my arms to keep me from falling.

"Do you need us to call a doctor?" Brenda asked.

"No, this isn't my pain. This is someone else's—someone here." I gazed around the table and allowed my eyes to rest on Emily, who was rubbing her thumb back and forth across the locket she was wearing. "This pain is yours."

She was feeding me information without even knowing. The locket, the melancholic set of her eyes—there was far more to this than just a simple daily blood clot medication.

"This was also the pain of a loved one." She began to cry, and I was shocked at the force of it. She nodded and gave out a small "Yes."

Here was the risk. The leap of faith. Would she fill the silence and give me another morsel, directing me where to go? Or would she remain silent aside from her small huffs and sniffs, leaving me to guess wildly? I let the silence sit. *Come on.*

"Both my siblings," she said as she opened the locket to reveal a smiling man and a straight-faced woman. "We have a hereditary blood disorder." The sitter next to her placed a hand on her shoulder as she continued to cry.

Another leap, another guess based off the split-second sighting of the pictures in her locket. "Your sister's energy is very stern." Emily chuckled. *Okay, spot on.* "She's telling you to take your medication. Same time every day."

She laughed. "Of course she is." Her tears abated into something like relief. "She was like a second mother."

"She says goodbye for now," I said, and Emily thanked me with a tearful smile. Someone in the crowd clapped three times, then stopped as they realized the others were too mesmerized to join in.

The lights flickered, and there was a collective gasp. *Thank you, Stevie.* "Someone is here that passed very recently," I said in a low voice. "They want to speak with us."

The sitters shifted in their seats, a small act at each séance that clued me in to their willingness and sparked a thrill in me. They were preparing themselves for the unknown.

I curved my spine inward, bowing my head so it was nearly touching the table. "Andrew," I said without raising my head.

"Yes?" His voice wavered, the question in his voice a sign of both fear and desperation for comfort.

I raised my head slowly and exhaled deeply as I opened my eyes. "John," was all I said.

The beat of following silence was tense as he tried to keep the disappointment out of his voice. "Who?"

"This is the name that keeps coming up. John, John, John . . ." I trailed off into a whisper as I closed my eyes again.

"Sorry, not ringing any bells," he said flatly. The audience was picking up their proverbial pitchforks, ready to call me a fraud, but I knew exactly what I was doing.

I opened my eyes and said to him, "'Do not let your hearts be troubled.'" He visibly gulped, certain I couldn't be right about this. I continued. "'You believe in God; believe also in me.'"

In unison, his voice booming in disbelief and mine calm and reassuring: "John fourteen, one through three."

The curtains behind us rippled gently, a pleasant detail that I'd later praise Stevie for. The other sitters and the audience were sneaking looks at each other as though we'd gone mad. After the perfect amount of whispering in the crowd, I spoke. "Andrew, your father is here to speak with you. Mark wants you to know he is at peace." Andrew's eyes brimmed with tears. I took a chance next, hoping it would land based on the humor he'd attempted to use earlier. "And he's glad you picked a short verse at his service."

A tear fell from his face just as a burst of laughter erupted, causing the other sitters to jump.

"He hated long funerals. 'In and out,' he used to always say," Andrew said with a sad smile.

I'd reached the end of Stevie's reconnaissance and needed to draw the séance to a close. There were three sitters who still leaned forward eagerly, but I had nothing for them. Perhaps they'd come to the shop for closure later on.

"It seems our time has come to a close. I no longer sense any spirits willing to communicate. Please, everyone, join hands as we sever any form of communication so that no negative energy can attach itself to you."

Someone in the crowd gave a sigh of disappointment, and I looked out, trying to see their face so I could target them for future readings. The only face that stood out, however, was the tight-lipped, smug face of Woolridge, the overly muscular and overly rude detective who'd interviewed me after I submitted the tip.

My palms grew clammy in the hands of the sitters beside me, and my confidence faltered. I tried to pick back up when something fell from the ceiling, smashing into the floor so close that I felt the breeze it created.

All the peace and closure I'd created was severed by gasps and screams.

* * *

Stevie

Shit.

I stared down at the broken stage light that had landed only a foot away from the séance table. Half the sitters were frozen with shock while the others craned their necks, trying to see what could have caused the fall. I tucked my head back, holding my breath.

"It's all right," Jade said, urging the sitters to calm themselves. "We need to close the séance immediately. When I have a very strong connection during a séance, the spirit can be a bit . . . unwilling to depart. Let's join hands."

It was a beautifully quick pivot to cover up my mistake. I scrambled off the rigging above the stage as quietly as I could, making sure to stay behind the layer of curtains as I moved through the back rooms and returned to the lobby.

I tried and failed to slow my breath and remember our plan. Jade spoke the phrase that was the cue for me to open the doors to the lobby. But due to my unfortunate mishap with the light, I was almost a full minute off my cue. I rushed, panicked sweat building as I made it to the lobby and swung open the doors, my breath frantic.

I froze as I was met with a brick wall of a man standing in the doorway. "Stevie Crawford?"

"Yeah?" I said before I could think any better. He'd used our real last name, and I'd just confirmed it.

"I'm Detective Woolridge with Forsyth PD. Do you have a moment to talk?" he said.

"Yeah, I remember you. And no, I'm a little busy," I said tersely as I pointed to the crowd meandering into the lobby. It seemed as though the crashing light had worked to our advantage as I heard amazed whispers among the audience members.

"I guess she's not full of shit after all," a young man said to the woman he'd locked arms with.

"Told you so," she said proudly back. "She can make things move with her *mind*."

"She's a psychic, not a wizard, Jenny."

Woolridge eyed the couple as they walked past us. "Could you tell me where you were on September twentieth?" Woolridge asked.

I'd never been questioned by the police in any fashion and blurted out, "Probably at work, I don't know. Why?"

"Since your sister submitted the tip about the councilman that turned out to be correct, we just wanted to tie up any loose ends. Now, when you say work, do you mean at the bar or the work you do with your sister?"

I bristled. How much had he looked into me? That in combination with him using our real last name was sending me into a panic. "I—"

Jade interrupted, nearly bumping me out of the way. "Detective Woolridge, so nice of you to join us. I don't remember your name being on the guest list."

"Great show," he said.

"If you don't mind, we're very busy. Please feel free to make an appointment."

Jade whisked me away to the table we'd arranged in the lobby. As I made appointments and sold overpriced crystals to the audience, Woolridge stood watch in the corner before eventually slipping out the door into the night.

CHAPTER

24

Stevie

I STOOD AT THE bar, my stomach twisting with nausea. The medicinal smell of alcohol and malty beer wasn't helping. I couldn't do this. I'd told Jade I could do it, but as I stood behind the bar, I was doubting myself. It didn't help that I'd been so worked up after the success of our séance tonight that I hadn't been able to eat more than a few bites of dinner before heading out for my late shift. My phone vibrated in my pocket, and I pulled it out. It was a notification for twenty new followers in the last hour alone.

Ian Stellman was sitting at the far end of the bar, nursing his fifth Budweiser. His gut was far larger than when he was my teacher, and his cheeks and nose had become a sickly shade of purplish red. I studied him as I swept a rag around the inside of a pint glass. He glanced up at me, meeting my eyes, and I jerked, dropping the glass at my feet.

"Watch it, Stevie," my manager grumbled as he closed out a customer's tab.

"Sorry." At least I hadn't dropped the glass in the ice bucket like the new hire did last week.

We were closing in a little over an hour, and Stellman didn't show any signs of leaving. He was watching the women in the bar, but mostly me. It made my skin crawl. I was never more than superficially polite to him, giving the same "How we doin'?" and "What can I get you?" questions that bartenders give in every language around the world.

How was I supposed to convince him to follow me? Wouldn't it be obvious that I was up to something if I was suddenly flirting after everything that had happened?

As I bent over to clean up the glass, bile rose in my throat. I could just leave. Tell Jade he didn't come. But where was the sense of justice in that? Jade had taken care of me like a parent, even before Dad went to jail. What had I done in return for her? Rigged a couple of cheap scares for séances and watched the shop when she couldn't? I had to do more.

I threw the glass in the trash and walked to the end of the bar where Stellman sat. "You need another one?"

"How'd you guess?" He lifted his empty glass. I wanted to take it and smash it over his head.

"I guess I'm psychic."

"Not sure those exist, but you make me want to believe."

I forced a smile. "You want to believe for real? There's a psychic parlor across town. Come with me after I close." God, I wanted to throw up. I wanted to slap him, throw up, and quit this fucking job.

He studied me, a look of confusion and hope muddling his expression. "You sure?"

No, I wasn't sure about *any* of this, but if Jade was, then I needed to pretend. "Yep. Meet me outside in about forty-five minutes. I'll grab your beer."

In that moment, his smile reminded me of how he'd been as a teacher—charming and bubbly, enthusiastic to a contagious degree. It was easy to see how he'd lured so many students into a sense of comfort. I heard so many whispers and derogatory comments about the students while working, and all I wanted to do was protect them, to tell them I understood. Charm and narcissism went hand in hand. It was easy to get wrapped up in the facade these types of people put on.

I begged the clock to slow as the minutes ticked by. Usually it was the opposite, silently begging customers to leave so I could start cleaning tables and glasses. My manager made the announcement that we'd be closing soon, and my stomach twisted as the late-night stragglers filed out. Stellman smiled at me as he took the last sip of his fifth beer and left to wait for me in the parking lot.

* * *

Jade

Stevie opened the shop door with all the color drained from her face and Stellman trailing in behind her. Gone was her initial excitement to help lure Stellman to the shop and in its place was a clammy, panicked Stevie, white-knuckling her way through anxiety for me. I appreciated her more than ever in this moment. We had a chance to prove to the cops that there was some sort of connection between Stellman and Nichols, that maybe Stellman was responsible for his murder. I had the voice recorder on my phone rolling already, tucked under the table just in case.

Although I'd never been one of his students and he hadn't even been hired until after I dropped out, I'd put together a disguise of sorts. I'd curled and teased my wig and my eye makeup was more severe than ever, the black eyeshadow buffed out nearly all the way to my eyebrows. I looked nothing like Stevie or myself, which made it perfect.

"Welcome. How can I help you two?" I asked in a slightly sultry voice, playing into his lascivious nature.

"We just wanted to check out the shop. He's not a believer." Stevie pointed to him. She was smiling, but I knew her well enough by the quiver of her lip that she was on the verge of tears. A bit of an overreaction, I thought, but Stevie was always full of surprises.

"I believe in science," he said, dragging out the *s* with a slur.

Let's loosen you up even more.

"How about a reading, then? At this hour, every reading comes with a glass of wine. On the house."

"Maybe I do like psychics," he said with a hiccup. He rested his hand on the shelf of candles to his right, and the entire shelf teetered. He jerked his hand back and waited while the shelf straightened out and settled. "Oops."

"Can I use your bathroom?" Stevie asked.

"Sure," I said after hesitating. "Up the stairs on the right."

She turned, displaying two shiny braids down each shoulder. Nice touch, I thought. By the way Stellman's eyes trailed over her body, it was clear he'd noticed. *Creep.*

"Why don't you take a seat at the tarot table? I'll grab your wine." I already had a bottle and a glass ready behind the curtain to the stairs and met him at the table.

"Would you like to get started?" I asked when I sat, handing him his wine.

"Sure. Wait, on what?"

"Tarot. I'm going to read your cards."

He rolled his eyes ever so slightly and took a messy glug of his wine. "Sure, why not."

"Deep breath for me as I shuffle. Focus on what's been happening in your life."

I shuffled, then placed three cards face down between us. Of course I had no idea what they would be, but even if it was a positive reading, you could twist tarot cards to mean whatever you wanted.

Usually I would flip the cards over one by one, explaining as I went, but I needed to know how to weave my reading to get a reaction out of him. When I scanned over the cards, the rise and fall of my chest quickened with disbelief. The cards actually applied.

"I'll explain each card as we go, and if you'd like, we can talk about how they apply to your life. You're in control of the reading." He didn't respond. "The first card is the Devil." I tapped the horned figure with a naked man and woman chained together beneath him. "This card is showing me something within that you're fighting every day." I waited for a reaction, but there was none, aside from his slightly defensive crossed arms. "There's an addiction you struggle with—whether it's someone else's addiction that affects you or your own."

Stellman sat there tight-lipped, just staring at me. It made me uneasy, and the hairs on the back of my neck stood on end. I wondered if Stevie was on the other side of the curtain, listening.

"The next card is a reversed Magician. There's a con man in your life, is there not? A trickster." I relished in the question as I reeled him into my web. He reached for his wine, nearly knocking it over, then took a sloppy sip.

"This trickster is lowering your quality of life. The things you used to enjoy—they now feel ruined. Tainted. Is that right?"

His face reddened. We both knew I was talking about him. He just didn't know that my words were weapons, sharp and pointed right at his throat. I knew exactly who he was.

"That's . . . true, I guess." *Jesus Christ,* I nearly shouted in frustration. This man was giving me so little, he might as well have not even been here. He finished his wine.

"Would you like another?"

He nodded, and I went behind the curtain to fetch the wine, fully expecting to see Stevie, but she was still nowhere to be found. She needed to come down soon, or Stellman was going to get suspicious. There was a light switch at the bottom of the stairs that connected to the landing's ceiling light, and I flicked it on and off two times to get her attention. For a moment I thought I smelled the skunky scent of weed smoke, but I didn't give it any further mind as I poured Stellman's hefty second glass of wine and returned to the table.

He took a gulp as soon as I handed him the glass, nearly drinking half in one go. It was a cheap red wine, but strong.

"Your final card is the Seven of Swords." I pushed the card closer to him, my finger tapping the long swords that a devious-looking man was attempting to carry. "This indicates someone in your life who keeps getting away with something. Unfortunately, this usually means something criminal. Something harmful. Is this true?"

"He really wasn't a bad person," he slurred.

I stiffened. *Wait . . . what?* This reading was supposed to be about *him*, and he was referring to someone else. Did he think this entire reading applied to the councilman?

Beads of sweat were forming around Stellman's receding hairline. The heat had kicked on as soon as Stevie went upstairs, and although I was sweating too, I silently thanked her. A little sweat went a long way in convincing sitters they were experiencing something substantial—something that affected them to the point of visible physical symptoms. My father had been keen on drugs to induce vomiting or fainting, but I played a little nicer, a little gentler.

I needed him to talk more. "All three cards together form a picture in my mind. I believe the person with the addiction is you.

The other two cards lead me to believe it's affecting other people. Maybe family and friends?" I knew damn well it was more than that. Innocent students. *Their* families and *their* friends.

His eyes watered, and he cleared his throat. I'd hit a nerve. "Yes. That's right." His entire face turned crimson. "My family's been going through a lot lately."

I resisted the urge to grab him by the collar. *Say it. Say what you did.* "What has your family been going through?"

"Aren't you psychic? Shouldn't you already know?" he slurred.

I dug my fingernails into my knee under the table, trying to keep myself from digging them into his face. "Nobody can know everything."

"My cousin," he hiccupped. "He's dead." His eyes were watering.

I froze. His cousin? If the councilman was his cousin, I wasn't sure if that would make it more convincing for the police to investigate or less. He was so close to spilling everything out, telling me all his secrets. I just had to push him.

"If you'd like to discuss his passing, we can pull more cards. Gain more clarity."

He gestured wildly, knocking over his empty wineglass, sending it crashing to the floor. "I don't need any more fucking clarity. It's done. It's too late."

"Sometimes admitting out loud what ails you can lift the weight off your shoulders. Make it easier to process."

"Process? What fucking good would that do?" He pushed himself back from the table, his shoe crunching on the broken wineglass. The curtains to the stairway swished slightly, followed by footsteps sprinting up the stairs. I was frustrated with Stevie—Stellman would eventually question why she'd never come back. It would be easy enough for him to discover her connection to the shop, especially if his interest in her grew.

"Ian, wait," I called out, desperate for him to admit what he'd done in front of the recorder. But there was no use.

His head whipped around, eyes narrowed. "I never told you my name."

Blood rushed to my cheeks as I realized my mistake. "It came to me during our reading," I lied.

"Crazy bitch," he muttered under his breath as he stumbled to the door. As Stellman swung open the door and left the shop, I swore I could hear sobs and sniffles upstairs.

CHAPTER 25

Jade

AFTER LAST NIGHT's reading with Stellman, I was grateful that the new client sitting in front of me was a textbook example of a simple cold reading. She was a young woman who was stuck in a dead-end cycle of dating. She'd picked cheater after cheater, and although I wanted to tell her that maybe her picker was broken and that she should go for the exact opposite of what she wanted, I was gently coaching her through her mistakes.

She flipped over her final card and gasped. I was used to this type of reaction when new clients pulled the Devil card, just as Stellman had, and I readied my usual spiel, ready to cater it to her dating troubles.

"I know it can seem troubling, but the Devil card isn't always bad. The card is upright, so in your case, it can mean one of two things. It could mean you're chasing after men based on carnal desires. Lust." She turned red and giggled. "I'll take that as confirmation?" I smiled.

"Well, I do have a type." She laughed. "Hot and dumb."

"It's all right to enjoy life's pleasures, but not when it causes you or others pain. And in this case, the one in pain is *you*, so you need to make a change. The second meaning could be an addiction. In this case, codependency with your romantic partners. How long has it been since you were single?"

"Maybe like twelve years?"

I tried to hide my surprise. "It's time for you to spend some time on your own. Fall in love with *yourself*. This will help you attract better partners."

Her eyes grew glassy. "You're right. I don't even know who I really am."

She began to cry, and I reached out my hand. "I know this is—" When our skin touched, a vivid image came to mind, and I became lost in it. I couldn't finish my sentence. I tried to keep the image in my head, to dissect it.

It was a dark room—so dark I could hardly make anything out except the outline of someone with a blanket pulled up to their ears. A violent shiver rippled over my body at the sight of someone else standing in the corner of the room, the shadowy outline of them almost lost to the deep black of night.

I jerked my hand back, and my client jumped and asked if I was all right.

"Yes, sorry." Now was the time to talk about a vision, to rope them into some grand scheme. But I did that when I had a plan. When I had a *fake* vision. Was that what that was? A vision?

Don't be ridiculous.

"Do you ever have nightmares?" I asked. Since the image popped into my head when I touched her, it had to be something I was picking up from her. I faltered, surprised by myself. Was I really starting to buy into my own bullshit? I needed to get more sleep.

"Not really. Years ago when I had a fever."

"No sleep paralysis?" I asked my client.

Her brow wrinkled. "Sleep *what*?"

"Sleep paralysis. When you wake up and can't move. Sometimes it's accompanied by the sensation that someone or something is in the room with you."

"God, no. That's disturbing. Why?"

"I just . . . I saw something when I touched your hand. I could be picking up on someone else's energy. It could even be about myself." I gave a fake laugh, trying to comfort her. She was clearly unsettled.

"I guess that makes sense," she whispered. "Well, I better get going. Thank you for the reading. I'm glad I stopped by." She set a twenty-dollar bill on the table—double the rate for a run-of-the-mill reading—and I thanked her before pocketing it.

It was mere moments before another new client walked through the door, the bell chiming brightly. I was growing addicted to the sound and the feeling of the wad of cash in my cardigan pocket. My risk with the tip hotline for the councilman was truly paying off, and I knew wherever Mom's spirit was, she was smiling proudly.

Spirit, I chastised myself. *Seriously?* I'd never believed in spirits, but lately I'd been thinking about spirits, ghosts, and all sorts of supernatural mumbo jumbo even when I wasn't working. Usually when I closed the shop and logged out of the medium app, I didn't even think about that kind of stuff. I wanted to think logically, to only talk about things that were here in this very moment—things that I could touch and see.

Perhaps it was just the increase in customers—I'd had to perform more than I ever had, and I was worried that I was starting to believe what I was saying.

To add to that, I had been noticing strange things happening around the apartment and shop. Little things that were truly meaningless, like misplaced or missing items, or strange noises coming from empty rooms. These were the products of a normal, everyday life, I told myself. It wasn't a supernatural being punishing me for profiting off them, for pandering to the grieving and desperate.

After I'd finished up another simple reading, the client walked across the street to her car, and I had nearly gotten up from my seat when a familiar face caught my eye. It was the owner of the bar across the street, pointing to our shop as he spoke to a young woman.

The woman turned around, and my stomach dropped. It was the hound dog reporter, Maria, armed with her notepad and pen. They both stared directly at the window and I wondered if they could see me through the reflection of the glass. I raised one hand slowly, testing to see if they could see me.

Much to my dismay, Maria raised her hand in a stiff wave. I wondered how often she happened to be on my street, talking to my neighbors. Had she talked to my clients?

Meddling asshole.

The anxiety in my body had turned into anger, and all I wanted to do was march out there and tell her to mind her business. I exhaled forcefully, blowing the first two cards off my stack of tarot. I reached for the cards so I could straighten my workspace, and out of curiosity, I flipped them over.

It was an upright Seven of Swords and a reversed Tower.

"Oh, fuck off," I said out loud as I flicked them straight off the table.

Not only did an upright Seven of Swords mean that I or someone in my life was being deceitful and I would soon be cornered by said deceit, but the reversed Tower was even worse.

The reversed Tower meant that crisis was looming and no matter the avoidance, it would catch up to me. The Tower was built on faulty foundations. Sooner rather than later, the Tower would fall.

* * *

Stevie and I sat in the kitchen, quietly eating our lunch. Well, Stevie was, but my coffee had long grown cold in front of me as my stomach churned. I couldn't stop thinking about my cold reading earlier. What would I even call that? A premonition? An overactive imagination? A shiver went up my spine at the notion that it was a hallucination and that this experience was going to be the first of many where I slowly but surely lost touch with reality.

"Are you okay after last night?" I asked Stevie. She kept stirring her coffee on autopilot, staring blankly at the crinkled newspaper in her hand. "Earth to Stevie?"

She came back to life in that moment, her eyes unglazing, and her incessant coffee stirring came to a halt. "I'm fine. Just tired." Her eyes were rimmed with red and a hint of purple, the skin raw and angry like she'd been crying all night.

"Stellman said his cousin died during his reading. If he and the councilman are related, there's something there that we can take to the cops. Get them to look at him instead of us."

Stevie sighed. "Being cousins isn't really cause for a warrant, Jade," she said, zapping the buzz of excitement right out of my body.

"Do you want to talk about anything?" I asked.

"No."

A beat of silence ensued, both of us surprised by the bite in her swift answer.

"I had a weird reading earlier," I said, trying to pull her out of her mood.

"Hmm?" The stirring began again, and my jaw set in frustration at the sound of the spoon clinking against the mug.

"Yeah, I was doing a cold reading, easy as pie, but at the end, I touched her hand and—" The stirring sped up, and my heart matched it from sheer annoyance. "God, Stevie, could you please stop that? You've stirred your coffee enough."

She stopped instantly, and much to my happiness, she rested the spoon down. But much to my *unhappiness*, she set the wet spoon directly on the table that I had just cleaned this morning. "Sorry. What happened when you touched her hand?"

I fought the urge to ask her to wipe the tiny puddle of coffee up from under her spoon and continued my story. "When I touched her, I had this really strong image pop into my head. It was like déjà vu but times a thousand. Almost like it was on a projector right in front of me."

"What was the image?"

"I was in a dark room looking at someone sleeping in a bed, but I couldn't tell who. But the scary part was that there was someone in the corner. Or something. Just a tall shadow facing the bed. I truly felt fear all throughout my body. It was insane."

"Sounds like your night terrors," Stevie said softly. "Maybe you're possessed."

"Shut up," I laughed. "Probably just an overactive imagination."

"Sure, could be that. Or Lisa's moldy ghost latching on to your brain."

I stood from the table, trying and failing to keep the smile off my face. There was nobody who could get under my skin or make me laugh quite so quickly as Stevie. And the worst part was that she knew it.

"Peace be with you," Stevie said as she made the sign of a cross as she left the room.

Even though Stevie hadn't been convinced I had enough information to take to the police, I had to try. I dialed the number for the police station and asked to be connected to Detective McCade.

"Woolridge speaking."

I grimaced at his voice. "Oh, I was trying to get in touch with Detective McCade," I said.

"He's on lunch. I can pass a message along."

I took a steadying breath. "I have some information that might be helpful for the Nichols case."

"Okay."

"The teacher that was suspended recently—Ian Stellman. He came by the shop for a reading and was upset about a family member that died. I think he and the councilman are cousins."

"They are." He couldn't have sounded more disinterested if he tried.

The confirmation should have buoyed my confidence, but it wilted at his tone. "I think you should look into it."

"Interesting." He was typing quickly, and the phone rustled. "And why do you think this is relevant?"

I reeled back at his brusque tone. "Well," I stuttered, "Stellman seemed so upset, guilty even, when he came into the shop. I'm just trying to help."

"Last time I had somebody try to help this much with a case, turned out they were the murderer."

My face flushed. "That's not at all what this is. I don't appreciate—"

"We'll be in touch," he said, and hung up. My face burned with embarrassment and regret. I should never have called. Stevie had been right—what we'd uncovered was meaningless until we had more information. There had to be more; I just didn't know what.

I checked the time on my phone, and the date glared back at me: October 3. At the end of this month, we'd have to pay the increased rent, and even though Stevie hadn't attempted to reenroll in college, I was still determined to set something aside in case she changed her mind. The biggest dent to our recent earnings had been the ceiling repair, and at this point we couldn't afford the increased rent, much less Stevie's tuition.

And with that panic-inducing thought, another day full of new clients continued, as well as another day waiting for the Nichols family to deliver the much-needed reward money.

CHAPTER

26

Jade

I STOOD ON THE sidewalk, flipping through the mail as gusts of wind blew the papers in my hands. Another rent increase reminder, as if the first one hadn't embedded itself into my psyche. A speck of rain splashed onto the stack of envelopes, followed by another gust that ripped the rent reminder out of my hand, dragging it down the street.

I shot after it, not wanting to give Phyllis an excuse to berate me for littering. As I caught up to it, I was sticking out my foot to stomp it to the ground when a shiny brown leather boot beat me to it. I said thank you as the woman bent to peel the paper from her sole. She slowly righted herself, and when she did, I was met with a familiar eerie gaze, two bright-blue eyes peering out.

"Hello," she said plainly, the lack of emotion making me take a step back. I wanted to turn on my heel and run. "I was just stopping by to see you again."

She was the client who'd visited last week to ask about her cheating husband, only to leave in a fit of frustration after not liking my answer. Maybe I'd been right and she was here to sing my praises.

The raindrops quickened, and she placed my rent notice over her head. "May we?" She motioned to the shop.

As I turned to the shop, I saw a flutter of movement in Phyllis's window as the curtains fell back into place. She'd always had a proclivity for eavesdropping and observing me, but it seemed like every time I left the shop these days, her eyes were on me.

Once inside the shop, I asked with a wary voice, "How can I help you?"

"I'm here to bring you your reward money."

I involuntarily jerked my hand, knocking over a half-used candlestick. "Sorry?"

"I'm Pamela Nichols. The late Thomas Nichols's wife."

The air in the shop stilled just as the rain picked up outside, water lashing into the shop window.

"Oh my God, I didn't realize. I'm so sorry for your loss."

She tilted her head, and at first I took it as a silent barb: *But you're happy for your own gain.* It was clear I was wrong, as her eyes brimmed with tears.

"*I'm* sorry. Our last meeting—I was out of control. I came here thinking awful things about him; meanwhile, he was already gone." She let out a sob, and I reached out to touch her shoulder. She was skin and bones underneath her sweater, and I guided her to a chair, afraid she would faint at any moment.

"I wanted to personally deliver the reward money so that I could thank you. If you hadn't, God only knows how long he would have been left to the elements." She inhaled sharply and held her breath, trying to abate another looming bout of tears, then reached into her pocketbook to retrieve a check.

She placed it on the table between us and I stared at it, not believing my eyes. There it was. Two thousand dollars. And she handed it over like it was nothing.

"Go on," she said. "Take it."

I dragged the thin paper rectangle of riches toward me with shaking fingers, convinced it would turn to ash at my touch.

"I have another favor to ask of you."

"Yes?"

"I want you to hold a séance. You're not the only one I need to apologize to."

* * *

As soon as she left, I barged into Stevie's room with a notebook. We needed a game plan for the séance: choreography, information, the works. To my surprise, Stevie was curled in a ball on her bed. Loud music spilled out of her headphones as she sniffled.

"Stevie, what's wrong?" She couldn't hear me over the music, so I approached her slowly. She startled and ripped off the headphones. She was trying to pull herself together—wiping her nose with her sleeve and blinking away tears.

"You okay?" I asked.

"I think I have a cold," she said as she sat up straight.

"A cold so bad it made you cry?"

"Don't be an asshole." She shut off the music, and the room was suddenly too quiet.

I gave her a look and let her squirm in the silence. "It's just work. I think I'm going to quit."

"What? Why?"

"I'm sick of the drunk assholes, night after night. The men expect me to act like their loyal girlfriend while treating me like trash and pestering me. I just can't fucking stand looking at them anymore. I know my job is useful for you, but I can't do it anymore."

I rubbed her arm. "I'm sorry, Stevie. I don't want you to be miserable for the sake of the shop. It's not worth it. You should start applying for other jobs if you think it's for the best." I could hear my own voice, and my performance wasn't convincing. The thought of losing her intel made me itch. "Or maybe this is a sign you should reenroll," I said tentatively.

She waved off the thought like a fly. "What's the notebook for? You dressing up as that annoying reporter for Halloween?"

"You remember that creepy woman you almost escorted out of the shop?" She nodded. "She just stopped by again. That was Mrs. Nichols—the councilman's wife. And she wants a séance tomorrow night. We need to plan."

"Oh, shit."

Over the next few hours, we planned the choreography of the séance, all the way down to when to play audio and the cues we'd use when I was ready to move on to the next trick. This was a huge opportunity, either to flounder or convince everyone we were the real thing.

We had no choice but for it to go perfectly.

CHAPTER

27

Jade

"HELLO, JADE."

I whipped my head around, not expecting anyone to speak to us while running errands.

"Hi, Maria," I said to the reporter with an evident lack of enthusiasm.

"How are you doing?"

"I was doing great before I realized someone was following me around town. I didn't realize someone from Charlotte would do their grocery shopping in Winston-Salem."

She gave an unamused smile. "They have great fruit here."

"And the best sidewalks in the state are right outside my shop, I'm guessing?" I asked, to which she smiled ever so subtly. Underneath her lips, her tongue darted across her teeth like she was hungry for a kill.

Stevie wandered over from another aisle, freezing when she approached Maria and me, both of us with our arms crossed as we sized each other up. This was one of the reasons I thought I hated her the most: She was just like me. She wasn't afraid to use silence as a weapon, waiting until the other person was uncomfortable enough to spill their secrets. She knew by now this wouldn't work on me, but I thought she was growing amused with our mirrored tactics.

"I'm glad we could run into each other," she said. Stevie approached cautiously and stood next to our shopping cart. Maria didn't even bother to say hello; she simply glanced at her before returning her gaze to me. "I wanted to ask you about Ian Stellman."

Stevie flinched, dropping a can of soup, which rolled into Maria's foot. Maria rested the ball of her foot on the can and kept it there, despite Stevie scrambling to try to pick it up.

Keep calm, Stevie, I silently begged. There was no way Maria could possibly know about us trying to weasel information out of him at the shop. We'd barely gotten anything out of him—it had all been drunk, vague nonsense. Nothing useful or relevant enough to get the cops off my back.

Stevie yanked the can out from under Maria's foot with a huff and put it back in the cart, her face red in annoyance, nervousness, or maybe both.

"What about him?" I asked.

"The school district said he missed an important meeting this morning—one that was supposed to potentially end his suspension. Nobody's been able to get in touch with him."

I blanched at both the prospect of him going off the rails after our meeting and the fact that they were considering letting him back into the classroom with minors. If they knew what he was capable of, how could they allow it to happen again? At that point, it would just be plain encouraging.

"That's odd. Why was he suspended?" I asked, but she narrowed her eyes at me as if she knew better.

"Oh, come on, Jade. You know so much about everyone with your *gift*." She put a bite on the last word, tilting her head slightly. "Don't act like you haven't heard the rumors."

"I know a lot, but I don't know everything."

"That's a real shame. Maybe if your gift was more powerful, you could stop bad things before they actually happen. Not just make money on them after the fact."

I blinked at her, surprised by her sudden regression into cattiness. She must be getting desperate if she was changing tactics. "Why are you asking me about him?"

She tilted her head, sizing me up. "I thought maybe you might have had another little vision."

"I don't know anything about it. Well, Maria, as always, this has been a pleasure. I hope his family is able to get in touch with him soon. You take care now." I gripped the handlebar of our cart, backing it away from her, but she clutched the end of the basket, stopping me in my tracks. Stevie stiffened beside me.

"Your séance with the Nichols family is tomorrow, right?" she asked.

I gritted my teeth in annoyance, but I was also impressed by how this woman knew almost everything. It was only this morning that Mrs. Nichols had stopped by the shop to give me the reward money and request a séance. I myself had barely digested that information, much less expected it to travel to a reporter from Charlotte.

"I'd like to be there. I asked the Nichols family, and they approved."

I hated the way she didn't even ask. She was telling me. I was stuck.

"If that's what the family wants, then great. We don't allow photography or recording, so you'll just have to bring your little notepad." I motioned to the pad and pen sticking out of her cross-body bag and wished I could grab it and rip it into shreds. I was so sick of seeing it, and the thought of watching her scribble on the thing while I was trying to focus on the Nichols family increased my anxiety tenfold.

"Perfect." She smiled, but it didn't reach her eyes. "See you there." Without a goodbye or asking what time the séance was—because of course, she already knew—she walked off.

"The least she could do is pretend to be shopping. Hold a handbasket or something, weirdo," Stevie grumbled.

I made a noise in agreement, trying to shake off my irritation. I could handle Maria at the séance, as annoying as it would be. What I couldn't handle was even more eyes on me with another man going off the radar. The detectives had already questioned me twice and attempted it a third. Even though they had nothing to pin on me, it was clear they didn't like or respect me. I was an easy target if they decided they needed one.

"What the hell is this about Stellman being missing?" I whispered to Stevie.

"Pfft. Missing is a strong word. You saw how drunk he got. He's probably just on a bender."

I crossed my arms, fighting the chill that came from the refrigerated section nearby. "He worked at your school when you were there. Did he seem like he would . . . do something to himself? Maybe the guilt was just too much and he . . ." I stopped, realizing I was babbling.

Stevie stared at me, her lips so pursed that they were nearly invisible. "He's probably fine. Plus I'm pretty sure he was at the bar yesterday during my shift."

"I wish you would have told her that. Did he say anything to you?"

She looked into the cart and shuffled items around, only to shove them back. "Nope. He was drunk though—was long before he even got there. The other bartender had to cut him off, so he left shortly after he arrived."

"You're right. Probably just a bender."

"Mm-hmm. When will people learn they can't just drink away the guilt?"

I laughed, knowing she was referring to our dad. "They never learn."

* * *

The pawnshop's doorbell chimed as I entered, and the Pulaskis immediately buzzed me in. Ever since the Pulaskis had called to tell us the ring had sold, it had acted as a salve to my anxiety, but I needed the money in my pocket to have any real relief. And even after that, there was still more we needed, but we were so close.

I'd been nauseous from both excitement and guilt all morning—excitement to get the extra cash and guilt from executing such an intricate con on poor Lisa. She'd been so earnest and trusting and believed me to be the same. Big mistake. Never trust a Crawford.

"Jade, welcome back," Mr. Pulaski said as he pulled off his reading glasses. His ledger sat in front of him, fresh ink on the page for our two pending transactions.

"Where's Mrs. Pulaski?"

"In the back giving your new ring one final shine. Only the best for you."

We made small talk for a few minutes before Mrs. Pulaski walked out with a black velvet ring box in hand and a proud smile on her face.

"Might I say, Jade, this is my best work yet."

My hand trembled as I took the ring box. I pulled it open, and unsurprisingly, the ring was perfect. I'd never had a lack of confidence in her skills. Only a lack of confidence that Lisa wouldn't be fooled and I wouldn't end up in jail just like Dad had.

The cheap metal and fake diamonds were somehow much more vibrant and shinier than the original, likely due to its heavy wear. I could tell Lisa I buffed the ring for her as a free add-on. I'd tell her I often had to buff my crystals, I thought as I prepared myself for the lie. "You did a fantastic job. Thank you."

"I do my best." Say what you wanted about the Pulaskis, they were the best at what they did, even if that was partly criminal, just like my line of work.

I handed Mr. Pulaski one hundred dollars for the replica as he meticulously counted out seventeen hundred in cash, stacking the bills on the glass counter with the flourish of a magician.

"I have to be honest. The last time we spoke, I really didn't think the ring would sell."

He made a wet, airy noise of disbelief. "We have connections everywhere. When we want something gone . . ." Mr. Pulaski made a *poof* motion with his hands before picking up the money and handing it to me. I stared at it in awe, the thickness of the stack almost making me salivate.

Don't get ahead of yourself. This isn't finished yet.

"You go straight to the bank and put it away before something bad happens."

From anyone else, I would have taken that as a threat, but I'd known the Pulaskis for years and had watched my parents do business with them hundreds of times, not even to mention the dozens of high-end jewelry pieces I'd pawned to them.

"Of course," I lied.

He sighed. "You know, Jade, it's a shame things didn't work out with you and Chris. You would have been a great addition to the family."

Although the Pulaskis would have been great in-laws and it would have been nice to have some semblance of a family again, their sons hadn't been gifted an ounce of their kindness or normalcy. Neither of them had made an appearance since the renaissance fair, and I was hoping that would stay true.

Mrs. Pulaski smiled softly as she noticed my grimace. "You take care of yourself, okay?" she said just as a loud thump resounded in their upstairs apartment.

"You sure y'all didn't open up a bed-and-breakfast upstairs?" I laughed nervously. This was the second time I'd heard noise from their apartment when both of them were in the shop.

"Ha, no. Just an old building, you know," Mr. Pulaski said. At this point, I was sure he was lying to me. It had to be Chris or Adam up there, and the Pulaskis and I both knew how little I wanted to see them. Before I could question him further, Mr. Pulaski spoke.

"Good luck with everything, Jade."

I thanked him, and as I began to walk out of the shop, I reached into my bag to touch the cash once more. I was afraid it would somehow spontaneously vanish, that all our new clients would disappear and everything good that had happened would have been a figment of my imagination. But no, the cash was there—a thick wad of beautiful bills.

As I stepped out into the brisk air, a smile spread across my face. I'd never experienced this amount of hope before, and it was like the opposite of a panic attack, where you're sure your chest is going to burst from anguish. This time it was near to bursting with something good, like pride, maybe.

I'd intended to go straight home, but instead I turned on my heel and nearly skipped to the coffee shop, where I splurged on an overpriced latte and cloyingly sweet pastry.

I deserved it.

CHAPTER

28

Jade

TIME SLOWED PAINFULLY as Lisa swung the front door of the shop open. Her face was stoic and unreadable. Were her lips clenched from the effort of opening the door, or was she here for a confrontation?

I'd called her to arrange giving her back her cleansed ring and, little did she know, hear her reaction to her newly painted ceiling. If my mental timeline was correct, she'd returned to her house last night. I inhaled deeply, steeling myself for whatever she was going to say.

"Lisa, welcome. How are you?"

She set her purse on the register counter, where I'd been restocking our new arrivals: rosewater sprays and hand-carved incense holders—something we'd never been able to afford to stock until now. She took a sharp breath, readying herself to speak, and I *still* had no idea what she was going to say.

"I've never been better," she said with a relaxed sigh. Her mouth formed a satisfied smile, and her shoulders slumped like she was releasing weight from her mental load.

"That's great to hear. What's been happening to make you smile like that?"

"The sage worked better than I could have ever imagined. When we got home from my sister's, the house had an entirely different energy. Fresh and happy and . . . empty. And you'll never guess what else. Or maybe you will." She laughed. "You're a psychic, after all."

"I did have a dream about your house, but there wasn't much to go off of. It was just a bright, sunny day, and you and your husband were eating breakfast in the kitchen. You looked happy."

"Happy is exactly what we're going to be from now on. The stain on the ceiling is gone." She clasped her hands together in prayer, and I feigned shock. "Completely gone. You have a miraculous gift. My husband has changed his tune about it. He's telling everyone he can about you. You're going to be even busier—if that's even possible."

"Well, tell your husband thank-you. Here's your ring, by the way. It was tough work, but the ring is fully yours now. No more bad energy." I pulled out the velvet box from behind the counter and handed it to her, focusing all my energy on keeping my hand from shaking.

She opened the box and pulled the ring out, holding it in the palm of her hand. She was utterly silent.

"I gave it a shine for you," I said to fill the painful silence.

Her eyes narrowed as she inspected the ring. "It feels lighter," she stated with no inflection.

Oh, God. I chastised myself for being too cheap and using too light of a metal. I smiled and nodded, searching for something to say.

"Lighter, just like the air in the house. You are truly amazing." Lisa smiled as she slipped the ring on her finger. She turned her palm away to admire it, then paid me the remainder of her bill as we said our goodbyes.

Another job done and one more worry to rid myself of. Maybe this would make me feel lighter, I hoped without conviction.

I knew one thing that would absolutely make me feel lighter: returning the files to Daniel's office. I'd held on to them for far too long, but I had my notes on them if I needed them in the future.

It was just after twelve. Daniel walked to the nearby sandwich shop for lunch every weekday right at noon. Now was my chance. I grabbed the files and flipped the shop sign to CLOSED. I darted outside and up his steps, then gently opened his front door. I sighed in relief as I observed the lobby: The secretary was nowhere in sight, and Daniel's office door was slightly ajar and dark, while his two coworkers' doors were closed with white noise playing. They were busy with patients. Perfect.

I slowly pushed open his office door, praying it wouldn't creak, then slipped inside. His desk was empty, so I'd have to find each file's place in the file cabinet. I gripped the handle for the drawer labeled *S-T,* but it wouldn't open.

Shit. A key—I needed a damn key. I tried and failed to keep my breath calm as I began opening his desk drawers, fumbling around in the dark for a key. The first was just pens and other office supplies, so I moved on to the next. Paperwork and receipts. *Shit!*

The third drawer was my last chance, so I slid it open and immediately saw the glint of a silver key. This had to be it.

With shaking hands I darted back to the file cabinet. It slid in with ease, and I turned it, almost melting with relief as the drawer opened. I slid the Stellman file into its spot, shut it, and relocked the drawer.

Almost done. Stay calm.

My curiosity got the best of me at the sight of a file partially sticking out of the drawer labeled *B-D*. I tested the drawer to see if it was locked, and it slid open. It was labeled *Cranston, H.*, a name I wasn't familiar with and probably wouldn't be of use to me for work.

My breath hitched at the sight of a familiar name: *Crawford*, the inky-black handwriting read. There was no first initial. I'd never met another Crawford in Winston-Salem—was it a normal thing for a psychologist to start a file on a romantic partner?

No, I decided as I slid the file out and opened it. A rush of adrenaline coursed through me, narrowing my vision on the file so it was all I could see. It was a sheet with basic information: name, address, occupation. There was nothing else. But the file wasn't for me.

It was for Stevie.

Voices in the adjoining office grew louder, like they were wrapping up the appointment. I needed to focus. I dropped the key into Daniel's desk drawer and did a quick scan of the room. Everything was just as it had been when I arrived, so I slipped back out into the lobby, cracking the door behind me.

One of his coworker's white noise machines cut off, and my heart dropped into my gut. I took four long strides to the front door, then froze.

"Can I help you with something?" an old man's voice asked behind me.

I took a breath and turned, forcing my face to form a smile even though I felt like I was going to throw up. "Oh, hi! I'm the neighbor, Jade. I was going to drop off something for Daniel, but he's not here. I'll come back later."

"I can put whatever it is in his office if you'd like," he said. The doctor dismissed his patient, who opened the door and exited behind me. I was tempted to dart out there with them, so fast the doctor couldn't protest.

"That's okay, I don't want to be a bother."

"It's no bother. Really," he said as he stepped closer.

"That's so kind of you," I said. I reached into my back pocket and handed him a bar of dark chocolate. Daniel had mentioned it was his favorite. I thanked him profusely and showed myself out, wincing as cold wind blew against my hot, sweaty skin.

I blew a huff of air out as I walked back to our shop, relishing in the feeling of weightlessness after returning the files. It hadn't been a perfect delivery, but it had worked nonetheless. I hated when my father's advice drifted through my head, but this time it had saved me.

Every lie needs a cover story.

That night I expected to be able to relax after ridding myself of both the ring and the file, but I'd been kidding myself.

A loud bang resounded from somewhere in the shop, and I shot up in bed, straining my ears to listen. What time was it? I was still in my jeans and sweater and had no memory of going to bed. The good news was that my recurring nightmare of the figure in the corner hadn't shackled me to my bed again, so I shot to my feet and crept to the door.

Another noise, but softer now, like the creak of the wood floor under someone's cautious foot. I knew every floorboard in the building at this point and could map them out with my eyes closed. It was coming from downstairs, either from the séance room or the prop room.

My palms were slick with sweat as I crept downstairs, praying that Stevie would stay asleep or was at work. I swung open the door to the séance room, hoping to take whoever it was by surprise, but it was empty and utterly undisturbed.

Exhaustion swept over me from the nights of broken sleep and nightmares. I only had myself to blame for it. That's what I got for meddling in everything from criminal investigations to the occult.

I leaned into the wall, and the room spun with the heady mix of sleeplessness and adrenaline. I turned on my heel at the sound of another creak in the prop room. I stomped to the armoire and swung open the door, not knowing what I even expected to see.

I crawled inside and pushed open the back of the armoire, but it didn't budge. I gave it a thump and shrieked as the armoire's doors clicked shut behind me, leaving me in the pitch-black. I pressed harder against the back of the armoire, my breath escalating into quick, anxious puffs. I pushed my entire body into it with no luck.

Breathe. But I couldn't. The air was thickening with each breath I took.

"Stevie!" I shouted, wincing as my voice reverberated in the small space. I continued pressing on the back panel for a few minutes as my panic grew. Stevie could be at work and I'd be trapped in here until midday tomorrow when she finally woke up. "Stevie, help me, please!" I screamed as a last-ditch effort.

I knew I should still my breath and listen for her, but I lost control and began to sob.

My heart leapt at the sound of the séance room door swinging open and footsteps pounding toward me. "I'm here. Stay calm." She yanked on the armoire doors. "They're stuck. Hold on."

Another minute passed, and the window in the prop room creaked as Stevie climbed in from the outside.

"Get me out of here," I cried. Within seconds, the back panel clicked open and I spilled out into the prop room covered in sweat.

"Are you okay?" Stevie asked as she crouched down to meet me. I nodded, which prompted a more aggressive, "What the hell were you doing in the armoire?"

"I thought I heard somebody down here," I whimpered. I glanced around at the empty room. Nobody could have come in or out without Stevie seeing them. The armoire doors shutting was just a case of bad luck and old hinges. I took in the sight of her typical work outfit. "Why aren't you at work?"

"I was about to leave for my shift—it's not even nine yet. You passed out about an hour ago, so I thought I'd let you sleep."

I was just hearing things. Was I even awake? Was this a nightmare, a continuation of the ones I'd had night after night? I pinched my bicep, desperate to wake up, but it changed nothing. I lay flat on the floor in resignation as Stevie sat on the floor with me, rubbing my arm. Despite the small amount of comfort her touch brought me, I was certain I was losing my grip on reality.

CHAPTER 29

Stevie

It was nearly one in the morning as I walked the few blocks home from work. My feet ached with each step, so much so that I slowed my pace to a crawl. The streets were empty, and a thick haze of fog smothered the chilly night air.

As I walked by the street with the Pulaski Pawn Shop, I wondered how Jade's meeting with Lisa had gone today. Mrs. Pulaski always did great work, but a part of me still doubted that Jade would be able to pull this off. I hoped I was wrong.

I nearly passed the street entirely until the sight of a man trying to unlock the pawnshop door caught my eye. It wasn't one of the Pulaskis, not even one of their sons. It was an older man, his familiar brown jacket making my blood boil.

There was no way my dad was stupid enough to break into the pawnshop. It was widely known they had a security system and guns they weren't afraid to use.

I stomped toward the pawnshop, hoping desperately I was wrong. It couldn't be him. If it was, did I really want to talk to him? My train of thought spiraled, and somehow I began guilting myself for being so angry with him. Why did this always happen?

"Hey!" I shouted when I was a few feet away. He was struggling with an obnoxiously large key ring and I wondered how many places he'd broken into with his collection of pilfered keys.

He jumped and turned to me. A jarring whirl of anger and excitement filled me as I approached Dad. The little girl I used to be wanted to see him still, to hug him and ask him to come back into our lives. But the jaded Stevie who had been forced to become an adult too soon was furious with how he'd wrecked our lives so profoundly.

"Stevie," Dad said breathlessly.

"Please tell me you're not breaking into the Pulaskis' place. You'd have to be insane."

He paused. "Okay, then. I'm not breaking into the Pulaskis' place." The whites of his teeth flashed, but the smile didn't reach his eyes.

"Then what are you doing?"

He took his hand off the door handle and tucked the keys in his pocket. "They're letting me stay with them for a few days. One of their sons is moving back in with them for a while, so tomorrow is my last day."

"Where will you go?"

"Does it matter?" he grumbled. I took a step back at the hint of annoyance in his voice.

I shuffled my feet and shifted subjects. "Hey, listen, I know I said we should keep our distance, but I wanted to ask you something important."

He blew into his hands and rubbed them together. "Shoot."

"Did you ever experience anything . . . strange in the apartment or the shop?"

"Strange?"

"Odd sounds, stuff moved around. Nightmares?" I thought of Jade's episode earlier. I'd nearly called out of work for fear that she was having some sort of nervous breakdown, but when I'd hauled her back into her bed, she'd fallen asleep immediately.

"You think the building's haunted or something?" I jumped backward at his sudden bark of a laugh. My cheeks flushed. "How old are you now, twenty?"

"Twenty-one," I corrected with a whisper.

"That's twenty-one years too old to be believing in shit like that. And if you do, you're in the wrong business. Maybe it's a guilty conscience."

The irony of *him* saying that made my blood boil. He took the keys back out of his pocket and turned his focus to the door handle. "I need to get inside. Don't want to wake the Pulaskis up." He found the right key and cracked the door open.

"Okay," I said quietly. "Do you have somewhere to stay?"

"Good night, Stevie," he said, not answering my question for the second time.

"Night," I said to the door that was already closed as he disappeared into the dark shop. I grimaced as soon as the pathetic words left my mouth: "Love you."

CHAPTER 30

Jade

"STEVIE!" I SHOUTED into the shop as I entered. I'd been running errands all morning, buying Halloween decorations now that the water damage was repaired. I was met with silence, which wasn't unusual when Stevie had just worked a night shift. Except today I knew for a fact that she didn't have a shift at the bar. She was supposed to have a shift *here*. At the shop.

"Have you set up for the séance yet?" I yelled out, just to meet more silence.

I marched up the stairs, the anger building with each stomp. Not only had she ghosted me, but she'd left the front door to the shop open. I knew something was going on with her lately, but how could she be so careless?

When I reached her door, I didn't bother knocking and yanked it open, expecting to see her lounging in bed with a joint. But she wasn't in her room at all.

I was disoriented by how different the room was. Stevie had always been a bit messy, but there had always been a method to her mess—her life separated into piles and stacks that made sense only to her. Now the room was sheer chaos. Her bedside lampshade was askew, exposing the blinding bare bulb. None of the clothes all over the floor were black, so this wasn't the typical scene of her rushing to get ready for work. This was the scene of someone having some sort of nervous breakdown or temper tantrum. Or someone looking for something.

A bubble of nausea rose in my stomach as my mind wandered to the worst-case scenario. A break-in? No—nothing else in the house was in disarray.

Stevie had been acting strangely lately, but it was all easily explained by the shit show the last two weeks had been. At least that was what I'd been telling myself. The scene in front of me was eating away at me, though, convincing me there was something else going on.

I began tidying her room—not out of duty, just to settle my nerves. My annoyance from only minutes ago was replaced with worry. Once I'd finished, I dumped myself onto the edge of her bed, my shoulders slumping forward. My body was exhausted, but my mind was moving at a startling pace. Stevie was all I had and I'd done all of this to give her the life she deserved, one with comfort and stability. Yet with each day, a new problem arose and we circled right back to the beginning: on the edge of a disaster.

I stood, a pile of freshly folded clothes tumbling off the bed, followed by a string of curses from my mouth. I bent to pick them up, pausing at the sight of Stevie's high school yearbook partially sticking out under her bed. It was bizarre to see that she still had the books, since those were the most miserable years of her life. She'd been relentlessly bullied, almost to the point of dropping out. But I'd pushed her to keep her head down and power through. I'd never gotten my high school degree and regretted it every day—how I'd squandered my dreams of ever getting a normal job, since not having a high school degree made it nearly impossible. I didn't want that for Stevie.

I flipped the yearbook open out of sheer curiosity, thumbing through the glossy pages, until I found her class's page. Her goofy smile in her portrait was still the same, but there was no confidence in the way she was holding herself like there was now. She'd grown so much in the past two years since Dad had gone to prison, and I couldn't watch her regress. That was what the past two weeks had felt like: progress with finances but regression with everything else.

I let the pages flip closed, but the blank page at the end had a handwritten note. I was surprised to see any signatures—not in an insulting way; she'd just withdrawn so much from her classmates that I was surprised she'd given any of them the opportunity to sign it. I began to read, praying it would be something positive.

To Stevie, the brightest and most beautiful star in her class.—I.S.

My eyes widened in surprise. I'd had no idea that Stevie had formed a romantic relationship in high school. It had been so long since I'd even seen her genuinely flirt with anyone that I'd begun to wonder if she just wasn't interested in sex or romance at all.

Who was I.S.? I flipped back to her year, my clammy palms leaving fingerprints on the shiny paper. I scanned through the rows of pictures until I got to the student surnames that began with *S*. There was the usual group of Smiths, a few Singhs, but none of the first names began with I. Could it have been a J? I hastily flipped to the note to check, but it was clearly a neatly written uppercase *I*.

After checking the years below her, it was clear there were no students with initials matching the note. Irritation bubbled, and I slapped the front cover closed, staring broodily out the window with the yearbook in my lap.

A thought was bubbling and I pushed it away, unwilling to give it any energy. Yet it persisted, pecking at my brain like a bored toddler poking at their parent's arm in demand of attention.

Maybe it wasn't a student that wrote the note. *Stop.*

It could be a teacher. *Shut up. That would never happen to Stevie.*

That wasn't something that just *happened* to kids. Adults sought them out, picking their target strategically. Stellman had done just that to those students this year.

The initials are just a coincidence. You're being paranoid.

I turned the pages to the staff section, my hands slippery with swelling anxiety. I wanted to crack open a window and stick my head out into the morning air. I couldn't catch a full breath.

Stevie would never have agreed to luring him to the shop if he'd done that to her.

Or maybe it had been more than revenge for those young girls. Maybe it was also revenge for herself.

My eyes again darted up and down each page until I reached the *S* surnames of the staff, then checked each for a first name beginning with *I.* As his photo stared back at me, I could no longer argue with myself. His ruddy cheeks, his bow tie perched slightly crooked between his jacket lapels. His smile was wide and proud, his name etched beside his picture.

Ian Stellman.

* * *

Throughout the afternoon, a few new clients had trickled in, but I could hardly focus as the sun dipped in the sky, nearing the Nichols séance. During each reading, I couldn't keep my brain from returning to Stevie's yearbook, getting stuck in an endless what-if loop about Stevie's possible connection to Stellman. Stevie had never put on any airs of secrecy except for lately, as she'd become increasingly anxious and cagey. And all that secrecy didn't even include her file in Daniel's office. I'd been meaning to ask her if she knew about it, but every time I tried, something interrupted us. I hadn't seen Daniel since then, which was a relief. Even if I had seen him, it wasn't like I could ask.

I'd taken a break, hastily flipping the sign on the shop door to CLOSED so I could have a moment to think. I was slumped on our couch, my body sinking into the crack between the two flat seat cushions. My tailbone pressed painfully into the hard base of the couch, but I couldn't conjure the energy to move. Stevie was walking up the stairs, her footsteps hesitant, like she knew I was waiting for her.

She skirted into her bedroom, then her footsteps faltered and reversed. When she entered the living room, her face made it clear she'd seen what I'd left on her bed.

She stood in the doorway, her arms wrapped across her middle. I sat there waiting for her to say something, but she did the same. We were too similar in that regard: stubborn enough to keep silent until the other broke the ice but impatient enough to blurt out whatever it was we were thinking.

We spoke at the same time, our words layered over each other in a garble.

"Where have you been?"

"Did you go through my things?" Her words were barbed, claws hidden beneath each syllable. She got like this when she was defensive, and it just made me more sure that my suspicions were correct. A beat of silence, each of us reconsidering our approach as we heard what the other had asked.

"I did go in your room, yes. I was looking for you because you were supposed to be working at the shop, and I found . . . that." I pointed off in the direction of her bedroom, where I'd left the yearbook splayed open on her bed, displaying Stellman's signature. "Your room's a mess. What happened?"

"You didn't do that?"

"Of course not."

She blinked back at me, both of us clearly wondering the same thing. If neither of us had done that, then who had?

"Who is I.S.?" I asked.

She uncrossed her arms, looping them behind her back, then brought them back in front of her. She was restless, her eyes wide like she was considering running back down the steps and out the door.

I cleared my throat. "Are you okay? What's going on with you?"

"Nothing. Jesus, why are you interrogating me?"

"Stevie, please, just tell me who I.S. is. I feel like you left it out for me to find. I want to understand."

"I didn't leave my yearbook out. Why would I ever want to look through that thing? Just admit you were digging through my stuff."

I shoved away the confusion bubbling up. "That's not important right now. Can you please explain who this person is? They seemed to have cared a lot for you."

"He didn't care about me at all. Or the fifteen other girls he did this to."

My heart sank. I wanted so desperately for my suspicions to be wrong. "Are you talking about Ian Stellman?"

Her eyes reddened and grew shiny before she bowed her head. “Yes. The multitalented man: my groomer and the reason Mom’s dead.”

I swore for a moment my heart stopped beating just so I could hear better without it pounding against my chest. “What?” The first part, I had unfortunately come to terms with, but the second knocked the breath out of me.

“That night when Mom and Dad were in the car accident, they weren’t just fleeing a failed break-in at some random house. It was Ian Stellman’s house.” She rubbed her eyes, smearing a black line of mascara onto her temple.

“What are you saying?” I knew exactly what she was saying, but my brain wouldn’t allow me to believe it until I heard it directly from her mouth.

“They were going to scare him. Try to get him to quit his job, move out of town. That was the night I told them what we’d been doing. What he’d been doing to me,” she corrected.

Blood rushed into my face, and every hair on my scalp stood on end. This was all too much. There were too many connections. “The councilman, Stellman, Dad. This is all related, isn’t it?”

She sighed. “Yes. Nichols is the only reason Stellman didn’t get convicted after that last girl came forward. He’s the reason why that pervert still has a job.”

“Jesus Christ.” I pressed the heels of my palms into my eyes until a burst of color danced behind my eyelids. “If the cops know that’s where Mom and Dad were coming from, or what he did to you, it’s no wonder the cops think I killed the councilman.”

“They definitely don’t know about me and Stellman. Mom and Dad made me promise not to tell anyone what happened, even you. Said it was nobody's business and it would only be trouble if more people knew."

"I can't believe they made you keep this to yourself." My stomach was rolling at the thought of her dealing with this for years, and all those times I'd nagged her to get out of bed and help me, to smoke less and be more responsible. This whole time she'd just been trying to cope all on her own. "So you knew this whole time they were related?"

She nodded. "I'm sorry. I wanted you to know, but a part of me still has this allegiance to Dad, like if I told you anything, he would immediately know. Or it would put you in danger. Clearly that happened anyway." Stevie slumped over in her chair, lifeless and frail like her previous teenage self.

I cleared my throat. "Can I ask you a question?" She nodded. "Do you know who killed the councilman?"

Her eyes darted from her lap to my face, eyelids squinted. "Are you kidding me? After all this, you're going to ask a question like that?"

"I'm not accusing you of anything. Think about the timing: Dad gets out of jail, then the councilman turns up dead. Now Stellman's supposedly on a bender. I'm just trying to understand how this all ties together. I'm sorry for asking," I said with my open palms facing her, a sign of peace.

Her anger gave way and she threw herself back into her seat, the dam of tears broken and streaming down her face in full force. She grimaced as she cried, and I knelt down, my hands resting on her knees. "I'm so sorry I never knew about this. I'm sorry I couldn't protect you."

"We were trying to protect *you* from knowing. Those two families—they're not good people. The councilman didn't want anyone to know about it either; otherwise it would ruin his campaign to have a pervert family member running around town, so he kept it all out of the news and under wraps. We thought if you knew, you might do something stupid. It was just too dangerous for you to know. This has been rotting inside me for years."

Tears spilled down her cheeks, and her chin quivered in the same way it always had when she was little. But this was bigger than a scraped knee or a broken toy. I wrapped my arms around her and gripped her shirt in my hands.

I stayed as still as possible, not wanting to disrupt the moment. I could tell this was the first time she'd ever truly let herself cry. I let her release it all for nearly fifteen minutes before her sobs turned into stuttering, wet breaths and she was wiping her tears away.

"God, Stevie, why didn't you stop me when I said I wanted to bring him in for a reading? I never would have made you lure him here if I'd known."

"It wasn't fully your idea. Once you started to connect the dots between the councilman and Stellman, I nudged you in the direction of wanting to get proof. I wanted to hurt him. He's gotten by with no repercussions. I thought I could do it. But it was too much."

"I'm sorry." I hugged her, whispering into her hair. "I'm so sorry."

A few hours later I sipped a cup of ginger tea, my thoughts viciously circling while I mentally prepared for tonight's séance. I'd tried to convince Stevie that we should just cancel, that we could close the shop and watch a movie together in bed, but she wouldn't let me. There was too much riding on this. I reached for a cracker, desperate to soothe my nervous stomach, but as soon as the flaky saltine touched my tongue, my body tensed, holding back a dry heave.

Stevie sat at the kitchen table across from me, cautiously lowering herself onto the chair. "You all right?"

Stevie's raw eyes matched my own after her confession earlier. "My stomach's a mess. I need to get it together for this séance."

I was so sick with exhaustion, both physical and mental, from the last two weeks of hell. Before all this, our lives had been chaotic, but never so much that we were afraid for our own safety. And now that I knew about what had happened to Stevie in high school, I was sick with the thought that I could have done more.

"I can make you some toast," Stevie said in a near whisper.

I conceded, not from the actual desire to eat but from the gentleness in Stevie's voice. I should be the one comforting her, not the other way around.

Stevie got up and rummaged through the fridge for bread, finally pulling out half a loaf. "Ew, this has mold on it."

I put the back of my hand to my mouth, the thought of it making my stomach roll.

"I'll run to the shop and get some more," she said, her shoulders back and confident like she was the older sister. Maybe I never gave her enough credit. Maybe I'd just babied her too much and now she was starting to feel more independent.

"Thank you," I grunted. "Don't forget the séance tonight. I'll need some help with prep work." I slumped forward, resting my forehead on the cool wood of the table.

"Already done. I set up all the props this morning, so we should be ready to roll."

"You're the best," I said into the table, lifting my fingers off the wood to give a pitiful wave. I breathed through my nerves as the door chimed downstairs. The sound was hopeful—Stevie stepping out into the cool autumn air to save the day. I'd always thought she was the one who needed saving. It seemed I was wrong.

CHAPTER

31

Jade

"GOOD EVENING, EVERYONE," I said to the roomful of sitters, my voice hushing their subdued chatter around the séance table. Their eyes shone in the candlelight. "Thank you so much for coming tonight. It's a privilege to share this time with you, and I hope I can provide insight and closure."

I make eye contact with each sitter—Councilman Nichols's wife, Pamela, and their two college-age sons, Samuel and Benjamin. I cast a cursory glance at Maria, who much to my dismay had shown up early, pen and paper in hand like a sword and shield. While everyone else sat stick-straight in their chairs, leaning ever-so-slightly forward, already hanging on my every word, Maria reclined in her chair with her arms crossed, making it known how much of a farce this was to her.

Stevie was closing up the shop and soon the front door deadbolt thumped into place, followed by the faint sound of the prop room's external window opening, then sliding shut. Stevie was hitting her mark.

The two Nichols sons shifted in their seats, inching forward even more. I couldn't tell if their eagerness was because they believed I would give them the answers they sought or if, like Maria, they were eager to see me fail. Although I hadn't known it was her at the time, Pamela had made her derision of my career clear during our first cold reading. At that point she believed her biggest problem was a cheating husband. Now here we were, eagerly attempting to commune with his spirit.

Maria's presence was enough to pit unease deep in my stomach. I'd hardly eaten today because the anxiety building in my body made me dry heave every time I tried.

"I understand some of you are skeptical." I turned my head slowly to Maria, challenging her sharp stare. I summoned all the confidence I possibly could. She was in my territory. I was good at this, and she was going to witness it. "I urge you to set aside your doubts tonight and be present in this process, which depends heavily on the energy in the room. If anyone is silently making a mockery of this, the spirits will know and may not feel welcomed."

This was both a dig at Maria and my easy way out if something went wrong. The spirits didn't communicate? Blame the nonbeliever.

"I'd like to begin with an opening incantation to invite the spirit we seek to communicate. It also protects us from any unwanted visitors."

Pamela and her youngest son murmured under their breath, looking nervously across the table at me.

"There's no need to be frightened," I soothed. The statement was both for them and for me. *Unwanted visitors,* I thought, my stomach heaving despite its emptiness. I couldn't stop thinking of my nightmares, the looming figure in the corner. The nightmares had bled into day, noises behind walls in my imagination almost sounding real. At least I tried to tell myself they were my imagination.

"Spirits, please be open to our communication. We only welcome those we call upon. Any others are unwelcome, especially those with bad intentions." I typically didn't say that last bit, but sometimes a small dose of fear spurred the imagination, making it easier to convince folks that my tricks were real.

"Mrs. Nichols, we're gathered with the goal of communicating with the late Mr. Nichols. Is that correct?"

"Yes," she said with a forced casual tone, but I could see the hesitation in her eyes that she was desperately trying to hide.

"Everyone join hands, please." The sitters created a circle of clasped hands, some a bit more hesitant than others. "Thomas Nichols, are you here with us tonight?"

A beat of silence, then one long scratch down the wall was followed by two hard knocks, sending ripples of awe and astonishment through the room. *A real spirit communicating with us,* they must be thinking. But I knew that signal for what it was. A distress signal.

Stevie and I had come up with a series of noises or visual signals to communicate with each other from the other side of the walls. Some meant mundane things, like Stevie was moving on to the next prop, or that an icy chill would soon blow through the vent, sending shivers down the necks of the sitters. The signal Stevie had just done had never been used, and fear coursed through me, making me shudder. Hopefully, the sitters assumed it was a side effect of mediumship.

"I believe he's with us now," I said, buying time while I tried to calm my breath. I needed to think, but the damn group in front of me was starting to whisper, the suspense building so much that it had to burst soon.

Stevie rattled the vent before a gust of cold air billowed in, causing the single candle in front of us to dance. The shivering flame cast moving shadows on the sitters' faces, mutating their true expressions into overexaggerated grimaces and scowls.

"Thomas Nichols, your family is here to communicate with you. They seek closure after your death. Do you have a message for them?" The word *message* was a cue for Stevie to start the recording. We'd spliced together the councilman's voice from a handful of his television appearances, which had been replayed on a loop as the news covered his murder. We'd added gritty, distorted effects and would play it through the hidden speakers in the ceiling.

But no voice came from beyond, only another long scratch and another two knocks: the distress signal again. Something must be wrong with the tape recorder or the sound system.

We were going to have to do this the old-fashioned way, communicating through our convoluted codes of knocks and scrapes. We could do without the technology, just like my family did for generations. It wouldn't be easy, but it could be done.

* * *

My memory darted back to my first interaction with Mrs. Nichols. She'd been convinced he was cheating, not that he was in any danger. I could use that to my advantage.

"Mrs. Nichols, this is directed to you." I rubbed my hand over my sternum. "I feel it in my chest, the pain of missing you. He knows you doubted his loyalty."

Mrs. Nichols's eyes glistened with tears, and she pressed her lips together in a tight line, trying to keep the tears of guilt from overflowing.

I continued, "He wants to make it clear that he was always faithful. His disappearance had nothing to do with your relationship. He wishes he was home with you."

She let out a pitiful gasp, like someone had hit her in the chest and knocked the air out of her. The sitters were enthralled, except for Maria, whose beady little eyes were scanning the room, no doubt looking for evidence of tricks or deceit.

I added for good measure, "And sometimes he *is* at home with you. Just not in his earthly form."

The room stirred with emotion, and I knew my hooks were sinking into them. *Draw the tears out, pull their heartstrings.*

My reverie was interrupted by the reporter's voice. "So if his disappearance—his murder—had nothing to do with his marriage, what was the cause? What was the motive?" Her annoying, aggressive tone cut straight through the emotion, and the others blinked away their tears.

The Nichols family nodded in agreement, egging me on to answer. Shit, Maria had sucked the progress right out of the room. We were back to square one.

I closed my eyes against the panic. *Think, think, THINK.* I conjured up the memory of the detectives questioning me, searching for any information they might have given away that I could use to convince the Nichols family and the reporter that I wasn't a fraud.

There was nothing in my head. God, it was blank. I was frozen. I was too tired to do this.

Can you see any political enemies in these little visions of yours? Detective Woolridge had thrown out a handful of jabs, and I'd brushed them off in annoyance. Maybe that wasn't so much of a jab; maybe it was where they were directing their investigation.

My voice came out lower, as if his voice were partially peeking through. "I've made enemies, he says." I blinked my eyes hard against the fatigue washing over me. *Push through.* I thought of Stevie's confession and the revelation that the councilman and Stellman were related. Nichols had bastardized his political power to keep his family's reputation clean, just for Stellman to continue to drag their family through the mud. "Despite all the good I did, it wasn't enough. I used my power in a way I wished I hadn't."

Mrs. Nichols widened her eyes, turning her head slightly to make eye contact with her son, who looked equally weary.

I took a deep breath and continued in my own voice now. "He made a sacrifice and it backfired. This is the cause of his death."

My tongue was dry and stale as my anxiety sharpened. I reached for the chalice in front of me. I told sitters it was a special mixture of herbs to open my mind to the spirits, but tonight it was just ginger ale that had gone flat from sitting out. My mind spun as I tried to remember all of our tricks that didn't require tech—many of them outdated and easy to mess up or make too obvious.

Every séance, I wore the same pair of pants that Stevie and I had sown extra pockets into for props and tricks: a small remote for the sound system, crystals, tarot cards, and luckily a magnet. Before our first séance, we'd sown a heavy-duty magnet into the knee of my trousers, the awkward bulkiness disguised by the black fabric and the darkness of the room. I hadn't used this trick in ages, but Stevie was clearly scrambling behind the scenes, and I needed to take full control.

I took a sip of the flat ginger ale, then set it on the table, my knee perfectly below it under the table. "Benjamin," I asked the younger of the Nichols sons, "can you please tell us a memory of your father? This helps build a connection between the group and the spirit."

I raised my knee as Benjamin spoke, straining my core so I didn't move my upper body. The magnet in my pants attached to the chalice's magnet through the table. We'd had to use the strongest magnet we could find to make this work, and sweat built as I strained to shift my knee slowly under the table.

It dragged across the table, barely a centimeter, but enough to draw attention. I reached for the chalice, as though I wanted to stop the spirit from moving it, but before I could wrap my fingers around it, I applied more force with my knee, using the motion of leaning for the chalice as a disguise to exert all the force I could. The chalice jerked two inches closer to Benjamin, the liquid sloshing over and dripping down the sides onto the wooden table. The sitters around the table took a collective intake of breath, music to the ears of any psychic medium.

"Your father appreciates you sharing the memory, Benjamin," I said in a low, soothing voice, despite the fact that I hadn't heard a word of what he said. "If anyone else would like to share, please feel free." *Except you,* I silently stabbed the thought at Maria, whose smug facial expression had lessened slightly. Maybe I'd convinced her.

A slam behind me caused everyone around the table to jump in terror. I shot out of my seat, spinning around to see what had happened. Neither Stevie nor I had given each other a signal. My heartbeat quickened and blood drained to my feet from standing too quickly—this was true fear, not a part of the act. I slumped back into my seat, dizziness taking hold.

I rested my forehead in my palm, realizing the irony of this being one of my usual tricks, only now the exhaustion and the sheen of cold, clammy sweat were real. "I'm sorry," I mumbled, a dry heave coming without warning. I hadn't had an anxiety attack like this since Mom died, and I'd forgotten the toll it took on my body. Benjamin reached for the chalice, supposedly for something for me to vomit in, but before he could reach it, I snatched it away so nobody would see the magnet attached to the base.

"Are you okay?" Mrs. Nichols said to me in the same moment the older son, Samuel, said, "This is fucked up." Mrs. Nichols glared at him, but a momentary glint in her eye said she agreed.

This was what I wanted, I thought. To strike fear into them, letting it erode their doubt. I hadn't expected it to be at my expense and to feel truly ill, but as my mother always said, *The show must go on.*

"I apologize," I said. "Sometimes communing with a recently passed spirit, especially one who had their life stolen from them, can take an extreme physical toll."

"Maybe we should call it," Mrs. Nichols declared. She put both hands on the table like she was about to push herself up and run out the door.

"Only if that's what feels the best for you. We need to close the séance."

The younger son leaned over to his older brother and whispered, "If she barfs, I'm gonna barf." Benjamin rolled his eyes.

"Is everyone ready? I need your focus." I pinched the skin on my thigh to distract myself from my panic. Everyone around the table straightened their backs like children chastised by a fed-up teacher.

"Please join hands." I reached my hand out to Maria and the younger son, and while the son loosely gripped my clammy hand, Maria's fingernails dug into the back of my hand. "We thank the spirit of Thomas Nichols for communicating with us today. Our time is now over, and we wish you to go in peace."

I leaned forward and blew the candle out, leaving us in darkness for half a second before Stevie turned on the chandelier overhead. The sitters squinted in the light and released their hold on their neighbors. I thanked them for coming and encouraged them to stay if they had questions.

The younger son stood first, eager to get away from the crazy dry-heaving psychic, and the others followed suit.

Once the sitters were out of the séance room, Stevie appeared in the doorway. Her face was gray and her lips were set in a tight line.

"Jade. I need to speak with you." Her voice had the thick, tight sound of someone who'd been holding back tears. "Now."

CHAPTER

32

Stevie

MY HANDS SHOOK as Jade said goodbye to the Nichols family in the shop. We'd never had a séance go so horribly wrong. Had the sitters noticed? I usually sat in the prop room, watching the séance from a hidden camera while eating snacks, but not this time. The cord between us had been cut.

"I'll stick around for a bit, if that's okay," Maria said.

I could practically see Jade's haunches rise, but she covered it with a smile and said, "Sure. I'll be with you in a minute."

Jade followed me into the séance room and locked the door behind her. I opened the armoire doors and pushed the back panel to reveal the opening to the prop room. My back protested as I hunched through the small doorway.

Unlike me, Jade wasn't prepared for what she saw when she entered the prop room. She let out a groan as she took in the state of the room. The tiny surveillance television had been smashed in, glass sprinkled on the floor below like crumbs. The table with all of our tech, including our tape recorder and light machine, was in shambles. Cords were cut and frayed on the floor, severed from their machines, which were cracked and dented.

Most of our manual props were also destroyed. Jade bent over to pick up the ripped arm of our cardboard cutout—the one shaped like the average middle-aged man. I'd intended to use it tonight, but obviously that hadn't happened. Fishing wire sat in a tangled ball by my chair, and scraps of black fabric were ripped into strips and tidily draped across the back of my chair. It made it clear there was a message—this mess was purposeful. It wasn't just a break-in. There was no burglary.

"Who would do this?" Jade asked, the cardboard arm bending in her tense hand. "The mess in your room too—it must have been the same person. What would anyone gain from doing this? Are they looking for something?" As she spoke, her grip tightened, and the arm folded with a quiet *snap*.

Guilt swelled in my stomach at the only person I could think of. I opened my mouth, my voice croaking out.

"Dad?" I said at the same time Jade said it, except mine was a question and hers was a declaration.

"But what reason would he have to do this?" Jade asked, frustration raising her voice higher, her throat clenching tighter.

Was she blind? How could she not see it?

"I'm the reason he went to prison. I'm the reason Mom is dead." My voice came out flat and hollow. The admission of guilt was something I'd never said aloud before. The words were acidic on my tongue but also sweet with relief. I'd believed it all along and I'd finally gotten it off my chest, where it had been festering with each day. Even though I resented him for what he'd done, a part of me still wanted him to be a part of my life—to give him a second chance at being a father. That was why I'd picked him up from prison, but the reunion hadn't been what

I'd pictured a thousand times each night as I lay awake in bed. Jade stared back at me, an expression of disbelief on her face, like I'd had a break with reality. "That's exactly why he did this. He blames me. He must hate me more than I've ever realized."

She took two steps forward, closing the space between us. She rested her hands on each of my shoulders, and while the gesture was supposed to comfort me, it made me feel claustrophobic. I'd been cornered like that far too many times.

"What happened is not your fault, Stevie. Did you break into Ian Stellman's house? Better yet, were you the teacher that abused his power to convince *little girls*"—she paused, letting those two words sink in—"to do whatever the hell he wanted?"

I shook my head.

"No. The only reason they got in an accident was because *Dad* convinced her to come along to intimidate Stellman. You don't put people in danger if you love them."

I silently blinked at her. She was right, but how many times did I have to hear it before I believed it?

"Say it." The tips of her fingers dug into my shoulders, the sensation on the precipice of pain. "Say it's not your fault."

I blinked away the burning sensation in my eyes, and her fingers dug in deeper. "It's not my fault," I conceded.

Another admission, but this was one I didn't believe.

* * *

A knock on the door to the séance room made Jade rip her hands away from my shoulders in a panic. Jade and I both knew how flimsy the locks in this building were. If Maria got through the door, the mystical facade would be broken. We'd closed the armoire doors behind us but left the coats pushed to the side. With the lights in the prop room on, Maria might be able to see light peeking through the cracks of the armoire door.

"Shit fire," I whispered. Jade's wide eyes met mine. If she got through the séance room door, we'd be ruined.

The doorknob jiggled more forcefully this time, and she called out in a frustrated huff, "Jade? I know you're in there."

She roughly twisted the doorknob a few more times, then finally, her knocking ceased and we crawled silently into the séance room. Jade reached to open the door to the shop, but I grabbed her arm. "Wait," I whispered. "Either she thinks we were ignoring her, or she's gonna realize we left through a hidden door."

"I'll handle it." Jade swung the door open and sauntered out. I paused behind her, trying to instill confidence in my posture that I definitely did not have, then followed behind her.

"Sorry to keep you waiting. We do a private, ceremonial prayer after each séance. You know, shake off any bad energy that might be lingering." Jade accompanied the jab with a smile.

Maria's arms were crossed, and although she smiled politely in response, her eyes were sharp and knowing. We weren't tricking this woman with anything.

"Did you have a good experience at the séance?" Jade asked.

"It was"—she paused—"informative."

"Fantastic. I hope you have a great rest of your evening."

"I have some questions, actually." She pulled a small notepad and pen out of her bag and flipped it open. "I was wondering if I could go back in the séance room. I just want to get the descriptions accurate for the article."

"The article?" Jade asked.

"Yes. I'll be writing an article about the councilman, of course, but now I'll be writing a separate piece about you. The local psychic hero." The last sentence was drawn out, invisible punctuation between each word dripping with sarcasm. "So, may I?"

I widened my eyes at Jade and smiled nervously, trying to signal that we had to let her in. If we didn't, it would be too suspicious and only make her more curious. Jade's jaw clenched in response, the message clearly received.

"Sure," Jade said, her voice falsely sweet. "We'll show you around."

"No need. I'll just look around myself."

"Nobody is allowed in the room without supervision. For their own protection," I said, the power in my voice surprising me. I hadn't intended to speak, much less sound so ominous.

"Fair enough," Maria said as she marched into the séance room, Jade and me trailing behind. She scribbled notes on her notepad as she looked at the occult paraphernalia around the room.

Jade caught my attention when Maria faced away from us, studying a painting on the wall—a cheap reprinting of Henry Fuseli's *The Nightmare.* With her hand low and hardly moving, she pointed to the armoire door, which was cracked open. My breath halted and I shooed her away. With whatever sisterly telepathy we had, she immediately engaged Maria in conversation, positioning herself so Maria would have her back turned away from the armoire.

I took three quiet strides, careful to not hit any of the creaking floorboards that I'd mentally mapped out over the years, and twisted the knob to retract the latch bolt. I pushed it closed and breathed a sigh of relief when I let go. I was about to return to where I'd originally been standing when Maria's head whipped around at the noise of the latch bolt.

Shit. I'd forgotten it could get stuck and let out an obnoxious click after fully releasing. How many times had Jade asked me to spray WD-40 on it? I knew that was exactly what she was thinking and that I was in for an earful later.

I tucked my hands behind my back and gave Maria a lazy, confident smile, followed by a sigh that let her know I'd grown bored. In reality, it was the opposite of the truth.

Jade's goblet was still on the table, sticky with spilled ginger ale. Jade's eyes met mine and followed my gaze. I grabbed the goblet and mumbled, "I'll clean this up," as I walked out of the room.

My hands shook as I hastily sat the goblet under Jade's tarot table, hidden by the thick tablecloth. I'd get it later.

I nearly jumped out of my skin as the front doorbell chimed and a man stepped into the room. The streetlights cast the person's face in shadow so that all I could see was their broad shoulders, their hair mussed from the heavy wind.

I stepped out from the dark tarot cubby to get a better view. "Oh, it's you," I said to Daniel. He smiled at me, his happiness uncomplicated and his excitement to see Jade plainly written across his face. I wondered what it was like to have someone so obviously infatuated with you in such a pure and wholesome way. There didn't seem to be any strings attached, excluding the one where Jade had secretly gone through his patients' files. I wondered if there was any chance someone with a PhD in psychology could really believe Jade was psychic. To be fair, men's logic had been blinded by pretty women since the beginning of time.

"How's it going? Is Jade here?"

"She's in the séance room with a reporter," I said. "Actually, can you do me a favor?"

"Anything," he immediately said. God, what an interesting person. No negotiation? No tit for tat? With the scumbags I'd had in my life so far, it was always the former.

I lowered my voice to a whisper. "Could you pretend to be a client? This woman will *not* leave us alone, and we need an excuse to get her out of here."

He winked and said in a booming voice without hesitation, "I'm here for my appointment."

"Welcome! Let me get Madame Ravencroft for you," I announced loudly. He took a seat in the tarot cubby and remained in character despite his cheeks growing rosy with restrained laughter.

I peeked my head into the séance room. "A client's here for their appointment." Jade smiled knowingly, a silent thank-you exchanged.

"Another client? It's almost midnight," Maria said in disbelief.

"This is a business of the night; what can I say?" Jade smiled and made a sweeping motion to the door, but Maria stayed planted, her jaw grinding in frustration.

"I'll walk you out," I said, and approached closely behind her—not enough to be threatening but close enough to make it clear she wasn't welcome anymore. She'd had her chance to uncover whatever truths she'd thought she would find, but she'd blown it. She resisted but shuffled into the shop, notepad clenched in hand.

Jade froze at the sight of Daniel, her facade of confidence breaking for only a split second. "Thanks for coming, Maria," Jade said as she took a seat at the tarot table.

"Get home safely," I said as I opened the front door. She started to protest, but I closed the door behind her and flipped the OPEN sign to CLOSED with a flourish.

CHAPTER

33

Jade

AS SOON AS Stevie flipped the sign to CLOSED, Maria stomped across the street to her car.

"God, she's like a horsefly," Stevie mumbled. "After that, I *definitely* need therapy. Daniel, is the offer still on the table?"

"The offer?" I asked, hyperaware of Daniel's gaze on me across the tarot table.

"I booked an appointment with Daniel the other week. I figured it was time to grow up, ya know? Move on."

"It was a shame you never showed," Daniel jabbed playfully. Stevie held her hands up guiltily. "And yes, the pro bono offer is still on the table."

I hadn't even realized I'd been holding so much tension after finding that file in his office, but it left me in that moment. Of course he wasn't taking notes on Stevie, or worse, stalking her. He was trying to help her.

"Thanks, Daniel. I'm going to bed."

"We'll figure everything out tomorrow, I promise," I said to Stevie.

"What do you have to figure out tomorrow?" Daniel asked after she ambled up the stairs.

I studied his innocent face, which was slightly tilted to the side, mirroring his crooked smile. Should I tell him the truth? I was so used to doing everything on my own and casting mistrust on anyone who tried to enter my hypervigilant personal space that I could hardly remember what it felt like to share something with someone other than Stevie. Could I trust him?

A wave of shame hit me as I realized my hypocrisy. This man sitting across from me should be asking himself that same question. I'd already betrayed him by going through his private files and using that information for my own gain. He'd let me into his life, and just like Dad, I'd immediately found a way to twist it for my personal benefit.

"Someone broke in." The words came tumbling out of my mouth as I decided *yes*, this man did deserve my trust. He'd given me no reason to believe otherwise.

"Oh," he said as he leaned forward, propping both elbows on the tarot table. "Are you and Stevie all right? What's missing?"

His concern warmed the cold pit in my stomach that had been sitting there all day. As my nausea wore off, I was starting to realize this could have been worse. What if the intruder had barged into the séance? What if they'd hurt Stevie and used all of our props to sabotage the entire thing? Although they'd nearly ruined the séance, they'd missed the mark. Still, though, they had left me with that unsettling feeling like everything in the parlor and apartment was tainted, a vulnerability of our sacred safe space being broken.

"Surprisingly, nothing is missing. At least that we've noticed. They rummaged through Stevie's room a little bit but didn't take anything. They broke a bunch of our equipment, though."

"Equipment? Like what?"

My heart stuttered as my mistake became clear. Daniel still didn't know I was an impostor, or at least if he suspected, he didn't seem to care. "Um, just like EMF readers—electromagnetic field readers for paranormal activity—and tape recorders and stuff. It'll set us back, but we can manage."

"You need to file a police report."

I thought of Stevie and me calling the police just to tell them that our secret little scammer room had been broken into. There was no way to file a report without screwing ourselves over in the process.

"I don't think so. They haven't been very friendly when we've talked to them about the Nichols case."

He sighed. "That's fair," he said as he studied my face. "I still think you should, though."

"Will you stay the night?" I asked quietly. "For safety, of course."

He laughed softly as he stood and took my hand. "Anything for you."

CHAPTER 34

Stevie

IT WAS JUST after one in the morning as I sat perched on my windowsill smoking a joint when I heard Jade's bedroom door open and quiet footsteps move into the living room. Curious as to what Jade could be doing, I stubbed out my joint and left the window open to let any remaining smoke clear.

I cracked open my door and followed as quietly as possible into the hallway. I stayed in the dark hallway, waiting to catch sight of Jade and leap out to scare her, as childish as it was. To my surprise, it was Daniel, clad only in a white T-shirt and plaid boxers. I blushed, feeling like I should look away from someone who clearly didn't know he was being watched, but for some reason, I stayed.

He fumbled around until he found a light in the kitchen, where he filled a glass with tap water and drank greedily. I couldn't take my eyes off him—he was constantly at ease, even in his underwear in someone else's house. He probably never thought that maybe someone was watching him, and definitely never felt looming anxiety that someone was out to get him at any moment.

I nearly retreated, assuming he'd make his way back to Jade's room or our shared bathroom. Instead, he walked into the living room and froze as he stood over the coffee table.

What was he looking at? It was papers, but I couldn't tell what they were. He reached out with one finger and flipped back a page of a notebook, then furiously rubbed his face with both hands. My breath hitched when he picked up the notebook, his grip so strong on it that it was bending. It was Jade's notes on his patient files.

He tossed it back on the table and stomped toward me so quickly that I stumbled back, retreating into my room. From my cracked bedroom door, I held my breath as he marched furiously to Jade's room, opening the door and disappeared into her dark room.

I don't know what I expected—shouted words, thrown objects—but it surely wasn't complete silence. My panicked brain told me to run out and check on Jade, make sure he wasn't pressing a pillow into her face or something else ridiculous and wildly out of Daniel's character.

A minute later he emerged, dressed, with a scowl on his face. I waited for the shop door to open and slam shut, and even though I knew it was coming, I flinched anyways.

* * *

Jade

"Jade," a voice said in the grayish-blue dark of early dawn. This had happened so many times in my dreams that I clenched my eyes and hoped the nightmare would end.

Two hands gripped my arms and shook as they hissed my name again, louder this time. "Jade, wake up. Now!"

The feeling against my flesh wasn't just my imagination or a dream. I let loose a primal scream as I kicked them off me. I was surprised this time by my ability to move—every time this had happened before, I'd been paralyzed with that sickly disorienting combination of sleep and fear. I kicked again and made contact with something.

"Oh, shit," they croaked out as they fell back on my bed, the breath knocked out of them.

I shot upright, panting with fear. I patted the side of the bed where Daniel had been sleeping, noting it had long gone cold. Where had he gone? I glanced at the alarm clock on my nightstand. It was five in the morning. Too early for him to get ready for patients but a reasonable enough time for him to go on one of his usual jogs around the neighborhood.

"I'm so sorry," I said when I realized it was Stevie. "I thought I was having another nightmare."

She held up a finger, making it clear I would have to suffer with her through the anxious seconds of breathlessness. Finally, she took a desperate gasp, and in true Stevie fashion, her first words were "What the fuck?" I mumbled my apologies before she cut me off, mumbling that it didn't matter. "Daniel left. Maybe thirty minutes ago."

"Okay?"

"He got up to get a water from the kitchen, and he saw your notes on his patient files."

I rubbed the crusty remnants of sleep from my eyes as if it would somehow make me hear clearly. "What?"

"He knows you stole the files. You just left it out in the open like you wanted him to see it. What the hell were you thinking?"

I sat up straighter, growing defensive to match her accusatory tone. "I didn't leave it out. Are you calling me dumb?" I winced at the immature question that hearkened back to our childhood arguments.

"Of course I'm not. But I didn't leave it out. So it had to have been you. You've been exhausted—mistakes happen. But this is a huge mistake."

"Maybe I've been exhausted, yeah, fine. But you've been high every day for the last two years, so why should I not accuse *you* of leaving it out?"

Her cheeks flushed red. "From the second you showed me the papers, I wanted nothing to do with them. Why the hell would I get them out of your hiding place—which by the way, I don't even know where you were keeping them—and set them out in the living room for anyone to see?"

It was my turn to blush, embarrassed by the fact that she'd heard us and that I'd lobbied out such a baseless accusation. "You're right. I'm sorry."

"Sorry doesn't matter. You have to fix this. He could call the police about this. He could get you arrested."

My mouth hung open, the unspoken statement of *He wouldn't . . .* not making it out of my mouth.

"He could and you know it."

"I'll go over there now," I said as I shot out of bed, not caring that I was stark naked. I threw on whatever clothes were strewn across the floor and ran down the stairs, my feet pounding in time with my racing heart as I ran out the door and the few steps to Daniel's building.

I glanced up, noting there were no lights on in his building. It took me one frantic, lunging step to get up the stairs to his stoop, and I knocked on his door, polite at first, then frantic. The guilt was bringing tears to my eyes, the horrible, dishonest things I'd done, ruining the beautiful night we'd had last night and every ounce of happiness I'd found since we'd watched that movie together.

There was no answer, and my polite knocks with knuckles turned into furious pounds with the sides of my fists. "Daniel! Please answer the door," I shouted uselessly. A light on the street came on, and my curmudgeonly neighbor Phyllis came out to stand on the street, her arms crossed and her jaw set in disgust at my behavior.

"Keep it down! It's not even six in the morning," she shouted at me.

I didn't respond and kept knocking, weaker now as resignation settled in my chest.

"You young women these days are despicable. Desperate for attention—"

"Mind your business, Phyllis," I yelled back, my voice cracking pathetically as I spat out her first name, knowing it would infuriate her to be addressed so casually. As she stomped back inside, I noticed Daniel's car wasn't parked in front of his office or anywhere on the street. He was reliable in his habits, so this meant he'd gone straight from my apartment to his car and fled. Where, I didn't know, but the thought of him driving away from me, fully aware of the type of person I was, made me cry harder. I wanted to lie on his stoop and cry, but that was too pathetic even for me, and Phyllis would love to use it as an excuse to call the police on me.

I stumbled to our apartment, the few steps feeling like miles as I dragged my heavy, tired limbs across the pavement. Stevie opened the door before I even had the chance and took me into her arms.

"I'm just like him, aren't I?" I asked as I sobbed into her T-shirt.

"Who?"

"Dad," I bellowed.

She didn't answer, but the tight grip of her arms across my back was enough confirmation for me.

* * *

My life was completely out of control, and it was undeniable that most of it was my fault. Daniel still hadn't returned to his building, so without a chance to speak to him, the dread was becoming more intense by the minute.

Searching for a sense of control, I got out a notebook and began going over the mess of our finances. To the benefit of my mood, we weren't barely skating by and we weren't in the negatives. The hidden soup can filled tight with bills was proof. Today I would send in the rent money for the shop and finally open a bank account. No more hidden stashes of money. We were going to start living the way *we* wanted to live, not the way our parents had taught us—in fear of banks, the police, everyone around us.

Stevie was pouring herself a bowl of cereal, and I called out to her without looking up, "Will you go get the cash out of the stash for me? I have to send the rent in."

"Cash stash. Has a ring to it." She hoisted herself onto the kitchen counter and opened the cabinet, rustling around inside for the can. Aluminum scraped against the wood cabinets, and I could tell by the low sound of the scratch that the cans were full. "Have you seen Daniel yet?"

"Don't want to think about that right now," I said mindlessly, fighting to maintain my focus on the numbers in front of me. "The can's all the way in the back. The chicken noodle."

"Yep." The shifting continued, even more quickly now, with the occasional glug of liquid as she shook the cans to check for the money.

The familiar sound of an aluminum lid scraping against skin let me know she'd found the can, yet she wasn't climbing down from the cabinet. "You need help?"

I glanced up from my notebook to see Stevie staring into the can, her face so pale it looked like she might faint. "Are you dizzy?" I shot up to help her, putting both hands on her hips to steady her in case she might fall.

With my help, she stepped down but teetered, holding the can out to me.

"Thanks. You all right?"

She didn't say anything as I took the can. I peeked inside, expecting to see the thousands of dollars we'd made over the past weeks. My stomach roiled, my coffee threatening to come up.

The can was empty. The overhead light shone off the bare aluminum and I squinted dumbly, searching for the cash like it had shrunk or fallen deeper into the can.

"This isn't funny, Stevie. Did you dump it out?"

Stevie shook her head silently. Dread filled my chest, making it hard for me to breathe. Despite the evidence right in front of me, my brain denied the truth of what I saw.

"This must be the wrong can or something." I threw the empty can onto the floor and hoisted myself up to the cabinet. After minutes of shifting around the cans, it was clear this wasn't a prank or a mistake.

All the news pieces and talk of the hotline tip had made us a target. It had made everyone aware that we had earned a reward, and although those same news pieces had flooded us with new clients, it had also damned us.

Someone had broken into our house and stolen the money.

CHAPTER 35

Stevie

I NEVER SHOULD HAVE mentioned the money to Dad. To be fair, I hadn't been the one to bring it up. He'd shown up randomly again one day when I was running errands and had asked me if we needed money. It had taken me aback, the kindness of it burning warm in my chest, blooming into admiration, drowning out all the negative memories. Of which there were many, I might add.

In retrospect, it was clear he'd been digging. *How could I be so stupid?*

I always reverted back to being a little girl when I was around him—trusting, wide-eyed with pride that he was my dad. So tough! So brave! No, not at all. He wasn't any of those things. I was just a gullible idiot.

Jade stared at me while I pored over what I'd told Dad. Was this really my fault?

"You need any cash, sweetheart?" he'd asked after we'd run into each other at a nearby deli. His mood had been so warm that I'd dumbly asked him to eat with me.

"For the first time in forever, we're actually good."

"Not dealing with the banks, right? Professional corporate thieves, believe me."

"Nope, it's all stashed safely away."

"That's my girl. Same way your mother hid it, I assume?"

Oh God, here it comes. Here's me fucking up again.

"Money's like chicken soup for the soul," I'd chimed, imitating Mom.

"Stevie, for fuck's sake!" Jade yelled, breaking me out of my stupor. She'd torn the apartment to shreds looking for the money.

"This is my fault," I said pathetically under my breath. Jade got annoyed often, yes, but she rarely got mad. And when she did, she went nuclear. She'd once torn a fistful of hair out of a girl's scalp when she'd seen me getting bullied in high school.

Jade's lower jaw jutted out as she flipped over the couch cushions, exposing a graveyard of crumbs and coins. "How the hell is this your fault?"

"I might have accidentally given someone a clue that we keep our money stashed in the apartment," I said cautiously.

"Are you going to keep speaking cryptically, or am I going to have to beat it out of you?"

"I accidentally said Mom's little jingle. The one about the soup."

"Who was it?" I hesitated and she took a step closer, her shoulders and elbows pulled back like she was ready to strike. "Who did you say it to?"

My chin trembled. I took a deep breath and finally said what I'd been wanting to admit all this time. "It was Dad."

Jade's eyes glistened with the beginnings of angry tears. "What do you mean?" She took another step closer to me, but I stayed steady on my feet, even though my entire body was shaking. I'd never been afraid of Jade until now.

I held my breath like she would smell the lies on my breath, rotten and ugly. “I’ve been in contact with Dad a little bit since he got out of prison.”

“For how long?”

“I picked him up from prison. I told him I didn’t want to speak to him after that, but I don’t know . . .” I sighed, both at how pathetic I was and how it wasn’t the full truth. “I just folded. I always do.”

Jade’s head bowed in disappointment. She’d always criticized me for letting people walk all over me, but I’d always reminded her that it wasn’t *all* people. The drunk regulars at the bar knew not to mess with me, as did creepy clients that came into the shop. There was something in Dad and a select handful of people that just made me crumble. I wanted to impress them, I wanted to be loved by them. And I always picked the people who never wanted to do that.

“What the fuck, Stevie? You let him in the house, didn’t you? He’s the one who put my notes out. And your yearbook. He’s the one lurking around.” Her eyes were wide and manic. I hadn’t noticed until now how tired she looked—how close she was to breaking.

“I promise I never let him in. He must have found a way in on his own.”

“He’s the one threatening us. It’s been him all along. He killed Nichols.”

I began to sweat, panic building. “He kept telling me to mind my business when I mentioned the tip about Nichols. I thought it had just been advice at the time, but maybe it was a threat.”

“We have to get the money back. We need to find out where he lives. Once we have the money, we tell the police it was him. Send him back to prison where he belongs.”

"The police won't be able to do anything. What proof do we have? Also, if you haven't noticed, they don't think very highly of us."

She sighed, knowing I was right. "It's still worth a shot. We just need some sort of proof first." Jade interrogated me about my conversations with Dad, asking where we'd met. I told her he just showed up; sometimes at work, the other day at the grocery store. I hadn't wondered until now how he always seemed to know where I'd be.

I glanced at the window, the lack of privacy leaving us exposed and vulnerable. I darted to the windows and snapped the curtains shut, leaving us in the dark behind the thick velvet shield of curtains.

"Where is he watching us from?" Jade grumbled, reading my mind.

I scanned the street through the sliver of curtains. "Some of those buildings have fire escapes. He could have snuck in through there, posted up on the second floor with a sleeping bag and binoculars. He stayed with the Pulaskis for a few days, but they kicked him out."

Jade scoffed and mumbled under her breath. "I knew someone was up there," she said without explanation. "We need to find out where Dad is as soon as possible. I have some stuff I need to do. Can you work on it before your shift tonight?"

I didn't correct her and tell her I didn't have a shift tonight. I'd asked a coworker to cover for me. "On it."

"Good. I'll ask around. For now, keep all the curtains closed. And for the love of God, Stevie, stay the hell away from him."

* * *

Anyone with siblings knew that whatever they told you to do, you did the opposite. And that was exactly what I was going to do. It didn't take me long to find out where Dad was staying. I conjured up my Girl Scout days, going house to house, knocking on his old friends' doors and asking if he was there.

Was it stupid? Yes. Was it dangerous? Also yes. But it worked.

On the fourth house, my heart sank when the wife of my dad's friend said he wasn't there but she knew where he was. She gave me the address of a trailer park between Winston-Salem and Wallburg, and I immediately hopped back in the car and headed straight there. My poor coworker, Alexa, had hundreds of new miles on her car because of me, and I wasn't looking forward to paying her back.

It was approaching nightfall as I drove to the trailer park, too distracted by the nausea rising in my stomach to appreciate the scenery that stretched out on both sides of the road. There were fields of crops to the left and at least a hundred goats grazing a grassy field on the right. Normally it'd bring a smile to my face, but I just pressed on the pedal harder.

How could a father do this to his own children? Not only steal their hard-earned money but then go on to try to make their lives miserable with harassment and threats? And they weren't even the bravado threats of someone pounding on your door, ready to scream in your face. It was all hocus-pocus from the shadows, as he was too chickenshit to show his face. I'd thought prison was supposed to make people tougher, but it appeared I was wrong.

I came to a rolling stop as I pulled into the gravel lot of the trailer park: Old Oak Hollow Estates. I didn't see a single oak, and it definitely wasn't like any estate I'd ever read about or seen on TV. Most of the mobile homes were well kept and you could tell the owners took pride in their homes, but any curb appeal was robbed by a handful of neighbors who left trash around their homes and whose metal siding was rusting and peeling into the dead grass below.

I checked the piece of paper the woman had given me: *Old Oak Hollow Estates, Wallburg, NC, Lot 48.* I stepped out, locking the car behind me. A few residents sat in lawn chairs around a fire pit, sipping beers and grilling. They looked like they were having a good time, at least until they saw me. I was well aware of the burn of their stares as I walked down the gravel road, silently counting the lots while I looked for nonexistent lot numbers on the mobile homes. *Just my luck.*

When I got to what I could only assume was lot forty-eight, I knocked on the front door.

"Who the hell are you?" the old woman demanded when she swung open the door. "Don't you know it's rude to stop by unannounced?"

"Sorry, ma'am, I was just knocking to ask if Bill Crawford was here?"

"Who's asking?"

"I'm his daughter." Out of the corner of my eye, I saw a bright light in another trailer go dim. The curtains on a small window swished before stilling. That must be lot forty-eight.

"He's not here and I'm making dinner, so why don't you go on now?" She waved me off with one hand, and the door slammed shut.

I cautiously walked across the road to the opposite lot, my eyes searching the windows for any other movement. My anxiety had been usurped by indignant anger.

You think you can just sit in there and hide from your daughter? The one you abandoned, harassed, then robbed? Not a chance.

I pounded on the door three times, rattling the metal frame. This home was more run-down than the others, and the owner had done little to maintain the lot. Beer cans were strewn about, broken bottles scattered in the ashen fire pit near the chain-link fence.

There was no answer, so I gave one more knock as I asked, "Hello? Dad, are you in there?"

Before I could finish the question, the door swung open and I was met with the swollen, bruised face of my father.

C H A P T E R

36

Stevie

WE STARED AT each other wordlessly for what felt like minutes but was only five painfully stretched-out seconds.

"What are you doing here?" he asked as I spoke over him. His lip was swollen, giving him a slight lisp.

"What the fuck is wrong with you?" My voice was loud enough that neighbors' front doors swung open, ears eager to listen.

"Whoa, whoa. First of all, lower your voice, and second, don't talk to your father like that."

"At this point, it's a joke that you call yourself my father."

His face tensed, the comment landing like salt in an open wound, just how I'd wanted it to. Someone in the back of the home was moving around in a way that made it obvious they were trying to keep quiet. "You got a secret family hidden in here? Maybe two sons like you always wanted?"

"I never cared about having sons. I was perfectly happy with you and Jade," he said. "I *am* perfectly happy with you two," he corrected.

"Then why are you trying to ruin our lives?" I bellowed, my throat tightening. I focused on the muscles, trying to loosen them so I didn't sound like a pathetic child.

"Can we go somewhere more private? You're drawing a crowd." He motioned to three women who were halfheartedly pretending to weed a small communal garden between the lots. "There's some picnic tables over there. You can yell all you want."

"Fine."

He ushered me off the road and down a dirt path covered by trees. There were four picnic tables and two rusty grills. I sat at the table least covered in bird crap, every ounce of sullen teenager energy I had before Dad went to prison coming to the surface. He made me feel like I was regressing on all fronts—all the confidence and the bravery I'd stored up dissipating. I resisted the urge to flee and sat still in my seat, every muscle tense as the confrontation approached.

Before Dad sat, he flicked on a switch, turning on lines of fairy lights that dimly illuminated the perimeter of the communal space. "Nice, right?" he said as if he'd built it himself.

"Magical," I muttered.

"So what is this about me trying to ruin your life?"

"Don't play dumb with me, please. I'm too tired for that."

"Stevie, you know I only want the best for you. I'm trying to get a job so I can afford my own lot here. Do you know how pathetic it feels for a fifty-five-year-old man to beg for a place to sleep? I'm supposed to be living with my family."

There it was, the guilt trip. I didn't know how he was turning this around on me, making himself the victim. "Does sound pretty pathetic. But that's your own fault."

His jaw flexed as he tried to calm himself. "I know I've made a few mistakes that I can never fix, but I'd never try to bring you girls down with me. Why would you ever think I wanted to?"

"A *few* mistakes? You've stolen so much from me. You stole mom. You stole *my dad*—you! And now you steal our money? You're sick in the head. You're a sociopath."

The space between his eyebrows narrowed and he opened his mouth to speak, but a deep voice behind me interrupted.

"What's all this commotion? Don't you know there are easier ways to resolve disputes?" The words themselves were harmless, but the man's tone was ice-cold.

I started to turn around to see who he was, but two heavy hands gripped my shoulder, freezing me in place before I could turn around to see his face.

"Take your hands off her. We can handle this on our own."

"You've made it clear you can't handle shit, not even your two little girls. Looks like they could run circles around you." He applied the slightest pressure to my shoulders, making it clear that I was powerless against him. Every hair on my body stood on end when he grazed the back of my neck with his rough, callused thumb. I tried to shrug him off, but he pushed down harder. I whimpered from the force of it, my spine curving in response so I was slouched over the table.

"I said get your fuckin' hands off her."

"Okay," he said in a glib, apathetic tone. He released his hands from my shoulders, and just as I started to sit up straight and move away from him, the man gripped my ponytail, snapping my head back. I took in the thick ridge of his eyebrows and dark-brown eyes for a flash of a second, just before he slammed my head into the picnic table and everything went black.

* * *

I wasn't sure how much time had passed, or if any had passed at all. I was in a limbic state, blackness clogging my vision as my head floated along, interrupted by the sharp slice of pain with each heartbeat. Even that felt distant—a part of my brain sending signals that something was terribly wrong, while the other part of my brain was telling me it was okay. This was the end. Don't pay attention to the pain.

"What are you going to do—" I heard my Dad's voice somewhere off in the distance yet so close by I swore his breath danced across my face. But his voice faded out, his question never finished.

I wanted so badly to open my eyes and look at his face. To stare into his eyes and silently ask him how he could put his daughters in constant danger like this. From the moment we were born, he'd grown more reckless, increasing the stakes and putting us more at risk. And now here I was, the damp cold of soil leeching through the fabric of my shirt as my limp body was dropped to the ground. I wanted to ask to be picked up, to be cradled before it all ended.

Instead, there was arguing. More violence. My head throbbed with the sound of it. Two meaty hands gripped my ankles and for a moment I felt relief—Dad was getting me off the ground. I would be okay.

But deep down I knew those hands weren't his. I knew as I faded in and out, now aware of the sounds of a car, that wherever I was being driven to wasn't safe. I would be there forever, whether I wanted to or not.

Nothing had ever gone the way I wanted it to. Maybe I'd not tried hard enough. Maybe I'd put myself in harm's way too many times. This could be the relief I was looking for.

I stopped bothering to try to decipher the sounds around me as I slipped in and out of consciousness, finding that whenever I came to, I wanted the blank darkness to return.

I eventually let it, settling into it.

What was the point in trying anymore anyway?

CHAPTER 37

Jade

WHERE THE HELL is she?

It had been nearly twenty-four hours since Stevie had been home. She wasn't answering her phone, but I kept telling myself not to panic, since she wouldn't be able to call or text without WiFi. I thought maybe she'd taken on extra shifts at the bar after we discovered our money had been stolen, but when I'd called the bar, he had no idea where she was.

"She hasn't made it to her past two shifts," her boss had said. He continued, frustration mounting. "If she misses the next one, I'm afraid we're going to have to—"

I'd hung up before he could finish.

I'd been in and out of the shop, running errands and hoping by some chance that I'd run into her, but she was nowhere to be found. Or maybe she didn't want to be found. I was growing restless with waiting, and my tailbone ached from the hours of sitting next to the window, hoping to catch sight of her walking up the street to our apartment. The muscles in my limbs were twitching, a deep itch of anxiety not letting me sit still for more than a few seconds.

I forgot about every ache and pain as Daniel's car pulled in front of his building. He slammed the car door and dashed up to his stoop, glancing to the side as though he were looking for someone. Or avoiding someone.

He didn't want to speak with me, but I had no choice. I had to explain myself.

"Daniel!" I shouted as I swung our door open. He ignored my call, but the slight turn of his head made it clear he'd heard me.

Before he could close the front door on me, I shot up his stairs and put my hand in the doorway. If I were him, I would have slammed it into my fingers just to hear the crack of wood against bone, but he was too kind to do that. He was rightfully angry, but he wasn't like me or my family. He was a good person.

"We need to talk," I said, the words interrupted by quick breaths from my dash up the stairs.

"I don't think so, Jade."

I was shocked by the lifelessness in his voice. He was avoiding eye contact, but as I studied his face, I could see the rim of purple beneath his eyes, like he hadn't been sleeping. That made two of us.

"Please. I want to talk about what you saw."

"You mean the patient files you stole from me that could ruin my career?"

I froze, startled by the swift change of tone in his voice. I'd never heard him angry before, but the shift was sharp and biting.

"Yes," I said pathetically. What else was I to do? Deny?

He gripped my arm that was blocking the door from closing, and although his hand was gentle, it was firm enough that I didn't resist as he pulled me inside. He ushered me into his office and motioned to the couch. Instead of sitting in the chair across from me like he'd done when I'd opened our rent letter, he stood in front of his desk with his arms crossed against his chest. He didn't bother turning the desk lamp on. After a full minute of silence, he motioned with his hand, a silent demand to speak. So I did.

"I took your patient files. There's no denying that, and I'm sorry. But I can explain that there was more behind it."

"Let me guess, you thought you could use their private information about their mental health to make money with your parlor tricks?"

Blood rushed into my cheeks like he'd slapped me in the face. It wasn't so much that it was a dig at my career; it was more that he was right. He'd read me like a book, and I couldn't help but wonder how long ago he'd figured me out. Had he known all along that I was a fraud and a cheat but just not care because he wanted to sleep with me?

"One of the patient files—Ian Stellman." My voice cracked when I said his name, and Daniel stood straighter, like deep down he knew what was coming. "He took advantage of my sister when she was in high school. It was a few years ago, and I didn't know until recently."

His eyes widened, and he reached up with one hand to pinch the bridge of his nose. "So what was your plan?"

"I wanted to mess with him—get him to admit that he'd done that to multiple girls. It's not fair that people end up in prison and he gets to run around free just because his cousin is—*was*—a politician." By the time I'd finished the sentence, I was shouting.

Daniel stared at me, his eyes darting around my face like he was searching for truth. "Do you have anything to do with the fact that he hasn't shown up to his past two sessions? Or the fact that a detective called to ask if I've seen him?"

"No, we have nothing to do with that. He was a drunk. He's probably in a ditch somewhere sleeping it off."

Daniel sighed, knowing I was right. "I don't think I need to explain myself when I say that whatever we had is over. Right?" he asked softly.

"Right," I whispered back. "I'm sorry I ruined this. I make a perfect case study for self-sabotage."

He laughed softly, but his lips were pulled tight in a wince. "You know." He paused, looking down at his feet. "When you were reading my palm, if you had told me we'd end up together for good, I would have believed you." He finally met my eye. He was fighting back tears.

I choked down a sob. He could have screamed at me. He could have called me a fraud—all of which I deserved. But without knowing, he said the words that cut deeper than any screaming match could. We had been right together. But everything about me was wrong.

"We should keep our distance," he said. I bowed my head and let my tears stain his carpet.

Whatever unspoken rule was forming underneath the conversation to keep him from going to the police about what I'd done wasn't to be tested or questioned. I stood, yearning to touch him as I walked out of his office.

I returned to the shop and trudged to the bathroom to wash the tears and makeup from my face. It did no good, because as I scrubbed roughly at my face, the tears continued, making my skin sting.

Looking up into the mirror, I took in how pathetic I looked. Red skin, swollen eyes. Under the surface was even more pathetic: no money, no real friends, no boyfriend. *I'd* done that. *I'd* stolen Daniel's files because I lacked self-control. Because I was a snake.

I swung my fist into the mirror, sick of my reflection, sick of myself. Cracks splintered outward from where I'd made contact. I didn't even feel the pain as blood trickled down my hand, glass wedged into my knuckles.

As I seethed at my reflection, a shadow passed behind me, a quick flash of black across the doorway. I spun around and tore through the house after the shadow—after what was likely our father manipulating us and messing with our heads.

"Where are you?" I roared as I checked each room, expecting to find my father smiling over his success. He'd done it. He had our money and my sanity. But every room was empty and silent.

I slumped onto the couch, continuing to cry as I waited for Stevie. The only person I had left.

CHAPTER

38

Jade

THE DAY CONTINUED without a sight of Stevie. I remained on the couch, drifting in and out of a sleep as I waited, until I finally gave up and opened the shop. I was pretending everything was fine as I was at the midpoint of a reading with a somewhat new sitter. This was her second reading—the reading where clients either cemented their belief in my ability and their willingness to give me money, or doubt and suspicion crept in, driving them away forever.

Just as I was pulling her third card, two detectives let themselves inside. Much to my dismay, it was McCade and Woolridge. I let the client know she could wait or she could return later for a free reading, and of course, she decided to stay so she could soak up every detail of my conversation with the detectives.

The detectives didn't bother with pleasantries. Woolridge said, "Do you have any idea how suspicious it looks that you're forming so many connections to deaths in the area?"

"Sorry?"

Woolridge repeated himself, the question exactly the same but his tone even more aggressive.

"We've already talked about the Councilman Nichols case in great detail, and I've spoken to numerous journalists—more than I care to, to be honest—so I'm not sure how else I can help. I'm in the middle of a reading, so if we could wrap this up . . ." I motioned with both hands, indicating my rush as my client stared at me, her mouth slightly ajar at the mention of death. Wasn't that what she was here for? The macabre beings lingering beyond the veil?

"This isn't about Councilman Nichols. This is about your sister."

The force of the word *sister* was like a punch straight to my sternum. "What do you mean?"

McCade spoke, his tone and volume far more gentle. I didn't like the soft look in his eyes. It reeked of pity. "This was dropped off at the station in the middle of last night. Nobody saw it delivered, but we can only assume that it was your sister." He handed me a piece of paper that was tucked into a clear plastic pouch. I stared at it, not wanting to touch it. When he pushed it farther toward me, I took it and began to read.

Please forgive me. I don't wish to be a burden on anyone anymore, especially after I'm gone. I've gone far away so you won't have to see what I've done to myself. I never wanted to hurt you, but I know ending my life will and I'm sorry. Now that I'm gone, I want to confess something that has been haunting me: I killed the councilman. We were having an affair and an argument got out of hand. I'm sorry for planting the idea to call the tip line. I should have never dragged you into this. I love you and I'm sorry.

Stevie

I dropped the letter as my vision blurred. I hadn't taken a breath the entire time I was reading, and now I'd forgotten how—my lungs weren't working, my brain was freezing, there was no way Stevie would do this. There was no *fucking* way. I needed to tell them that. The detectives had to know this was all bullshit.

"No," I said as I shoved the letter back into the detective's hand. "This is typed. We don't even have a printer. She didn't write this."

"She could have used the library or a friend's printer. We have no reason to believe this has been forged."

"You do have a reason, and that's me telling you she did *not* write this."

"I understand that this is a shock, but this is all the information we have for you."

"You understand? You think you *understand*?"

"Ma'am, there's no need to get aggressive," Woolridge snapped.

McCade put a hand out to shush him. "I misspoke. No, I don't personally know what you're going through. But we've seen this type of thing before—troubled individuals leaving their final note but not wanting their body to be found."

"Have you even tried to find it?" *It.* My stomach churned at the use of the word. "Have you tried to find her?" I corrected.

"We did send out three officers to do a sweep of the town, but we weren't able to find anything. We spoke to her manager, who allowed us to look in her locker. It was cleaned out, with the key and padlock left behind."

"But nothing in the house was cleaned out."

"Are you sure? May we take a look at her room?"

Every ounce of self-preservation told me not to let them in, that they needed a warrant. But I was scrambling and desperate and wanted to prove to them that she didn't do this to herself.

"Fine," I conceded, showing them to her room. "Go ahead," I said as we arrived at her closed bedroom door. They would find it exactly as it always was—unmade bed, a pile of clean clothes tossed onto the floor, three or four empty lighters strewn across her vanity.

"It's pretty cleaned out. Is she always this tidy?" Woolridge asked.

Tidy? There was no way anyone would ever describe Stevie's room as tidy. I took a step into her doorway, and the sound was sucked out of the room, leaving a high whining pitch in my ears. I gripped the doorway and found myself bending over at the waist, my nails digging into the doorway. The muscles in my thighs twitched, threatening to give out.

"Ma'am? Are you all right?"

All her things were gone. The bed was made, with crisp, neat corners, and there wasn't a single item on top of her vanity, bedside table, or chest of drawers. Her closet door was open, displaying the brutally empty wire hangers inside.

"It's all gone."

Both officers were asking me questions, but the whining noise in my head had grown louder as I glanced around, desperately searching for something of hers—even a pair of shoes. There was nothing. She'd never had much anyway, just the basics: clothes, books, and toiletries. She was the type to cherish the few items she had. There was no way she would just get rid of them.

The sound rushed back into my ears with a snap, both officers waiting for me to answer the questions that I hadn't even heard.

"She would never do this to herself. We've had trouble lately—threats. Stolen money. My dad just got out of prison."

"Whoa, whoa, whoa. Slow down," McCade soothed. He sensed my growing agitation and spoke. "Why didn't you report the theft or the threats?"

The question was like a slap in the face, feeling like the equivalent of asking a woman what she was wearing when a strange man grabbed her ass. "You questioned me multiple times about the Nichols case, and as you can remember, they weren't the kindest of conversations. I didn't think I'd be taken seriously given the fact that you practically mocked me to my face and implied I had something to do with the councilman's death." My words came out like sharp hisses, only to be met with a sneer from Woolridge.

I imagined the rest of the police force in the office, giggling over how pathetic I was, kicking their little feet and having a grand time. I'd told Stevie we should talk to the police about Dad, and she'd been right—there was no way they would take us seriously.

"Let's go take a seat and we can ask you a few more questions. Seems we have a lot to talk about," McCade said.

They led me to the living room as if they were the ones who lived here, and I followed. It took me a few minutes to gather myself, many of their questions going in one ear and out the other as I tried and failed to get a grip on the truth. Stevie was gone forever. And she'd done it to herself.

* * *

I sat at the kitchen table, my cup of coffee long grown cold. I hadn't bothered to make breakfast or lunch. There was no point. My stomach was hollow, but there was no hunger. I was just a shell without Stevie. And now I didn't even have Daniel. I was completely alone.

A blow to the door downstairs made me cower in my chair, throwing my hands over my head. I released my arms from my head. It was just a postal worker dropping off a package. I hadn't ordered anything and wondered if Stevie had. The simple thought of her name on a package made me begin to cry again.

No matter what the detectives said, I still didn't believe Stevie had done this to herself. Someone had done it *to* her. Why would she nudge me to call in a tip when she was the one to murder the councilman? It made no sense. She would never take me down with her. I was even more confused by the idea that she would be having an affair with a man our father's age.

I dragged myself downstairs to get the package, shielding my eyes from Stevie's open bedroom door as I hurried past it. I didn't bother wiping the tears from my cheeks as I opened the door and grabbed the package, trudging my way back upstairs. I hadn't looked in the mirror since speaking with the detectives, but I could tell just from the way my tears stung my cheeks that I'd rubbed the skin raw. There was no point in keeping myself together anymore.

I took out my phone and opened my email. I took a sip of coffee just to spit it back out. There was an email from Maria with a link and one single sentence: "Thought you might like to see this."

"Hero Psychic's True Past Uncovered: A Family History of Deceit," read the headline. A high-pitched whine escaped my throat. I'd known deep down I'd be caught eventually, but not in such a public capacity.

"The Crawford family's penchant for scams goes back decades, as far as the early 1900s," wrote Maria. I'd known from the second I saw her that she would be the end of me, yet I'd entertained her anyway. Self-sabotage. That was what I'd been doing all along.

Maria continued, detailing my ancestors' psychic businesses, but the real meat of the article was about my parents. "Bill Crawford, recently released from prison after serving only two years for one charge of breaking and entering and another for vehicular manslaughter, was the face of the Crawford family crime ring for years before his wife was killed in a fatal car accident after fleeing a failed robbery. Despite their daughters' best attempts to distance themselves from their family history by rebranding as the Ravencrofts, their predilection for scams quickly spiraled out of control."

I set my phone down and placed both palms on the table, digging my fingernails into the cheap wood as I let out a scream of frustration.

I'd done my best to separate myself from my parents, and that had only been possible due to my parent's complete lack of marketing the shop. Changing our last name to Ravencroft had been a precarious separation from our past all along, but now it was over.

I had nobody in my life to care for me, and now my only source of income was shot. There would be no reason for anyone to come here, other than to gawk and shame me. I had no other life skills, no degree. Nothing that would help me get another job.

I rested my head on the table and sobbed, not knowing how much time passed before the banging on the front door began.

* * *

"How *dare* you, you little fraud!" Lisa screamed in my face as I stood frozen in the shop. A small group had formed behind her with equally foul, glowering faces. Some of them were unfamiliar, likely Lisa's family, but I recognized the others. They were my clients.

"Lisa, please come inside, and we can talk in private," I pleaded.

"Not a chance," a man behind Lisa said as he held the shop door open, pulling it back so much the hinges gave a sickening pop. "Whatever bullshit you're going to spew to her, we want to hear too. No time to rehearse your lies this time."

The man pushed past me, knocking me into the wall. An ache radiated through my shoulder and up my collarbone, but I just stood there dumbly clutching it, wishing they would all disappear. There was no point in trying to stop them or trying to explain my behavior away like my job truly had purpose. They were all correct.

I was a liar. I was a thief. A scammer. A con artist. A Crawford.

I gave people temporary pleasure and false hope. Sure, I tried my best to give advice so I could help them improve their lives, but in the end, maybe I did more harm than good.

Two people had rushed in after the man, and in the blur of movement I recognized Lisa's son from the photos on her wall. They looked around wildly for a moment, tension building, then finally, a silent decision was made.

The first man took a portion of my stack of tarot cards and ripped them in half, tossing them at me. They fluttered to the ground and he repeated the process again and again, shouting insults and expletives with each rip. Lisa's son swiped his hands along a shelf full of crystals, and I pressed my face against the wall as they fell to the floor, smashing into smithereens.

"I trusted you. I let you into my home," Lisa said. We were both crying now, but hers were tears of righteous anger and violation while mine fell down my cheeks in resignation. "Then you broke into my home, violating my trust. You made everything worse in the long run, you know that, right?"

I held my breath, waiting for her to bring up the replacement ring, but there was no mention of it. I knew damn well that any theft over one thousand dollars in North Carolina constituted a felony, so I kept silent so I wouldn't end up in jail just like my dad. Maybe I belonged in there. What else was I adding to the world other than suffering? All I did was take, take, take, and now the universe was snatching it all back.

"I know you and your little rat of a sister painted over the mold on the ceiling. The neighbor across the street showed me the footage from their doorbell camera. There was never a haunting, was there? Never a spirit or bad energy. I should have listened to my husband. You brought the devil into my home with that nonsense."

Anger boiled in my blood at the mention of my sister. I wanted to tell her that the only reason I'd been able scam her was because she was willfully blind. Her desperation had made her stupid and weak and I'd been there at the right time with the right words. But thoughts of Stevie made the anger fall away, replaced by crippling grief, and I knew that every awful thought I'd just had about Lisa was what I'd heard my dad say about his targets, not what I actually thought about her.

I studied the faces of everyone who'd come to confront me. Their features were contorted with anger, but underneath it all was hurt. They were suffering and I'd preyed on it, and I deserved every bit of this.

I sank to the floor, pressing my side into the wall as I cried, pathetic sobs coming out in breathy heaves. I stared, removed from myself and from the moment, as they tore apart the shop. By the time they were done, nearly everything had been broken, shattered, and ripped to pieces. The velvet curtains had been wrenched from the ceilings and walls, and the shelves teetered over on their sides like a blast had gone through the building.

I hardly noticed them leave, pummeling me with their final exasperated curses as they stomped out of the shop. I sat there for what could have been hours, my body aching from my slumped position as I stared at the flickering overturned lamp on the floor next to me.

What could have been minutes or hours later, I trudged up the stairs and threw myself onto my bed, not caring that my stomach growled as the sun began to set. I knew I wouldn't sleep tonight. Or if I did sleep, it would be infested with nightmares and anxieties, just like it had been for the past weeks. I'd pushed the splintered front door back into the doorframe, but any man or spirit could easily push their way through to wreak havoc on me as I lay helpless in bed. I didn't care.

As I lay there, the sky shifted to pitch-black. I clamped my eyes shut, praying for the sweet bliss of unconsciousness. But my prayers were never answered.

CHAPTER

39

Stevie

THE INCESSANT POUNDING in my temples woke me, making me want to scream. I just needed to sleep. To stay in the dark black bliss of not caring, not knowing, not having to act.

I shifted, a feeling of damp seeping through my clothes. My first thought was that I'd wet the bed—something I hadn't done since I was a little girl. My head ached fiercely, a pain so deep and sharp that I let out a groan. Had I been drinking last night? My head spun as I shifted, my limbs meeting resistance from something on top of me.

There was a foul smell all around me and I gagged, immediately groaning at the pain from all my muscles clenching.

"Jade," I tried to yell out, but my mouth was so dry it came out as a scratchy, ghostly wail.

It was then that I realized that despite my eyes being open, I couldn't see. Memories flashed through my brain, fast and nonsensical. A picnic table, a string of fairy lights above. Where had that been? My father across from me, a look of horror on his face. Why was he scared?

I wasn't blind, which had been my first thought—some sort of freak accident in my sleep. No, there was something blocking my vision. I struggled to raise my hand to my face to feel around, but I could hardly move my arms an inch before being met with resistance.

I was underneath something. Multiple things, I judged by the different weights and textures around me. Tiny pinpoints of faint light shone through above me, filling me with hope.

I used the inch of space around my arms to keep shifting, the process taking ages. Without access to my watch, I had no idea what time it was or how long it took, but there was no way it was shorter than thirty minutes just to clear the debris from my face. I sighed with relief when I pulled away the last piece of debris, confusion lodging itself in my throat like a rock. It was a wad of plastic grocery bags.

Panic began to take hold as I looked around me, unidentifiable lumps blocking my legs from movement with only pinpoints of light to make sense of my surroundings. It was trash. Trash and dirt and filth. I was in a dump, left to rot with unwanted produce and soggy, soiled tissue paper.

More memories came to me as my pulse quickened, worsening my headache to the point where bile rose in my throat. The stench around me wasn't helping either. A thick, meaty hand on the back of my head. A man's rough voice. The sick, crunching *thunk* of my skull against the picnic table before everything went black.

Who was he? My dad had shouted at him, I remembered that much, his voice tight and panicked as they argued. My vision swam as pain rattled through my skull with a vicious force I'd never felt in my life. The muffled sounds of two grown men arguing, then two sets of hands dragging me into a car.

I wasn't going to sit here and try to remember. It took every ounce of energy, which I had nearly none left, as I fought against the debris around me. Inch by inch I cleared space for my legs, removing bags of trash and pieces of broken furniture from my body.

I growled in frustration as trash shifted, falling into the space I created, forcing me to start all over. But at least this time I had my arms and one leg free. After resting for a moment, I started pushing my way up, gagging as unidentifiable liquids dripped into my mouth, the taste rancid and foul.

I pushed my way toward the pinpoints of light, and for a moment, my brain told me my body was done. It had been through enough—just rest, just stay. There was no point. But I fought against the useless voice and continued, my head finally breaking through.

That bastard—whoever the hell he was—had thrown me in a landfill. *A fucking landfill* like I was a piece of trash.

The moon shone bright above as I looked around at the mounds of trash and metal scrap. I had no idea where I was or how to get home. But one thing was for sure. My dad had a part in this—whether this was the end goal or just that he was too chickenshit to stop this man from doing it—and he was going to pay.

CHAPTER

40

Jade

I'D NOT MOVED an inch in hours as I stared at the ceiling, barely enough energy to blink. In the time since I'd learned Stevie had committed suicide, I'd floated outside myself, my mind and my body two separate entities. How could my heart continue to beat, doing its job so steadfastly? How could my lungs be so persistent that they made me keep breathing when I had no desire to at all?

There were noises all around me, and I wasn't sure which of them were real anymore. I was now comfortable in the fact that I had no grip on reality and my sanity had failed me. Maybe it was temporary, caused by grief and shock. Maybe it would last forever. My great-aunt Melody had suffered a psychotic break after her husband died, and she never came out of it. She died thinking there were rats living behind the walls, eating their way through drywall to get to her.

This was nothing like rats, though. It sounded human, like someone was trying to break in. Rattling door handles and thumping fists. Maybe they were previous clients, trying to break in to trash the place again. Maybe I should just let them come up here and end it all for me. A sort of poetic justice. Psychic fraud murdered by victims in her parlor, like a noir novel from the 1950s, the kind that had a beautiful woman fleeing into the night on the cover. Except I wouldn't flee. I would just take what I deserved.

Glass broke downstairs and I shot upright, certain that the noise was real. I'd told myself I'd let it happen, but my damn body was a puppet to the adrenaline, making me move when I just wanted to wallow.

I crept out to the landing, listening to the rustling by the front door. The door handle rattled. Whoever was breaking in was seconds from unlatching the lock and stepping inside.

I took the stairs two at a time, not thinking, just letting my body go into defense mode as I grabbed Stevie's baseball bat and poised myself behind the curtain that separated the stairs from the shop.

The door creaked open. A footstep on the broken glass and then another.

I took a shuddering breath and ripped the curtain back with the bat in my other hand. The urge to scream was rising in my throat, a roar of grief and anger and fear and sheer exhaustion.

I faltered, realizing in that moment that I'd gone fully insane and there was no coming back from this. This was a full mental break.

She stood in front of me, dried blood encrusted in her hair and along the outside of her face. Her clothes were torn and soiled.

It was Stevie.

* * *

"Stevie?" I asked with a whimper. My arms were still holding the baseball bat but had gone limp, the bat extended straight forward at my waist like a dowsing rod.

She didn't answer me, but a groan came out. This wasn't real. Ghosts weren't real, no matter how much money I made off the idea.

She fell to her knees and I raced forward. Even if this was a hallucination, I couldn't just leave her to suffer with her knees pressed into the broken glass. When I touched her shoulder, I expected nothing, maybe a feeling of cold mist, some added detail to my hallucination. Instead, I gasped at the warmth of her skin. So warm it must have been feverish, her skin producing enough heat to break through her cold, damp T-shirt.

Was this real? It had to be. I lifted her up, not caring about the rancid smell coming off her, like days' worth of trash out in the summer heat with the sharp iron tang of blood. She cried softly, like someone about to wake from a nightmare but not quite able to break out of it. Tears rose in my eyes to match hers. There was no denying this was real.

Together we walked over to the tarot table, where I sat her down and raced to turn on lights.

"What—" I began to ask, but I didn't know which question to choose. *What happened? Who did this to you?* There were too many things left unanswered, and I didn't know which to address first.

"Water," Stevie croaked. Without responding, I raced upstairs to get her a glass of water, spilling half of it on myself as I shook uncontrollably. I refilled it and hobbled down the stairs, still dazed, to see Stevie's head hunched over with her chin nearly touching her chest.

I lifted her head up by her chin. "Here." I held the glass of water to her mouth, and she took a timid sip at first, then drank greedily. It had been almost forty-eight hours since she'd left the house. Had she not had any water this entire time?

I asked the question aloud, followed by a string of others, each one more frenzied.

She ignored them. "I need food. And a bath."

While we waited for the tub to fill, Stevie ate a bowl of cereal despite hardly being able to hold the spoon. When her water was ready, I took her to the bathroom and helped her undress.

"Oh, God." I inhaled sharply at the sight of her bruised and cut body. Along with the gash in her head, they were purple and red finger marks along her neck, arms, and torso. To my relief, they didn't go any lower.

"I'm starting to think God doesn't like me very much."

How much of that was our own fault? I deserved every ounce of it, but Stevie had never done anything willingly. She was always dragged along, the innocent accomplice.

After nearly an hour of soaking in the tub as I sat on a stool making sure she didn't fall asleep in the water, I dressed Stevie and put her in bed. Before I could even start rattling off my questions, she spoke.

"I went to confront Dad," she said. I tried to hold back a sigh, but it came out anyway. "His friend did this to me."

"Who?"

"I don't know. I never saw his face. Dad just let it happen. Or maybe he'd wanted it to happen. For all I know, he helped hide my body."

My blood boiled with anger, and heat flushed into my face. I reached out to grip her hand. Her fingernails were still encrusted with dirt like she'd dug herself out of a grave.

"Why did his friend attack you?"

"He said we knew too much and were poking around. He was talking about the councilman's death. I think he and Dad did it together and were afraid we'd get them caught."

I took a breath, trying to digest the information. "And the dirt all over you?"

"They dumped me in a landfill. Covered me with trash."

My mouth hung open dumbly, and for some reason Stevie smiled.

"Why are you smiling? This isn't funny." I was holding back tears.

She giggled, delirious from the past forty-eight hours. "He put me in a fucking trash pile. What the actual fuck?"

We'd entered that strange, rare moment that only happened when people grew too tired or something so dark happened that it felt out of the realm of possibility. A smile crept up on my own face, and despite me fighting it off, Stevie's delirious giggling made me join in.

"This is ridiculous," I huffed out, trying to stifle a laugh.

"Oh my God, our family sucks."

Anyone looking in on this moment would have thought we were insane. One woman battered and bruised, with a sister sitting next to her who only moments before had thought she was having a full psychotic episode. And here we were, somehow laughing.

Eventually it petered out and the seriousness of the situation sank back in. That split second of time after laughter when reality returns with a biting vengeance.

Stevie looked up at me, all hints of levity gone from her face. "We have to make him pay."

I squeezed her hand. "We will."

CHAPTER

41

Stevie

"WHAT MAKES YOU think he's going to be there?" Jade asked. "Don't you think he would . . . I don't know, flee after doing something like this?"

"Fair question, but when has Dad ever won the battle against his own ego? He's so stubborn and egotistical, he probably thinks his hands are already clean."

"I'm sure he does. When the cops told me about your death, they said it was a suicide. Well, all they had was a note. No body."

"I obviously never wrote a fucking note," I seethed. Jade nodded, chewing on the inside of her cheek. "So what are we going to do?" I asked. I already had ideas. Many of them. But I assumed Jade's wouldn't end us up in jail like mine would.

"We do exactly what he taught us. We haunt him."

I blinked at her.

"Remember the client in our neighborhood that Mom had—the widow? How Dad learned her schedule, then would get into her house to shift things around, mess with the electricity, until it got so bad that her children checked her into a nursing home for dementia patients?"

"Yeah, then all her symptoms disappeared as soon as she got there. She never realized what was going on, just said the house must have been haunted."

"Exactly. That's what we're going to do."

"That might be possible, but he's staying in one of his prison buddies' trailers."

"So we learn his schedule just like Dad did the widow's. And he would never expect to see you. When I saw you, I thought you were a ghost and that I'd finally lost my mind. We can use that to our advantage."

Later that night, we drove over to the trailer park. The grounds were quiet and only a few people were outside, but we walked along the outskirts of the estate just to be safe.

Our feet crunched against the leaves and our breath puffed in front of us in thick plumes. I pulled my black hoodie down lower over my face as we approached the trailer my dad was staying in. "This is the one."

There was only one dim light on at the left-hand side of the trailer, and it cast a glow on the faint outline of a man's head.

"I'll circle around and try to see if anyone else is inside," I whispered to Jade. "Keep watch and let me know if you see anyone coming."

I crept around the side of the trailer, immediately tensing as I lost the cover of the trees. Thin, gauzy curtains were drawn over all the windows, but as I moved farther to the left, I could see inside, but only barely. I crept farther out into the open, glancing around for anyone who could catch sight of me.

With a light step—which was not easy on a gravel path—I moved toward the window with the light. I held my breath as I approached out of fear, but when I peeked in, I was holding it out of sheer rage.

There was my father, alone on the couch, watching television while he shoved fistfuls of popcorn in his mouth, interrupted only by greedy gulps of beer. That was not the behavior of a man who'd just watched his daughter be killed, or worse, helped to kill her and frame it as a suicide. Shouldn't he be panicking? Grieving? I wanted so desperately to slam my fists against the windows and watch his pathetic popcorn go flying, or better yet, to stop his heart and watch him drop to his knees.

A car door slammed in the distance, and my dad turned his head at the noise. He was on watch too. As far as I could tell, he was the only one inside. Was he waiting for someone to return?

He turned farther and I dropped below the window, just in time to see the light on the gravel brighten as he peeled back the curtains. My heart thumped in my chest, and I wondered how much more my body could go through before it gave out. I'd never treated it well, and others certainly hadn't either.

The light dimmed on the gravel once more as the curtains fell shut and I waited for my thumping heart to calm before getting to my feet. I made my way around the back of the trailer, trying to peer into windows to take inventory of possibilities. I needed to think like him to take him down.

A window was cracked open in the back, and the stench of a full ashtray hit my nose as I approached. My vision blackened with rage as I took in the sight of a stack of eerily familiar tarot cards. The distinct art style and significant wear around the edges were unmistakable: It was the same stack as the card that was stabbed into our front door.

If he wanted to play the game of fear, he'd finally met his match.

Don't think, just act. I licked my finger and stuck it in the ashtray, coating my fingertip with the foul ashes. It took effort to write upside down, but as I dragged my finger along the windowsill, a thrill crept up my spine, making me forget about the pain still radiating through my body and the sorrow and disappointment infesting my thoughts. When I'd picked him up from prison, I had believed in him. I'd thought he'd truly changed.

I tilted my head to see the finished product from the angle of the person who would eventually find it.

Killer.

After admiring my message, I wiped my hands on my jeans. I froze as a rock flew toward me, landing with a small thud at my feet. I looked around, stepping backward to stick my head around the trailer, out into the open gravel road between the rows of homes. I squinted into the dark woods as another rock flew at me, this time hitting me in the chest. As my eyes adjusted, I saw Jade's frantic waving as she crouched on one knee behind a bush.

"Hurry up!" Jade whispered with hushed fury.

Forceful footsteps approached, angry and quick on the gravel as they neared the trailer. I flung myself onto my hands and knees and rushed to the trees to meet Jade, who was panting with alarm. From this vantage point, we could only see a man's large black boots as he stomped up the trailer stairs and swung open the door, not bothering to greet our dad as he spoke aggressively.

"They stopped by the shop again."

"Who?"

"Who the fuck do you think?"

Neither of them spoke, and I imagined a strained, tense glare being exchanged. My father never backed down for anyone, but the fact that they were still exchanging words instead of fists meant that Dad was afraid of this man, as he should be. After all, he'd watched him kill his daughter. Or so he thought.

The man raised his voice. "I told the cops—again—that I haven't seen you since before your sentence. They're starting to put two and two together because of your daughters."

Dad responded, but he'd lowered his voice to an unintelligible level.

"We need to leave," Jade whispered. We crawled along the trees and bushes. My hands and feet were throbbing with cold, the partial numbness causing me to stumble over even the smallest of branches. I winced as one snapped below my palms, the dry wood releasing a loud crack as it broke into two.

"What was that?" The man's low, deep voice rang out, laced with paranoia.

"Run," I whispered to Jade, and she didn't hesitate. We launched ourselves to our feet and sprinted along the trees, only a few feet between us and the row of trailers to our right.

Dad's trailer door creaked open and slammed shut, footsteps pounding down the stairs.

I couldn't help myself. I glanced back, desperate to get a glimpse of the man who'd thought he took my life. If he had given just an ounce more of his strength, he would have succeeded.

We were nearly to the car, but as I faltered and turned, all I could see was the enormous shape of a man dressed in all black, his face shaded by a baseball cap. Jade's hand gripped my arm and pulled me along to the safety of the car. As Jade sped down the road, the only sound was the engine and our heaving breaths of relief.

* * *

I awoke in the middle of the night to the sound of my own voice. It was the same warbled sentence over and over again.

"Daddy, please help me."

My skin erupted in goose bumps so intensely that my skin ached. I threw back my duvet and touched my feet to the cold floor before cautiously making my way toward the sound.

"Daddy, please help me."

It was coming from the living room. Had I actually died? Had this whole plan with Jade been some postmortem hallucination? This time, the sentence was spoken again, but my voice was lower and warped. "Daddy, please help me."

I swung around the doorway of the living room, only to see Jade sitting on the floor next to the coffee table with a tape recorder and some of our séance equipment in front of her. Their plastic shells were still broken but taped together, barely restraining the mess of jumbled wires inside.

"What the hell is this?" I asked.

Jade jumped, nearly spilling the cup of coffee on the floor next to her.

"It's almost two in the morning," I said when she didn't answer. Her hand was over her chest as she slowed her breathing.

"I know. You were having nightmares. Crying out for help, yelling. I couldn't sleep. But it gave me an idea." She pressed play with a devious smile as my voice rang out again, slightly tinny and small like a child this time.

"Daddy, please help me."

I shivered at the sound of my own desperation.

"We're going to play this while he sleeps. This is the pièce de résistance."

"That's horrible. I love it."

"Everything before this is small potatoes. This is what will send him over the edge."

I rested my hand on her head. "Let's get started."

* * *

Over the next three days, Jade and I slunk into the trailer park like ghouls, wreaking havoc on our father. Each time he left the trailer, he came back to his items moved or missing. We began by moving his everyday items and furniture just a few inches—enough to disrupt his muscle memory and throw him off. Then we graduated to bigger tricks, like stacking items in precarious towers that teetered to the ground as soon as he entered the room.

We wrote messages with soapy fingers on the bathroom mirror so he was greeted with curses and hexes as he stepped out of the steaming shower. If we had anything to do with it, he would never feel clean again.

It had been child's play to tamper with the trailer's electricity. We made the lights flicker as he ate microwaved dinners in front of the TV every night and turned on all the lights while he was sleeping. By today, the third day of our haunting, he was exhausted and paranoid.

"Do the speakers," I ordered, relishing in the power of being the one to finally make a command.

Every night, we'd been opening the trailer windows while he slept, ensuring he'd have a poor night's sleep from the freezing cold along with the eerie sensation of cold spots in the trailer. On the first night of opening the windows, I'd reached inside, connected my phone to his speaker's Bluetooth. We'd worked quickly while Dad shivered in his sleep. Even though his friend was routinely nowhere to be seen, every preparation or trick we pulled to haunt Dad was coated with a thick layer of terror that we'd be caught. Nevertheless, the joy behind torturing Dad still shone through.

Jade connected to the speaker, and it began to play. Dad gripped the couch cushions next to him as his wedding song began to play: Roberta Flack's "The First Time Ever I Saw Your Face," which we'd added reverb to and slowed down.

"Wonder if he remembers their anniversary was last week," Jade whispered with a sneer.

"He does now."

He rushed to turn the speaker off, only to stumble to the floor. He scrambled to his knees and groped for the power button.

"Lights," I ordered.

Jade yanked on the long extension cord we'd rigged up to the trailer, and the power shuddered out—everything except for the speaker, which had a rechargeable battery. It was lucky our dad had such lovely, caring daughters who had remembered to charge it for him.

"What the fuck!" he yelled as he jumped to his feet. He stumbled over empty bottles, the glass tinkering under his panicked steps.

The song stuttered out, repeating "your face" again and again. Dad whimpered. I smiled as Jade rewound the song over and over until even I began to find it chilling. I rubbed the goose bumps from my arms as I watched him cry.

They were the same silent, pathetic tears he had been crying for the last few days, only keeping it together when his mysterious friend came around. As soon as he was alone, he cowered with fear and what I hoped was guilt. The TV stayed on but the food gradually disappeared, only to be replaced by cigarettes and more bottles of liquor that he left scattered around the trailer at his feet.

I was ready. It was time.

"Do it," I told Jade. My heart beat in my chest, and I welcomed the heady rush of blood coursing through me. This was the revenge I'd been looking for.

Jade switched the audio to the digital recorder and pressed play. There was a moment of silence, and Dad released his hands from his ears, only to be met by my voice.

"Daddy, please help me."

CHAPTER 42

Jade

"DADDY, PLEASE HELP me," begged Stevie's distorted voice for the fiftieth time.

"Please!" Dad shouted inside the trailer. "I can't fucking take this anymore!" His voice ricocheted off the walls, sending forest creatures skittering deeper into the woods. He screamed in frustration as he threw an empty liquor bottle at the wall.

The noise of multiple trailer doors opening then shutting would have been comical in any other situation—their unabashed nosiness, the universal desire to eavesdrop. But now we needed them gone.

"Stop the recording. He's had enough," I told Stevie.

Her eyes sparkled against the light of the faraway streetlamps, reveling in the sound of her own pitiful voice lashing our father with pain. For a moment I thought she wasn't going to listen. But she turned it off, disappointment wiping the glint from her eyes.

"I'm sorry," he wailed now, more softly than his previous shouts. A woman across the gravel street went back into her house, assuming this was just another case of a drunken temper tantrum. "I'm so sorry."

Without even having to ask, Stevie reconnected the trailer's power, sending the lights shuddering back on. There was only one dim light on inside, but it was enough for us to see the shape of him sitting on the couch, his head in his hands.

"My baby girl," he cried out, then spoke no more, just silently crying.

"Let's go talk to him," Stevie whispered.

"What? No."

"Let's see what he has to say. I'm going with or without you." She stood and marched to the front door, opening without a knock. I trailed behind her, rushing to meet her inside.

"No, no. God, no," Dad wailed as he took in the sight of Stevie standing in his doorway, still and furious. She was wearing all black, and the dim light from the single lamp gave her the appearance of a reaper-like specter.

"How is this happening?" He clutched his hands in his thinning hair as he stared at her in shock.

"How could you do this to me?" Stevie growled at him.

"Stevie? Oh God, I'm losing it." He rubbed his eyes, then smacked his palms into his forehead. "I'm losing my fucking mind."

My eyes darted around, taking in the crumpled beer cans and ashtrays filled with cigarettes. In the window were the remnants of Stevie's message written in ashes: *Killer*.

He rubbed his eyes. "What the hell is happening?"

"You and your friend should have buried me deeper," Stevie said with a snarl.

"I . . . you weren't breathing when I checked. Your lips were blue. I tried to stop him—I begged him to take you to the hospital, but he told me it was too late, that you were already dead. I almost ended up in the dump with you." Judging by the bruises covering his face and the long, oozing split in his lip, he was telling the truth.

"Stevie, sit down. We all need to talk. Calmly," I said.

Dad's head hung low, his fingers shakily rising to wipe away a tear. He raised his gaze. "I tried to convince him that you two knew nothing, that your tip to the cops was just a shot in the dark for the reward money. But he wouldn't let it go. I did everything I could to keep you safe, but it wasn't enough."

"Everything you could? Seriously?" Stevie bit back. Dad started to speak, but she interrupted him. "Who was he, anyway? Who did this to me?" Stevie pointed at the gash on her forehead that led to a purple-and-blue bruise around both eyes and into her cheekbones.

"It was Adam."

The air was sucked out of the room, and neither Stevie nor I dared to take a breath. My mouth grew dry, and when I spoke, my tongue stuck to the roof of my mouth. "Adam Pulaski? There's no way. He's antisocial, but he would never do that."

"Why? Because you used to date his brother? People change," he said pointedly. "When's the last time you two even spoke?"

"Last week. He was with the crew that helped repair some water damage at the shop."

He sighed and rubbed his eyes. "I told him to stay away from you both. A bunch of fucking good that did." He motioned to Stevie's face, then his. "Not sure how he even got in with that crew. He's never done maintenance or construction in his life. Not exactly his skill set."

We all sat in silence, and the sound of us each taking anxious breaths was growing to be too much. When Dad spoke, it was too loud. Too desperate. "You have to forgive me. I tried to protect you. I tried to keep him away from you, but he kept threatening to come after you."

"So was it him who was fucking with the shop? Who stabbed the tarot card into our front door and stole our money?"

"The more you talked to the police and the media, the more aggravated Adam got. He wanted to scare you off." He rubbed his eyes roughly. "He was convinced you had some sort of proof related to Nichols' murder hidden in the shop—maybe he thought I gave you something to hide there, I don't know. So he wrecked the shop looking for it. Thinking the reward money might be there was just an added bonus."

"How'd he get in?" I asked, accusation simmering underneath.

"He had a key. I don't know how he got it."

The repairs, I realized. Both my dad and Chris had seemed so surprised to learn he was on the crew for our ceiling repairs; then he'd miraculously disappeared, and the rest of the crew had no idea who he was. He was never supposed to be there at all. He got what he needed, then got out.

"How did Adam drag you into this? Why didn't you just say no?"

Dad sighed. "He was blackmailing me."

"With what? What did he have over you?" Stevie asked.

"I was there. When he killed Nichols."

"You looked me dead in the eye and told me you didn't kill him," Stevie said in disbelief.

"I didn't kill him. When I got out of prison, the Pulaskis let me use Adam's room, just until I found my own place. One day at the crack of dawn, Adam woke me up and asked me for a ride. Didn't say what for, but I figured I owed him because I'd been sleeping in his bed, after all."

Dad continued. "So he's just sitting in the passenger seat, telling me what turns to take, still no explanation. When we got to Salem Lake, he told me to pull into the parking lot and wait.

I didn't realize what we were there for until he came back to the car, dragging the councilman by his ankles."

"Why did he do it?"

"Burying his family's bad behavior wasn't the only crooked thing Nichols did. He took under-the-table payments all the time to help people get their way. Anything from expedited permits to reduced jail time. His hands were filthy, and I'm surprised someone didn't get to him sooner."

"So Adam paid him for something? What?"

"Not Adam. When his friend got arrested, Nichols took money and said he'd get his charge dropped, but never did. His friend went to prison a couple thousand dollars poorer, and only a few months later . . ." Dad dragged his thumb along his neck. "So Adam went after Nichols."

"Jesus. Can't you just call the police and tell them what he did?" I asked.

"He has proof that could put me away forever, Jade. He took Nichols' wallet and his wedding band and made me keep it here in the trailer. He wiped his prints and told me if I ever stepped out of line, he'd tell the cops I did it and then he'd come after you. He comes by randomly to make sure I haven't tossed them. I'm under his thumb, at least until the investigation is over and he tosses the evidence."

It was astonishing to see him as a pawn in someone else's scheme, just like we had been for him when we were children. Just like Mom had always been and just like all the women in my family centuries back.

"Does Adam have anything to do with Ian Stellman being missing?" I asked. Dad's eyes widened as he glanced at Stevie. "I know what he did to Stevie. Don't bullshit me."

He cleared his throat. "No. Adam doesn't care about Stellman. Just the councilman."

I sighed, not willing to spend any more energy worrying about where Ian Stellman was. We had more important things to think about: not just staying out of prison, but being able to afford to live. "Is there any way we can get the money back? Or is it already gone?" As I spoke, Dad gave a tired smile. "What's that look for?"

"Adam hadn't told me he'd been breaking into the shop, but one night he'd been drinking and let it slip. He was breaking in almost every night looking for it, and I knew he had to be close to finding the money, or even close enough to losing his shit and hurting you two. Stevie let slip that y'all hid it in a soup can just like your mom, so I took the money before he could. It's safe. You'll get it back."

"Father-of-the-fucking-year award," Stevie grumbled, and stood, pacing in a circle like a caged animal. "You couldn't have just told us everything? For once in your life just be honest?"

"The more you knew, the more danger you'd be in. Even if you'd had all the information laid out in front of you, it's not like the police would believe you without any proof."

"You've kept me in the dark before, and look how that turned out," I said as I made eye contact with Stevie, who winced.

"I know I've made mistakes before and I've put my family in harm's way, but it's never been on purpose. I know I'm responsible for your mother's death, but it was because I was trying to protect you," he said to Stevie. "In the wrong way, I see that now, but I'm trying to learn what the right way is. I want to learn how to be a good father. But you have to let me."

As messed up as this all was, the part of my brain that wanted to believe in him was overtaking every ounce of logic and resentment. I didn't want him to know I was on the verge of understanding and maybe even forgiveness. Not yet. I didn't know if there was any coming back from this fully, but we could try, no matter how painful it was.

We sat in silence, Stevie and I silently asking each other *Do we let him?* Stevie nodded. "Here's what's going to happen. You're going to sit here and call Adam, tell him you have a problem and he needs to come over."

He looked at me with wild, wide eyes. "I don't want you anywhere near him. He's dangerous."

"We won't be anywhere near him. But the cops will."

"No. No way, I don't like this. He'll take me down with him."

Stevie retorted, "You said he made you keep some of Nichols' stuff—we take that to the police station and that's how we convince them to help us."

"Go get Nichols' stuff," I said. "Wipe your prints and use gloves to put them in a bag. We'll drop it off at the police station. Time to submit another tip, everyone."

C H A P T E R

43

Jade

WOOLRIDGE AND MCCADE stood in front of us, their faces drained of color. The Ziploc bag of Nichols's belongings was growing slick in my hand, and without asking, Stevie reached out and loosened it from my tight grip.

"She told you I didn't write the note," she said as she placed the bag on McCade's desk.

Both detectives were studying Stevie, and I was torn between wanting to berate them for not listening and wanting to cry. I landed somewhere in the middle, my chin quivering. "We know who killed the councilman, and they tried to kill Stevie too," I spat out.

The detectives reeled back, and I took a steadying breath as I continued to explain Adam's link to the councilman and his attempt to avenge his friend's death. To my surprise, Woolridge's eyes were still wide and his cheeks were flushed with what I could only imagine was embarrassment. I pictured him at his desk behind mountains of paperwork, being forced to document how badly he'd bungled the case.

"Well, I can't say I've ever experienced anything like this in my career. This is an unfortunate situation for your family," Woolridge said.

Stevie huffed. "Is that how detectives apologize?"

I put my hand on her arm to quiet her. We couldn't afford an argument right now. "You can make it up to us. We need your help."

* * *

Back at Dad's trailer, I wasn't able to sit still as we went over the plan one final time. We'd gone over the details at least fifty times, and in just a few minutes, Dad would light the fire that started it off.

"Are you ready?" I asked him.

"Yes, go in my bedroom and lock the door. He has no reason to go in there." He shooed us off with an authoritative voice, despite his hands shaking as he picked up his phone. Stevie and I were nervous too, but the fact that the police were aware of what Adam had done and who was in danger put me at ease. They said with one call, they would be here in less than ten minutes. They technically couldn't go after Adam without a confession or proof he was actively committing a crime. So that's exactly what we were going to do: get a confession, then call the police to report Adam for trespassing. We'd failed at this with Stellman, but we weren't going to this time. We couldn't.

Stevie and I locked the door and sat between the bed and the wall. Stevie's hand hovered by the old landline on Dad's nightstand, ready to dial 911 at the first sign of trouble.

"I need you to get over here now," Dad said into his cell phone. "It looks like someone broke into the trailer."

It technically wasn't a lie—Stevie and I *had* broken in the first time, after all. We barely breathed until we heard boots stomping up the stairs twenty minutes later.

"What happened?" Adam asked breathlessly.

"They wrecked the place. I think they got into the safe," Dad said.

"That's where Nichols' stuff—"

"I know," Dad interrupted.

More footsteps as Adam stomped around the trailer, taking inventory of possible missing items or damage.

"Goddammit, you're right. They took everything. We're fucked. We're so fucked." The panic in his voice was clear even through the walls, the anxiety tightening his throat to the point of gasping for air. I could picture his face contorted in frustration, so eerily similar to Chris's.

More footsteps. Were they coming toward us? "They didn't touch anything in my room," my father said.

The encroaching footsteps faltered. "Oh really? Thought you said they'd wrecked the place."

"Yeah . . . why are you giving me that look?"

"How convenient for you that none of your shit's wrecked. You're one lucky guy." The doorknob rattled and my mouth grew dry, my heart racing. Stevie shivered next to me. "Why's the door locked?"

My dad had started stuttering, trying to explain, when Adam threw himself into the door with a crashing thud, so loud that I nearly screamed.

"You need to leave," my dad shouted, trying and failing to sound authoritative. It didn't matter, though. We just needed to have it on record that he'd told Adam to leave and Adam had refused so 911 would have cause to dispatch officers.

"Stevie," I whispered, hoping she remembered the next steps to the plan.

Once more, he threw his weight into the door, but it resisted. Without thinking I rushed to the door and pushed my palms against it, not bothering to do it quietly. There was a huff of surprise on the other side of the door, followed by a quiet laugh that slowly grew louder.

"Well, well, well. Looks like our little burglar is still inside. Couldn't find a way out, huh?" he shouted into the door. "Or is daddy's little assistant staying for a family sleepover?"

With the last word he shoved himself into the door one final time. The cheap wood around the lock splintered and gave way. I braced against the door, trying to keep it closed, but I was no match for his strength. He had over one hundred pounds on me, but I pushed back anyways. I couldn't let him hurt Stevie. My dad could fend for himself, but Stevie couldn't.

I braced against his next push as he slid my body across the floor effortlessly and I fell to the floor. The door was open enough now for him to get in. I glanced back, relieved to see Stevie had hidden and that the landline was missing from the bedside table.

"Hello, Jade. Can't say I'm surprised to see you here." Adam took two steps and gripped me by my hair, dragging me up to my feet. The shock of it made me gasp, and I clawed at the doorframe, then the kitchen counter as he dragged me out into the living room and pushed me down into a chair. My dad sat across from me, resisting the urge to stand and fight.

"You sure didn't think it through when you submitted that anonymous tip, did you?" Adam asked. I didn't respond. "No thoughts running through that pretty head of yours, huh?"

My dad was pale with worry, but I met his eye, urging him to keep to the plan. Let Adam think he was in control. If Stevie had followed through with her part of the plan, the police would be here in less than ten minutes now. That's all I had to survive. Ten minutes.

"Why are you doing this?" I said through gritted teeth as he shoved me into a chair and stood behind me, his meaty hands pressing down on my shoulders. My collarbones ached from the pressure, and I squirmed underneath him.

"Because you don't know how to mind your fucking business." With the last biting statement, he dug his fingertips into my collarbone and I yelped, trying to squirm away. He lowered his face to my ear. "Don't even think about moving, or I'll tie you to the fucking chair." The calmness in his voice was more chilling than the actual threat.

He sat on the couch next to my father and eyed me sitting still in my chair and gave a sickly-sweet smile. "Good girl, sitting there like you were asked. You're as much of a pushover as your father." He slapped him on the back like this was a family barbecue.

"Whatever you think is going on here, I can assure you that you're wrong," I said, doing my best to sound confident, although I was on the verge of tears. I'd never experienced violence from another man like that. Sure, I'd been groped, but the feeling of being dragged around like a weightless doll made me feel so powerless that I wondered what we were even trying to accomplish here. There was no way we could best this man when he could clearly wring my neck with little to no effort.

"So after all these weeks of you trying to take me down, I'm supposed to just believe that you were here, hanging out in your dad's bedroom—which if that's true, that's fucking weird, by the way—when your dad calls me and tells me I've been robbed?"

I gulped and my dad spoke, but Adam held up his hand. "Shut the fuck up," he said calmly, as though he were asking a waiter for a glass of water.

"I wasn't trying to get you in trouble. I just called the tip line for the reward money, and it was a lucky guess."

"Sounds pretty unlucky to me with the way this is all going to end for you two." He turned to my dad and smiled like he was about to tell a joke. "Do you realize how much of a fucking pain in the ass you've become? I mean, it's truly amazing."

How much time had passed? Surely at least five minutes. Only five or less left to go. I needed to get Adam to confess, but more than that I needed to keep him calm enough so he didn't do anything to me or my dad. Or worse, discover that Stevie was still hiding in the bedroom—the same Stevie he still believed was dead.

"Whose wallet and ring was in your safe?" I asked with a gulp. It was a risky question, but I was running out of time. "You sounded worried—maybe I can help."

"You know. Don't you, Jade?"

Subconsciously, my eyes darted to the coffee table, where my phone was duct taped to the underside, recording and waiting for a confession. He must have followed my gaze and paused. He tilted his head.

"What are you looking at?" he asked pleasantly, his voice at odds with his clenched teeth and veiny forehead. I swore I could see his heartbeat in the large vein shooting from the crown of his head to his eyebrow. He was about to snap.

"Nothing," I answered, trying to sound as casual as he did. "I'm sorry, you're just making me nervous."

My stomach dropped as he jumped up and lifted the table a few inches off the floor and peeked below. When he finally spoke, a deep, violent rage boiled beneath and my body readied itself to flee, even though I couldn't. "You fucking Crawfords. Like fucking rats always sneaking around, taking whatever you want. How long has this been here?" He ripped the phone off and flipped the table over completely.

He shut the recording off, then turned and gripped my dad by his shirt collar and reeled his other fist back, landing one solid punch to his jaw with a sickening crunch.

Two minutes. Surely there's less than two minutes until the police get here. If they come at all.

"You want me to do to you what I did to fucking Thomas Nichols?" He punched my dad again. "I already killed one daughter. Do you want me to kill another? Make you watch before I kill you?"

Despite the fear coursing through my body, I glanced at the floor under my father's seat. Knowing Adam might find my phone, we'd started a voice recording on Dad's phone and hid it under the chair. This was our last chance to get the recording, or we would look even more guilty than we had before.

"*You want me to do to you what I did to fucking Thomas Nichols?*" We'd gotten it. We'd gotten the confession. Not just for Nichols, but his attempt to kill Stevie, who he had no idea was hiding under my dad's bed, very much alive. We had the confession—as long as he didn't find Dad's phone.

Adam reeled back again, punching my father so hard he went limp. If he didn't stop, he would kill him.

"Stop!" I launched myself at him, trying to pull his arms away, but it was no use. I clung onto his back, so desperate that

I wasn't thinking about the outcome of this or how stupid it was for me to try to overpower him.

I thought I heard the crunch of tires on gravel in the distance, but there was no time to keep listening before he threw me off and my tailbone slammed into the floor, the back of my head hitting the chair's armrest on the way down.

* * *

I groaned in pain, my vision skittering. There was an explosion of noise, and I wondered if this was what dying was. Not a gentle pull toward the light but a violent auditory hallucination of all the moments in your life, experienced all at once.

There was light, but no, wait. It was a flashlight, beaming on my face through the window. I followed it as it trailed over my father's face. The noises continued, the shouts of numerous people so loud that I didn't bother following.

"Adam Pulaski, you're under arrest," a policeman shouted. I let loose a sigh of relief, wanting it all to end here. But instead of finality, there was a heightened tinge of desperation in the room—an increase in panicked breaths and obstinate arguing.

I pushed myself up to sitting and was hit with a wave of vertigo. I turned, noticing a bloody mark on the wooden armrest where I'd struck my head. I tried to count the amount of police in the trailer, but my vision doubled, making it impossible. I pushed myself out of the way, pressing my back into the wall, and breathed out a sigh of relief.

There was a blur of movement as Adam tried to push his way through the police in the trailer. Sounds erupted from every angle—Adam's fists making contact with the officers, then his struggled breathing as they slammed him to the ground. A metallic click of handcuffs accompanied by chatter on the police radio while sirens sang in the background. It all sounded so beautiful. It sounded like relief.

We'd done it. We'd gotten Adam's confession on tape, and although the three of us were covered in wounds, both physical and emotional, we'd made it out alive. It was over.

EPILOGUE

Stevie

Although the police said his confession wouldn't have held up in court on its own, the police had found enough evidence on their own to send Adam away for a very long time. Adam had left a trail of data with his cell phone location, linking him to not only the location where Nichols's body had been found but to weeks before when he'd been following Nichols, waiting for the right moment to strike. But the final nail in the coffin had been the single hair on Nichols's body that they were able to match to Adam. Despite Adam constantly telling the police that my father had helped cover up the murder, there wasn't enough proof to pin anything on my dad.

It was nearly a full year later and he hadn't been sentenced yet, and I dreaded the day we would be dragged into court just to relive this all again. Although, I did crave the moment where he would lay eyes on me, whom he still thought dead—a fact that Jade and I found hilarious. His attacks on my family would only add to his sentence, something that brought me great joy as I fell asleep each night.

The Pulaskis, including Jade's ex, Chris, had been horrified to hear what Adam had done. They were constantly trying to make it up to us, leaving dishes of pierogis and potato pancakes at our new apartment that the three of us shared.

After deciding she couldn't cheat people anymore, Jade sold the shop and got the normal, boring job she'd always craved at a local grocery store. Even though she'd always told herself she was helping her former clients, we both knew it was still dishonest at its core. She didn't want to stay in this position forever, but maybe somewhere down the line she'd realize what she really wanted to do with her life. Until then, we were both happy with the pleasant mundanity.

Despite enjoying the direction her life was taking, she still spoke often about Daniel. Jade had come to terms with the fact that he would probably never forgive her and certainly never want to speak to her again, but as she went on first dates and came home rolling her eyes with disappointment, it was clear her guilt still brutalized her and she might never get over what could have been with Daniel. Despite their distance, he still agreed to help me get affordable therapy, and I was now having weekly appointments with his coworker at a severely reduced rate. I was still amazed that he hadn't asked for anything in return. No negotiation. Just kindness.

My dad had been disappointed at our career change at first, but he was slowly coming to terms with it. Together, the three of us had normal jobs and normal lives, although the new friends I was making at school thought it was highly abnormal for our dad to be paying *us* rent. But it was working well so far, and it was only until he could get his own place. And yes, the rent money he paid went to the bank and not to a can of soup hidden in the pantry. Everything was going to be blissfully normal from here on out. No tarot cards, no cleansings or palm readings. No more revenge.

Now, as I sat at the breakfast table while Jade got ready for work, I stared down at the newspaper Dad had silently placed in front of me.

"The Nichols-Stellman Family Curse Continues: Local Teacher Takes Own Life."

The reporter—luckily not the one that had practically hunted Jade and I—detailed the sordid history of the Nichols and Stellman family, uncovering more of Nichols's under-the-table deals with local criminals.

The article went on to describe Stellman's fall from grace as a respected teacher—I scoffed at the term, glad I could finally laugh instead of cry at the mention of him. After the councilman was found dead—Stellman's cousin and close friend since birth—Stellman's family was quoted describing his increase in drinking and withdrawal from everyone around him.

"He spent every night alone, drinking his pain away," his mother was quoted as saying.

Poor Stellman, suddenly showing up at my workplace, begging for forgiveness. Mumbling a pathetic, slurred apology at me. "I'm sorry, Stevie," he'd said. "It was wrong. I was wrong."

The first time he'd said it, I'd been so taken aback that I'd pitied him. After the tenth time, I'd grown angry at his meager tears. *I* was supposed to be the one crying. *I'd* been the innocent, ignorant girl he'd taken advantage of. Why should I feel bad for him? Why should I forgive him? He hadn't come back to the bar after his reading at the shop, but I'd only grown angrier.

The look in my dad's eyes as he'd given me the paper said it all. He was proud of me. Of what we did and what we finished. And I was proud too. Stellman deserved what Dad and I did to him—the revenge we finally got for me and those other girls. For Mom. For Dad's time in jail. A year later, and everyone still believed he'd taken his own life. But Dad and I knew the truth, and we would take that to our graves.

I tucked the newspaper away as Jade and Dad left for work. Chris Pulaski had gotten him work in repairs, ironically working for the same company that fixed the shop's ceiling. In an hour I had class, something I was still nervous for despite this being the third week of my first semester. After the dust settled with Adam, I'd called the school and asked for a year-long deferral.

We were all breaking our habits, trying to be better. Maybe deep down we were the same, but we were making an effort to be better people and finally move on.

We all deserved a second chance.

Well, most of us.

ACKNOWLEDGMENTS

I'D FIRST LIKE to thank my agent, Katie Shea Boutillier, for her guidance, support, and patience. Additional gratitude is owed to Rachel Saylor, whose brainstorming and spot-on opinions helped my infant drafts turn into a grown manuscript. To Holly Ingraham, who edited this book with me until nearly the end, and to Thaisheemarie Fantauzzi Perez, who arrived in time to see the book home—your help and guidance are appreciated every step of the way. Thank you to my copyeditor, Rachel Keith, for your keen eye and comb that is expertly fine-toothed. I'm grateful for the artistic work of Dana Steele, who executed my vision for the cover. And to the rest of my Crooked Lane team, thank you for your hard work behind the scenes to bring this book to fruition.

Thank you to my extended family and friends, especially the Deckers, the Trents and Dawn, the Turners, the MacFarlanes, and the Boyds. To my best friends from college who love me no matter the miles in between: Catherine Anne, Margaret, and Hilary, with additional thanks to Hilary's husband Peter for help with Polish nicknames. Your support and excitement has spread to new readers, and I couldn't thank you enough for being my "street team." A huge thank-you to the lovely author Shannon Morgan for help with my epilogue; your perspective is exactly what was needed when I was blinded by stubborn myopia. To my readers, thank you for taking valuable time out of your lives to spend time with my stories. To those of you who have reached out after reading *The Engagement Party*, you have no idea how much your kind words bolstered me to keep going and have confidence.

And finally, but most importantly, thank you to my family. To my husband, Tyler, thank you for cheering me on whenever I second-guessed myself and for listening to me huff and puff through brainstorming sessions while walking through the neighborhood. To my children, Ellie and Roman, don't tell my books, but you're the best thing I've ever created.

A VERY COLD WINTER

Fausta Cialente

Translated from the Italian by
Julia Nelsen

Introduction by
Claudia Durastanti

Published by Transit Books
1250 Addison St #103, Berkeley, CA 94702
www.transitbooks.org

ISBN: 979-8-893380-23-1 (paperback)
Cover design by Jared Bartman | Typesetting by Transit Books
Printed in the United States of America

9 8 7 6 5 4 3 2 1

Introduction

As World War II ended, Italian publishing houses found themselves flooded with memoirs and semi-fictional accounts of what had happened to the country. Neorealism quickly became the lens through which writers and directors were keen to represent the stories of the poor and the working class: most of these accounts were based on first-hand experience or inspired by conversations in bars and public spaces. Italian cities were now occupied by an army of storytellers writing novels they were never going to publish, but their contribution was essential in establishing a new artistic form. One of the storytellers that did publish a war novel was the young Italo Calvino: his debut, *The Path to the Spiders' Nests* (published in 1947, when Calvino was twenty-three), is a typical product of that time. It's a tale of the Italian Resistance seen, fable-like, through the eyes of a child. Almost twenty years later, when Einaudi reissued the novel, Calvino wrote a famous introduction to reconsider what neorealism had done to fiction. He now felt that his debut novel was born anonymously from the "general atmosphere of an era." Part of him wished he hadn't given away his memories of World War II so early; the war should have been kept safe for his final book. It seems that Calvino was wondering about a larger question: how does war age in the mind of the artist? And how long does it take for a war to get into a novel properly? Although neorealism might provide a coherent perspective of Italian literature in the aftermath of war, reading a literary map drawn around conflicts can be a fractured experience. One could assume that nothing and everything happened at the same time. This is true for our ancestors as much as for us—forgetfulness is not a privilege acquired with distance. The objectivity of war is blurred by one's own perception of time and the wavering faith in what's truly conveyable through language. Sometimes dreams and nightmares go undercover as useless spies until they resurface in times of peace. How long does it take for a war to get into a novel? The answer is usually too late, or too soon. This is why, perhaps, Calvino had his regrets. Declaring neorealism over, Calvino admitted that the true and important war novels came much later, especially Beppe Fenoglio's *Una questione privata* (*A Private Affair*, 1963) and *Il partigiano Johnny* (*Johnny the Partisan*, 1968). His reasoning was straightforward: in order to fill the gap between the reality of war and its representation, a writer needed time and space to distill collective memories into something more sophisticated and unique.

But timing was more complicated than that: sometimes war novels could feel out of place simply because as the years went by, people wanted to move away from war altogether, maybe they wanted to forget. For Primo Levi, in fact, the question was less about when a book about war should be written and instead when it should be published. The manuscript for his memoir *Se questo è un uomo* (*If This Is a Man*), about his arrest and incarceration in Auschwitz, was turned down by both Natalia Ginzburg and Cesare Pavese for publication in 1947, with the thinking that it was still too close to the war for such an account. A small press took the book on instead, until it was finally reissued in 1958 with a larger house. Looking back at what happened, Natalia Ginzburg would later say, "We've been guilty imbeciles."

Women writers were also trying to capture the collective experience of war. In 1949, Alba de Céspedes published *Dalla parte di lei* (*Her Side of the Story*, originally published in English in 1952 with a different title, *Best of Husbands)*, an ingenious book about a woman's recognition of life through the fascist and partisan years and what came next. In over five-hundred pages, later to be cut and re-edited by the author herself, de Céspedes played with the conventions of the coming of age, romance, and noir novel to deliver an entirely credible female character. For women writers, engaging with autobiography in the general context of neorealism could feel tricky and encourage literary critics to dismiss their work under the pretense that it was too personal, domestic, akin to a journal. This is why de Céspedes went for a bulky novel and a "parallel" autobiography, to prevent its content from being weaponized against her. No wonder, then, that it took Natalia Ginzburg quite some time to open herself to the possibilities of explicit autobiography: in her own words, she approached the genre with slow "wolf steps," circling around it for a long time. After several first-person novels, *Le piccole virtù* (*The Little Virtues*, 1962) and *Lessico famigliare* (*Family Lexicon*, 1963) arrived: both are unforgettable lessons in how to use a family as a narrative device to enter a larger collectiveness. One feels this especially in *Inverno in Abruzzo* (*Winter in the Abruzzi*), a wounded elegy on displacement and reinventing families after the death of her husband Leone Ginzburg. It might be the reason why Ginzburg's first judgment on Primo Levi's memoir had been too harsh: she'd recently lost her husband to the fascist regime, and Levi's manuscript might have felt too raw. Looking back on the Neorealist period, it feels like women writing at the time were keener on going undercover or mixing different literary genres.

A Very Cold Winter is Fausta Cialente's interpretation of war, family, and of womanhood.

The novel came out in 1966, after a five-year hiatus. Her previous book, *Ballata levantina* (*The Levantines*), lost the prestigious Strega Prize to Raffaele La Capria by a single vote in 1961. Cialente was careful to stay outside of literary society and took her time with the next project, which traded the crowded streets of Alexandria for an entirely new setting: an occupied attic in derelict Milan, in 1946.

The appearance of *A Very Cold Winter* must have been a very curious sight.

The avant-garde literary movement Gruppo 63 was waging an open battle against any form of writing that was sentimental: Umberto Eco, Edoardo Sanguineti, and Nanni Balestrini, among others, were trying to kill the novel just like the French (it didn't go too well in either country). Everything revolving around intimate relationships was labeled as romance (and one could only wonder what Gruppo 63 would say about the pervasiveness of romance today). To them, even Elsa Morante was writing romance—her war novel, *La storia* (*History*), came out in 1974 and was massacred by intellectuals and beloved by readers—as well as Giorgio Bassani: it was not a gender-based critique, but it was powerfully misogynistic all the same. And yet, two years ahead of the counterculture movement and the revolution of radical feminism—Carla Lonzi and the Rivolta Femminile would come to the forefront in 1970—Fausta Cialente managed to write a postwar novel centered on a female character that didn't feel like a throwback. How did she manage to achieve this? Cialente is agonizingly prophetical in her quietness. Her focus is on the narrative's texture; her patterns are recognizable and dense with matter.

The book takes place in an attic in Milan, a year after the Liberation. In a city heavily bombed by the Nazis, war destroyed the traditional family nucleus that would reaggregate in larger and amorphous formations, where strangers or distant relatives were forced to live in close quarters. (In cities like Milan, where this practice is currently resurfacing among people in their forties and fifties in response to the expensive rent market, the setting of *A Very Cold Winter* is now fashionably called "co-living.")

Camilla, the reluctant matriarch of the house, calls it *albergo dei poveri*, a poorhouse, where she lives with her three children—two daughters, Alba and Lalla, and a son, Guido—Regina, a young mother who just had a baby with Camilla's late nephew Nicola; another spiritless nephew, Arrigo, married to a mannered French-speaking girl named Milena. And then two neighbors: Enzo, a young Italian anarchist born and raised in Egypt who already appeared in *Ballata levantina*, and Rosso, the country gentleman. (Cialente's brother, Renato, was a very successful actor who died in a car crash after playing in Maxim Gorky's *The Lower Depths* at the Teatro Argentina. She probably had this episode in mind when she visualized the attic).

Under the gray and filthy fog of Milan, we are immediately absorbed by Camilla's attempts to become a new woman in a new life. She's experiencing the uncanny state of being deserted by her husband Dario. She's not widowed, he's just disappeared. The idea of *desertion* can refer to an abandoned woman, but also to a voided space or the act of defecting from war: in Italian, *disertare* could refer both to dismissing a cause or dismissing a lover.

Over the course of the novel, even the attic will be deserted and somehow acknowledges this, as if it were a sentient being. The word *desertion* is also close to one of Cialente's favorite landscapes: many of her novels interact with the Egyptian desert; some of her characters live and die shoeless, with dusty feet. This is especially true of the colonial triptych *Cortile a Cleopatra* (1936), *Ballata levantina* (1961), and *Il vento sulla sabbia* (1972), set in Alexandria and in Africa, where Cialente lived for twenty years and witnessed the in-betweenness of being a foreigner in a new country.

In *A Very Cold Winter*, Camilla's hot scorch of a husband, Dario, first appears while lying on the beach. Every time he is recalled by his wife or daughters, he's placed in an exotic Mediterranean setting or maybe in Sudamerica. The sand is the precise counterpart of the run-down and leaking attic where Camilla lives: something apparently warm and desirable, but also open to the void, and with unstable patterns.

Acquaintances often described Fausta Cialente as a loner. In the novel, Camilla perceives the same kind of judgment, which feels surreal to her as she's always taking care of someone or something. But as a recurring theme in her female characters, the act of living has its demands. While staying at her mother's, whose cold behavior pushed Camilla and her late sister to be hyper-affectionate in their marriages, she has a one-night stand with an American soldier: "She'd gone there with maternal compassion and left with fire in her veins." Here's the freshness of it; the scene is genuinely felt, bodily perceived. Camilla's not particularly faithful or unfaithful to her vanishing husband; it just *happened*.

Cialente draws many images from the idea of war: occupying a house, deserting a relationship, being deserted, conquering space, conceding space. The attic is made of scraps, and even its inhabitants feel like scraps. When Regina and Enzo collide into each other, these words are spoken: "I've always thought of us as two shipwrecks . . . It had to be this way."

Enzo is the character with the clearest political function in the novel, embodying Cialente's personal meditations on what it means to be truly and fully Italian: he speaks the language, Italy is the land of his ancestors, but he was raised and exposed to a very different culture for most of his lifetime. He's unmistakably Levantine, and he wonders if he could achieve the right amount of "cunning" to adapt to Italy. This is the author speaking about herself and raising the question that haunted her whole life.

Fausta Cialente was truly the twentieth-century cosmopolitan nomad: born on an island, in the city of Cagliari in Sardinia, she spent her childhood in Trieste, among the decadent crumbles of the Austro-Hungarian Empire. This part of her life is magnificently evoked in *Le quattro ragazze Wieselberger* (*The Four Wieselberger Girls*, which did win the Premio Strega in 1976), centered on her wealthy mother and aunts, who once met Italo Svevo during a dance and later appeared in *La coscienza di Zeno* (*Zeno's Conscience*). In 1921, Cialente married Enrico Terni and moved to Alexandria for twenty years. She experienced fascism abroad, among expats, colonizers, and people on the run. She embraced communism and became an activist: she worked for the dissident Radio Cairo and directed a magazine for Italian prisoners called *Fronte unito*.

With her 1930 debut novel, *Natalia*, a love story between two women, she witnessed the censorship of the regime firsthand. After she moved back to Italy, she divorced and later left for Kuwait with her daughter. After some time back in Rome, she moved permanently to England, where she died in 1994, after translating Henry James and Louisa May Alcott.

Like Enzo in *A Very Cold Winter*, Cialente was bitten by the fear of not having real access to Italian culture, although she wrote in that language. In 1946, she was not living in Milan, she never saw the city under siege, but she collected stories; she rebuilt a city through oral accounts and many conversations. Weren't all writers doing the same to write their war novels?

In Calvino's new introduction to *The Path to the Spiders' Nests* in 1964, he stressed that most Neorealist novels were possible thanks to oral history, gossip, war folklore around the fire late at night. Cesare Pavese never fought in open battle—communist intellectuals like Giancarlo Pajetta accused him of being a "coward and deserter," and yet he wrote beautiful novels on the aftermath of war.

Regardless of their experience, to turn the war into art these authors paid attention to memories played through dialects, mannerisms, class inflections, the intricacies and cacophonies of multiple languages in the same street.

This is why, perhaps, *A Very Cold Winter* is such a musical novel. It starts with recurring exclamation marks: they almost recall a bell on the counter of an old shop; every character rings the bell while walking by and falls into their inner monologue—the bell often signals surprising or intruding thoughts. In this rhythmical coming and going, Camilla stands out as the owner of the house, "managing" her extended family through her excellent listening skills.

Her daughters require different melodies: Lalla wants to become a writer, she mustn't "get distracted by flashy details or seduced by form over content." She wants to write, and she is written with fewer adjectives. Her older sister Alba, on the other hand, is beautifully sad like one of Cesare Pavese's girls. A little ornamental, her gaze is mostly aesthetic but also tragic. No wonder, then, that she will be the first to leave the house. A less skillful author would describe a scene of Alba being undressed by calling the buttons on her dress "rosary beads": Italian novels are full of girls with rosary beads all over them. But Cialente describes these buttons "popping open like peas under his fingers." It's a small detail, in a novel full of such visual brilliance.

A Very Cold Winter conveys the distinctive feelings of *Vermiglio*, Maura Delpero's prize-winning independent film set in a small village in the Alps during World War II. It's the tale of an extended family, dealing with the arrival of a foreigner, a Sicilian deserter. A war story taken from family lore. If Cialente's novel is mostly musical, *Vermiglio* owes a lot to its enchanted and hazy light. Although there are several seasons in Cialente's book and Delpero's film, we seem to perceive only two: the lower depths of winter and the volatility of sunny days. In contemplating these works of art, the question is: what does it take to be *atemporale ma non inattuale*, timeless but never outdated? This is the mystery and balance which Fausta Cialente's novel treads.

The Italian women writers that mean so much to us today—Ginzburg, de Céspedes, Lalla Romano, Fabrizia Ramondino—they are not modern because we wish them to be. The reason why their work, so easily dismissed and neglected at the time, is startlingly current is because they were not afraid to imagine womanhood fully on the page, with all its consequences.

—Claudia Durastanti
Rome, 2025

Cast of Characters

Camilla, head of the family
Lalla, **Guido**, and **Alba**, Camilla's three children
Arrigo, Camilla's nephew, orchestra violinist
Nicola, Arrigo's late brother, Resistance fighter
Milena, Arrigo's wife, originally from Paris
Regina, Nicola's widow, mother of baby **Nicoletta**
Enzo, Camilla's neighbor
Matelda, longtime friend of Camilla
Dario, Camilla's estranged husband
Grandmother, Camilla's mother
Rosso, Grandmother's neighbor
Martina, Grandmother's caretaker
Sandro, Alba's lover

A VERY COLD WINTER

PART ONE

I

A faint glow on the sweeping horizon announced the autumn sun that was about to rise over the city, cloaked in rippling banks of fog. All night, the fog had stubbornly hidden the stars in the dark, impenetrable sky, but now the sliver of light widened little by little into a luminous band, a hazy phosphorescence that slowly spread and took over. As if on cue, a flock of mourning doves took off, gliding over the crumbling rooftops and run-down balconies, around the blackened chimneys where pale wisps of smoke had yet to rise, and traced jubilant circles around church spires and bell towers with their fast-beating wings. From up there, the doves could see the vast city's aching wounds, the sooty remnants of doused fires marking the blazes of war, the rubble of burned and razed houses whose insides had caved in, where debris choked the street-level windows and sometimes reached the upper floors. The liveliness, the happiness of their flight tempered the sadness of the silent city, so grimly disfigured by disaster that it still seemed numb and dazed at having buried so much life, while the hungry doves were already looking for things to feed on as they fluttered across the pale, empty sky. As the last rusty leaves fell from the trees in the parks and historic piazzas, the birds swooped down, rummaging and pecking and shaking their feathers, then flew off again with quivers of delight.

Front doors began to open onto building entryways, revealing deserted courtyards inside. The clatter of rising shutters echoed through the empty streets, the occasional rambler scurried past, along the walls, bundled tightly in his coat, women walked by with milk bottles tucked in shawls wrapped around their chests. The cold was biting at that hour, and people hurried about, thinking of autumn—a season as bitter and disagreeable as a sour apple that could nonetheless hold a beautiful day or two in store before the freeze set in, a sudden blue sky washed clean by the wind or rain. With vague hope, they looked down the streets erased by the fog, only to see the ashen specter of the long, fierce winter that already lay in wait.

One of the doves perched on the balcony railing, catching Camilla's eye as she peered through the curtains from inside. The bird had come, as it always did, looking for the breadcrumbs Camilla would scatter on the tiles, though she'd forgotten to the day before. It was too late now: the rickety fixtures of the old house creaked and squeaked terribly; if she'd tried to open the glass doors to the balcony, she would have woken Alba, who might still be asleep behind the flimsy wicker partition. Since she had also left the shutters open that night, she could now glimpse the dawn breaking in the sky, which looked frozen and distant against the dove's restless pecking.

It was mid-November. The sun won't rise before seven thirty, Camilla thought, as her gaze drifted bitterly over the nearby rooftops and domed churches in the distance. Down in the courtyard, hidden from view, gloomy, skeletal trees stood shrouded in a fog that was unmistakably Milanese: gray and filthy, like lint. The loose bricks on the terrace looked wet, as if it had rained overnight. Along the cracked, mossy wall stood a row of terracotta pots where a few withered, dull leaves drooped from weedy, bare stems, and a tangle of dark branches twisted around the iron rod at the edge of the railing: no one would have believed it was a rosebush, filled with lush scarlet buds during the warmer months.

The warmer months! In reality, winter had barely begun. They'd have to spend it in that attic again (for the second time since the war ended) and consider themselves lucky to have found somewhere to live that hadn't been bombed, so soon after the catastrophe.

As she leaned against the window frame and looked out over the city's stark angles, knowing there was nothing behind her but an old attic, Camilla had that same fleeting vision: a southern beach under a blazing sun, and Dario, lying half-naked on his stomach, letting his bare back burn, a canvas cap drenched in saltwater resting on the nape of his neck.

Alba wasn't born yet, she thought, so it must have been . . . yes, it must have been the first year they were married.

She drew the curtain back over the window (useless, those daydreams of hers, useless, idle thoughts), startling the dove that had hopped down from the railing to peck at the tiles. As it flew away, she turned and saw that the morning light had meanwhile settled on the dreary walls of the large room and over the furniture that emerged gloomily from the shadows. The night before, they'd all argued around the table that was now barely visible in the makeshift dining room, right by the front door (in fact, if a visitor came in while they were eating, he'd practically fall face-first into the dinner plates). Argued was too strong a word, perhaps . . . they grumbled as they talked. It was an unpleasant conversation about how they'd survive that lousy, wretched winter—as if one of them (she, perhaps?) were solely to blame for all their troubles, as if they were the only family in all of Milan having a hard time! Alba and Milena grumbled more than the others, as usual, in tones she could no longer tolerate, prompting her to chide them, much to the children's satisfaction. Arrigo, instead, surly and withdrawn as always, mumbled those incomprehensible phrases of his—not that anyone paid him any attention, not even his wife.

Right, Milena. The woman acted like she was born who-knows-where, in a lace-lined crib, waited upon by fairies! Lalla and Guido had every right to mimic and make fun of her: *pensez-vous, dites donc . . .*

"Stupid kids, the both of you," Milena snapped and turned up her nose. "No one can ever talk with you two around. Go on, Camilla, you'd better send them to bed."

It was truly useless to wonder how her nephew Arrigo could have fallen for a woman like her. The heart works in mysterious ways, every family has its differences. And yet they had to get along and pretend all was well, that the latest addition was the missing piece they'd lacked. Regina was the latest, actually; Milena was there first.

She isn't just lazy, she's a snob, Camilla thought, and she makes that dolt Arrigo feel like the crème de la crème, being born and raised in Paris, where her parents ran a luxury accessory shop for haute couture—feathers, tulle, sequins, the works . . . She's well-dressed, Camilla had to admit, she'd even look good in rags, that's why she and Alba get along so well, because Alba's wild about all that luxury stuff, about anyone who knows fashion. Unfortunately.

Alba was still asleep on the other side of the partition. Soon Camilla would brew the coffee and wake her, and she'd start grumbling again about getting up early, the fog, going to work . . . "Blessed are those who can stay in bed as long as they please!"

Everyone's unhappiness was so depressing, their eternal discontent! Thank goodness for Regina and the children. If anyone had reason to worry, in fact, it was Regina, starting with the matter of how to keep warm in that attic. It was Regina's first winter there with the baby. Always tactful and accommodating, she'd hardly said a word that night, except to point out that they could easily store a week's worth of coal and firewood on the balcony under the roof eaves, covered by a sack or two. Camilla suggested the same, since there certainly wasn't enough room in the kitchen—that tiny kitchen—and leaving it out on the landing, as Alba and Milena had proposed, was an open invitation for the other tenants to steal. Those two even had the wild idea of piling the wood outside the toilet door, where the balcony turned a blind corner.

"How clever!" Camilla said. "So I won't even have the satisfaction of seeing the face of the thief who's stealing my coal and firewood!"

"You always think the worst, Mamma," Alba scoffed, taking offense. "We already look like we've survived an earthquake with the toilet out on the balcony."

"War's far worse than an earthquake, my dear."

Regina was about to speak up in Camilla's defense but held back. Camilla felt sorry for her, knowing perfectly well that Regina forced herself to keep quiet because she felt like a burden, almost like an intruder there with her baby girl, and not who she truly was: Nicola's widow. If not for Camilla, who'd gone out of her way to take Regina in, even letting her share the bedroom with her and Lalla, the others wouldn't have welcomed her—not out of spite, no, because none of them were spiteful after all, but out of indifference, selfishness, plain and simple. Oh, how quickly the solidarity of war had faded—the only good thing those bitter years had brought to light.

Besides, even if she wanted to, Regina wouldn't have had the chance to say what she thought, because Guido started teasing Alba: Could such graceful, delicate lips utter a word—gasp—like *toilet*? Annoyed, Alba shoved him out of the way, and the conversation was cut short.

It was true that Lalla and Guido didn't take things too seriously and pestered the grown-ups. But what could you expect from two vivacious, outgoing kids who spent the war hiding out in the country, managing to carry on with their studies (Lord knows how), and now found everything about the city exciting? Nonetheless, they'd grumbled too, the night before. Like Alba, Guido had to sleep in a nook thrown together with wicker and wood panels at the far end of a makeshift passageway that separated him from the "honeymoon suite." Despite the partitions and flap doors, Milena and Arrigo had far less to gripe about than the others, since they could make use of the spacious adjacent room with two windows that opened onto the balcony (one of them, luckily, let air and light into Guido's nook) and even had its own entrance from outside. They had nothing to gripe about, nothing at all. And what about poor Lalla, who slept in an old bed with her mother, in the same bedroom (so to speak) as Regina and the baby, behind a partition in the corner? It wasn't sharing the bed that Lalla complained about, so much as not having a quiet, private space to study. Clearly, such a thing was impossible in that vast space, divided up with curtains and partitions, which looked like a poorhouse with the baby's clothes hung to dry by the wood-burning furnace when it rained outside.

The room was brighter now, and Camilla could see everything more clearly. The ceiling beams, for one, so charming and picturesque, those wide, sooty beams that slanted down toward the room's outer edges, but when it rained or snowed . . . The landlord, that crook, did everything he could to throw them out after the Liberation, when they rushed back to the city and occupied the loft—squatting, if truth be told. In the end, he'd left them alone, since Nicola was wounded and fell ill—wounded in those last days of fighting, what bad luck!—but then got even by refusing to fix the roof and leaving them to deal with it. They built all the partitions themselves, and divided the space into roughly equal halves. On one side was the entrance from the balcony, through a tiny attic door, where they arranged a table and chairs and a rickety sideboard; on the other, a tatty sofa, two armchairs, a bureau. "What a dump," Alba scoffed when she first saw the place. Her daughter's vocabulary was hardly refined, who knows where she'd picked up such language, Guido was right to tease her. But what did they expect, all of them—brand new furniture, salvaged from a bombed house and left in a musty basement for years? They were lucky to find such a large space at all. The partitions fit under the slanted beams so that the makeshift rooms were almost fully sealed off, but it hadn't been easy to set them up, map out the doorways, and install a gas stove on the only plaster wall that enclosed the kitchenette by the front door, so the vent pipe could pass through and heat up the space—otherwise, they'd have frozen to death. The sink and shower were tucked in a dark corner behind a few slapdash panels, which she'd covered with floral wallpaper so no one could peek between the gaps. It was thanks to Camilla, really, entirely thanks to her that they'd found those things when they did, when everyone refused not only to make themselves useful, but even to listen! Luckily, the weather was warmer then. After occupying the loft, she sent the children back to the country house with her nephews, even Nicola, and supervised the construction, cleaned up, claimed the old furniture and sent for the rest of her belongings. Though those things were hers, her mother, stern and suspicious as always, inspected each and every item. The summer was nearly over when they were all reunited, but of course no one thanked her; all they did was grumble and complain. Wasn't she a mother, after all? Mothers have to grin and bear it. They should have thought twice before bringing children into the world, too bad for them.

Ringing in her ears, over and over, was the tacit accusation people make to a woman whose husband left her on her own: that an abandoned woman's useless, even to her children, a good-for-nothing who can't accomplish anything in life, a wreck. Milena, for instance, would never let a man leave her—easy enough, of course, with a man like Arrigo. But to deal with the likes of Dario! Fact is, a man like Dario would never look twice at someone like Milena.

I shouldn't act like a mother-in-law toward my nephew's wife, Camilla thought. After all, who she is or isn't, what she does or doesn't, is no business of mine.

Now she couldn't recall exactly how many days she'd spent there, alone and in peace, amid the dust and cracked plaster, forced to carry bucket after bucket of water up from the courtyard, one after another, with no electricity to pump the water to the upper floors, let alone to the attic. Sitting on an empty crate, she'd have a piece of bread with a few slices of mortadella, or a glass of milk at night before retiring to the mattress she set down on the brick floor. Slightly less filthy than the ones on the balcony, those bricks could have used a coat of paint. Still, the balcony was a wonderful thing to have, a breath of fresh air when the weather was nice. That summer, Regina's baby, then a newborn, had spent the end of August there in her bassinet, spared from the heat inside, where only a sliver of sun would hit the eastward wall in the early morning. There was no baby yet the summer before, when she toiled away. But Enzo was there. He'd helped her with the water bucket one day as she climbed the stairs, taking it from her and carrying it himself. Later on, he knocked on the door to ask if she needed more. Of course, she said, and having absolutely nothing to offer in return, except for some bread and mortadella, she invited him to sit with her on the balcony, in the moonlight, to escape the heat. There were no plants, no flowers, nothing at all: just the two of them, sitting on two shabby pillows against the wall, talking late into the night as the moon set. They'd been neighbors for a while; in those days, a neighbor like him was priceless. Like her, he occupied (more or less lawfully) a room at the far end of the balcony, around the corner, near the door that opened onto the sink and toilet—right where Alba and Milena wanted to store the firewood and coal. His room had a sink, too, but it ran dry, without a single drop of water. Though he chuckled telling her about it, she noticed that he rarely ever smiled. He offered her a water bucket, and she accepted. What times, those were. Nearly deserted streets, half-empty trams; the only people to be seen were in the Galleria and Piazza della Scala, at the busiest times of day. Along Via Brera and Via Torino, wherever you looked, walls and gates hid tidy piles of rubble from collapsed houses, but fever-bearing mosquitoes buzzed in the courtyards of those old palazzi. When the workers took breaks and Camilla had nothing to do, she'd sometimes go on walks with him—the foreigner. For Enzo was practically a foreigner, an Italian born abroad, raised between Egypt and Paris, who had made his way back to Italy with the Allied forces before the war ended, as far as she could tell. As they ambled along the destroyed sidewalks, side-stepping potholes and trenches, she told him about the city that was once orderly and organized, run by rich bureaucrats who spoke in a snobby dialect—and yet were still to blame for the war and all that rubble. He seemed intrigued as she spoke, taking her arm, like a friend. She knew she was repeating Nicola's words—if Nicola said so, he must have been right. Milan was now a vast, wounded city, she said, that no longer smelled of burning but wore the sad colors of extinguished fires; he could see for himself. They stopped outside the wrecked buildings, where nothing was left standing except the exterior walls. Looking up, they saw the hazy sky through the gaping windows, like dark eye sockets that opened onto nowhere. Staircase landings with wrecked, dangling railings stood suspended in the void, and strange chasms took the place of the furniture inside the grand apartments of the grand palazzi where those rich people once lived with their orderly ways and snobby dialect, where faded scraps of wallpaper fluttered gently in the summer sky that was either quiet and drizzly or dry and dusty.

"It's like Judgment Day, isn't it?" she muttered, "And all for nothing. You'll see."

"Come now, don't be such a pessimist," he answered with the glimmer of a smile.

One evening—or night, rather—as they sat on those pillows against the wall, after a long silence, he asked, "Are you really on your own?" This surprised her, for they'd shared fairly long and frequent conversations which gradually alluded to every member of her family, the people she worked so hard for to put up those partitions and paint the walls . . . Her three children, first of all: Alba (though she hadn't mentioned her eldest was very beautiful, she was sure Alba's beauty surfaced in her stories one way or another, as it always did); then Lalla and Guido, fourteen and twelve. Then there were her nephews, Nicola and Arrigo, the sons of her sister Anna who died young, left fatherless years back and raised in boarding school. Camilla always looked after them, as a mother would: before the war, for instance, they spent almost every summer with her at their grandmother's in the country—they were much younger and easier to please back then. Nicola was her favorite, she loved him like a son. (But to Enzo at the time, she must have said: I *love* him like a son, in the present tense, since Nicola was ill but hadn't died yet. He wouldn't have been living with them either; he was engaged to Regina, a nice young woman whom she was fond of. They'd soon marry and be off to Sardinia, where Nicola worked as a schoolteacher.) Arrigo, instead, had already married a middle-class young woman, who despite being half-Parisian still had the tired, backward mentality of a provincial Italian girl. Her family had left France when the war broke out, and they were among the evacuees near Camilla's mother's house in the country. That was how those two had met and fallen so in love that they'd married before the war ended.

Camilla was sure she'd told Enzo the whole story, so that question—"Are you really on your own?"—gave her pause. He also seemed to regret it the moment he asked.

"What do you mean, on my own? Can't you tell I've got tons of people around?" she laughed. "And not one has a cent. Not even the newlyweds." Nonetheless, she thought, here we go again, another man wants to know if I have a husband. If he were dead, the dear soul would come up right away, "My poor husband used to say this or do that," and they'd soon find out if she was a widow.

"I can tell you're fixing up the place for lots of people. But you know that isn't what I meant," he said. Maybe he'd given a wry smile.

Again, a silence fell between them, neither awkward nor aloof. Camilla looked up at the moon. He blew a puff of cigarette smoke away from her, as if to stay out of her way, yet still with an air of anticipation. "You want to know if I have a husband, don't you? I did. But he left," she sighed, with a wave of her hand as if something had suddenly vanished. "No one knows where."

He laughed after a moment, affectionately. "I like the way you put it. Like a girl who's seen a magic trick. Oh, forgive me!" He had taken her hand but pulled away. "I didn't mean to offend you, forgive me. You seem so youthful and calm, but what you've told me could leave a woman broken and embittered. It doesn't seem to have affected you."

"Oh, it affected me. Even if it doesn't look that way." She turned to him, imagining that she must have seemed youthful and serene in that instant. "I loved my husband. Maybe I still care for him." A pause, then the truth. "But I can't show it, you know. Because nobody in here"—she gestured toward the dark, empty room, which smelled of freshly sawed wood, paint, and glue—"nobody wants to hear such things."

"He must deserve to be loved," Enzo answered, with his strange lilt. (She later learned that was the way Italians from the Levant talked.)

"Maybe not. But what does it matter? You don't love someone because they deserve it, imagine that! The world would be so dull if that were true. All the good people on one side, loving each other, and the bad ones . . ."

She trailed off. He stared straight ahead, silent and impenetrable, with hard, gleaming eyes. (Goodness! she thought, has he seen a ghost?) An excitement began to stir inside her, awakened perhaps by his kind words.

"What about you?" she asked politely. "Are you on your own, too? Are you with someone?"

He reached to put out his cigarette on the damp bricks, with more force than needed to extinguish such a tiny ember. She worried her question was too vulgar, the kind of line a servant and soldier might exchange at a town dance. "Are you with someone?" How could she! Yet Enzo seemed neither surprised nor hurt. In the growing darkness, as the moon disappeared behind the eaves, his voice sounded so bitter that he must have been scowling.

"I should put it the same way you did, Camilla. There was someone . . . a woman I loved very much. But she disappeared." It sounded like he'd dreamt it, like he was telling a fairy tale. "No one knows where."

She stared at him in stunned silence. Was he serious? Hurt and unmoved, he added, "Wherever she went, all I know is she's never coming back."

He had called her Camilla for the first time. They would always call each other by name from then on. Once the others arrived, they called him Enzo, too, and now they were almost all on friendly terms. They considered him part of the scenery, like the old furniture salvaged from the bombings, though he lived alone in that solitary room at the far end of the balcony. Guido followed him around like a puppy, from the very first day, always knocking on his door. As for Alba, who Camilla thought would make an impression on him, Enzo barely paid her any attention—no more than anyone else, at least.

The coffee! Camilla gave a start. As she tiptoed past the tiny doorway to the big room where Lalla and Regina were still asleep, she heard cautious footsteps. Perhaps Regina had gotten out of bed, trying not to wake the baby.

The kitchen was so dim, she had to turn on the light. She picked up the coffee grinder and found it full. Regina must have ground the beans the night before—no one else ever thought to help. As she lit the stove, Regina came in and whispered good morning, wrapped in her robe.

Even after so long, Camilla was still moved at the sight of her, so graceful and petite, with that thin, waiflike face. The poor girl. Regina was standing by the window now, looking even more gaunt under the artificial light of the bulb behind her and the faint glow of the sunrise in front, which barely managed to filter through the balcony awning. As usual, she fiddled with the tortoiseshell headband that held back her thick hair, ashy brown streaked with blond, then shoved her hands in her pockets with a shiver. She must have felt cold in the silken robe that was a bit too long and loose-fitting, draped over her shoulders to accentuate her almost childlike physique; actually, she'd easily given birth to a beautiful, healthy baby girl, and the robe hid milk-heavy breasts that she began to massage, grimacing as she turned to Camilla with a pained look.

"Are you leaking? Don't fret, Nicoletta will wake up soon and empty them out, like she always does—you'd feel worse if she didn't."

"I know. The trouble is washing up afterward. The water's so cold." Regina looked down at her swollen, red hands. "Not just the baby's clothes, mine too."

"Give it time! Heat up all the water you need, don't worry." (In truth, needing so much hot water every day was a real problem.) "Everything will get easier in a few months. This damned winter will end." As the coffee pot on the stove began to whistle, she laughed. "Unfortunately, it's barely started. You heard them last night, didn't you?"

"Of course I did, Camilla. You should stop asking their opinion and do as you please. You always do things right, anyhow. They certainly couldn't do any better. It makes me so mad, every time!"

"I could tell you were upset. But you didn't speak up."

"You know I can't, Camilla, and not because I'm afraid to."

"I know that isn't the reason, but it's no good acting so withdrawn, as if you weren't part of the family."

Regina stared out the window without answering, deep in thought. Her melancholy look, if Camilla had seen it, clearly expressed that she didn't feel part of the family—at least not yet.

The kitchen had two small windows, one facing the long balcony, where the glass doors opened onto the bedrooms, and another facing the corner under the awning, by the toilet and sink. Regina stood in front of the window overlooking the void that plunged down to the courtyard below, beyond the balcony railing. The window was the only source of light, suddenly blocked by a tall shadow bundled in a coat and scarf. With a quick tap on the glass, the figure vanished down the stairwell at the other end.

"Enzo," whispered Camilla, "already out at this hour. He's an early bird." She picked up the breakfast tray. "I've got to wake Alba or she'll be late."

Seeing her holding the tray by the door, Regina shook her head. "What's this! Why serve your daughter breakfast in bed? She should be the one serving you."

"Oh, I don't mean to spoil her, but she always gets in the way and makes a mess in the kitchen . . . she's so irritable in the morning."

"So you toss food in her cage, to keep her quiet!"

"She isn't a wild animal, the poor thing, let's not be dramatic. She's just difficult, like everyone in here. Maybe it isn't their fault, it's because of the war . . . Would you switch off the lamp when you leave? You can light the furnace before the baby wakes, to boil some water."

"But it's early!" Regina seemed alarmed by the suggestion. "We'll run out of firewood if we light it too soon, and everyone will complain if the house is cold tonight."

"They'll complain no matter what. Just make sure the room's warm, if you want to give Nicoletta a bath."

"No. We'll wash up in the evening from now on." Regina tightened the belt of her robe, as if to emphasize her sudden resolve. "I know it's best to bathe her in the morning, at her age, but the house is always warmer at night."

"You're right," said Camilla as she pushed open the door and left with a smile, holding the tray.

II

With her eyes still closed and the covers pulled over her head, curled up in the warm bed, Lalla had been awake since she heard her mother get up and tiptoe away. Then she heard Regina leave the room. For a while, she listened to the familiar sounds coming from the kitchen and the soft whispers on the other side of the partition. Opening one eye, she could see a faint light filter through the partition and the shutters of the kitchen window overlooking the balcony, signaling the usual leaden sunrise, she knew. But she wouldn't let it upset her. She was enjoying the coziness under the covers for a bit longer that day, because school was starting later and the first session was French, thank goodness, a class she always enjoyed and felt prepared for, thanks to Enzo. He was kind in his own way, that cold fish: he wasted no time on jokes or small talk, but she knew from the start he could be counted on—Nicola would have liked him too, she was sure. But Milena! She would never say, come here, let me help.

And to think Milena knew French even better than Italian! She'd only deign to speak it with Enzo: pensez-vous, dites donc . . . What a snob! And that fool Arrigo, who looks at her as if she were a gift from God.

Not that going to school is pleasant. All those broken windows in the classrooms, patched up with strips of cardboard and aluminum that block the light, the old furnaces put back in commission (radiators are still a luxury, this year at least) with smoke that stings your eyes, holes in the floorboards, and the toilets . . . oh, best not to think about the toilets, they're revolting. No gym, there's nothing left, the janitor says the Germans turned it all into firewood. And no money for repairs, we've just got to resign ourselves and wait. They've been saying so since last year. Then everything will go back to the way it was before, they say.

But not everything will be the way it was *before*. Nicola died and her father didn't come back, not even after the war ended. *Before* is a place so far away and long ago that sometimes Lalla can't see herself there. Or Alba. She can picture her mother and father as sweethearts, for example, hand in hand . . . her young mother, beaming and beautiful, as she still is sometimes, saying yes, she'll marry him, her father, with the proud swagger he has when things turn out well. Lalla barely remembers him, but she's sure he was tall, handsome, elegant. He gently twists her wrist and makes her let go of the grasshopper trapped between her fingers—a real memory, vivid, she knows it happened at her grandmother's in the country. As a little girl she was never squeamish, always catching caterpillars, toads, even cockroaches, trying to shove them inside her mother's collar and down the boys' shirts. They all ran away screaming, even Arrigo and Nicola. Chasing them off was her way of doing what she pleased in peace. The only one who was never frightened nor disgusted was her father. At the beach he had fun sticking slugs on her bare legs, bait worms, tiny flaccid jellyfish that looked like dirty rags . . . She remembers the warm golden sand where they lay, and those long legs of his, motionless. He seemed to be asleep, but then he'd reach out without warning and playfully grab her arm.

She heard what sounded like a soft sigh and lifted her head from the pillow to listen for a moment. Had the baby moved?

If she's awake, she'll start to whine, Lalla thought, Regina will come in and I can't pretend to be asleep much longer.

Perhaps it was just the bassinet creaking. She rested her head again. Fortunately, no one snored; how would the baby manage to sleep, otherwise? She'd get used to it, that's all. How do poor people manage? Don't the poor sleep seven, eight, twelve to a squalid room?

"Overcrowding," Nicola used to say. "The scourge that rots this society."

First her father, then Nicola. A house without men. Arrigo didn't count—maybe he did, but only when he played the violin or discussed music. Guido was just a boy, and Enzo . . . Enzo was outside the family circle.

But he seemed to understand what Nicola's death meant to her. Often she'd mention a lesson learned from him. One day Enzo said, "So, Nicola was a teacher to you," and when she pointed out that teaching was actually his profession, he interrupted, "That's not what I meant, you know," half teasing, half exasperated.

In fact, Nicola was the only one she could talk to about the things that interested her. She couldn't tell anyone else, not even her mother, that she aspired to be a writer, for example. Nicola suggested what books to read, and how to read them, without getting distracted by flashy details, or seduced by form over content, "which happens at your age," he'd say, "you'll have to choose wisely with a critical eye, remember even the best writers can pander." When he corrected her essays, he cut out half the adjectives, with no mercy for superlatives or diminutives. "Your style should be spare, razor-sharp, never pandering." But it was wartime and he visited less and less. He even had to hide out, then fled to the mountains, and she didn't see him again until after the Liberation, when he was already wounded. After all, she couldn't expect him to worry about her and her problems, with everyone else around, especially Regina.

Lying on her back, Lalla stared up at the shadow nestled between the ceiling beams. It hadn't been easy to swallow the news about those two, whom she thought were just involved, but in fact were already husband and wife. Not that Nicola would have confided such a thing, she neither expected nor wanted him to . . . But to keep it from Mamma! He'd gotten Regina in trouble, that was it—and then he died. Perhaps they'd give him a medal, but this was all he'd earned for now. Everyone was up in arms when the secret got out, shortly after he died, and yet Mamma took Regina's side. Though Lalla only heard whispers, she understood that due to some "missed menses" (which were normally regular, apparently) Regina hadn't realized what was happening right away . . . By then it was too late. Nicola was buried underground, and up here was the girl, alive yet abandoned, *pregnant*.

An ugly word, truly, a slimy word. Meaning the belly enlarges and swells, losing its shape. Yet you see it depicted in paintings of the Annunciation, beautiful angels kneeling in blooming meadows, holding a lily, a young Virgin chastely bowing her head. It was a difficult word to say, one Regina refused to say to her family. So Mamma intervened: they'd have to help and protect her, take her in. She was practically Nicola's widow, and they'd follow the requisite procedures to give the father's name to the child-to-be.

That's an odd word, too—child-to-be—meaning something will be born but we don't yet know what. The child-to-be turned out to be a girl. Guido made the strangest face when they showed her to him, as if he'd seen a white rat. Not that he was oblivious, even if he never talked about what happened. All he cares about are movies and plays, he's wild about them, the only things that ever affect him happen on a stage or screen. She sympathizes: even in novels, life is so much better than reality. But you're not supposed to say so.

The most surprising reaction of all was Enzo's. The day Regina moved in (no one would have guessed she was pregnant then, she was hardly showing) Enzo picked her up in a taxi and carried her luggage upstairs, though it should have been Arrigo, her brother-in-law. It wasn't clear why Mamma, who was usually so reserved, had confided the family secret to a stranger. For that's what Enzo was—a stranger—even if they all liked him. Almost. (Alba looks down on him, but that's her way, she likes to pretend she belongs to different circles outside the house.) While Regina was in labor, on a sweltering night in late July, Enzo was there keeping Mamma company as she waited outside the maternity ward. And he was there again a few days later, calling another taxi to take them home: the two mothers, their things, and the baby in her basket, all decked in pink. No one repaid him for those expenses, as far as she knew, but it was also true that Enzo was a frequent guest at the table for lunch or dinner. (She likes the idea of giving and taking without keeping count, she even wants a communal piggy bank for the house, like the alms box at church, for everyone to put money in or take out as needed. They'd all share . . . not Alba, though, who always talks about clothes as if they were the most important thing in life and could easily drain the household savings for a new wardrobe. Milena wouldn't share either—stingy or not, Lalla can't tell, but she always keeps to herself.)

The baby cooed in her bassinet. Lalla leapt out of bed and slid the partition away from the window to let some light into the room. Awake and staring out with an anxious pout, the baby rested her gaze on the shadow bent lovingly over her and smiled with big pink gums. Nicoletta was a beautiful baby, with a pale, sweet little face and eyes that glistened like ripe blackberries.

"You're awake, little one!" Lalla patted her gently and felt a damp wetness, but it didn't disgust her at all; as she rubbed and tickled her belly, the baby gurgled and drooled, squirming and kicking her feet.

"You want to be picked up, don't you! I know, but you'll have to wait, Mamma's on her way."

The baby was about to cry when Regina hurried in and opened the window.

"Good thing you're here. She's all wet," Lalla said, and jumped back under the covers. "Brrrr, another cold day."

Regina picked up the fussy baby and held her on one side as she laid out the dry laundry on her bed. Lalla nervously studied her movements.

"Quick . . . Make sure she doesn't catch cold . . . What do you need, the talc? Here it is, on Mamma's nightstand. She's crying. Why's she crying?"

"She's hungry. Can't you tell?" Regina had untied her robe and pulled a chair by the bassinet, where she sat with the baby on her lap. "I wanted to dry off, too, but this one won't let me!" Lalla watched Regina unclasp her bra and let it fall to the floor, stained with milk. The baby latched on while she pressed a terrycloth onto the other breast to stop the leaking, shaking her head and biting her lip.

"Does it hurt?" Lalla asked, intimidated by the baby's ravenous suckling.

"Of course not," said Regina, with a piercing gaze and rueful smile. "There's nothing to be afraid of. It's a natural thing." She looked down at the baby as her mind went elsewhere and the smile began to fade. Lalla peeked out from the sheet that she'd pulled over her face. Sure, it was natural, but . . .

A door slammed, angry whispers. Then her mother peeked in. "You can use the bath now, Lalla. Alba's done."

"Princess Alba!" Lalla complained as she climbed out of bed. "You have to get up at the crack of dawn, or wait while she takes her sweet time in there."

"Go on, you're next in line," said Regina. "And try not to fight, if you can help it."

"Talking, not fighting! Didn't you hear the door slam? I'm sure it was her. It's her way of flaunting that she's made for luxury apartments, not hovels with outdoor toilets. Mamma's right when she says the roof will cave in one day, with all that slamming." Lalla gathered the clothes strewn about, then stopped in the doorway and sneered. "Well, I don't mind this hovel, if you can believe it! Call me crazy, like Milena does, but if we ever leave this attic we're all sharing in this strange way . . . so *theatrically*, Guido says, I'd probably miss it, to tell the truth."

She left the room without an answer. Regina was busy tickling the baby's chin to keep her from falling asleep so she could nurse at the other breast. A while later, under the lukewarm spray (it was Lalla's turn to shower that morning, the shimmering water was always hypnotic), her mind drifted amid the usual thoughts: that miserable existence nobody wanted; the dead and missing who wouldn't return; life that must go on, as her mother liked to say; "natural things," Regina said, that didn't hurt.

She'd learn to write about them in a spare, razor-sharp style, those natural things. Life (pregnant young women, milk-swollen breasts?); death (cold, silent tombs, from which no words of encouragement would ever emerge again?); the harsh, ruthless silence surrounding the name of her good-for-nothing father . . . The water was getting cold.

"Mamma!" she cried, "Turn up the heat or I'll freeze to death!"

"You've showered long enough!" her mother's voice replied, "Don't you know how expensive the gas is?"

III

Slowly chewing a mouthful of bread and butter, coffee cup in hand, Arrigo leaned against the kitchen table.

"Why eat standing? Can't you sit for a while? It's still early," Camilla said behind him.

He kept chewing, swallowed deliberately (to delay answering her for as long as he possibly could, she knew), and finally cleared his throat, responding in a hoarse voice. "It's late, Auntie. Milena wouldn't stop gabbing, as usual . . . and the time flew by."

"What's she complaining about today?" Camilla asked coolly from the sink, rinsing the dishes. He furrowed his brow. It was true that Milena always complained, so he'd better not look Camilla in the eye: she was most certainly smiling.

"You know what. They wake her every morning, and she can't fall back asleep."

"Is that right?" Camilla replied under her breath, dryly. Arrigo sensed his irritation mount as it had moments before, when he had to listen to his wife—only that Milena had felt so soft and inviting in the lacy folds and ribbons of her still-new nightgown when he leaned over to kiss her, and the warm scent of the bed that tickled his nostrils gave him a passing thrill.

"It's not easy to sleep undisturbed until ten o'clock, in a house full of people leaving early for work, kids going off to school, and a newborn!"

"Don't exaggerate, Auntie. Not until ten. After all, why get up early in this cold weather? What is there to do?"

"Oh, there's plenty to do in the morning and all day, if only one cared to."

He hated it when she uttered simple truths like that with polite, stern restraint. It was relentless. He'd rather she be irritable or aggressive. Instead, she walked over, set the dishcloth on the table, placed her hands on his shoulders, and looked affectionately into his eyes (or was there more sarcasm than affection?). Her fingers fluttered to adjust the knot of his necktie.

"Guido's the one who wakes her, I know—guilty as charged, every morning. Actually, to keep from bothering you two, the poor boy walks around barefoot in the cold. He doesn't have a pair of slippers, so he waits to put shoes on. But he has to finish getting dressed and gather his books in there, and everything creaks and squeaks, the doors and windows, no matter how hard he tries to stay quiet. I don't know where else to put the child, to keep from disturbing Milena."

"But, but I . . ." Arrigo said, "No one's asking to throw him out, Camilla." He regretted raising the subject.

"Of course, no one's asking to put him on the balcony, the only place left besides that nook of his! Go on, lighten up, don't make that face," she chuckled, giving him a playful shove. "You know very well, while we live in this state for who knows how much longer, tantrums aren't allowed—not Alba's, not Milena's, not yours." She caressed his cheek, with a melancholy look in her eye. "Poor Arrigo, you don't deserve such a scolding. You never threw tantrums, not even as a boy."

When she talked to him that way, touched him, he felt overcome by a strange languor, far different than what Milena's affectation stirred in him—a baffling happiness he tried to resist, as if striving to break a bond too tight to loosen. A taste of the past, that's what it was, and Camilla *was* the past: his childhood, his mother, the dead.

She looked at him without saying a word, tugging on his suit sleeves. His suits were always too dark and too tight, recalling the austere attire of an Anglican pastor. He shouldn't have worn such form-fitting suits, his neck being too short for his lanky frame, with hunched shoulders (one sat higher than the other, the left, where he rested his violin). He even had the bad habit of jutting forward his large, round head, which looked almost ape-like underneath that shock of black hair. Sleepy lids drooped over the dark, mild-mannered eyes that dotted his broad, pale face, and a hesitant smile stretched the ashen lips that covered his big white teeth. Camilla always thought no two people could ever be so alike and, at the same time, so unalike, as Nicola and Arrigo. Nicola stood tall, head high, with smoldering eyes, a whip-like smile, a voice as sharp as metal; Arrigo always had to clear his throat before speaking, having to repeat himself since no one ever heard him the first time. There was nothing left to compare, now. Dejected, Camilla let her hands fall and went back to the sink. Nicola lay in the ground, his brilliant life and joyous strength gone forever, while Arrigo, unsure and visibly unnerved, exhaled his angst through those cavernous nostrils, answering her affectionate words with exasperating complaints.

"I don't know why everyone always asks for my opinion on this or that! Lalla's right when she says I act like I don't want to have an opinion! In fact, I don't want to weigh in on all your . . . your hassles. That's all they are, hassles. Everyone's always complaining about something . . . I know, Milena does too, most of all. You say so every chance you get. She's an only child, a spoiled brat, I know. But I've got to focus on my work, Camilla. I give private lessons because the music school doesn't pay enough. It's not the conservatory, just a humble little school, but it's all I can find for now, they won't hire me at the radio. All your concerns . . . the house, the family, every single nuisance . . . it's all a bother, and I *can't* be bothered, Camilla. I can't be swept up in so many things, down a thousand streams . . ." He gestured as if a thousand streams were rushing around him. "Music—that's all. And Milena. But that's really the end of it." He walked toward the door and shot her a furious glare. But he wasn't actually furious, and he struggled to speak.

Camilla felt sorry for him. He was a poor fellow who had a hard time simply existing, she could tell. The war had frightened him, though he'd spent most of it in an office, having been declared unfit for duty. She never understood how he dared find a wife. If he did, it must have been because that shy, lumbering body of his, always cloaked in dark colors, was driven by a powerful sensuality that was hard to restrain.

"I've done the best I could," he added from the doorway, sullen and tense. "I moved the wardrobe against the partition between us and Guido, and I put the big old coat rack in the entryway, the one you wanted to throw out, all for some privacy. As if that were possible! That boy!" he sneered. "Do you think we enjoy making love behind a wicker wall, always worrying he'll hear? Don't you think I might need to give lessons at home, or at least study, sometime? Has it ever occurred to you? And you're shocked when Milena complains!"

He paused for a moment, worried he'd been unreasonable.

"I'm sorry about Nicola, truly. But the dead . . . the dead can't do anything for anyone anymore, can they? Why should we care so much about the mess they made?"

"Arrigo!" Camilla said in dismay, but he had already stopped talking, blinking as he breathed a heavy sigh.

"What do you mean?" she asked, more gentle than stern. "Regina and Nicoletta are people, not 'messes.' They'll have to find their place in the world, and we've got to help them. That's that." As he stood there, downcast and humiliated, she took a step toward him and caressed his cheek again. "Go on, dear. Don't be late on my account. You've explained what's stopping you from working on your music as you'd like. Don't think I'm not aware. I'll even forgive you. Go on." She shooed him away as he shuffled through the kitchen and disappeared behind the balcony door. She cleared the table and tried rinsing his cup in the sink without getting her hands wet—the water stung like a porcupine, so cold and harsh.

The bleakness she felt wasn't just because of the gloomy morning, the freezing water, the dull and tedious chores, everyone's selfish complaining. It was something sinister that followed her, lurking in the dark kitchen and nuzzling against the squalid walls. She caught whiffs of its vile scent here and there, in the drain, the trash bin, the dirty stovetop where Regina had burned the spilled milk, and now it flashed upon the cooking pots, the copper and aluminum lids that hung from the nails on the wall; those humble metals weren't shiny enough to justify such a bright glare. It was the memory of a faraway sun that blinded her that morning, as she watched the sunrise from the balcony—a jealous and possessive sun, like a lover come to carry her away from the cares and worries of her family, the here and now, taking her hand in its sweet warmth to lead her back to a southern beach.

"Look at her dig," he said, sitting at the edge of the waves with his feet in the water. He hugged his knees and rounded his slender bare back, damp cap pulled over his eyes. (This was after their first year of marriage; squatting in the sand, a hundred-odd meters away, Alba dug and dug, looking for seawater at the bottom of the hole.) Camilla said nothing. The light of her youth gleamed on the horizon, and everything was blue, sea and sky. The air burned solemnly, the sand sparkled like a diamond, a perfect silence all around, except for the gentle lap of waves on the shore. They always chose secluded spots like that, apart from the rest of the world. She felt beautiful and happy, nearly naked herself, hips and breasts barely covered for the little girl's sake—otherwise they'd skinny dip and play in the water, far out from shore, like two dolphins in love. But the girl sulked. He loved his daughter's pout, however; he'd scoop her up with a playful spank, and ended up making her laugh. Alba was a sullen child, who always wanted something different than what she had, to be in a different place than where she was. But he breathed contentment.

"So, Camilla, did you do the math?" he asked in a lazy voice. "Can we afford to stay for the month?"

She didn't know whether they could afford to stay for the whole month, but she said yes, she'd done the math. She was the only one who did, after all. But without resentment. What did money matter, anyhow? They always seemed to have enough, and he always managed to make a living, despite his elusive air, head forever in the clouds. That was another thing they agreed on: to spend their money this way, on blissful secluded getaways and modest trips to places no one else went, on performances (gallery seats, of course, or upper balcony) and books.

"Oh Camilla," he sighed again, looking happier than

before, "If only we could stay all month long. Only you could work such miracles."

She'd certainly worked her share of miracles, all those years, without ever thinking that's what they were. Handiness, practicality, good judgment: the qualifications any good housewife should possess to steer the ship through the end of every month, without hitting too many waves or sprouting leaks in the hull. She never thought of those qualifications as virtues. She still didn't. She wiped her hands again on the dishcloth.

"You're too good, too devoted!" Matelda always said, her friend since childhood. "Buy yourself a new dress, instead of listening to that hunky husband of yours!"

"For starters, I forbid you from calling my husband a 'hunk,'" Camilla laughed.

"You think men are grateful, that they recognize the sacrifices we make for them? Selfish, that's what they are. They cheat on us and then pull the wool over our eyes." Matelda always said the same things, stung by the brazen infidelities of her rich, free-spending husband, who—even despite not having children—she never brought herself to leave, out of laziness and a fondness for luxury.

"So leave him," Camilla replied, turning the tables. "What are you still doing with that hunky husband of yours, knowing what you know?"

"Oh, sure. Then where will I get my cash?"

"Working for a living never occurred to you?"

"You must be crazy!" Matelda looked at Camilla as

if she truly was. "He'll never scratch the itch, my dear. I make him pay for every tryst, really I do." She gazed down at her soft hands, with her beautiful, perfectly polished burgundy nails. "He can't just hang onto me; he's got to treat me like royalty. Am I his wife or am I not?"

"If this is the kind of wife you've chosen to be . . ."

"Cash, my dear, and social status. In Italy, a woman who gets separated or divorced cuts a bad deal, believe me. If we separated, he'd pay alimony, wouldn't he? A pittance! And who would I go out with at night, without a husband? Men steer clear of single women of a certain age. I make it very clear that I'm his wife, trust me. Not a peep from him. He pays and keeps his mouth shut."

Once, Matelda had confided, with an odd sense of pride, that her husband no longer touched her, as if that, too, were an asset.

"I certainly don't want to catch a disease from those dirty women of his."

"You could easily treat it, with all that cash. Perhaps you shouldn't give him such free rein."

Conversations from long ago, when Camilla thought she was safe. When Dario ran off to France and sent letters and money at first (but then disappeared, once the war broke out), Matelda had completely surprised her with a show of friendship in which Camilla sensed not only compassion, but bitterness. As much as her friend vaunted unshakable cynicism, she realized her wrecked marriage had caused Matelda pain. Once, when the runaway hadn't sent word in a while, Matelda sighed, "You know, Camilla, if someone had predicted that Dario would leave you and the children this way, I wouldn't have believed them. I thought yours was a real marriage, to last a lifetime. I suppose that's impossible."

"I still think it's possible, though things went wrong for me, too. At least I hope so, for my daughters' sake."

Alba was just a teenager then, Lalla a little girl. The war had dispersed everyone. Matelda and her husband went all the way to South Africa to wait it out (the things you can do with money!). When they met again a year later, a slightly aged but still lavish Matelda (her husband had found a way to rake in cash there as well), exclaimed at seeing Alba, who was all grown up, "Oh, this one's nothing like you, my dear! She'll keep the men on their toes! She'll get even for you, trust me!" As if Camilla ever longed to get even, imagine the ideas people got in their heads . . . As if keeping men on their toes were a feat worth achieving.

"All I ask is that you not say such things around my daughter. You sound like a kept woman."

Now, to Camilla's amazement, Alba—of all people—is carrying the breakfast tray back to the kitchen. She sets it brusquely on the table, tense and irritable, a bit unsettled. Yet she still looks so elegant, in that hand-me-down suit (it was practically brand new, when Matelda gave it to her). It fits her so well: defined shoulders, slender waist, soft around the bosom, lightweight. And that scarf, which perfectly matches the suit and her splendidly flawless skin.

"Don't leave without your coat or a rain jacket. It's cold out."

Alba glances outside, though there isn't much to see through the foggy kitchen windows.

"Definitely a rain jacket. It might pour. The fog's just as wet, in any case."

Camilla senses her daughter has more to say as she lingers by the window (as if looking outside could change the weather!), then pauses again by the door to put on her gloves, one finger at a time. She wants to say something, too, to compliment her looks and healthy complexion; despite the gloomy haze in the kitchen, Alba's glowing, she uses nothing but water and a gentle soap on her face, not even blush, a natural look she's proud of, so uncommon and unique compared to those made-up women. Even Regina uses lipstick to freshen up, but she's so pale. Then there's Milena, with that heavy, sophisticated makeup, "the way Arrigo likes it." (Nonsense! She likes it that way, Arrigo has no say, not even in this, and whenever they go out he's always waiting for her to get ready—she takes forever!—shuffling around, tight-lipped and irritated.)

"I may not be home for supper. Don't expect me."

(Oh, that was it.)

"How do you know? It's still early."

"Oh goodness," Alba snaps. "I know how much of yesterday's work needs to get done. You know I can't make calls from here without a telephone."

She's right; it's not her fault they live in such a lousy building without so much as a telephone, not even in the custodian's quarters! A hurried goodbye from the kitchen; the door creaks open and shut.

I've got to oil those hinges, Camilla thought. Why must everyone feel so ashamed at not having enough money—enough cash, as Matelda says—and act as though it's someone else's fault? We've got no telephone, no bathtub, no elevator. We may even run out of bread . . . Well, that's a bit much, we haven't reached that point. But we could run out of coal, and I'd love to see their faces then! I'd feel sorry for the baby, though, she isn't to blame . . .

She listened for a moment. The house seemed silent, not a sound could be heard. The early risers had all left, willingly or not, Milena wouldn't show her face for a while, Regina must have been lulling the baby back to sleep, and then she'd surely offer to go to the market. Having made everyone's breakfast, Camilla almost forgot about her own. She poured a drop of coffee into the warm milk, tiptoed to the chair by the window in the main room, set the cup on the table and reached for her sewing tin. A quiet moment before starting her usual routine. She took a sip, looked outside, and saw the doves tottering impatiently up and down the balcony on their pink feet. She really ought to scatter those crumbs.

It's so quiet up here, she thought as she picked up her mending. Not at all like Milan.

London was like that too, her husband used to say, or Paris. All you had to do was leave the hubbub of the city center to find a quiet corner where it felt like you were exiled in a faraway provincial town.

But she preferred the country. She knew before, but the war confirmed it. The family was the only reason she came back to the city. Though it had to be done, she'd much rather have stayed there in the country—forever.

"There" didn't mean her mother's house, for Camilla certainly didn't enjoy living with her mother—a strange, selfish old woman! Who knows why she'd married and had her two daughters so young . . . Not terribly young, now that she thought about it, practically a spinster, raised by an Englishwoman, who'd died before the wedding. Her mother must have been forty by the time Camilla was born; her sister Anna, the eldest, had come a few years before. She didn't seem to suffer the death of her husband, poor Papà, and not even poor Anna's, which had been far worse, perhaps on account of her upbringing, that typical Anglo-Saxon reserve. Even her grandchildren seemed as bothersome as smoke in her eyes, and the only reason the war affected her at all was because she'd been forced to give up her independence and take them in after they evacuated, forced to share the eggs from her hens, the vegetables from her garden. Chestnuts were the only thing she was generous with. No wonder—they fell from the trees, and she certainly hadn't the strength to gather them all, so the kids could have at it and roast them, on the condition they'd stay outside, under the portico, since she wanted no mess in the house. The war was of no interest, if she even noticed. "Are we fighting Poland now?" she asked once, when a group of Polish soldiers passed through. In her mind, the fascists were nothing but a pain in the neck, causing a stir for no reason and always getting in the way. Nicola enjoyed teasing her. "Go on, Nonna, tell us who we're fighting!" She was inimitable, in any case, with a worldview all her own. Dario's disappearance hadn't upset her terribly, though she'd seen Camilla struggle, with three young children to raise. She never said much about it, aside from the early days, occasionally asking if he'd sent word; once she even muttered, perhaps to cheer her up, in her own way, "People get tired, sometimes," as if it were normal for Dario to have left because he was "tired" of his wife and children.

Camilla's mother never uttered a word of blame, for that matter. Any condemnation for whatever serious offenses people might commit seemed to lie outside her moral standards, if she had any at all. (You couldn't help but wonder!) Any show of intolerance or reproach was reserved for things of no consequence: closed doors that should have been kept open, or vice versa; wet footprints on the floor; spilled milk on the stove; the children's messes; their "awful" manners. Then, her gaunt old face would turn a mean shade of red. One night, she startled Camilla who had snuck into the dark kitchen from the portico, on her way back from the barn where she'd met that young American soldier, an escaped prisoner of war in hiding for days. Her mother knew he was hiding out, awaiting help to flee to Switzerland. Camilla found her mother in the kitchen, smoking the last puffs of a cigarette as she stood by the smoldering fire, wrapped in a thick woolen shawl. It was the last winter of the war. The young soldier fell for Camilla right away, after she translated for him and brought food to the hideout—bread, milk, salami, and thick slabs of polenta that he dipped his fingers into, flummoxed—along with a washbasin, soap, and a towel. It was her usual maternal instinct, thinking how pleased she'd be to know Nicola was also cared for by some loving mother while away fighting in the Alps. Plus, the American was so far from home, thrust into a war that must have seemed particularly senseless and absurd.

The soldier took her in his arms and said she looked just like a loved one he'd left behind in the States, apologizing even as he held her tightly, trembling all over. Unable to deny him the little bit of love he wanted, she agreed to a rendezvous that night. They'd never see each other again, anyhow. As she lay there in his arms, the warmth of pleasure overcame her, lust awakened.

A sudden flame raged, sure enough, and the sex, the pleasure, left her in a daze. No one had touched her since her husband disappeared, and not because she felt obligated to stay faithful to him. She'd never had such qualms, that was simply the way things were, but she couldn't deny that a flood of passion somehow cleansed and washed away the cold ashes of a long abstinence. She'd gone there with maternal compassion and left with fire in her veins. That rapturous delight must have been written all over her face when she came home and her mother surprised her. Camilla dreaded her judgment: only country girls had trysts in haystacks. Instead, after a long silence, her mother said impassively, "I couldn't sleep and felt like smoking this last cigarette, but there weren't any matches in the bedroom." It was nearly one in the morning, and freezing cold, and there was no possible explanation for Camilla sneaking in at this late hour. "That's life, isn't it?" her mother said with a smirk, and tossed the cigarette into the embers. As she brushed past with her thick woolen shawl on her way up the stairs, with Camilla not knowing where to stand or where to look, she added, nonchalantly, "Weren't you cold, dear?" and rested a wrinkled hand on her shoulder. "Go on to bed."

That was her mother—and those were perhaps the only times she felt any love toward her. Yet the endless frustration of familial relations, especially between the two of them, drove Camilla to leave home young and prove herself as a married woman. She knew Anna had done the same. Long before her sister died, each admitted to the other that their excessive affection toward their husbands and children was the result of this complex they suffered. Thus, Camilla's fleeting affair, which she never regretted or felt ashamed of, sounded an alarm. Her mother must have thought so, too, that such behavior was a problem to be solved, since after the incident she began to sing the praises—openly, and with a notable lack of subtlety—of a well-to-do resident of the area, her neighbor, a wealthy landowner who discreetly and steadfastly courted Camilla from afar for quite some time. Rosso, they called him, on account of the vivid red color of his thick, curly hair. Tall and muscular, forty-five or fifty, he was always out and about wearing country clothes, corduroy and boots with a rifle slung over his shoulder, since he was also an avid hunter—of game and women, naturally. He lived alone in a solitary house, in the middle of a vast estate, with stables, kennels, and a library. On her evening walks, if she happened to pass the perimeter wall, she'd catch a glimpse of him through the window—open or with the lights on, depending on the season—standing in front of those packed bookcases. He had invited her over, a few times, but she never went alone. So, after catching her by surprise that night upon returning from the barn, her mother implied that if she was determined to let loose, if she had no qualms, she might as well make it worthwhile. Perhaps she had a point, but Rosso had always intimidated her, with that brute physicality he could hardly contain. She had little faith in his love for books, his Latin quotations, his classical records. He was a country gentleman, to be sure, and an attractive one at that—but what else might she learn, at the dinner table and in bed? And what would she tell her children? In a country as rotten as Italy, a woman of her age and social standing had nothing left but the thrill of an escapade—and in this case, she told herself, better to end up in the barn, the only risk being some hay in her hair. Eventually, once the war ended, the time came to return home to the city, without having to cut any ties. Rosso let her go without making advances, with a look of genuine sadness she didn't think him capable of.

She set the sewing on her lap. The milk had turned cold, the doves had flown away.

A woman on my own. That's what I am.

But that irrepressible feeling of being alive, of expecting something from life, never left her. It's there when she wakes up in the morning, when she goes to bed at night—the true companion of her solitude. She thinks of her father (who wasn't as quiet and guarded as her mother, no) and the times he used to toss her from the boat into the water, so she'd learn to swim. Her father was right—she did learn to swim, and well—yet still it feels like she's cleaving, one long, calm stroke at a time, through a vast space that keeps pushing her farther and farther away from youth.

IV

If the furnace ran at a low temperature during the day, with the valves and vents almost fully closed, especially when the weather was mild, at night it ran at full blast. The flames glowed red through its open mouth, and hot air rumbled through the pipes when the house was quiet. But it was hardly ever quiet. Though everyone went to bed fairly early, they usually huddled together for a while in the main room to warm up after dinner. Camilla had put up a partition in the corner by the furnace, which hid a chair piled high with pajamas, nightgowns, robes (whoever was lucky to have one!). Each of them would undress, one by one, hidden from view—first the children, on school nights—and then head off to bed, clothes and shoes in tow. Camilla came to love this odd bedtime ritual. It began as they sat on the sofa and armchairs, tatty yet still plush, and the chairs they dragged from the kitchen to the center of the room, trying not to wake the baby who was already asleep. As for smoking, as a rule they did so as little as possible, to avoid spoiling the air. In any case, the only smokers were Enzo (who wasn't always there), Arrigo, and Milena; sometimes they'd go out on the balcony before hurrying back inside—brrr!—shivering and warming their hands by the furnace. Whoever began changing in the meantime would linger for a while and chat from behind the partition that was low enough for their heads to peek over. The children often played a game, studying each other's hidden gestures to guess which article of clothing they were wearing or removing. "You slipped off your socks!" they cried, or "You pulled down your underwear, rascal!" It was one of the rare occasions when Arrigo laughed his head off. One of them might shower before bed and towel off the wet hair around their ears; another might yell, no, I'll wash up tomorrow, I'm too tired! Camilla directed traffic as she always did, acting stern and fatigued when in fact that was the best part of her day. She had a heart-wrenching feeling that it would all end soon enough, and they'd all go their own way, as they should, after all; she wished as much. Though she knew well (they all did) that some people lived that way all the time—if not worse off, with little hope of things getting better—she realized such assertions wouldn't appease the children when they started complaining. They were all children to her, even Milena, Enzo, and Regina. Actually, those two never complained; Regina came from a strict, straitlaced family that kept her in line, even after the baby was born, and Enzo liked to act tough.

But he also knew better, Camilla could tell. Life was much easier, practically speaking, in that colony of sorts where he was born and raised, if only for the mild climate. She was sure he couldn't stand the cold, even if he wouldn't say so. Whenever she noticed him come home late in the evening, without having had time to heat up his room, she'd leave a note on the door: "Come for dinner, don't freeze in there!" They were all on friendly terms by now, except for Alba who snootily insisted on using the formal address: "Pardon me, Mr. Enzo . . ." For a long time, he made it a point to call her "Miss Alba," until she finally said, "You can cut out this 'miss' business. I can tell you're doing it on purpose, trust me. We can be formal and still call each other by name."

". . . Five thousand lira a day is plenty, isn't it?" Alba whispered as she gazed distractedly at the flames flickering through the furnace door. "Can you live well on five thousand lira a day?"

She was talking to Milena, as usual, but Arrigo overheard and snickered. "Why, has the office raised your pay to five thousand lira a day?"

Alba shook her beautiful head. "No, silly," she replied, sounding secretive, "but I know someone who earns that much."

"Doing what?" Camilla furrowed her brow.

"Sales, I think." Alba hesitated. "I'm not sure, exactly. Office talk."

"If it's clean money, she's lucky," her mother said harshly.

"Alba doesn't seem to know if it's clean or not, do you, Alba?"

Enzo had spoken up. Alba spun around, bristling. "I said, I don't know," she frowned, and turned her back.

"Sure, five thousand lira is a good living, these days," Milena chimed in, late as usual, between yawns. Regina was untangling a knot from the ball of yarn that Lalla was holding. Lalla was already ready for bed; she was the first to change her clothes behind the partition, and now sat wearing her coat over her pajamas.

Alba noticed, irritated. "Why won't you buy her a robe, Mother? Send her to bed. She looks ridiculous in that getup. If someone were to come over . . ."

"Don't worry, no one's coming, certainly not at this hour! It'll be a while until we buy Lalla a robe, my dear. I don't make five thousand lira a day."

"What a getup!" Lalla laughed. "I'm dressed the part for this poorhouse. It's almost too elegant. Look, not a single rag."

"Right, no patches covering your ass," said Guido.

"Guido!" Camilla scolded. "Don't get carried away, as usual." But everyone was laughing, even Enzo, who gave Guido a playful whack on the head with his rolled-up newspaper.

"I've had it!" Alba shot out of her seat as if that was her cue to leave, clearly exaggerating her irritation. "No one can ever talk in this house. I'm going to bed. A good night to all of you, heroes, saints, and martyrs!" she paused in the doorway and scowled.

"Sorry to see you go, with that sense of humor," Camilla said calmly. "Where did you have breakfast this morning?"

Alba kept her back turned. "At the dining hall, didn't I tell you?"

"No, you didn't mention a dining hall."

"Really!" Enzo replied, surprised. "I thought I saw you at half past near Via Speronari . . . Am I mistaken?"

"You certainly are. It wasn't me." Alba shut the flap door. The thin partition creaked and shook for a moment. They could hear her close the shutters, open a drawer, drag a chair—then something fell with a thud. Camilla was knitting a sweater for Nicoletta from the same ball of yarn that Regina was untangling. When the conversation resumed, she whispered to Enzo, sitting nearby, "Are you sure it was her on Via Speronari?"

Enzo was reading the newspaper (or was he pretending?). He glanced up and seemed confused for a moment (or was he pretending?), then shrugged, quickly lowered his eyes, and kept reading. "I must have been mistaken." Camilla continued, as if talking to herself, "That girl's too sullen, too irritable. She has no reason to be, all things considered. I . . ." she paused, as if swallowing a bitter pill. "I let her keep almost all the money she earns, you know, because I hate to see her suffer this . . . this rage, whatever it is. I don't understand it."

"Don't get too upset, Camilla. You know Alba's got a bad temper. She wishes she could have everything she wants, and she wants plenty of things . . . all of them material! The easiest things to get." He smiled. "And she doesn't yet realize she won't ever be satisfied, even once she gets them."

"None of this is any consolation, you know."

"You shouldn't need consoling, Camilla." He folded the newspaper, almost angrily. "Let her make mistakes and fix them on her own."

"That isn't good advice, Enzo. So what am I here for?"

"You're setting a good example. You always have. So much the worse if she doesn't appreciate it."

Now Camilla was the one laughing. "We sound like a schoolbook lesson. When have parents ever set a good example for their children, Enzo? I'm certainly not deluding myself anymore with that wishful thinking. It's enough that they tolerate us." She noticed Regina watching them, ignoring Lalla who was trying to get her attention. "Enzo's right," Regina said, and Camilla knew she'd heard everything. "You get too upset and torture yourself." Regina set the yarn on her lap as Lalla rubbed her now-empty hands together. "You shouldn't give her the idea that you don't trust her, that you keep an eye on her. No wonder she's got a bad temper."

"Who are you talking about?" Lalla asked, curiously eyeing the three of them.

"Your sister."

"Why not say 'my daughter'?" Lalla laughed. "That snob. I don't understand why you worry so much, always on her case. Just let her be!"

"Go on, dear, it's past your bedtime."

"It's still early, and I'm not sleepy at all!" Lalla pouted. "You know I can't even read in bed, with the lamp in the middle of the room. You won't even let me light the candle on the nightstand."

"A candle's the last thing we need, with wicker everywhere!" Regina sounded concerned.

"You're afraid I'll set Nicoletta on fire, that's why you don't want any candles."

"Nonsense. The furnace worries me enough."

"Speaking of which," Camilla interrupted, "I won't add more firewood, that's enough for today. You'll all have to go to bed when it gets cold."

Milena and Arrigo weren't paying attention. Instead, they were teasing Guido, who was reciting by heart the showtimes of every film and performance happening that night, and not just in Milan—he even knew what was on in Florence, Rome, Turin. "Mais il est toqué, cet enfant," Milena said in her mellifluous voice, and Arrigo nodded his big head. "Your schoolwork!" he chuckled. "Can you recite your lessons this well?" He turned to his wife, pointing at the boy. "Whenever I see him out and about, he's always reading the playbills. That's what he studies, this kid."

"Sure. Don't encourage his antics!" Camilla said as she stood from the table and gathered her sewing, the knitting needles, the newspaper. Regina followed and took down the clothes hung to dry by the furnace. Only the baby's things hung there during the day, for decency's sake, but when everyone went off to bed, sheer stockings appeared, bras, underwear, all fluttering on the clothesline overnight in the warm, dry air. Enzo walked to the door with Guido hanging on his tall shoulders, looking as if he were floating above the floor. They went out on the balcony but didn't linger in the cold. ("Don't you follow Enzo out," Camilla chided, begging Enzo to shut the door behind him, since the boy would disturb Milena and Arrigo if he didn't go straight to his nook.) They all whispered goodnight so as not to wake the baby. Alba was still awake—they could see her lamp through the wicker partition, a lamp Lalla envied her terribly, for it rested on the nightstand where Alba could adjust it as she pleased. Camilla and Regina were the only ones who stayed up to hang the clean laundry from the basin. In silence. Another day was done, and there was nothing left to say but the same dull phrases, go through the same motions. The laundry on the clothesline started to drip. "Leave it," Camilla whispered, when Regina noticed the wet spots on the floor. "It'll be dry in the morning. I'll clean up tomorrow."

"I'll do it," Regina replied. "You're busy enough, aren't you?" Meanwhile, Alba had turned off the light.

So, everything sank into darkness and silence, an urban silence, more like a faraway thrum, of wheels whirring, the piercing wail of screeching metal, things falling with a thud, an indistinct clamor that floated up to the attic as if from another world. It wasn't raining, so the gutters made no sound, otherwise the only nearby noise would be a faint drip from the roof, or the long, endless gush of an autumn downpour.

Alba gazed into that darkness but couldn't see the hazy figures that gradually emerged in the night as her eyes adjusted. Words and phrases from the recent present flickered around her like letters written in fire, then a mist or fog began to gather and they disappeared, only to resurface in different shapes and luminosities.

Indeed, she had been on Via Speronari; for now, her only deceit was having accepted the invitation. She saw herself sitting at the table in the smoky air of a simple trattoria, with plain glassware and burnished steel utensils set inelegantly on the wine-stained tablecloth. She was the one who had suggested meeting there, hoping no one would see her, while her companion looked around with an air of disapproval, as if the place were beneath her. The woman's fleshy hands rested on the tablecloth, somewhat coarse yet carefully manicured, with perfectly polished blood-red nails. Now and then, she crushed a long cigarette, of which she'd barely taken a few puffs, into a saucer. (Arrigo and Enzo smoked every bit of their cigarettes, no way they'd waste them like that . . .) Yet she had an enticing face and smooth silky skin, a true blond—and so well-dressed! A perfectly tailored coat, made of soft shearling wool, a gorgeous satin scarf, and those gloves, that handbag . . . The shops already stocked such things, if you could afford them, and hers must have come from Via Montenapoleone. A far cry from the clothes rationed by the UN . . .

I'm not doing anything wrong, Alba thought, why worry? But a vague uneasiness wouldn't loosen its grip on her during that lunch. If I never mentioned this woman at home, it's because . . .

Alba rolled over suddenly in bed, as if something had stung her.

She hadn't said anything for a reason. Months before, the woman had quit the office, "for her health" (this made everyone laugh, she being the picture of health!); she couldn't stand the strain, the hours were too long, so she decided to work as a translator, having good connections with certain publishers who needed technical expertise. Before leaving, the boss assigned her to train Alba, who would take on some of her duties. One day, early on, Alba overheard the woman bragging to the office ladies ("my colleagues," she pompously called them) that she'd earn far more in no time after leaving that job. Opportunities present themselves when you move in certain circles, she said; wealthy foreign businessmen would soon flock back to Italy, as they had before, and they'd need secretaries who knew languages, stenography, *et cetera* ("*et cetera*, indeed!" her "colleagues" said), they paid well, and even took them on business trips!

"The whole package, in other words," the ladies laughed. "We know about those circles!"

Alba and the woman shared a desk at the office and grew quite friendly during those weeks of training. The woman seemed indifferent to the insults of her fellow employees, while she was affable and warm with Alba from the start, as if taking her under her wing, giving advice, building her defenses against something Alba didn't quite understand. Subtle, persuasive whispers followed Alba day after day, like a spell in her ear.

"You know, I was shocked when you first came to work here, such a young and beautiful girl, among these witches. Aren't they hideous? Let them fiddle with their fountain pens and inkwells . . . that's all they're good for, with their bad breath! They could kill flies a mile away . . . But you! Do you want to be stuck here forever? You can do much better, trust me. Learn as much as you can, whatever's useful, then cut and run. Fast. The sooner, the better."

The woman visited now and then in her free time, but stopped showing her face once she sensed her colleagues' suspicion. "Free time," they said in the break room. "Can she really afford those clothes on technical translations? Who's she kidding?"

Some weeks later, after a chance meeting, the woman invited Alba out for a glass of vermouth at an elegant bar in the city center. Spring had given way to summer, the weather was warm. "How lovely! You cut a fine figure," she said, eyeing Alba's cotton dress, a striped chemise suitable for the office. Then she resumed her subtle questioning. "What are you still doing there?" Didn't she realize, she continued, that the best that could happen to Alba was for the boss's son to woo her and make her his mistress? Oh, she wouldn't advise it at all! (Again, that spell in Alba's ear.) The man was nothing but a lout from up north, and they were all a bunch of cheapskates. Even if she got pregnant (Alba shuddered at the possibility, presented in such stark terms) and he married her, it would still be a bad deal.

"He'd keep you stuck at home, churning out babies, the way Italian husbands do. You'd never, ever see the Côte d'Azur or Taormina."

"Why, have you been?"

"Of course! Listen, one of my last affairs . . . business trips, I mean, took me to London. In May. The city's still destroyed, worse than here. But I saw Admiral Nelson's statue."

The woman lit a cigarette and blew the smoke sideways, narrowing her eyes. She was well taken care of now, she admitted, with someone to look out for her; but as for getting started, she'd done that on her own, without a leg up. She said so proudly—"No one gave me a leg up." When Alba asked timidly, "Not even your family?" she replied with a dismissive shrug. "Those people! Hmpf!"

She had a few relatives down south in Le Marche—vaguely mentioning them during their early conversations, when they sat at the same desk—but who they were, she never said.

But she did tell Alba about the gold, later, when she came by on occasion to wait outside the office, trying not to let the other ladies see her, or phoned when she knew Alba was about to leave. Let's meet at this or that café, she'd say, always footing the bill.

She certainly has plenty of free time! Alba couldn't help but think.

A jeweler the woman knew well had sold her some gold at a good price, despite knowing she would pay in installments. She used part of her last wages to make the first payment, and then, with a month before the second was due, pawned the gold to pay off the rest. The money was enough to rent a small furnished apartment where she could finally live on her own, no longer at boarding houses ("Those crooks!" she called the owners) or inns, where "you live a rotten life without enough cash."

(She called it "cash," just like Matelda.)

Her initial earnings managed to cover the hefty installments, and she even redeemed the gold she'd pawned after a while. "I sold it for a profit, go figure." It was during one of those conversations that she told Alba about Nelson's statue, with the obvious satisfaction of a child sucking on a sweet. "I'm already making five thousand lira a day," she boasted. "I'd love to tell those big mouths who used to gossip about me . . ." But she suddenly had second thoughts, as if the sweetness turned bitter on her tongue. "Don't say a word, they'll jump to all sorts of conclusions." Then, as Alba gathered her things, she said "Leaving so soon?" And Alba, who always felt somewhat uneasy around her, grew suspect: was this woman weaving a web—or setting a trap?

"Five thousand lira a day." The words lodged in her throat. The woman sensed Alba's shock and trepidation, realizing how she must have held her in the grip of her piercing gaze—like a bird of prey. Slightly bothered, Alba had always tried not to let her surprise show. Why was this woman always sharing her affairs with her, of all people? Why flaunt her lavish gloves, shoes, dresses? Was that the trap she'd set? She sometimes seemed sincere.

"I wanted to escape the muck of poverty, understand? Things were tough, believe me! I didn't have much time to waste. The years fly by, for you and me both."

There was no mistaking how she earned five thousand lira a day, not at all. Which was why Alba never mentioned it at home—until that night. She now realized she'd been careless (especially since Enzo had seen her). She should have held her tongue, rather than talk.

Late summer had given way to the bright days of early autumn, and after weeks of silence, the young woman got in touch again. She phoned her at the office at the usual hour, as Alba was about to leave.

"I wanted to tell you I moved into a new place . . . With a telephone, too. Wait there, I'll meet you at the office."

Wearing a brand-new suit, she eyed Alba's modest autumn coat without a word, but wasted no time telling how she finally managed to rent a vacant apartment and furnish it herself: on the ground floor, with a private entrance through the garden, even a pergola! "So no one can spy on me from upstairs, and I don't have to walk past the porter unless I want to. They're always calling the police, those damn vultures . . ."

Alba couldn't help herself. "Why? What are you so afraid of?" The woman laughed, circled by wisps of cigarette smoke, and stared with those big rapacious eyes.

"Come visit sometime. I want to show you how well I've settled in."

It was a brief encounter, just a drink at the bar. Bothered by how the woman had eyed her coat, Alba wanted to leave right away, with the excuse that she was expected at home earlier than usual. As they said goodbye, the woman insisted, "Come visit, I mean it!" and whispered, "You know I'll buy a car soon? I'm already taking driving lessons."

Now Alba's eyes shot open with a shudder in the ghostly darkness. She didn't realize she had nodded off, and her sleep must have been nightmarish, for she could still see herself sitting at that table, staring at the wine-stained tablecloth, orange peels and walnut shells strewn across the dirty plates. She had given a start when the woman said, "All right, let's go." She was nearly as tall as Alba, but shapelier. "Let's call a cab," she said, and paid for everything as usual, breakfast, coffee, cigarettes. "You don't smoke, do you? And you don't wear any makeup." With a slight yawn, she concluded, "Nothing wrong with that."

The taxi had sped through the nearly deserted streets at that hour. Through the fogged-up glass, as they drove past familiar shops and window displays, and the grand entryways of the palazzi in the city center, Alba glimpsed iron gates half-covered in blackened winter leaves, bare trees, slender spruces, lonely sidewalks, all cloaked in the heavy, humid air. "What did you tell your family?" the woman asked at one point, and she heard herself reply, "That I'd eat at the dining hall, not at home. We don't have a telephone." She sighed—that she remembered well. The woman continued, snide yet sweet, "Was it you or someone else who told me your father disappeared?" Alba was silent. "Fine, don't answer if you don't want to," she added. "But that's the way life is, right? Even our parents can't be trusted." With a jolt of the brakes, the taxi stopped.

Alba anxiously switched on the lamp, as if something called out to her suddenly from the darkness. For a moment she almost couldn't recognize the sparse furniture surrounding her in that confined space: the closet, the wobbly nightstand with uneven legs, her reflection in the mirror, lying in bed, the dark slanted beams—but the dim light calmed her nerves. She heard a rustle behind the partition, perhaps her mother's soft footsteps, since she always got up at night. Stirred by the fear of hearing her hushed, sweet voice ask, "Why aren't you asleep, Alba?" she reached over and turned out the light.

The other scene took shape in Alba's mind: the gloom of winter hovered over those rooms, just like this one, and a delicate fragrance lingered in the tepid air. Was it almond-scented soap? The radiator was warm to the touch.

"The furnace works? Lucky you! Many buildings still have no heat."

Yes, the woman replied, the apartment had a furnace. "It's in the kitchen, see." She burned wood during the day, and coal in the evening, to keep the rooms warm even when she left the house.

A faint light filtered through the shutters. The kitchen looked uninhabited, as if no one had ever cooked there. Instead, the attic kitchen was bustling at all hours, with baby clothes hung everywhere to dry.

It was just as the woman had described it, two rooms and a bath. That tiny bathroom—what she'd done with the place! Alba gave a start at seeing it. The tub was covered in delicate pink tiles. The porcelain sink and bidet were pink, too, even the toilet, where a colorful silk tassel hung from the pull chain, and the chintz-covered seat had a lovely, pleated trim. Peeking out of a ceramic box, a tissue fluttered like a butterfly's wing in the draft as the door swung open. The woman's soft, proud voice noted every detail. "There's even a boiler, see, it works perfectly when the electricity comes on. We make do until things get back to normal. If I need hot water during the day, I can boil some in the kitchen, that's what the big enamel pot is for."

(Oh really, Alba thought wryly.)

"Let me pour you a drink."

The apartment was newly furnished, Alba could tell, and flamboyantly so. (Her mother would have laughed, she was sure; there was nothing garish about the modest attic.) A fur pelt served as the bedside rug, for example—how delightful it must have felt to sink her bare feet into the cream-colored fleece, despite the bristles (goatskin, of course). The spacious bed was draped entirely in mauve faux satin, as morbid as a coffin. Simpering porcelain figurines adorned the lampshade, vase, and candy dish, while other framed figures sought to liven up the space that looked oddly cold, almost clinical. From where Alba sat sipping a purplish liqueur from a dainty glass on the austere sofa, upholstered in dark blue velvet, the immaculate bed in the next room resembled an operating table. Everything was perfectly neat and tidy, every surface sparkled, the scent of almond soap wafted through the air; the only thing missing was a surgeon in a white coat, rubber gloves and mask, flanked by a nurse holding a basin full of floating bits of something she couldn't see but which was certainly repulsive. I should act more excited or impressed, she thought . . . or envious, even!

"Delicious" was what Alba actually said as she raised the glass after downing its contents. "But I really must be going now." She set the glass on one of those polished, gleaming surfaces, with a smile that was more uncomfortable than friendly. It was time to put an end to this; the breakfast, and that visit, weren't for nothing. She was sure of disappointing the woman, who meanwhile ignored her and bragged about the total discretion with which she always conducted her affairs. No one ever visited—at least no one she didn't want to see. Alba was the exception. The dressmaker, the manicurist, the masseuse, no one was allowed in the house. "Everyone's so nosy, always trying to worm their way in." As soon as she could afford to start a business of her own, she'd be gone—"So long, ladies and gentlemen, you never knew me. I'll open a beautiful salon, a classy establishment, obviously." With a smug smile, she added, "I could even end up married, it's not out of the question."

She saw Alba to the door. It was then, as she turned the handle, that she said those words. "Do what you want . . . But for starters, I'd lose it if I were you . . . you know what I mean. You're an adult, for God's sake, it's your decision."

Alba thought she heard the woman laugh as the door closed. In the taxi (the driver was waiting outside, her return fare had been paid for) she noticed barely half an hour had gone by, so she wasn't late for work. Huddled in the back seat, she thought the ride must not have cost much, after all . . .

The woman hadn't uttered the end of that sentence, which simply flashed in Alba's mind. Was she frightened by the venomous clay that seemed to shape those words? It had begun to rain; the sidewalks gleamed, wisps of fog floated among the trees before gently dissipating. Then the buildings grew denser, their sharp edges, rooftops and cupolas rushed toward her in waves, ever closer, finally sealing her inside the city's lonesome din—the same she could now hear humming in the distance, keeping her awake.

Was that really the reason she couldn't fall asleep? Or was it the woman's foul words that burst in and shattered the darkness? "My *affairs* brought me to London, I saw Nelson's statue." The fiendish statue towered over her, amid dark gathering clouds that threatened to swallow her up.

"Total discretion . . . no one ever visits . . ." and yet here they are, surrounding Alba with their devious smiles, those dolled-up louts, the manicurist, the dress-maker, the masseuse, groping at her with their fleshy hands and tentacle-like fingers ("go on, lose it," they seem to say), as if ready to steal her away. Instinctively, Alba squeezes her thighs tight.

Like a dazzling gold star, the "five thousand lira a day" cut through the darkness. Somewhere, a door slams (a real one). Alba shudders (so Enzo really did see her), rolls over, and buries her face in the pillow.

• • •

Enzo, on the other hand, was sure he hadn't been mistaken. Could it really have been another young woman darting through the crowd, with that blue and white patterned scarf tucked into her raincoat? Not just the same scarf, but the same auburn hair falling in soft waves over her cheeks, a color he holds in his heart like the enduring memory of a wound. Enzo doesn't care much about Alba, he just hates to see Camilla worry—like tracing circles in water, all that worrying.

But Camilla's right, despite his attempts to argue otherwise and calm her worries: that girl's up to something, hiding a scheme, maybe. Does she have a lover? He can't see the signs yet . . . but he senses something's bound to happen. Alba's smart enough to realize he knows what's what, more than the rest of them. He couldn't care less about her. A smug pretty face, that's all she is. She has it coming, though he isn't sure what.

Enzo tossed and turned in the tiny bed, tucked under the meager covers. He needed to get more blankets and arrange for the porter to heat his room in the evening. Retiring to those damp, freezing attic walls depressed him. But he'd have to get by on his own. Paying for the porter's help didn't bother him; what did bother him was the charity of his neighbors who bent over backward and left notes on the wooden door. Doting Italian women, forever at the service of men! Even Regina, with all that men had done for her!

Outside, the sky must have been invisible, a shapeless floating mass of gray, fetid fog, punctured now and then by searchlight beams. Or the black velvet skies of his memory, gleaming with stars. The fleeting gold of the setting sun over the placid desert horizon; the silhouette of the Caliphs' tombs, domed roofs encircled by rosy clouds of dust; the scalloped shadows of white minarets cast against porous stones that smelled of the East, the scent of caravans, sesame and incense, spices, garlic and lamb, and old musk. Cool, shaded souks where cavernous stalls displayed glimmering copper and marvelous silver, and the spirals of exquisite rugs swallowed you like quicksand. The muezzin's call to prayer at daybreak or nightfall (Allahu Akbar, Allahu Akbar!), rows of camels atop violet dunes, clover and jasmine in bloom. And the drums of an Arabian feast beat in his heart to mark the unrelenting number of years gone by. Everything's faraway, finished, swept up by the waves that took everything from him—even her.

I can't fend for myself yet, he thought, as the cold Milanese night pressed on his closed eyes. The porter's from Milan, too, of course she speaks in that well-mannered dialect; though he pretends to understand her, he doesn't actually know when to say yes or no, always afraid of giving the wrong answer. He'll send for his parents from Egypt as soon as he can, he's already earning enough—he's nearly thirty-three, it's about time to prove he can take on this responsibility: to reunite the family in Italy, as he should. His mother's an old woman now (his parents married late and he's an only child, he once told Camilla, to paint a clearer picture of himself), and he wants the poor woman to face Europe's harsh realities in the best possible conditions, after having lived comfortably in the Levant for many years. With so much changing, best to get out while one can. Change is positive, historic, it should happen, and anyone who ignores it, who can't read the writing on the wall, is deluding themselves . . . The Arab people will suffer upheavals, make inevitable mistakes, the same way childhood illnesses are unavoidable, but Enzo can say in good conscience that he's always been sympathetic, even when deep down he felt like they were bigoted and xenophobic. You had to understand them, all the shame and betrayals they endured; now, they'd have to learn everything from A to Z. But it's the changes happening here that will affect him most—and his elderly parents, to some degree. Who knows how far they'll get with understanding and acceptance!

Though his father had been an anarchist in his youth, then a socialist who helped found the Italian community around the People's University, the emergency aid, the citizens' cemetery, Enzo could tell from his letters that both his parents had a postcard idea of Italy, where everyone would band together once the storm blew over, no hard feelings. That was dangerous.

In reality, Enzo's already suffered the deep sting of disappointment, it bit him to the bone, but he won't say so in his letters, imagine what his parents would think. The usual cynic, they'd say. No one could deny that some good things had happened, or it would have ended differently. Yet he's still on slippery ground, stuck in the muck of doubt and uncertainty, simple as that . . . He'll have to ponder, as he did in the past, whether the Italians were too cunning to really have been fascists then, and now the opposite . . . or almost. Back then, when he emigrated to France as a young idealist, he'd already battled certain fears and suspicions—especially the fear that the main target of blame wasn't just the bourgeoisie, as his father's teacher in Alexandria used to say. He'd sometimes visit the man at the apartment block on the edge of the Arab Quarter where he rented a sunny room with a balcony facing the East Port. For years the old anarchist would sit on that balcony in his rattan chair, from which he seemed to gaze over the entire universe from on high. "A class with no traditions and no honor," he'd say, "with no education, no culture, no shame, quick to barter and betray. But are intellectuals any better? Is society any better?"

The cries of vendors selling sour lemons and jasmine rose from the street below; the warm scent of sea salt wafted from the shimmering blue waters of the East Port, where feluccas floated by—a dream, to remember it now in that dreadful Milanese cold. Back then, Enzo didn't just fear others ("We're all to blame," the old man used to say, "remember, we're all to blame, the shameless bourgeois, the intellectuals who think they'll get off scot-free, in the aristocratic isolation where they invest their supreme futility, pretending not to know the jails are full and those who fled are dying hungry all over the world . . . and the people, who justify their actions with poverty, ignorance, and superstition, as the Church and State have wanted for centuries . . . they're also partly to blame"). It was also himself he feared. Born and raised abroad, despite short sojourns in Rome during his studies, he often wondered back then whether his spirit, his character, his upbringing made him an Italian like everyone else—and he didn't think so. "You're not cunning enough to be a real Italian," the old man replied with a smirk, when Enzo naively asked the question one day.

Then the war brought life to a halt, there was more to do than spew sophisms about suspicions and appearances. His heartbreaking affair with that woman had left him numb, or hardened; and he finally made his way back to Italy, once and for all. In the end, he couldn't escape the fact that if everything had changed from then on, it was because he had changed. Sometimes he wondered whether the ache of disappointment sprung first and foremost from having disappointed himself, with his own cold indifference, detachment, disgust. So he forced himself to remember when he flew down over the mountains of Abruzzo, hauling those heavy packs, the austere aid of those old shepherds (so much like Old Testament patriarchs) who hid him in a cellar where he survived on soft cheese. He remembered how it felt when the raft quietly approached the shore, waves lapping in the dense darkness, as he entered the water and patted his pockets to make sure he had what he needed, papers, badges, ration cards. Those operations, planned with incredible accuracy at the British offices in Cairo—he sometimes enjoyed them, even. Yet when he recounted those same events later, his teeth would chatter as if he had a fever. He even saw a doctor, who suggested he persevere and keep telling his story, all of it, to overcome his fears. He no longer had anything in common with that character now.

I could try, he thought bitterly, but what's the point? He'd slept with many women, each time going through the motions, a lonely release he was secretly ashamed of. Those women weren't always thoughtless or vulgar, some even told him off. ("Is it really worth the trouble to get undressed with a cold fish like you?") More than once, he thought, he wouldn't have said no to spending a night with sweet, kind Camilla (the bed was starting to feel warmer now), but he wouldn't dare, with all those kids and relatives around. He was a friend and yet still a stranger, somehow cut off. He wouldn't have minded Regina either, so supple and pale, who seemed to harbor hidden resentment toward that poor fellow Nicola, without realizing it. Lalla sensed that dissonance, and whenever Regina mentioned the dead man, hardly ever in fact, the girl grew defensive, as if fearing Regina would ruin her image of him. The flawed human heart! Milena had said the same about Enzo once: how he flaunts that broken heart of his!

Stupid Milena, he thought. Human bonds are broken, not my heart.

Sleep was finally approaching. Nighttime noises drifted away with a groan, memories ebbed and flowed, chaotic and unreal, long streams of light sparkled and swelled in waves, drawing ever closer, gushing from an unknown source, and as he tried to guess from where, a thick ash enveloped his tired brain, and everything went dark and fell silent.

Arrigo didn't care for the sight of Milena's face on the pillow beside his, covered in the greasy cream she used to remove her makeup before bed, but when he tried wiping it off with the edge of the sheet, she complained he'd make a mess . . . plus, the night cream was essential, didn't he know her skin needed pampering?

What he did know, now, was that this wasn't a nightly ritual. Sometimes she'd lazily say "I'll skip it tonight" if she hadn't gone out and done up her face that day, suggesting he could come closer—as quietly as possible, since the boy was asleep behind the partition. Her displays of affection were thus contingent on night creams and on the soft snoring of their neighbor Guido, who luckily almost always fell fast asleep the moment he got into bed.

With his black head of hair against the pillow, sitting upright, arms outside the covers, Arrigo drummed his fingers against the turned-down sheet as if marking the tempo of a musical phrase. As he whispered excitedly to the shiny, sleepy face next to his, a round eyelid opened now and then and a cerulean eye stared at him to say: still at it?

"He's a buffoon, an arrogant young buffoon. Sure, someone his age can't have much experience, but certain things come naturally to a true artist, and an orchestra conductor ought to be a truer artist than every last one of us, thirty and forty times over . . . This one's deaf as a post, damn it. What's one to do?"

The two eyelids, streaked with bluish veins and fringed with delicate blond lashes, opened in unison and languidly said they didn't know. Then, in unison, they closed again.

"An orchestra's like an army, see—cavalry, infantry, artillery—and each unit must function on its own. Rather, each unit must create a feeling of total harmony—first winds, then brass, then strings—a harmony to be enjoyed in isolation, before all the pieces may work as one. There are no ugly textures of sound in an orchestra, like that buffoon said today. They're all beautiful. *All of them.*"

A weak groan—"Did you have rehearsal?"—and an affectionate yawn rose from the pillow next to his.

"I did. With that tone-deaf idiot." Arrigo grew more incensed. "He ought to listen for the high notes, especially on the strings. I realize some notes call for an acute effect, but without being overly drawn out. That's when the music starts sounding ugly. It's the conductor's fault, not the instrument's. Today, at one point, I put down my bow and told him so. 'This note's too long, maestro, it's wrong,' I said."

He stared into the dark as if facing his archnemesis. The closed eyelids couldn't tell whether the rival had accepted the challenge.

"You mustn't demand a prolonged note with such license, see, even from the trumpet, the horn, the flute.

Your lips tire, you run the risk of the instrument not holding the note to the end. But he doesn't seem to understand. Some maestro he is."

The fluttering lids attempted to stay open but then fell closed again, at longer intervals. Those eyes were most certainly asleep. What Arrigo didn't hear, instead, was Guido snoring—was the boy awake? He stared dejectedly into the dark, wondering why on earth that asinine young conductor refused to follow—or to respect—the logic of musical composition.

The Greats have always composed—still compose!—with logic and clarity, without scorning practicality, he thought. So why not follow the composition to the letter and execute the notes? Ah, interpretation! Unfortunately, even a conductor belongs to the despicable ranks of the solo artist, because in some sense that's what he is. He aspires to tyranny. The Great Composer's work, with which he experiments, is simply a pretext . . . I'd say it even gets on his nerves. What really ought to reign is an understanding of the very work one performs, its laws. Technical mastery is one thing, but so is respectful deference, a sense of tradition . . .

To whom was he ranting, without saying a word? To the sleeping beauty whose smooth cream-covered forehead glistened like a marble tile? To the creaky, quivering partitions? Or to the boy on the other side, who listened and lurked like a rabbit? A charming boy, full of energy, he was a sharp one. When the call finally came to play the violin in the orchestra, Arrigo was so happy! But how he hated not being able to discuss music in the house, beyond "this is good" or "that's bad." He couldn't care less that Milena liked *Cavalleria* or *La Bohème*; tastes could be puerile, as long as they're sincere. But Harmony, Balance, Tradition must reign . . .

He turned off the light and slid under the covers. Those capital letters kept haunting him in the dark. His arms were freezing, and he began rubbing his hands together, massaging his fingers. They'd have to be warm and limber to hammer out the martellatos, accent the staccatos. The music school was an icebox, the students complained they couldn't play with numb fingers. Broken windows everywhere. The management had promised to make the most urgent repairs that week. A pile of rubble, this country. How he'd wrestled with feeling nothing but disgust and dismay during the war, incapable of denouncing one side or the other, mostly staying out of the fray, though never fully shielded from it, of course. But poor Nicola! He talked and talked, always so calm, generous, even-keeled. Whatever he said made sense, there was no disagreeing with him. But then . . . piles of wreckage, piles of bodies, gurneys carrying mangled flesh from the frontlines. And all Arrigo could hear, for some reason, was the opening adagio of Mozart's string quartet, or some other classical gem. He tried fleeing to Milan where the war affected him less, despite the bombings. All the best excuses in the world couldn't help him stomach that awful insanity, one way or another. Devious, despicable humanity—that summed it up. A spider devouring the fly caught in its web, in its tight grip (see it pierce and suck the flesh, under the microscope) is nothing at all, compared to what humans do to each other with that mind of theirs—a mind equally capable of composing an adagio or allegro of enduring beauty. If you were to pass those killers and torturers on the street now, they'd all seem normal; perhaps (he sneered in the dark) they'd even appreciate Mozart's string quartet, like nothing ever happened.

The baby's finally asleep, what a relief—I can stop rocking the cradle, or she'll get spoiled and never nod off on her own. Who knows why she's so alert after nursing in the evening, always wanting to babble and stay awake, the poor thing. What can I do, with four of us in this room, always so worried about bothering Camilla, or Lalla, especially, who has to wake up for school. Good thing she sleeps like a rock at her age. That little bedroom of mine! Thinking back, I can hardly believe I grew up an only child with a room to myself. All to myself . . . It was so quiet! No one ever talked about anything of importance: the weather, good or bad, the food, the neighbors—not many, actually, we never saw much of anyone. Aren't you hungry today, they'd ask, are you tired, perhaps, did you work too hard at the office, did you get wet in the rain—as if I were a doll meant only to eat, sleep, not catch cold. Plenty of ways to show you care, I know, but the war had already begun, and we kept to ourselves, apart from rest of the world, as if what was happening outside our door was of no concern. Maybe that's why I liked Nicola right away, at least he talked to me, dug deep inside, explained me to myself along with explaining everything else happening around us. Sure, he had no trouble getting me in bed, with his sweet talk . . . men are selfish, Camilla's right, and he should have thought twice, given the risk . . . Things went fine, as they always did, I was lucky until the end, after he got sick and I couldn't say no, and besides, who am I kidding, wasn't I fond of him, too? Enough—I shouldn't think it was sour luck, that would mean poor Nicoletta was a mistake. Why didn't my parents, my mother, ever talk to me about these things, not necessarily the risks a young woman faces, since they couldn't have imagined I'd do it—but at least tell me love's a natural, inescapable feeling, not something to be ashamed of. Camilla was right to tell them off after I came here! "All you've done is scare and punish her, instead of teach her about life. Now let her be. What'll you do, poison her existence day after day with your contempt and accusations? She's pregnant, she needs to be left in peace." I thought my mother would faint when Camilla said to her face that I was pregnant, just like that. But they couldn't blame me, I'd always been a good daughter, they only thought I seemed bored . . . Better to laugh about it than . . . not cry, no, I cried enough when he died, poor Nicola, and I can talk all I want, but they shouldn't have called him a rat who took advantage, saying they'd have bolted the door and thrown him down the stairs if they'd known what he'd do to me, instead of taking him in like a son. I'm ruined for life, they say, even if I'll be recognized as a Resistance fighter's widow and Nicoletta can take her father's name. Maybe they'll calm down when everything's settled, but these things take time, so drawn-out and miserable, as it always is when you have to plead with those officials . . . Having to tell your whole story to those stony faces who stare down their noses at you like you're a whore, leering men who might invite you to do the same with them, since you've done it before, you're easy. I'll have to watch out when I go back to work, they'll have free rein, no strings attached, they'll be all over me the minute they get the chance. Motherhood hasn't ruined my looks, just the opposite, my own mother even said so, the first time—the only time—she saw me after the baby was born. You're prettier now, she said. Enzo sometimes looks at me as if he thought the same, maybe I remind him of the woman he lost, who knows what she was like. Camilla seems to think she was very attractive, a seductive type. But me! I'm like one of those wrecked buildings, with the façade still standing, but empty inside. Maybe that's why Enzo always tells me about the horrors of war, massacres, death camps, as if to prove what happened to me is nothing by comparison. He talks like Nicola, says the worst thing is having killed and disgraced those souls, debased and corrupted them, while I'm safe, he seems to be thinking, with a beautiful baby girl. Yes, a beautiful baby girl. When she nurses at my breast, I feel she's all mine, so tenderly, it's true. But it won't always be this way, poor Regina, who knows what's in store for you, silly girl, that's why you're crying when you should be asleep.

• • •

Milena must have fallen asleep while Arrigo was talking; some time had passed since Guido heard her soft, sluggish drawl. They must have turned off the lamp, too, but he could only guess as much, since no light filtered through the partitions. The window in his nook glowed pale. There was no point in his mother saying the shutters kept out the cold; he didn't want them closed unless it was stormy and windy, and it wasn't the season for storms. Whenever he lay in bed, morning or night, he liked to look out at the slanted edge of the roof eaves jutting over the balcony, the trellis holding up the now-bare rosebush, and, at dawn, the mourning doves perched daintily on their pink feet, pecking away. Then, someone—his mother, Regina, sometimes Alba—would fling open the glass doors to the balcony to check on the potted plants or something else. Seeing the shutters open, they'd peek inside to see if he was up or wake him with a soft tap on the glass, to avoid rousing Milena whose neighboring window was firmly shut. She wanted to sleep until late, in pitch darkness, that snob.

He'd have liked to spend some time in Enzo's room earlier that night, since it wasn't late, but his mother wouldn't allow it, on account of his forced route through that pathetic excuse for a foyer that separated him from those two. Everything creaked horribly, it was true, except for the stone floor his feet knew every inch of, having walked upon it barefoot so many times.

The night must have seemed endless, had he stayed up until sunrise! He'd never tried; even when he made up his mind to, sleep would suddenly take hold and swaddle his head like a soft, warm blanket, and that was it. Slowly, slowly, he'd fall into the gray haze of an ever darker, more inviting chasm. Not even his desire to eavesdrop could keep him awake—but that was a topic no one was allowed to joke about, nor would they dare, truth be told, Enzo being too considerate, Regina too shy, Alba too indifferent . . . let alone his mother. Mamma had shot a glare at the handsome gentleman Matelda brought over the first time she came to visit. Seeing their living arrangements, compared to Matelda's luxury three-bedroom apartment on Via dei Giardini, the man had said, "You're in for a good show, kid!" Good or bad, Guido never overheard a thing, those two were as quiet as mice, but how could Milena never let slip a sound, with tall, lanky Arrigo weighing a ton?

"May I come in?" he'd ask from the balcony after knocking on Enzo's door, always sounding as nervous as the first time. "Of course, come in," Enzo replied, lounging on the bed, smoking and staring at the ceiling, sometimes reading, sometimes writing. Guido couldn't help but think how much he'd prefer to have him as an older sibling, not stupid, snooty Alba, who always looked right past him like he was invisible. Though he couldn't talk to his sisters about certain things, Enzo wasn't much for conversation either. Sometimes he'd sheepishly mention his favorite topic, the theater, but the conversation fell flat; besides his utter unfamiliarity with the subject, Enzo also seemed uninterested. Mamma often said Enzo was vacuous about certain things, and his lack of interest in theater and the cinema seemed to Guido like one of those voids. The few books he kept in his room on a musty, chipped shelf, the kind you'd find in a shabby kitchen, had such unappealing titles! He would have liked to lend Enzo his paperback Shakespeares, cheap copies where the type bled so badly you'd sometimes have to guess the words. He really would've liked to lend him those books and talk about them later. But he lacked the courage, and felt foolish and angry with himself instead.

Why shouldn't I? he asked the surrounding darkness, where only the windowpane shone faintly. No answer. Still, Enzo seemed like a character to him, not from a novel because he didn't read novels, those were Lalla's business, but one from the movies, a comedy, or drama, that was it. He'd rather be skinned alive than admit it, but sometimes he'd imagine Enzo making a commanding entrance, mid-scene. He could hear the captivating sounds of the silver screen, crystal clear. Footsteps climb the stairs, for instance, a door creaks open and shut. The leading man, a slender, handsome fellow (like Enzo), enters with suspenseful silence, sets a package on the ground and warms his hands by a flickering fire, while men sit around a table playing cards, let's say, cursing. They exchange words through gritted teeth, rapid-fire, all hell's about to break loose, but the young man (Enzo) turns around suddenly, eyes like daggers, and makes threats that leave the others stunned, scared stiff. In the corner, cowering on a bed or divan, there might be a frightened young belle who loves that young man—just an accessory, Guido thinks, fleshing her out would be unwieldy. Shakespearean queens are one thing, Hamlet's mother, Lady Macbeth, Cleopatra, they all carry a certain weight, not these young harlots who strut and shimmy around in short dresses.

Or another scene, just like the film *Port of Shadows*. Cloaked in fog, dark waves crash against a crumbling stone jetty—all that's missing is the smell of the sea. We see Enzo from behind, confronting the Jean Gabin type dressed from head to toe in a slick black raincoat, an older Gabin, who could be his father.

His father, of course. An important part of the friendship Guido wishes he had with Enzo, of Enzo himself—another topic he never mentions, perhaps out of respect, Guido thinks, or discretion. But what a movie it would make: a father who disappeared, just like that.

Guido and Lalla used to tell stories when they were younger, she was the only person he ever talked to. She was the one who told him, a long time ago during the war, that their father wasn't in France anymore, as his family quietly guessed, but probably fled to South America, Suddamerica, to avoid getting caught by the Germans. Lalla had quite the imagination! From then on, Guido would picture his father blending into a vibrant, cheerful crowd (there was no war down there, and everyone had enough to eat, lucky them!), crossing paths with people of every color, a crowd that walked under different moons, different stars, Lalla said, a peaceful, powerful crowd that swallowed him up. A place where butterflies were this big—at least the size of a melon, Lalla gestured with her hands—where if you planted a seed at night, it would grow this tall the next day. Brazil? Chile? Peru? Maybe, Lalla said. Maybe somewhere on the Equator, a line Guido imagined as a tightrope under a dancer's feet. Did their father tiptoe across, swaying back and forth? "Of course not," Lalla said, "he walks with two feet on the ground, silly." But she was sure his children's names were tattooed on his chest, under his shirt. And she admitted having nightmares where she'd seen him dead, poor Papà, lying in the gutter; the crowd parted, giving him some air, then someone bent over and unbuttoned his shirt, and there were the tattoos, the names of his three children . . .

Ever the novelist, that's Lalla. Who could say if their imaginations match reality, if knowing the truth would shatter those ghostly visions, muddling them to the point where nothing was familiar any longer? Was their father a man of vice, a gambler or drunk, maybe a convict? Behind the family's wall of silence, anything's possible, and life could take one down murky, depraved paths. Guido tells his own stories these days, Lalla hasn't for a while. Oddly enough, lately Alba's the one who cheers him up, secretly slipping him extra money for a movie or matinee show. Alba's sensitive to making sacrifices, they clearly weigh on her more than the rest of them. Though they rarely talk and she hardly seems to notice him, as if he were invisible, at least she's generous, saying "go on, have fun," as if it were all just a diversion. No—it's a bittersweet, heart-wrenching affliction, a dream so asphyxiating he can hardly stand it.

Guido pulled the bedsheets and blankets over his head, warding off the icy chill in the air. That way, he wouldn't hear the city's endless din in the distance, nor the calm, methodical gnawing of the mice nearby, humbly admitting he wouldn't stay up until sunrise, not even this time.

As she waved her tiny arms aimlessly in the dark, a trickle of spit-up milk dirtied her mouth and dribbled down her chin, into the folds of her neck, and onto the bedsheet. They were all asleep now, resting upon their sad memories, their biting heartaches and bitter hopes, innocent or shameful desires. The partitions breathed and quivered invisibly in the gentle nighttime breeze that seeped cautiously through the crevices, stirred the stockings and underwear hung overhead, crept around the bare lightbulbs gone dark, and sniffed along the floors, sending up invisible puffs of household dust. She slept, too, a perfect, formless sleep, undisturbed by the globs of curdled milk that formed on the quilt (infants mustn't sleep on pillows), nor by the warm wetness that spread out underneath her with its sweet babylike scent of ammonia. She slept with tiny clenched fists and chubby cheeks, innocently bald and softly plump. A tender, poignant nothing. What could she be dreaming, if not a geometry of light and shadows, the unconscious anticipation of waking in tears upon the bulging breast that would soothe and flood her with loving, liquid joy? The memory of the storm could make the others shudder in their sleep. For her, it was simply winter—her first winter—knocking at the door.

PART TWO

I

The first dusting of snow turned the gray sky white, resting on the grimy red rooftops and tar-black sidewalks, forming tiny heaps in the cracks. People grumbled that it was too soon (it hardly ever snowed before Christmas, and it was only the end of November); the good-for-nothing mayor should have acted more quickly to fix the wartime potholes, you'd risk a sprained ankle or even a broken leg at night. Instead of the sun, a dingy drizzle replaced the dancing sleet to melt that first white coat and reveal the drab roof tiles and asphalt underneath. But the respite would be short-lived. Dogs sniffed around buildings; pensive cats stared down from the gutters (a few fell into courtyards and ended up dead on the wet cobblestones); canaries cowered in their cages, tucked into their fluffed, feathery collars, and darted about with a flicker of their bright, mean little eyes. They knew hard times were approaching, while those hapless humans didn't know a thing.

In fact, no one knew (and how could they?) that a terrible winter already hovered amid the distant clouds, spreading its vast wings, preparing to descend and seize every last thing in its deadly clutches. Camilla, feeling a duty to keep daily life humming along, cast an uneasy glance at the hostile, impenetrable sky, with one eye on the calendar: winter shouldn't start until December 22, when the sun leaves Sagittarius to enter Capricorn. Though the sun's closer to Earth (her father taught her as a girl and she never forgot it, like when he tossed her into the water from the boat so she'd learn to swim), it's the coldest season because the warming rays fall obliquely, at their lowest angle. She kept an eye on more than just the calendar, where the images of the winter months were a woman draped in a shawl, or a boy wearing a garland of withered leaves and dried fruit. She also eyed the scant supply of firewood and coal in the corner of the balcony, green wood that burned weakly and quickly soiled the chimney pipes, producing lots of smoke but little warmth—and hard to come by, no less. The last batch cost five hundred lira per ton, but the price had gone up and she always got less than what she'd ordered, on top of having to light the furnace earlier and earlier every morning. Flour was in short supply, too, though the newspapers claimed rations would be guaranteed until mid-December—the same papers that suggested making do with cornmeal if white flour was scarce. Polenta instead of bread, basically. Luckily, she'd learned to bake during the war, but it was easier in the rustic oven at the country house, and the bread came out better; here, it was harder to bake with flimsy aluminum pans on the gas stove, the bread was always over- or underdone. Camilla was overcome by memories of the country, where winter seemed less fearsome and far less sad than in the city. The muddy, frozen furrows would glisten gold in the sun (low in the sky, sure, but sun all the same), and when they began to melt with a soft crackle, the black-and-pink piglets rolled around inside with their adorable squiggly tails. The wintry scent of the country could cheer anyone up, despite the war—the smell of wild smoke and wet forest, of pulpy leaves that still seemed full of life, of mulled wine and roasted chestnuts in the house. She couldn't fathom how people managed to hate each other in the tranquility of nature, but they did all the same, because they were fascists or they weren't, because they were or weren't in the Resistance, because this man stole from that one—ten years before, perhaps. Such deceit, such vengeance and cruelty in those chaotic final days of the war—and none of it had anything to do with the Liberation. "Basement fighters!" some sneered at the men who reappeared when it was all over, gaunt, pale, beards overgrown. Those phony partisans pretended to have fought in the Alps, when they were really hiding in their cellars, said the old gossips who had a bone to pick with everyone (like her mother, for whom the war had simply been a bother). But many really had gone off to fight, and even died, during and after the war. Like Nicola.

So long as the baby doesn't catch cold in this wretched attic, Camilla thought. Whenever Nicola came to mind, so did the baby, as if she were responsible for her, as if it wasn't enough to feed them, keep the place warm, all of it. And no one knew how little money was left. There was enough to last a few months, and then . . .

I'll go to the country and ask Mother for more, Camilla thought, she might agree if the timing's right, and I'll promise to pay her back as soon as I can, for formality's sake. Rosso would have wanted nothing more than for her to ask him, but she also knew what he'd expect in return. She'd been more easygoing with the American soldier, perhaps because their encounter had nothing to do with money; she'd fluttered that night from her bedroom to the barn, like a bird that flies only after dark, and this, she knew, was because something about that young man had stirred in her before, reminding her of the way Dario made her feel: a current flowing between them. It wasn't just because they had slept together or were about to, but something deeper and more mysterious—gone forever, in any case.

She turned her thoughts away from those memories (perfectly useless, she said to herself, unconvincingly) and back to the winter. In the city, the season was hardly ever blustery, no gusts of wind that hurled dried pinecones against the shutters and birds against the telephone poles; instead, it was a tedious string of ever shorter, grayer days, formless and strangely quiet against the urban noise. If the din outside happened to hush, it seemed as if the lonely old house floated in a noiseless world whose only sound was the persistent gnawing of mice. There was no risk of finding dried-up white spider's nests between the slatted shutters, or clumps of frozen iridescent wings, dead moths, hanging in the windows. Perhaps that was why she even loved the sound of the baby crying, a cough, a nose blowing loudly (they all took turns catching colds and spreading germs), or Arrigo's violin: *La fille aux cheveux de lin* was lovely, for instance, reminding her of an August evening, in a country far north, where the sunsets last forever.

After that first dusting, it snowed again, this time a blizzard that went on for hours. The vast city, all dressed up in white, was almost beautiful despite its deep wounds, and strangely silent, as always happens when a steady snowfall leaves a thick coat on the ground. The only sound in that submerged world was the clatter of trams and bicycle bells. As soon as the snow stopped falling, the shoveling began. Towering banks lined the sidewalks and filled courtyards; no one knew that they'd stay put all winter long, never managing to melt, since fresh flakes would cover the dirty snow beneath. Every house had an ample supply of ice. Outside the street-level and first-floor windows, the threatening snowbanks grew and grew; cats pawed cautiously, then rushed back indoors, mewing in alarm; dogs sniffed around and pissed, melting only tiny patches that steamed in the frigid air and left yellowish dents behind.

The attic began to creak under the icy weight atop the roof tiles. Since they couldn't run the furnace overnight, thick, soft layers of fresh snow settled not only on the windowsills in the morning, but around the panes encrusted with ice. After the heat was on for a few hours and the ice finally began to melt, you could see through the glass again, but drops of water seeped in and you'd have to sprinkle sawdust beneath the windows. Guido went looking for some at carpentry shops and warehouses, hauling the heavy sacks home and seeming to enjoy himself. "Do you see yonder cloud that's almost in shape of a camel?" he'd say as he climbed the stairs or stopped to catch his breath on the landing, and anyone passing by, puzzled, would look first at him and then at the sky, searching for the shape of a cloud or a camel. When he reached the top, he'd drop the bag with a sigh and declare, "Here is my journey's end, and very seamark of my utmost sail."

"Who were you talking to?" his mother scolded from the balcony. "Give me that, stop acting silly." Handing her the sack, Guido laughed like a shrewd Shakespearean clown. "Look you, the worm is not to be trusted but in the keeping of wise people, for indeed there is no goodness in the worm."

"If only you were as serious about your schoolwork! Go on inside, it's cold out here."

Every morning, the same routine: you had to remove the canvas covering the meager supply of firewood on the balcony, shake off the snow that settled overnight, and bring in the day's share to dry by the furnace. Regina wanted to help, but she was nursing and Camilla wouldn't let her, so Lalla was almost always the one to venture out reluctantly in her galoshes. Once outside, though, Lalla gazed in awe: everything had lost its usual shape and become unrecognizable, slightly rounded, as if inflated from the inside. The old wall was the only thing that retained its ghostly form in the dim morning. White flakes floated and flickered in the leaden air, the snowbanks glistened mysteriously. She hated to leave footprints behind, but the fresh snow would repair the damage later. Lalla went back inside, face and hands numb from the cold, shouting how beautiful it was—"Come out and look, lazybones!"—but they'd scold her for waking the baby. Milena slept in later and later. When she finally got out of bed, wrapped in her heavy robe, hands in her pockets, she seemed to take offense at the sight of the blizzard, as if what was unfolding outside the window were some sort of scandal. "Mais voyez-moi ça," she mumbled with a yawn, making Arrigo leave the house bundled up like an enormous sausage.

Alba grew more and more irritable. "My window's staying closed, you can open it later," she said sourly on her way out in the morning, after taking her coffee standing in the kitchen; that vague "you" meant her mother, of course. She rarely had breakfast at home and never gave a reason, but griped about the cold and bad weather, and expected an early dinner because she was tired and wanted to lie down in the evening. Camilla would have preferred to avoid the inconvenience of serving dinner in two shifts (Arrigo wouldn't be home until he finished giving the private lessons that often took him far across town), but Arrigo said not to wait, always indulging Alba, whose tantrums Milena also defended; he'd eat later, as long as they saved him some hot soup.

"I'll serve myself," Alba said. "Who asked you, anyway?"

"Fine, then. Wash your dishes, too," her mother replied. "You stay out all day, we never see you. You could at least pretend to enjoy spending time with us at night," she added dryly, with a hint of weariness and disappointment that made Regina feel sorry for her. Whenever Alba ate her dinner at the corner of the kitchen table, Regina fidgeted by the stove and whispered, "Go sit with the others, I'll tidy up." Alba either flatly refused, or she'd say, "Thanks, I'll help, so we'll be done faster," leaving Regina disheartened. Though Camilla pretended not to notice, sometimes she'd admonish, "Don't use up all the hot water, you two," when one of them would fill the kettle and go to the furnace. Though Alba joined the others begrudgingly, the conversation sometimes stalled (Lalla and Guido usually ignored everyone, lost in their books) and the only sound came from the whistling kettle as the water slowly started to boil.

"Go on to bed, you've made enough sacrifices for today," Camilla joked sympathetically, but when Alba disappeared into her nook with an apathetic goodnight, her mother followed, and the others winked when they heard Camilla's calm, affectionate whispers and her daughter's curt replies, satisfied at the sort of reconciliation taking place behind the partition.

How she loved tucking her in as a little girl, Camilla later thought as she joined the others, remembering not only Alba, but Lalla and Guido, when they'd hide the day's treasures underneath their pillows at night, whatever they found at the beach, or in the woods or the city park. She'd laugh and kiss their rosy cheeks, as elated as they were by the treasure trove: a giant seashell, a shiny rock, an old coin polished clean with salt and vinegar . . . Would they always be so happy, all together? And Dario would answer calmly, without glancing up from his book, "Why shouldn't we be?"

Of course they should be! But perhaps she had a premonition of what was brewing, the darkening storm clouds that would ravage them all. Already, she sensed that no one wanted to hear a word about what happened, the slightest mention of war made people uneasy. Even Regina spoke less and less frequently of Nicola, saying his name only when discussing the legal procedures to recognize the baby as his. There was a collective desire for things to "get better" as soon as possible, which she understood and even shared . . . there was so much she wanted for herself and everyone! But it frightened her, this desire to forget about feelings, which no one talked about anymore, and be better off, which was more than a wish, it was a fever, insatiable, blind and violent at its core, as if they all braced for whatever might happen and no one could wait any longer. The harsh winter all around wasn't the only reason she had the sensation of living in the middle of a barren, frozen plain, without horizons.

She truly believed that misfortune and suffering, the absolute void that death brought with it, would create a deeper unity among people, a lasting warmth.

A trance of sorts, Camilla thought, the euphoric light that colors my fondest memories, my happiness and my children's. I'm an incorrigible fool, I ought to learn to live the same way as everyone else and resign myself to what we'll all become one day, if we keep erasing feelings from our lives: icy stones at the bottom of a stagnant pond.

I shouldn't exaggerate, she then thought, pulling herself together. Lalla's right to want a desk in her room by the window, so she won't have to study in the entryway with everyone milling about, or the kitchen. I don't mind Guido's passion for the theater either. But I don't like the look Alba gets when she gawks at new dresses and Matelda's furs.

Camilla preferred that Matelda not visit her at home and that they meet somewhere in the city center instead, but she was always so busy, weeks would go by without a word since they didn't have a telephone. So Matelda, bored and unemployed, would often lose her patience and turn up at the attic unannounced.

"This poorhouse of yours doesn't even have a doorbell!" she grumbled on her way in, falling in a breathless heap onto the tatty sofa. "The custodian said you were home, how could I not believe her. You're holed up in here like a mole, always scurrying about! That custodian's a real sourpuss, cold as ice. What a grand idea, moving to the top floor with no elevator!"

The baby's clothes were almost always hung to dry and the ottoman was out of place, never over the hole in the rug where it should have been. Regina usually nursed there. During the day, she often put the bassinet near the glass doors to the balcony, so the baby could lie in the sun.

Matelda, who was sensitive to the cold, kept her fur coat on and cast suspicious glances at the furnace—"Is that thing on? You wouldn't think so!" She disapproved of everything: the crabby custodian, the missing doorbell and elevator ("But we've got a wonderful little basket and pulley to deliver our milk and bread, see?" Lalla joked, "And have you seen this beautiful hole in the rug? We hide it when guests come over, but we kept it uncovered for you, you're family!") Camilla was sure Matelda actually liked almost everything about the poorhouse, even the baby. She said foolish things when it came to children, not knowing anything about them. Regina half-smiled and answered politely, covering her breast when she was done nursing.

"You look like a Renaissance Madonna," Matelda declared, addressing her informally, and insisting that Camilla's children and relatives, including Regina, call her Auntie. When Matelda zeroed in on Regina's gloom, she dispensed advice for the future: she shouldn't waste her time on bureaucracy to prove Nicola was practically her husband and the baby was his. "In a country like Italy, you'll waste ten years proving it and end up an old lady . . . not a young miss anymore, at least. Don't go thinking this happy republic's any better than the monarchy that fell apart, regime aside. Find yourself a nice young man to marry, you're a pretty girl and so is the baby, he'll love you both. By the way, who's the fellow always hanging around here?"

"Come off it, Matelda, what a thing to say!" Camilla laughed and Regina forced an awkward smile, while Lalla stormed off in obvious disapproval.

"You always scold me for talking about clothes and my philandering husband . . . What should one talk about in here, I'd like to know!"

Camilla and Regina had criticized Matelda once, after one of her visits, but Milena had come to her defense.

"You think you're in the right, but Matelda's done the math, believe me, she knows what's good for her. All that cheating is worth gold."

Listen to her, the bourgeois! Indignant, Camilla complained to Regina after learning that Lalla and Guido asked, "Who came to visit today? Gold Coins?" when they guessed Matelda had come by.

"You see why I prefer that she not visit the house. We think the children pay no attention, instead they soak up every drop of this filth, like sponges."

Though she didn't reply, Regina couldn't help but think she and the baby set a far worse example than Matelda's inane chatter. Camilla seemed unconcerned, and Regina was grateful to her for considering her situation normal and respectable, so the rest of them would follow suit. Alba came home early that day and, overhearing her mother's comment, shot Camilla a glare that Regina interpreted as an act of defiance. Had Matelda really come over? Alba asked, as soon as the two of them were alone. What was she wearing?

Oh, Regina couldn't recall!

"Did she leave a note?"

"Not that I know of." But then she remembered Matelda asking what time Alba would return from the office and, on hearing the answer, saying, "It's too late, I can't stay." Regina told Alba, who sighed in irritation.

II

Winter wore on, dark and dreary. In the ashen daylight, any faint sun that might thaw the frozen snow disappeared so soon that the mounds would harden again immediately, piled high and thick in the courtyards, making your numb feet ache even more if you happened to stub a toe. The children took off their shoes the moment they came home, sitting on the floor and massaging their feet by the furnace as they cursed the frigid winter, only to rouse the itchy chilblains on their toes. Camilla came to the rescue with vials of camphor and iodine as the snow fell steady and soft outside the glass doors, without a breath of wind, casting a pall over the gloomy walls and rooftops.

The calendar announced that the holidays were approaching. Despite the awful weather, Camilla decided to spend a few days at her mother's in the country. With the excuse of bringing holiday wishes and the usual gifts from the city—a grill pan for toasting bread, new coffee filters—she'd get far more in return, for a change: a young Christmas turkey, eggs, focaccia, winter fruit, a jug of olive oil and another of wine. Guido would tag along to lend a hand and keep her company.

Milena and Arrigo also left town to visit her parents, who lived in the country, too, while Enzo would soon go to Rome to see friends from the war or from past adventures, Englishmen or Americans, as far as they could glean from the little he shared. Alba, Lalla, and Regina stayed behind. Regina's parents had sent gifts for her and the baby, but not an invitation to visit. Lalla should have consoled her, but she had a hard time showing sadness or sympathy for Regina's bitter tears when in fact she was thrilled about the Christmas gift she'd received: a neoclassical-style desk her mother bought from the secondhand shop—with a drawer and a key. Filled with excitement, she rushed to line the drawer with lovely floral paper.

"I couldn't hug you if I wanted to!" she told Regina, showing off her glue-stained fingers. "But look how beautiful it is, all cleaned up! Come on, help me tidy up and stop moping."

There was no Christmas tree to brighten the attic, only a few silver ribbons draped over the lampshades, a colorful ornament or two hung from the ceiling beams, and snowflakes cut from red and gold paper, pinned here and there on the partitions.

"See?" Lalla said, "If we had real walls, we couldn't stick pins in them like this!"

Regina finally smiled and joined her to cut out the paper snowflakes. Decorated that way, the attic looked "ridiculous but cheerful," Lalla said. Then, realizing there wasn't enough paper to finish the decorations, she went to buy more.

"I'll be back soon," she said, "and don't start whimpering again while I'm gone!"

Regina was alone, but there was no time for tears (perhaps she'd shed enough) when Matelda showed up with the surly custodian who helped carry the Christmas gifts upstairs. Really, the poor custodian was all smiles, bowing and shuffling out the door as she said a deferential goodbye.

"The least she could do, with the tip I gave her!" Matelda said. She was leaving the next day for Sicily, where her husband's relatives lived, at least they'd escape the snow and cold. Matelda arranged the gifts on the table in the entryway: a giant panettone in a golden box, bottles of sparkling wine in a basket festooned with ribbons, nougat, dried fruit, even a pack of firecrackers.

"So the kids can have some fun, even if that grump Camilla doesn't like noise. Speaking of," she continued, ignoring the look on Regina's face, "I'm glad to find you here alone. Do you have any idea what kind of debts Alba might have racked up?"

"Of course not," Regina answered, dismayed.

"Oh, I didn't mean to alarm you, don't get upset!" Matelda whispered how a few weeks before, Alba asked her to borrow some money—not much, really (how much, she wouldn't say). She found it odd that Alba's pay wasn't enough for her to afford small luxuries, since she knew Camilla let her keep almost all of it. Matelda got right to the point.

"It's probably nothing to worry about. Alba mentioned having to pay back a colleague before the holidays, someone who loaned her the money a while ago . . . She'll pay me back soon, too. But that's not the point, see . . . She looked so ashamed, just asking! Do you recall her having any big expenses?"

"N—no," Regina hesitated.

"I don't mean to judge, of course, a girl can treat herself. When I see something I like, I buy two!"

"I can't recall," Regina repeated, upset. "I hadn't noticed, I don't know."

"In any case, don't ask. Alba begged me not to tell anyone. I'm telling you because I feel some responsibility, you know, I'm not sure whether the money's for good or ill. You know how strict Camilla can be. And here's where that strictness leads: the girl's afraid of her mother!"

At that, Regina protested. "Listen to you, so quick to criticize! I came to Camilla when I was in trouble, not my mother."

"Right," Matelda agreed, surprised, after a pause. "That's true, I hadn't considered. It must be a matter of modesty, with one's mother. I've forgotten what I was like, if I talked much and who I talked to. All I remember is that I got plenty of spankings! Clearly, I said too much, then and now. Well, goodbye!" She stood and gave Regina a hug and kiss, handed her a tiny package wrapped in tissue and a pink bow ("It's nothing, just a trinket for the baby"), and left with holiday wishes: may they all have a wonderful time, Christmas comes but once a year, the war was a distant memory by now, thank heavens.

Alone again, Regina stared at the trinket—a pretty silver bell to hang in the crib—and the gifts strewn across the table, shimmering quietly in their shiny gold wrapping. Meanwhile, the baby had woken from her nap and was fussing behind the partition. Regina rang the bell to distract her; it worked. There she was in her bassinet, listening and staring wide-eyed into space. No, she wouldn't say a word, let things go their way, Regina thought, giving the baby a tender kiss. Christmas was just around the corner, and the war . . . well, it was long gone for Matelda, of course, perhaps it never affected her to begin with, but Regina—she held the baby tight. How could she not succumb to sadness: her strict parents, so cold and adamant, and now Alba's debts, which lurked like an ugly, growling beast in the dark corner behind her (how could she not tell Camilla?), the snowmelt's endless drip on the roof . . .

Lalla's cheerful voice broke the silence. She burst in with a slam of the door and shouted, "Ah, the custodian was right, Gold Coins really did come to visit! With Christmas gifts!"

"Shhhh!" Regina hissed from behind the partition. "If your mother heard! You know she doesn't like you calling her that."

The baby cooed, kicked her tiny legs, and laughed at the silver bell.

• • •

The fearsome winter weighed on the countryside, too. Everything was buried beneath the frozen snow, a dark fog enveloped the hills, crows and blackbirds hovered somberly over the skeletal trees, resting now and then on the dirty white ground. Motionless, they looked nothing like birds, camouflaged against the tangled, dark roots that surfaced from the snow, muddy rocks, and piles of rotted leaves. Farmers and shepherds wore knee-high boots and draped sacks over their heads like hoods, covering their shoulders; after tilling the fields and meadows, there was nothing to do but stay indoors and take care of winter tasks, sit around the fireplace at night, make wood carvings of strange figures and auspicious symbols to pass the time. Only the lumberjacks worked in the mountains, as the sound of rushing streams and axes striking tree trunks filled the silence.

Camilla would have liked to linger among the wintry sounds and smells of the countryside she so loved; instead, she had to get ready to head home the next day. She looked worriedly at her mother sitting by the fire in the kitchen. The old woman hadn't been well lately, as proven by the fact that the table was piled high with an unusual number of provisions destined for the city. Though her mother was never much for conversation, Camilla was struck now by her listless insistence on not talking, attempting to communicate as best she could by nodding and pointing at things to indicate what she needed and what had to be done: add logs to the fire, light the oil lamp on the cellar stairs, make tea, a ritual she never quit. She sank into the wide sofa, wrapped in the thick purple shawl that stirred so many memories. A heartbreaking sight. The woman was old and alone, and though she'd insisted on living by herself for years—defiant of everyone—Camilla now seemed to glimpse a vague dread in her eyes. A half-empty pack of cigarettes sat on the tiny round table she always kept by her side. After a long silence, she turned to Rosso at the far end of the hearth (Camilla sat between them, facing the fire) and said in a hoarse voice, "See? I'm not even in the mood to smoke. Bad sign."

Camilla glanced at Rosso, but there was no need to prompt him. That didn't mean a thing, he joked politely, smoking even made him queasy sometimes. Camilla looked down and quietly resumed her knitting. She didn't say much either, aside from a few words about that night's dinner, the house, the caretaker who helped with the chores and stayed the night when Camilla wasn't there. She knew her mother preferred tranquility and long silences. Out of everyone in the family, the only company the old woman truly enjoyed and desired was her own.

Guido spent practically every day outdoors since they'd arrived, building half a dozen snowmen. Having failed to unearth any old hats or pipes from the closets (no men had lived in that house for a long time), he crowned them with oak twigs and laurel leaves, so in the dim light it looked as if the snowy patch along the woods was dotted with busts of Roman emperors.

"Cannibal-emperors with sticks for pipes, sour apples for eyes," Guido laughed, looking out the window at whatever was still standing.

"Why didn't you come to my house?" Rosso asked affably. "You'd find all the raggedy hats you could want, and probably a pipe or two."

Guido's eyes sparkled with surprise (the fun he'd have!) before he turned quickly toward the dark window and answered shyly that it hadn't occurred to him. He knew they'd always kept a strict distance between his grandmother's house and Rosso's property, even during the war; it was mainly his mother, he recalled, who wanted it that way. Only recently would Rosso pay Nonna a visit, and Guido certainly didn't expect to cross paths with him that morning as he ambled around the snowy fields, nor that Rosso would invite him to visit the stables, the bare orchard (those scrawny trees, so neatly pruned, must have tons of fruit in the spring), and finally, his library. The shelves reached the ceiling, overflowing with books. Guido went straight for a collectible bilingual edition of Shakespeare's complete works. Why Shakespeare? Rosso asked, so he started talking. How foolish of him to open up to a total stranger, a country-dweller who might have come upon all those books by sheer coincidence, inherited from who knows where, books he perhaps never read. Whether he'd read them or not (Rosso didn't say, he simply let the boy talk), Guido was sure Rosso had listened closely, with a sympathetic ear. That was why he felt so uneasy now, worrying Rosso would tell his mother or grandmother—so he wanted nothing more than for him to leave. Better yet, Guido himself wanted to leave, to slowly slink out of sight, skirting the subject, in hopes Rosso might forget the conversation entirely.

He had already left the kitchen, hardly moving a muscle on the dark, rickety wooden staircase leading to the bedrooms, which creaked terribly with every step, when Rosso's voice mercilessly gave him away.

"So, Signora Camilla, that boy of yours is a real thespian."

A groan (it must have been Nonna), then his mother's soft, sarcastic voice. "How do you know? Did he say so himself?"

The traitor! Yes, Guido told me himself, Rosso said, revealing all: their encounter that morning, the stables, the library, and the boy's enthusiasm! Angry, on the verge of tears, Guido felt truly ridiculous, and saw that he must have come across as such.

No one will ever understand, he thought, it's my fault, I shouldn't have said a word. I'm a dope, a real dope. I should have learned, but I always make the same mistakes, I can't help it. Rosso seemed interested, asking this and that . . . and there I go, sucking up, like Lalla says. Nicola taught her that. Never be a suck-up.

Unable to make out their faint voices on the other side of the door, Guido went to his room and only showed his face again at dinner, though he heard his mother calling long before—probably to say goodbye to Rosso, which was exactly what he didn't want to do.

They dined in silence. Nonna barely ate some boiled

vegetables and a few spoonfuls of yogurt, then grumpily pushed her half-full plate to the middle of the table with trembling hands.

"Have some more, Signora, you're so thin!" said Martina, the caretaker who came to help at night, a young, full-figured woman who shuffled quietly around the house in cloth slippers and winked at Camilla behind his grandmother's back—stupid, useless winks, Guido thought, still peeved.

"Aren't you hungry?" Camilla asked. Ignoring her, the old woman grumbled that the fire had gone out. Guido stood and tossed a thick log onto the embers. Camilla knew better than to insist and changed the subject. Did Rosso come by often, she asked her mother wryly, or was that a special visit on her account?

"Don't be so sassy," the old woman snapped, and Guido realized they must have had the same conversation before. He had barely begun to wonder what had sparked his grandmother's frustration when she turned and poked him with the tip of the cane she always kept nearby. "You know, my boy," she added curtly, "there's no room for mediocrity in the theater. A mediocre actor is like a leper. You're either talented, or you're a traveling hack. A guitto. Know what a guitto is?" Her cheeks turned pink. "Hand me the dictionary . . . that one over there, on the shelf. It was your grandfather's . . . Right, you never knew your grandfather. You never really knew your father either, that's why you're full of silly ideas."

Guido glanced at his mother (he felt himself turn beet red), who glared with pursed lips.

"Really, Mamma," he pleaded indignantly, "why does it matter?"

"It matters, it matters . . . I want to read him the definition of *guitto*," said the old woman.

He brought her the heavy tome, which she picked up clumsily, dropping her cane under the table and shuffling through the pages, until she finally found the entry and read aloud in a shaky voice. "Etymology . . . theatrical jargon . . . ah, here: a third-rate, destitute traveling actor."

"I know what it means," Guido said, mustering confidence, "but we don't say that now, Nonna. There are no guitti anymore."

"Nonsense. There certainly are, mind you," she said, slamming one hand on the table with a thud. "They might be called something else now, but they exist. Destitute nomads. Like lepers. Goodnight to all. I'm off to bed, Martina," she called to the caretaker, shakily rising to her feet. "Fetch my cane, dear, and help me upstairs."

"I will, Mother." Camilla stood and Guido noticed she looked unhappy.

"No, you finish dinner. Keep your son company. And come say goodbye before you leave in the morning. I'll be awake." She poked her grandson again with the cane as she walked past. "I don't mean to discourage you. If you're talented, we'll see. And you'll have been right." Martina followed her out and up the creaky staircase.

They sat down again at the table. Guido kept his chin down, staring into a glass bowl filled with plum custard.

Camilla reached out and touched his arm. "My boy," she murmured affectionately, with smiling eyes. "Don't get upset. There's no use talking about certain things. The custard's delicious, I made it myself, have some."

"Mamma!" Guido said, with tears in his eyes. "It's that dummy's fault! What does he want anyway? I . . ."

Camilla turned serious. "Look, I don't want to defend him, but perhaps it was a bit rash of you to confide in . . . a stranger. Best not to talk about such things, maybe not even with family, unless there's a good reason. Go on, finish your dinner, and forget about it."

Guido reluctantly swallowed his portion of purplish custard (it really was tart and sweet) and studied his mother's sad, beautiful face, against his better judgment, knowing full well it was neither him nor Rosso's foolish intrusion that was causing her obvious worry.

They went to bed early. Their luggage lay open on the bedroom floor, half-full, straps unbuckled. Tomorrow was the day before Christmas Eve, the taxi would pick them up and take them to the train station in town. To conserve the heat, the two of them stayed in the bedroom with a wood-burning furnace, sharing the large double bed that Martina had kept warm with hot-water bottles. Guido was thrilled to have his mother all to himself, day and night.

The lights were out when he curled up next to her under the covers. She gave him a kiss and an affectionate nudge.

"Go on back to your side, or neither of us will get any sleep. There's plenty of room in this big bed."

"Wait," Guido whispered, nuzzling her neck, "Let me say something. Do you really think . . ."

"What?" She needed patience.

"Is it really wrong . . . to dream of it so much?" She rested her cheek against his hair, breathing in his youthful scent. What to tell him, she thought, my goodness. "Because I do, all the time."

"Nothing wrong with that, dear, as long as you're serious about it. Acting's a job like any other, maybe more demanding . . . riskier, too. We'll see how things turn out, sweetheart, it's too soon to say. Get back to your side and try to sleep."

He didn't move. Was he crying? She could tell he was hurt. He was her little boy, her youngest, still attached to her as if with a delicate umbilical cord. A muffled voice reached her.

"You . . . you won't stop me, will you, if I'm serious about it?"

"Of course not, dear, I'll never stop you from making a decent or respectable living, I just want you to be happy. Sleep tight . . . Don't fret."

"I love you more than anyone in the world, Mamma." His voice was clear again. "I won't ever leave you. I want you to know that." He let go and rolled onto his side. After a long silence, he went on, this time more sleepily. "It isn't true that I don't remember Papà. Sometimes I even think about him . . ."

Silence followed again, for real. She felt two teardrops run down her temples as she lay on her back and stared into the dark. Of course he would leave her, they all would . . . Far in the past, someone was asking, "Do you think we'll always be happy?" The voice was hers. Another voice calmly replied, "Of course, why shouldn't we be?"

She lay there listening. The country was so quiet at night! (Hush, her heart told those voices.) The gleam that traced a window in the darkness was the moon, the roving, blue winter moon that caressed the snow and made the muddy paths sparkle, illuminating the rows of bare trees, the tattered leaves left hanging on their branches. Then Camilla's thoughts shifted and she remembered, yet again since arriving, that she never dared speak of the hard times with her mother, the poor old woman. She should have. She hadn't come there simply for Christmas gifts or Rosso's compliments; she certainly wouldn't survive that winter on strength alone, unless she found part-time work soon, since leaving the house all day was still out of the question. She and Regina agreed to take turns, one would do the morning shift, the other afternoon, depending on the job—even if they did manage, it wouldn't be easy, Regina had to wean the baby before she could go out on her own. Camilla tried hard to convince herself that her life was more than an inert, wretched thing. Thorny, vexing thoughts stung her without really hurting, like the barbs of a prickly pear that get stuck on your fingertips when you rub them, burrowing deeper and deeper under the skin. Alba, who can't stand hardship, their "pathetic existence," as she called it, her nerves as taut as violin strings (making such unpleasant sounds at the slightest touch); Lalla, who wants great, passionate things out of life (she herself wanted the same, once), no matter the cost. And Guido . . .

Her dear boy had fallen silent, after trying to make her glimpse inside the enchanted door of his dreams. Since coming to the country, she felt ashamed of always thinking about cash, so menacingly linked to Rosso, imagining a cascade of gold coins down his tall, burly body like a precious gleaming stream—"Come get them, as many as you want," he seemed to imply, with suspicious chivalry—and then, a sensation even more shameful and unsettling than the dazzling gold, the thought of that muscular man, the vivid hue of his skin, rushed through her like a landslide.

She'd better try to sleep. The window darkened (a sign the moon was disappearing behind the corner of the house, she knew exactly where), nothing was visible, everything had melted into the night. She could clearly hear her mother coughing behind the closed doors and cold walls, the soothing breathing of her boy, asleep beside her. "Staying awake won't solve our problems, will it, dear?" she sighed. Meanwhile, the clock struck midnight.

III

If the first days of the new year were memorable at all, it was because of another blizzard. Tiny trenches of powdery flakes reappeared on the windowsills, iridescent frost on the glass. The dirty mound in the middle of the courtyard grew higher, and the soft, gleaming pile of snow on the balcony turned pure white. Lalla said the ghostly whiteness, that silent, white stillness, was starting to make her nauseous.

After New Year's and before the Epiphany, Arrigo and Milena came home from the country shivering, frightened by the cold. "Faraway ghosts dwell up there in the sky, glaring at us with menacing white eyes—menacing and deadly, even!" Lalla said, to scare them even more. The roof began to creak again; a few drops of dirty water fell on Alba's bed, which was moved to the middle of the room.

"I'll have to sleep under an umbrella," she said, with the same outrage and exasperation as whenever she encountered the slightest inconvenience.

"Why don't you go to a hotel, and ask the landlord to cover the damages?" Guido retorted without batting an eye. "If you ask with that face, he might even pay!"

"What do you mean 'that face,' dummy?"

"Not that you're pretty . . . but you might scare him."

They could hear Arrigo practicing the violin in his room. Solo or ensemble parts, the sounds floated gently through the immaculate whiteness, bearing a supernatural message—at least that was how it seemed to Lalla, locked in her bedroom. Pretending to finish her schoolwork, she wrote and wrote, tucking page after page in the desk drawer. There weren't many, actually; she decided her story would fill no more than ten or twelve sheets. Then she'd have to find a copyist, of course, and pay for a typewriter, paper for printing, carbon paper, all of which would cost quite a bit. After all, who would ever agree to read an actual handwritten manuscript? It had to be typewritten, so she wouldn't come across as an ingenue, a novice or starving artist. To afford it, she tutored a student two grades behind her, for a fee. Regina thoughtfully left Lalla in peace during the day, keeping the baby in the main room or letting her nap at Enzo's, since she had a key, so she could keep the heat on and he'd come home to a warm room.

"Regina's so kind and easy to get along with, isn't she, Mamma?"

Camilla smiled, stroking Lalla's cheek. "So are you, luckily."

When she finished her schoolwork, real or pretend, Lalla went to the baby. "I'll take her, do whatever you need to do. If you've got nothing to do, rest," she said to Regina, as she played with the baby who recognized her now, with squeals of joy. "Let me hold her a while," Lalla begged, "I know we shouldn't spoil her, but she's so curious! See how she looks at her reflection?" Cradling her head, she'd carry Nicoletta from the mirror to the window, where she would pat against the glass—breaking up the crusts of ice outside—and later, on the pots and pans in the kitchen. When Arrigo studied his music, Lalla swaddled her in a blanket and walked across the balcony to the honeymoon suite, where Arrigo would play a song or jig on the strings, and the baby giggled, wide-eyed, waving her arms.

"C'est une enfant très éveillée, pour son âge," said Milena, curled up idly on the sofa in her woolen robe.

Why did Milena have such a beautiful trousseau, when Regina didn't even have a warm robe? Neither do I, but it doesn't matter, Lalla thought, pretending to concentrate on the baby.

"Of course she's smart! Soon she'll recognize all of us. She already knows me!"

"Allons donc!" Milena replied, surprised, and Lalla mimicked her—"pensez-vous, dites donc"—bobbing along under the ceiling lamp as the baby looked up, mesmerized. Arrigo returned to his music. Without looking, Lalla thought those two made an odd couple: his dark colors (thick black hair and olive skin) must have been drawn to Milena's pale blond complexion—the color of yogurt, she and Guido concluded, noticing yellow undertones—and to her oval blue eyes, high-strung though they looked.

"Lalla," Regina called, tapping on the plaster wall—the Great Wall, they called it, since there were wicker partitions everywhere else in the house. Lalla returned the baby, who was starting to fuss.

"Tu vois, tu l'as fatiguée, tu l'as énervée," Milena scolded, but Lalla paid no attention to her banal remarks. Like Matelda, Milena didn't know the first thing about babies.

It was time for dinner. The windows were shut tight against the snowy trenches, the Christmas treats had given way to minestrone soups where noodles and potatoes outnumbered the fresh vegetables, far more expensive, then eggs, fontina and pecorino cheese, and cooked apples—tiny ones, firm and sour, that couldn't be eaten raw but didn't cost much and "tasted delicious with a bit of sugar, lemon zest and white wine," Camilla declared. Fresh fruit appeared on the table just once a day, at lunch; Alba was the only one to find a ripe apple or orange on her plate some evenings, if she was gone at breakfast. On one of those evenings, she announced, aloof, that the office might send her to Rome for a few days. "To do what?" Camilla spun around and asked from the sideboard where she was putting away the dinner napkins.

"Recordkeeping, I think. The archives are a mess, they need a hand." She looked down at her plate, peeling an orange. “They asked our office to send someone.”

“Someone! Why you? Do me a favor and decline. Say your mother won’t allow it.”

“Oh Mother!” Alba dropped her knife on the plate with a clang.

“Don’t start breaking dishes, now. You’re too young. Who knows where they’ll have you stay.”

“Somewhere it won’t rain on the bed, maybe,” Alba muttered through clenched teeth, staring her mother down with a look that frightened Regina.

“Don’t be ridiculous, it was just a few drops!”

(I should say something, Regina thought anxiously, what should I do, I really ought to say something.)

“And how frugal of them to pay for a ticket from Milan to Rome and back! As if they couldn’t find a temporary hire down there.”

“What do I know. Maybe they want someone from this office, with experience.” Regina sensed that Alba regretted bringing it up.

(Camilla should keep quiet now, she thought, Alba will only get more upset if she carries on.)

“We’ll see,” said Camilla calmly, changing the subject. Alba disappeared into her room and dragged the bed across the floor. Guido laughed, about to shout something, before Camilla put her hand over his mouth and whispered, “Leave her alone.”

The next day, a telegram arrived: the old woman was dying, and Camilla had to go back to the country.

• • •

Now that "it was all over," said the caretaker, if the Signora wouldn't be staying . . .

"No, I won't be staying," Camilla sighed, sitting in a sunbeam against the portico column.

. . . If Signora wasn't staying, they'd have to shut off the water and drain the pipes so they wouldn't freeze and burst, make sure to lock all the doors and windows, and the keys . . .

"I'll leave the keys with you. Martina can air out the rooms once in a while."

"Will Signora sell the house?"

"Oh, it's too soon, I'll have to sort things out and see . . . Probably best to wait until next summer at least, the children will be glad to visit again." Sighing, she added, "We've got so many memories here." The caretaker thought he'd better leave, if Signora was going to start sighing. And he could understand why! She'd buried her mother that same morning, and the old woman had spent practically her whole life there, from springtime to autumn until her husband died, then all year long. Now she lay in a grave, under a mound of dirt that the snow and rain would turn to soft mud; little by little, the mound would flatten and settle, and in time the family could have a handsome marble tombstone made, like the well-to-do families in town. Only he didn't know whether the dead woman's daughter was well-off . . . He'd ask Martina, she might know.

Alone now, Camilla shut the glass doors in the entryway and walked across the yard surrounding the house, toward the vast estate. She didn't know where she was headed, she just wanted to walk and tire herself out. Arrigo had come for the funeral with Alba and the children (not Milena, who'd caught a cold, nor Regina, who couldn't leave the baby), but they'd already left, and she had stayed behind to lock up and settle the bills. Her mother always kept some money inside a tiny chest on her nightstand, as she told Camilla the minute they were alone after her arrival.

"There's nearly fifty thousand lira to cover the initial expenses, so you won't need to go to the bank right away . . . Don't make that face." Then she added, "There's no will. Everything goes to you . . . You're on your own, and Arrigo is Anna's only child. Give him whatever he can use, if he ever buys a house of his own. There's plenty." That was all she said, in a rare moment of lucidity. Between naps, she'd wake up sulking, her usual demeanor in any case. Camilla had seen her smile so rarely in life that it would have been ridiculous to expect a different look on her face then.

She had been comatose for more than twenty-four hours and the final, drawn-out throes left Camilla exhausted, hardly able to eat and barely sleeping the whole time. Martina, another relative, and the doctor took turns at the old woman's bedside so Camilla could rest. Rosso asked after her, too, day and night, but Camilla didn't see him; she stayed upstairs, occasionally retreating to the room farthest away so as not to hear.

"Is there really nothing we can do?" she asked the doctor. "Isn't she in pain?" He shook his head without answering.

Martina sighed. "Do you think these doctors really know? No one's ever come back to tell us whether these moments are painful or not." Camilla shivered in horror and covered her ears when no one was watching. They kept a cup of sugar water on the dying woman's nightstand, using a cotton ball on a stick to drop some liquid into her half-open mouth and moisten her lips. Finally, the death rattle ceased. Waiting in the kitchen, the caretaker ran to call the nuns, who had already been alerted, and Camilla saw all the women in black come in, carrying basins, towels, washcloths, as she waited downstairs by the fire until it was time to see her. It was nearly midnight.

Her body washed and dressed in black, hands clasped, head slightly raised on a flat pillow, there was no longer any trace of the suffering the old woman had endured; she had already overcome the degradation of physical death. Now all one could say was that life had taken its leave of her. There she lay, calm, slightly less sulky than usual. Yes, that was it: the breath of life had left her, and thus she seemed so inanimate. Though everything was still—the bed, the blanket (only the flames on the candles flickered slightly)—Camilla had the impression of seeing her mother sail into an insurmountable distance. The silent wave that stole her away would leave her forever in the invisible world of the dead.

Then came the funeral, the black hearse and pallbearers, floral wreaths and crucifixes. In spite of it all, the crows seemed almost gleeful as they glided through the morning sky, where a faint blue peeked through the towering gray clouds. Some people came from town, as did Rosso, of course, calm and collected, sporting a smart suit for the occasion, an elegant one at that, though to Camilla it seemed odd not seeing him dressed in his usual corduroy pants. Everyone's eyes were on Alba, whose tranquil beauty gleamed the way ice gleams on the ground. But they were all there to pray for the body lying in that coffin.

"If I stayed, I'd miss her even more. I'd better go as soon as I can."

Camilla wouldn't pretend to turn her mother's death into a tragedy, inwardly or outwardly. She was sure her mother wouldn't have expected her to, always being so gruff—a gruffness directed at herself above all. Having chosen to harden her heart in life, all the old woman could expect from her family in death was a subdued, restrained grief—far off in the distance where that mysterious wave had carried her. But perhaps those who had come to the funeral—black blotches whispering among the cypress trees—disapproved of their restraint. The people in town already said that "city folk" too seldom went to church; who knows what they'd say to criticize the family now. They stared at Alba, and her, and Rosso.

Since Camilla didn't want to make a tragedy of it, her first thought was that the sudden inheritance—despite the hassle of selling or renting the house and land, the taxes and debts (she knew her mother had taken out a loan for renovations)—would help her face the immediate future with greater peace of mind. To get some liquidity, perhaps she could borrow money against the house. She'd ask Rosso for advice, he was shrewd and practical. Yes, no doubt she'd seek his advice; after all, she had no one else to ask.

Quickening her step, she walked along the firm dirt furrow dug between two trenches of dirty snow. The sun had already hidden behind the clouds, the air was turning white and cold. Up ahead, she saw the fog roll in from the far end of the meadow. I've really got no one, she paused and thought, Arrigo doesn't count, let alone Dario, who isn't around to give advice or anything else. I'm not asking for a sign. Being alone, too, is death, no different than the body we buried this morning.

Yet somewhere inside was a longing, still alive, awaiting Rosso's visit. She was sure he would come from the way he looked at her during the funeral, especially knowing she would be alone. When she tidied up after dinner (she told Martina not to come that night, there was no need) and heard the doorbell's faint chime, she opened the door without asking who was there. Rosso, standing outside, said how brave she was, and reckless, for answering the door like that at night, without knowing who it might be!

"I knew very well who it was," she answered, calm and serious. I won't act coy, she thought, nor pretend as if I've misread the signals.

Rosso tossed his cigarette, sending an ember flying behind him into the dark sky. As he wiped his shoes on the doormat he stared straight into her eyes—brazenly, perhaps?

He was just as serious. He was paying his respects. Hat in hand, he walked in, head high, standing tall.

IV

Camilla's return from the country was delayed without explanation, and a number of unpleasant things happened while she was away. The rusted pipe fittings froze, thanks to the poor insulation, so the house went without running water for a few days. To manage the inconvenience, they all had to carry buckets upstairs from the spigot in the courtyard, waiting in line with nearly every other tenant in the building, just like during the war. Enzo and Guido were the quickest and most diligent in providing these emergency services; Lalla and Arrigo made an honest effort whenever they could; but Regina, still nursing, was advised not to tire herself out. Alba and Milena stubbornly refused despite Lalla and Guido's objections that they be punished with a water embargo: Those two smug princesses should go fetch it themselves!

As expected, it was Regina who tried to keep the peace and soothe their tempers: Alba worked all day, they should understand ("What about us? Don't we go to school?"), and Milena . . . well, Milena was a piece of work, they all knew, and that pushover Arrigo would carry the buckets for her. Still, Regina couldn't talk to anyone about the thing that worried her most. Alba, with icy frustration, acted as if they were all to blame for that disgraceful situation, as if she were the only one affected. She hardly ate at home anymore, or had only a cup of tea for dinner, huddled at the corner of the kitchen table, "to avoid washing dishes, since there's no water in this dump, this hovel," as she dubbed the attic, when she didn't call it "the death camp."

"Oh, stop exaggerating!" Arrigo scolded in his good-natured way.

"It's no exaggeration. I wish I were dead, if you really want to know, at least I'd be done with all this!" While her morbid threats made the others laugh, they upset Regina.

Finally, the landlord made up his mind to have the pipes repaired and they survived the ordeal of having no running water.

"Thank goodness," they all sighed in relief, but hardly twenty-four hours went by (and Camilla still hadn't come home) before the furnace pipe caught fire. Soot had built up and overheated, they later learned, and no one thought to have it cleaned halfway through the winter.

That afternoon, the sudden roaring flames made Regina run out of the bedroom where she'd just put the baby down to nap. The pipe had come loose from the wall, a cloud of thick black smoke billowed through the room as the flames flickered and nearly spread to the old wooden beams above. Alone in the house, terrified, Regina immediately pushed the baby's bassinet into Enzo's room, then shouted from the balcony for help. The neighbors and custodian rushed over and managed to quickly douse the fire (it could have been catastrophic, with all those wicker partitions). An enormous oily stain blackened the wall where the fire had started, and sooty puddles of water filled the kitchen and entryway, soaking the old floorboards. That wet mess was a miserable sight, where Camilla had worked so hard to create the semblance of a home. Camilla was on everyone's mind that night as they all looked around in a daze, exhausted, bitter, caught in the grips of the cold. Since the broken, flooded furnace couldn't be lit, icy air seeped in from the rickety roof, blowing its vicious breath through the cracks and crevices.

Bundled in coats and scarves, they all stood around the table, even Enzo, and discussed what was to be done while the custodian mopped up the soaked floor, wringing out the water into a bucket, grumbling in Milanese. All of a sudden she leaned on the mop handle and said curtly to Regina, "You shouldn't nurse tonight, your milk's spoiled until tomorrow at least. Hand me the bottle. Signora Camilla would agree, if she were here." She shot a mean look at Alba, Lalla, and Milena, as if to say, Good thing I'm here, these women have no idea what they're doing.

"Cette femme a raison, ma parole," Milena droned. "Why are you crying?"

Regina had started to cry, in fact, with her back to them, so the group quickly reached an agreement. Not much had changed in the attic, at any rate, aside from the cold. Enzo would lend Regina his room for the night, so the baby could stay put with the heat on, and he'd sleep on the sofa in the main room with his own blankets. They'd unmake a few beds and share the covers to keep warm. The furnace was never lit overnight anyhow, and the chimney sweep would come the day after next to clean and reattach the pipe—a new one, evidently. Everything would be all right. There was quite a mess, of course, and the fire gave them all a scare, especially Regina, but it wasn't a tragedy, Enzo said, resting a hand on her shoulder. She ought to calm down and rest for the baby's sake, the custodian rightly advised on her way out the door, satisfied, holding the mop like a scepter.

Standing around the table with the others (Regina sat, stricken), Alba finally said, "I'd rather spend the night somewhere else, if you don't mind."

They noticed how pale she was (perhaps the fire had frightened her, too), and the unusual way she said "If you don't mind . . ."

"What for?" Regina replied anxiously. "Your room's clean and dry, it was spared this chaos."

"I'm freezing." Alba shivered in her coat. "The house is an icebox, with all the windows open. And I can't stand this burnt smell."

"Where will you sleep? A hotel?" Guido prodded. No one else thought to ask where she planned to go.

"At a colleague's house . . . She invited me over today,

when she heard what happened. Maybe Enzo could sleep in my room, instead of on that uncomfortable sofa." Her tone was more condescending than caring.

The accident had shaken them all, not just Regina. So while everyone was shouting, interrupting each other and bustling about, Alba, with her small valise, managed to slip out nearly unseen; you could say she vanished. The others noticed only later, when someone went looking for her but couldn't find her. No one believed they could have stopped her from leaving, it wasn't any of their business after all, they said. Thinking back on the evening, later, Regina grew worried again, recalling how unusually pale Alba looked, wondering how she'd managed to alert her colleague about the fire and receive an invitation. (A phone call, perhaps?) Regina hadn't told anyone what Matelda revealed; those debts still rustled in her mind.

As Regina dried off the silverware after a rushed dinner, Milena said a demon had taken aim at the attic with fire and water, leaving a fiendish black stain on the wall, as demons do. Hearing Arrigo's violin in the next room, as if on cue, she said goodnight and left, taking Guido with her, or else he'd disturb them later. Regina listened for a moment as the violin's faint melody filtered through the wall. "What's Arrigo playing?" she asked Lalla, who was carrying an armful of sheets and blankets from her bed to Enzo's room.

"Who knows! A Bach adagio, maybe."

After all the commotion, in that freezing room, with that nauseating smell (Alba was probably right to leave after all, while poor Enzo had to spend the night there), Regina felt a wistful calm wash over her soul with the sweet, soothing music. It was as if a wave carried her out to sea, toward a faraway blue where whitecaps rose and fell to the gentle rhythm, over and over, with heavenly precision, sharp and joyous in equal measure—a steady, unyielding joy.

"Right, it must be Bach," she said, picking up the sheets and blankets. "Thanks, Lalla, and good night. Try to get some sleep." She left without turning to look at the black stain, the devil's mark.

Milena had hit it on the nose, though she forgot having said so. A demon really had stolen into the attic to play its shrewd game—without fire or water this time.

Since the circumstances forced Regina to stay not only in Enzo's room, but in his bed, an air of mischief soon gathered like a cloud. Meaning well, they both thought it was the fog outside that began to soften the edges of the meager furniture, to dim the glare from the window that swung open or closed, or from the sad, lone mirror hung in the corner. But it was really the mysterious, tender lure of sex that clouded their vision with a strange unease. Since the baby would have to stay in that room until the furnace was repaired (the good-for-nothing chimney sweep hadn't come yet), Regina spent the days there, too. Her things filled part of the shelf; a few sheer articles of clothing were draped over the chair; the baby's bottle sat plunged in a pot of warm water on the tiny stove, covered with a napkin; and a newborn scent (wax paper, talc, rose water) softened the air. If Enzo came to lie down during the day, his pillow smelled different, like an infant's head. When the baby was asleep, Regina would go to the attic and leave Enzo alone, in case he should need to change clothes or fetch something. Since he wasn't very neat, she hung and dusted his suit, put away neckties left lying around, ironed out wrinkles. More than once, they happened to find themselves alone together in the room, which had quickly taken on the look of married life—one they couldn't help but notice, the same way they sensed the tumult that the unexpected scene would inevitably stir. Enzo was surprised at reactions he initially thought prompted simply by well-meaning sympathy, by the sense of compassion that Regina's situation and looks awakened in everyone. Still slender after the pregnancy, she looked youthful with that long, straight hair grazing her elbows, an almost childlike shade of blond, pulled back with a blue ribbon or a tortoiseshell headband—no one could believe that someone so thin and wan had given birth. Enzo thought his compassion was noble, that the tragic look in Regina's eyes sought only justice, justice that was hard to come by in a world short on mercy. But Regina's fearful gaze held a mix of elements he couldn't identify nor call by their true name, because he was a man. And she, a vulnerable young mother wounded by a bitter past, feared just one thing—the most natural, ordinary, and inescapable thing—with that demon roaming the house.

Meanwhile, after having spent the night out, Alba sent a hastily scrawled note to inform them she'd have to leave that same day for Rome, on her boss's repeated orders; by the time the message was delivered to the custodian by an unknown hand, she would already be gone on the noon train.

Right away, they all said the news would devastate Camilla, had she been home—but she wasn't. Her mother's grave was keeping her—a ridiculous excuse! Besides, there was plenty more to worry about. "Alba did well, in my opinion. It's warmer down south," Milena said, unperturbed, and everyone more or less agreed. The attic was an unpleasant place to be, in those days. Rereading the note, Lalla observed, "She doesn't say how long she'll be gone."

But Regina was hardly calm, following that conversation. She was the only one who remembered (though she didn't say a word) seeing Alba leave with a small valise. Why hadn't she come home to pack more things? Suspicious, she went to Alba's room, where Enzo was still staying, and opened the closet and the drawers, one by one. They were all nearly empty. Amid the creased paper that lined the bottom of the drawers sat old ribbons, torn stockings, tattered gloves; a few old sweaters hung in the closet, a skirt with a frayed hem. It was just as Regina expected, to tell the truth, but still her heart sank. There was no way Alba had come home to pack a larger suitcase; there wasn't even a larger suitcase to pack, since Camilla had taken the only one with her. So Regina supposed Alba had packed her things ahead of time—how and when, no one could say—and certainly before the fire. Something more distant and mysterious than fire or water had influenced Alba, and now Regina saw her hide and vanish inside an evil haze. The billowing smoke that had blackened the attic walls paled in comparison.

Matelda, the only person Regina could talk to, still hadn't returned from Sicily, though she sent the occasional postcard. "It's sunny and beautiful," she wrote underneath pictures of palm trees and blue skies. "Hope the weather's milder there, too."

Not only was the weather not milder, but it started snowing again. The chimney sweep came to take measurements and haul away the burnt pipe, but he hadn't yet returned with a replacement—that crook—and plugged the hole in the wall with crumpled newspaper to keep the rain and snow from seeping in. The temperature inside the attic wasn't fit for beasts, Lalla said, piling the bed high with every cover she could find, including her coat. They ate lunch and dinner in the kitchen, where the gas stove and boiling pots slightly warmed the freezing air. Milena spent all day in bed to avoid keeping the electric heater on too long. She let Guido and Lalla do their schoolwork in her room, "as long as you don't bicker," she warned. Actually, she said, "pourvu que vous ne vous chamailliez pas," and Guido shook his head, not understanding: What did she mean by *shamaié*?

Those daily nuisances, the snow's renewed assault on the doors and windows, the winter darkness, the groaning gutters on the balcony—all of it took Regina's mind off Alba's departure. That same night, or perhaps the following evening (if she'd wanted to tell the story, she couldn't have said for sure) Enzo knocked on the door. It was already late, everyone was asleep and she was ready for bed. The baby had finished half her milk and fallen asleep when Regina heard the knock, as she wrapped the still-warm bottle in a napkin. Enzo had left a pack of cigarettes in his suit pocket, there on the hanger, the only pack he had. He put on a coat over his pajamas to walk across the balcony.

"Sorry to bother you, but if I don't have my cigarettes first thing in the morning . . ."

They were whispering. Softly, she insisted he shouldn't worry about coming to get what he needed, the two of them—she gestured to the bassinet—were the real bother . . .

The lamp on the nightstand cast a shadow over the room. In the dim glow, with that ribbon in her hair, wrapped in a thick woolen shawl whose fringed edge matched the ruffled collar of her long nightgown, Regina looked like a schoolgirl who'd just emerged from under the covers.

"It's still toasty in here, lucky you!" Enzo placed his hands over the terracotta heater, which stayed warm for hours. "My hands are freezing!" As he touched Regina's cheeks, perhaps to justify the intrusion, she gave a start without moving aside. He pulled back, apologizing as he had before.

"Stay and warm up," Regina murmured. It was his room, after all, she acknowledged with some sadness, but Enzo thought he saw a hint of skeptical surprise in her eyes: there she was, thinking she'd been tricked by the reserved, heartbroken foreigner, and his vague excitement was tempered by a slight irritation at that impression of himself he'd worn for years, like someone else's clothes.

Suspicion hovered over Regina like a hawk spreading its wings. Was it or was it not a pathetic excuse to have come by at that hour, looking for a pack of cigarettes? But the hawk landed quickly—without talons. Enzo's firm hands pulled her close, his arms embraced her, his soft voice sighed into her hair. "Be a good girl, Regina, let me stay a while."

They said nothing more about needing to warm up, since that was exactly what they were doing. As they stood there, the timid warmth they shared could only grow and expand, comforting them from the dreadful cold and snow. Ice glistened preciously on the windows; in the silence, they heard the gutter drip, a mouse gnawing in a dark crevice somewhere. Enzo made her rest her head against his shoulder (being much taller than she was), and Regina hesitated for a moment but then gave in, being a good girl, as he suggested. Confused, she now sensed he'd been expecting such a thing for some time, but she hadn't imagined it would happen without advances, with hardly a word, the two of them so scantily dressed despite the cold.

"You know," he whispered, "I've always thought of us as two shipwrecks . . . It had to be this way."

A pair of ghosts were keeping watch: the young woman who'd vanished years before in the waters of the mythical, ancient river, whose death Enzo wore—unconsciously, perhaps—like a mournful flower on his lapel (a narcissus? a violet?); and Nicola, the fierce, eloquent Resistance fighter ("qu'il était bavard, le pauvre," Milena would say), who had left behind a tangible message on this earth—a token of sorts—as if he hadn't wanted to die completely. He'd risked his life, but also considered it essential. The warm scent of the bassinet proved it.

We drifted and drifted, Enzo thought, and ended up colliding, as wrecks do—but he didn't say a word. The description was inapt and might have upset Regina. In any case, his mind was engulfed by the mounting climax, and by a plainer, more charitable thought that justified the act: the desire to help her forget that poor fellow, whom she still might resent, unwillingly. Yet if he could have read Regina's mind, he'd have uncovered her fear, above all, of seeming too brazen, like someone not to be trusted: there she was, with a baby hardly six months old, already forgetting about the poor fellow.

"Let's go to bed," he whispered, all aflame, removing his lips from hers, "or we'll really catch cold."

In that room which had taken on the look of married life, Enzo calmly exercised a marital right that fate seemed to have established without their permission. But were they the only man and woman in the universe to share a bed, clinging to each other with disarming tenderness—or were they part of a vast concert? It was dark now. The glowing white snow that fell outside the window, with the shutters open, was a joyful accompaniment to the timid beginning of their embraces, inviting them to proceed, to tune their instruments.

The baby was asleep in the soft bassinet. Perhaps her father's image was already etched into her features, but it was too soon to tell and wouldn't have mattered much in any case. Unaware what was happening between those two, she would soon win her first fragile independence, weaning off her mother's tender breast. As for the two of them, despite the harsh experiences woven through them, the barely healed wounds, their mutual compassion, they obliterated the past (for life is far wiser than death). The blood quickened in their veins, the heavy sighs of lovemaking warmed the room. Then they rested, side by side, hand in hand, listening in silence before falling asleep to the flow of the silent winter night.

V

Camilla left her suitcase in the entryway. "No need to carry it upstairs," she told the custodian, "my nephew or Signor Enzo will help later." The custodian insisted she'd carry the bag herself as soon as she could, noticing the Signora wasn't wearing mourning clothes, though she looked pale and tired and seemed to be in a rush. Had she followed Camilla into the stairwell, she'd have seen that wasn't the case at all; Camilla climbed the stairs slowly, holding the banister, stopping at every flight—and there were many.

Though her thoughts raced during that sleepless night, and again during the short train ride home, Camilla wasn't ready to see them again; no one was expecting her, since she hadn't alerted anyone. She wanted to dwell a while longer on what had happened, the only thing on her mind, which kept stirring up anxious questions.

Alba's letter had arrived at the country house, the same evening Camilla agreed to join Rosso on that walk, knowing where it would lead—that coincidence alone seemed a terrible punishment.

If only I'd stayed in the city, Camilla thought, but no, I couldn't, my mother was dying. Still, I should have come home right away . . .

Dear Mother, read the letter which she now knew by heart, *When you come home, they'll tell you I sent word about leaving for Rome. It's true, I'm leaving soon, but not for work. I resigned from the office before Christmas and collected my last wages. It's not much, but hopefully enough to start a more lucrative venture. I even asked Matelda for a loan, maybe she hasn't told you, but I'll pay her back, rest assured. All I want is to be left in peace. I'm an adult, remember. Don't send anyone looking for me. You understand, don't you? Our father left, you've done everything you could and I'm grateful. But I can't endure the kind of existence you've all accepted. I'm determined to find something better. Just grant me this, no matter how impulsive my decision may seem and how much it upsets you. I promise I'll send news as soon as I have reason to. Hugs to everyone.*

Clear, straightforward, impassive: that was Alba's way. A stern, sharp beauty. But how would she carry that dangerous beauty of hers around the world on her own, without her mother, without Guido and Lalla and the rest of them? Or was that exactly what she resolved to do, carry her beauty and flaunt it?

Rosso implied as much, somewhat inconsiderately (how else could he have acted, after their walk in the woods?), when he found her that evening with the letter in her lap, seated in front of the unlit fireplace. She must have looked as if her world had fallen apart. He'd come to talk her out of leaving the next day, as she'd made up her mind to do, and she knew why he wanted her to stay. He lit a fire to warm the room and rouse her. "You don't want to freeze to death, do you, Signora Camilla?" Fortunately, he was using the formal address again, she wouldn't stand it otherwise. He'd been kind and thoughtful, putting on the kettle so she could at least have some tea. Was Alba looking for work in the movies? he asked. Oh no, Alba had no such interests, movies and plays were Guido's business, Camilla answered half-heartedly. Seeing she was in no mood to talk and clearly wanted to be alone, Rosso left, telling her not to lose sleep, nothing terrible had happened, kids always threw tantrums . . . Lord knows how many times he'd run away from home!

"It's different for a man," she muttered, dismayed.

He agreed. But he remembered how Alba was, ever since the family fled to the country during the war: smart and headstrong, even back then, averse to the sentiments of the times. Those years had been tough, but full of idealism, and Alba seemed unmoved by it all—in Rosso's view, at least. She took after her grandmother—certainly not her mother, so dissimilar, whom he'd already fallen for back then.

He kissed Camilla's hand on his way out, after saying so. He'd gone to the station that morning when she left for Milan, hoping to lift her spirits and set her mind at ease, the proper way, with the requisite formality. She couldn't deny he gave a sense of stability and safety, which she'd been lacking for quite some time—since Dario left. Remembering their walk now, all his advice about the house and estate somehow led up to what followed. It wasn't just the appeal of his muscular build and bright ginger hair, or the fact that he'd forced her (was *forced* the right word?) to yield to him on the cot at his hunting lodge, lost among the chestnut and birch trees. She now saw that night as the predictable outcome of her quiet, droll flirtation, gone on for too long. To tell the truth, she didn't dislike the memory of that lodge on the hillside, built from sturdy timber that smelled of the forest, as if still a living tree with roots in the ground; the raw animal hides strewn across the hardwood floor; the fire lit inside the stone hearth; the plaid quilt they lay underneath, afterward, as she closed her eyes to avoid the sneering trophies mounted on the wall, with their gnashing teeth and snouts painted red, the menacing shadows cast by an ibex's antlers, an owl's glowing yellow eyes. And then that letter, waiting when she returned.

Camilla stopped at the second-floor landing. The balcony apartments began one floor up; the luxury apartments below were spared the indignity of outdoor toilets, which Alba couldn't stand. She knew their pitiful existence had driven her daughter away. *Don't send anyone looking for me, all I want is to be left in peace.* Alba didn't want to cause a scandal, nor start a police search; she simply wanted to be better off, the same thing everyone wanted and always talked about, in their own way, which would lead to a life without feelings, as she feared. Alba had already erased all emotion, how else could she write with such cold detachment—*you've done everything you could and I'm grateful*—a dry acknowledgment of her maternal abilities, which nonetheless didn't stop her from looking for something better. Hopelessly naive, Camilla dreamed of a deeper unity between people after the war, a more enduring warmth, the lives of others fused with hers in one abundant swell, to make up for so much suffering. But the war shattered and destroyed everything. Nor had Alba, in leaving, spared her the insult or accusation—*our father left*—as if to imply, It's your fault too, what did you do to drive him away?

Camilla had done nothing, at least that's what she thought; she believed she wasn't to blame. She often rummaged through the memories of married life, searching for a reason why he'd left; for her part, all she found was an enormous amount of love, a love as naive as it was useless. Only recently did she consider it all a waste, her naivete a kind of clumsiness—perhaps that was her fault.

She paused at the foot of the last flight of stairs, holding the banister. There they were, the outdoor toilets that fouled the air, she could smell them from one floor down. All of a sudden, intensely, she began to imagine a most improbable thing: not that Milena, or Regina, or another relative would greet her at the door, but that it would be Dario himself, no longer as blond as he used to be (nearly ten years had gone by) but gray-haired and haggard, with a weak, nervous smile that would take her by surprise, since his smiles had always been triumphant.

No joy came of the wall of separation falling. Camilla felt her lips move and say, "You're too late, dear. Another man has taken me for a second time, and Alba's gone. She couldn't stand this stench any longer, suffering the cold and eating vegetable soup every night. She went looking for something better, don't ask what. It's your fault, too. A father shouldn't leave his children, unless he's dead."

She pressed the doorbell, sure he wasn't dead. Milena opened the door.

"She won't follow my advice and alert the police," Milena told Arrigo in their room that night. "En voilà une idée! She says since Alba left on her own, without telling anyone, she'll have to find the courage to come back on her own, too."

Arrigo cleared his throat and muttered something as he unbuttoned his sweater, frowning.

"Qu'est-ce que tu as dit?" Met with silence, Milena went on, with a lazy drone that offset any bitterness in her voice. "After coming home this morning, Camilla spent a long time in Alba's room. Nobody dared disturb her. Regina and I were the only ones here with the painter who was cleaning up the black stain on the wall. Maybe that's why she wouldn't come out. She won't let anyone read Alba's letter . . . Personne ne l'a vue, cette lettre . . . Did you know she wrote to her at the country house? Alba should have sent it here. I think your aunt's in shock, even if she tries to hide it."

"Obviously," Arrigo muttered, uninterested. Milena slipped out of her robe and into bed, maneuvering as she nestled against the hot-water bottle into her preferred position. Glancing up at her husband, her mouth half-covered by the sheet, she said, "You shouldn't have eaten so much at dinner, didn't you notice the others hardly ate a thing?"

"I was hungry," he complained, "I was tired and freezing at school all day."

"Le pauvre!"

He felt soothed by Milena's turns of phrase, those interjections in French that peppered her speech; he could understand them by now, and they felt comforting, though they all sounded the same. He'd read somewhere that middlebrow people like Milena had a scant, pedestrian vocabulary, always repeating the same words; nonetheless, whenever she exclaimed *le pauvre*, it was touching to feel her lazy heart warm up and sweeten the tired saying.

He needed a distraction that night, not just because he had suffered the cold all day at school—that pathetic excuse for a school—or regretted displaying his shameful appetite at dinner; he didn't feel shaken enough by the recent events, nor overly distraught, and worried that it showed. If it had, he regretted it, for Camilla's sake. As for Alba . . . Oh, Alba knew what she was doing, and Arrigo agreed that Camilla was right not to get the police involved (it made his skin crawl, the thought of those interrogating cops trying to mask their terrible Southern accents with phony Tuscan formality), but for different reasons: not for fear of causing a scandal, which certainly worried Camilla, but because he respected Alba's right to go her own way. Yet everyone else—especially Milena—was wary of the path Alba might have chosen. Had that wariness ruined their appetites, when they all looked so unhappy and regretful at dinner? He'd eaten heartily instead, and now hoped to savor an intimate moment with his wife and tell her about his day, how he'd again confronted his archnemesis, the arrogant, asinine young conductor, about his habit of adding more players to perform a piece of chamber music—cheap showmanship, Arrigo thought, or chicanery. What a brute.

Arrigo saw himself again in the orchestra pit during rehearsal, looking up at the Buffoon who towered overhead and announced the idea from the podium, disappointed at not being able to execute it. "Pardon, maestro, why do so?" Arrigo said from below. "In the composer's day, the actual number was thirty . . . thirty players, including the chorus." The conductor stood there, baton in hand, more surprised than irritated, as if to say, how would you know? (To which Arrigo would have readily replied, I teach my students such things.) Instead, the maestro shrugged and suggested it was now common practice; even Bach's *Passions* could have a hundred-piece orchestra and soloists. "A terrible practice," Arrigo opined, "and bad musical training, unless the composer envisioned a throng of players." Laughing sarcastically, he added, "Bigger doesn't mean better." Beside him, the first violin whispered, "Easy on the insults, he'll get angry." But the Buffoon didn't get angry. Full of himself like a true solo artist, the conductor couldn't imagine not being right, feeling supported and justified by the weight of custom, Arrigo thought grudgingly. He loathed using the word tradition to describe what he considered a betrayal of authentic tradition: case in point, not respecting the precise balance of sound the composer intended to achieve.

But he could hardly discuss such things with Milena, whose sleepy sweetness beckoned him to join her in the warm bed as soon as he could. Right then, she asked, with a dreamy look in her eyes, "For once, would you tell me about the infamous Dario? He comes up now and then, but I . . . mais je n'en sais rien, moi."

Thus their nightly ritual ended. He'd have to come down from the heights of contemplating the rigors of music and shut up about Faithfulness to Tradition, Respect for the Greats (there they were again, those capital letters!), which ought to remain untouched by the vain, petulant pursuit of useless or pernicious variations—and talk about a man who left under disgraceful circumstances.

But why call the poor man disgraceful? What did Arrigo know, after all? He was practically a boy when his Uncle Dario left, and he remembered him the way a boy might remember a much older relative he didn't have much in common with. At least, that was how he thought of Dario back then, though he must not have been as old as he imagined, now hardly older than fifty—if that.

A sudden, sinister creak made them look up, startling Milena, and reminded them that the deep freeze of the past few days had prevented the last snowfall from melting, leaving a heap on the old roof tiles that groaned and sighed under the weight of winter. Milena furrowed her brow. "If the snow keeps falling, the roof of this old shack will fall on our heads sooner or later."

She said almost every word in French, except for *shack*, which Matelda taught her, but Arrigo seemed not to understand. Spurred by Milena's question, his memory now led him back to his Uncle Dario: an intelligent man with refined tastes, who also knew a great deal about music. When he left, no one imagined they'd never see him again. They awaited his return for a long time, even Arrigo. He'd write, at first, and Arrigo heard he used to send Camilla money. Then, the letters came less and less often, until they stopped coming altogether. Camilla was the last to realize he wouldn't be coming back, or rather, the last to admit it. His grandmother, however, knew from the start, and soon began asking what that oaf was still doing in France. *Oaf* was what she called anyone who contradicted her idea of what was right. Even before the war broke out (when Camilla wasn't around, of course), she'd tell the others, "That man's long gone, believe me, he's already tired of his wife and kids." There were whispers of a scandal in the family, Arrigo remembered well, and after a certain point, for fear of humiliating her, they no longer said a word about it to Camilla—the poor woman.

Milena yawned. "He went to France, didn't he? What was he doing there?"

"Negotiating scrap-iron sales for a foreign company, I think . . . Scrap from dismantled ships, in Brest or Le Havre. But he dawdled in Paris. That made Grandmother suspicious. You know how Paris is." Arrigo craned his big head with a knowing look, as if to justify the man's perdition. "I doubt he had much of a work ethic. Camilla wanted him to have a good job, since he spoke several languages, but he couldn't stand keeping a schedule or following orders. He'd get out of bed at eleven, that I remember. How could he have held a job, of any rank? The family moved around now and then, but I only saw them for the holidays. We were all at Grandmother's in the country after the army's defeat, in 1940, and he was already gone. Some said he went looking for work in America, others said Brazil or Argentina. No one really knew for sure. All we know is that he didn't make his way back to Italy while the border was still open to reunite with his wife and children."

"C'est ce qu'il voulait, peut-être."

"Right. We all thought the same. Alba, the eldest, was just ten or eleven. She's the only one who's never shown any sympathy toward her father. The other kids romanticized him like a ghost, the opposite of their mother's completely unromantic existence, forever struggling with the most material preoccupations: staying warm, having enough to eat, pinching pennies . . . Enzo thinks so too. It's not right, but I'm worried it's true."

"Doing the right thing—imagine that. A rare occurrence." Milena yawned again, eyes half-closed, when she whispered, "Enzo and Regina are up to something, aren't they? I've noticed for a while now. It wouldn't be wrong, I wonder if Camilla also . . ."

The rest faded into a mumble that Arrigo couldn't follow—or didn't want to. He agreed to talk about the past with Milena because he didn't want to leave her with unanswered questions about his family, sensing her detachment. Her only reaction to Alba's departure (he loathed calling it her escape), for example, was the ill-advised suggestion to call the police. Good thing Camilla disagreed. But he wished Milena would shut up and fall asleep, to avoid further discussion. Alba, Enzo, and Regina flickered before his eyes for a moment and slowly faded (had Milena really said those two were up to something?), while the man who left under disgraceful circumstances, the poor devil, had already sunk into a dark fog. Arrigo hadn't savored the outpourings of affection from his wife that he'd hoped for earlier, while digesting his dinner and still feeling optimistic. Now feeling less full, with Milena asleep beside him, he felt much less optimistic, and hadn't talked at all—as usual!—of the clash with his archnemesis, nor shared his musical opinions. But were they really opinions, he asked himself, lying there in the dark (the roof still creaked miserably), or were they in fact questions and quandaries that left him anxious and distressed? Why couldn't he be content giving lessons, which paid well, and keep his part in the orchestra without worrying about young buffoons? He was just a pathetic, unknown violinist, tormented by his Respect for the Greats, Pure Aims, Perfection . . . all those capital letters!

Arrigo couldn't prevent such sacrilege, that much was true. But the Perfection he stubbornly aspired to existed, indeed it did. Others had the power to achieve perfection—and had done so countless times—each time bringing him the utmost joy. Recalling those moments, he felt a shiver of pleasure run through his bones, which he attempted to restrain by modulating the allegretto from Beethoven's Seventh more with his mind than his lips. Such journeys don't always end on barren and desolate shores of gray pumice, brambles and boughs lashed by the wind; some also reach shores of unmatched harmony, beyond description, where one drops anchor with peaceful happiness, where only Music may dwell, which no father or wild maiden would ever dream of fleeing.

VI

The view from the bedroom window was anything but beautiful: a massive suburban warehouse that escaped the bombs despite its size; a wide, muddy road (the countryside wasn't far away); enormous apartment blocks built the cheapest way possible, ugly and squalid, towering scrappily everywhere you looked. Run-down, rustic houses were being demolished to make room for new construction, since the vast city would soon have to welcome more inhabitants, on top of healing from the war's wounds, multiplying to infinity the number of windows that now lit up one after another as evening fell to illuminate meager, melancholy rooms. Laundry hung from clotheslines that stretched outside the windows and concrete balconies, freezing overnight in the dirty, sooty air. No, the change of scenery wasn't pleasant; the view had been nicer from the attic overlooking the historic heart of the city, with its tiled roofs and old bell towers.

The view down below wasn't much better. Beams of light fell onto the wide sidewalk from shop windows, the butcher, the grocer, the baker, the bar—the same bar she'd phoned from that morning, as agreed.

"I'll pick you up tonight," the usual voice said. "Dress for a night out. There will be four of us . . . Understood?"

She understood. Alba lay on the bed and stared at the ceiling, where yellowish blotches had begun to spread; with the lamp off, the stains would slowly disappear in the dark.

This isn't a nice place either. Two small rooms, a bath and kitchenette—just like the woman's apartment, only none of the furniture here is hers, nothing's hers, in fact, apart from some toiletries scattered about in the bathroom, a few dresses hanging in the closet, not one suitable for a night out, she thinks bitterly. The whole place is shabby, vulgar decor, furniture used by a long parade of strangers, an indefinable smell that lingers in the air despite a thorough cleaning. On the table in the other room is the typewriter she borrowed to pass as a traveling typist from out of town. Still, the doorman and landlord were standoffish, studying her with suspicious, prying eyes—especially the landlord. "You finally made up your mind!" the woman said, when Alba let her know she'd moved in. "Careful not to attract attention, though. Say you're from out of town," she warned. But before she can afford a nicer place, Alba will have to make hefty payments of her own, not to mention return the cash she borrowed.

Her thoughts freeze, twist and turn, retracing how she got here. The city's distant hum drifts through the quiet room, while nearby sounds pulse to a constant beat, upstairs, downstairs, next door: an object falls, a door suddenly slams, a child yells. A throng of people. Soon she'll be a nameless face, coming and going in the stairwell of an apartment block. It doesn't feel like she's still in Milan. She should leave the city for a while, the minute she can, widen the gap between what has been and what's to come—and not look back, never, for that would mean looking over a precipice and feeling an inescapable vertigo, a nausea she can't overcome. The woman brought her to the jeweler, that wasn't awful, but when she went to the pawn shop alone, there it was again, the same woozy feeling, like scaling a terrifying peak. And that same voice, those repeated phrases, like a fountain rising and falling. ". . . I'd rather be born an ape than poor in a world like this, built for the rich . . . Is marriage any better? Don't fool yourself, marriage can be a bad deal. See how your mother ended up?"

The room grows darker, the ceiling stains have disappeared and that chalky white looms above, as if slowly bearing down—to bury her. She burrows under the covers with a shiver. The heat only comes on for a few hours at a time, almost worse than the furnace in the attic. A hazy mirror hangs crooked in the corner, distorting the door's reflection, giving her the uneasy feeling that it's always about to open, ready to let someone in.

Her thoughts whirl and run amok, doubt closes in, relentless—it's only natural. Is that Reason pounding inside her head, demanding an answer? No—it's a woman pounding on a cutting board in a kitchen somewhere; the tiny apartments in these lower-class buildings echo like empty tin cans. Again, the gushing voice. "Believe me, we ought to charge the highest price for what they want from us . . . They haven't paid nearly enough for all our troubles and ills! All the hunger, fear, evacuations, because of their wars, just or unjust. As if war could ever be just . . . Those monsters! The first thing I need is a bank account, with all the cash earned behind their backs."

The woman's chatter echoed Matelda's, but worse, fretting about cash and disgusting men, seesawing from pity to contempt, a sense of camaraderie one might share with a business partner mingled with boundless suspicion, even hate. Who knows what's really hiding in her past: a zone of darkness, like a black lake. You read plenty of stories in the papers . . .

"Why do you read such things!" Camilla would ask, exasperated.

Her mother. Now, Alba feels like running away all over again. Something happened—she's in that room, on that bed, staring at the chalky white ceiling that slowly fades to gray—and there's more to come. She could still delay, postpone, not make a decision, but she won't go home or look back, never. It's as if the door reflected in the mirror were about to open and let in someone hiding on the other side, while she waits patiently—awfully, awfully patient.

• • •

Dinner wasn't especially terrible, though she sometimes felt faint, more out of hesitation and inexperience than anything. The other tables were mostly empty at that late hour; the deliciously aromatic dishes reminded her that it was late and she was famished, eager for a tasty hearty meal. Should she faint, let it at least be with a full stomach and warm blood in her veins. She'd felt cold and hungry all day, not because she didn't have money for food, but because she wasn't used to fending for herself. The kitchen was cold; the cabinets, empty . . . She hadn't had the time or the means to get settled, that was it.

There weren't four of them at the table, but five. When the car pulled up to her front door, the woman was sitting next to a man in the driver's seat. Alba couldn't make out his features in the half-light, noticing his bald head only when he lifted his hat to greet her. As she climbed into the back seat, she glimpsed two other people sitting in a second small car by the curb, which followed behind as soon as they drove off.

Now, at dinner, she could see them all. The bald gentleman was older, with the dignified and mild manner of someone confident in having the right advice to dispense at every opportunity. His eyes lit up with a faint glimmer of transgression as they rested on the young lady next to him, whose teeth, eyes, and nails sparkled as brilliantly as her costume jewelry. Alba sulked for an instant, feeling lackluster and listless, but soon perked up and flashed a smile at the two men, who seemed full of cynical curiosity, but gracious after all—prompted in part by the woman, who sternly arched her eyebrows as if to warn her it was time to smile.

"Did I mention she doesn't even wear lipstick? Look at her, she washes her face with soap and water . . . like being at boarding school with the nuns."

"I thought you'd forgotten all about the village convent!" said the bald gentleman in an affected voice, with a hint of crudeness. He turned and handed Alba the menu. "What would the lovely miss like to eat?" he asked politely. "What shall we start with?"

Alba quickly answered with a smile, daintily holding the menu between her fingers. "Lasagna with bechamel . . . Oh yes. And chicken alla diavola."

"Ehi! What's the hurry! Your friend seems to know exactly what she wants," he said to the other woman; if she was just as quick to act in other matters, so much the better. Alba froze and felt the smile vanish from her face as he politely suggested, "First the antipasto, my dear, and a nice wine to pair with it . . . Let's see . . ." He took the menu from her and mumbled to the waiter, who stood there listening deferentially.

(What if someone walked in and saw me here, Alba thought. But who do I know? Hardly anyone. I wouldn't mind running into someone from the office, that's over and done with. And the folks at home would never have enough cash in their pockets to set foot in a place like this.)

It was a lavish locale, with plush rugs and strange static drapes covering nonexistent windows, since the bistro was below ground, accessible only by walking down a long flight of stairs. Dreary flower arrangements filled large vases under the archways or on the windowless sills, reminding Alba of a cemetery. Yet the appetizer cart gleamed as it approached their table, and glorious tiered trays of reddish fruit cast a glow over the buffet. The red wine, fragrant and robust, felt warm running down her throat and into her stomach, which had begun to cramp from cold and hunger.

"1934," the bald gentleman read from the bottle. "A fine vintage to toast the young lady." He filled Alba's glass as she smiled at her dinner companions. Another gentleman looked to be the same age, but not bald. Thick, bristly eyebrows ran across his forehead (like two mustaches, she thought), with a shiny pair of eyeglasses underneath. Behind the lenses, the man's bright gaze occasionally rested distractedly on her, as if he were staring at an object, or at a graceful animal in a cage at the zoo. His thin lips formed a mechanical smile. After downing half a glass of wine, he began to talk business with the bald gentleman, and it seemed to her his only real thought the whole time had been to continue that conversation. She heard words like *insolvency, trustee, tariff plan, profit margin*—dry, homogeneous jargon peppered now and then with an aside: "Make no mistake, I won't let those people hoodwink me," or, "I taught him a thing or two, let me tell you." It was then that Alba saw the other woman withdraw into a tranquil silence, to which she must have been accustomed, and transform before her eyes into the same object or exotic animal that she herself had felt like moments before, under the polite gaze of those two old men. She realized the woman's behavior was a technique, which she perceived as a sort of initiation: the business talk was her cue to retreat into a deferential silence (which didn't at all match the venom she spewed at other times) and wait to resurface and rekindle the sparkle in her eyes, her teeth, her jewels when they turned their attention back to her. As the woman hid a long, dainty yawn behind her polished nails, Alba turned toward the third man. He was much younger than the other two, she noticed earlier, but only now could she see him more closely.

This younger forehead has the same thick, bar-like eyebrows, reminding her that outside the bistro, earlier, the older gentleman introduced him as "my nephew," hence the resemblance. But his youthful face is shaped by a delicate touch, with softer, more refined edges. His eyes shine sky blue below those lighter, expressive brows; clean-shaven cheeks delineate the slight smile on his sharp masculine lips. He looks like a scruffy young student, and the conversation he strikes up reminds Alba of being in school, though his manners reveal an unsettling trace of sympathy and skepticism toward her. Perhaps because she isn't wearing makeup, her nails aren't polished, she isn't dressed as lavishly as the other woman, he seems to be asking: What are you doing here? How did you get here?

Though the surroundings suggest order and substance—down to the large, shiny dish whose lid the waiter lifts ceremoniously, releasing a delicious aroma of baked cheese, ragù, and cream, as he elegantly plunges the serving spoon into the warm lasagna—she feels like she's drifting through a fluid space, no longer solid herself, but merely the reflection of something she can no longer define, as if she had become the aroma of one of those delectable dishes.

Thinking back, afterward, her memory of everything was hazy. At one point, for example, she remembered asking herself, anxiously, What am I doing here, really? Am I throwing my life away? She recalled her mother telling the story of being tossed into the water as a girl so she'd learn to swim. Nonetheless, despite her taut nerves and the pangs in her heart, she ate with a hearty appetite. After the champagne was served, she was savoring a bite of cake when the man's uncle left the table to take a call (one that must have been quite important, as he had mentioned it several times during dinner), then hurried back, downed the espresso at his seat, and gesticulated as if giving a blessing.

"An exquisite meal . . . I hate to leave this wonderful gathering, but I really must go . . ."

Amid the hubbub, as the others lamented his departure, there was talk of meeting again later at another location. The gentleman and his nephew conferred on their way to the door, half-hidden by the cascading flowers. Alba saw the older man rummage around in his wallet and the young man return with a hand in his pocket, a more pronounced smile about to form on his lips. As he sat and moved his chair closer to hers, that hint of a smile gave way to a look of gallant affection. It was then that she imagined—perhaps on account of the wine and champagne buzzing between her temples—in the shadow of the funereal flowers under the archway, that the man had slayed an old dragon left writhing in a pool of dark, steaming blood, and come back to her, triumphantly wiping his hands clean. Like a fairy tale. But hers was no fairy tale.

VII

Though Camilla was the most distraught by what happened, Lalla and Guido were the most unsettled, as much as they tried to hide it. They were clearly shaken by their mother's pain—the dazed look in her eyes when she'd walk into a room with something in her hand and stop suddenly, unsure of what she was holding and what exactly to do with it; her unusual irritability; those pitiful silences; the streaming tears she lowered her head to hide whenever she appeared in the doorway of what used to be Alba's room, where she now slept, alone. It bothered them—as an itch would, or something terribly uncomfortable—to see the empty seat at dinner, despite Regina and Milena's attempts to spread out the chairs when they set the table. Lalla and Guido were never especially close with Alba, but her disappearing that way, without warning, made them feel as if a part of their bodies—something that once functioned so normally that they could ignore its existence—had somehow broken down or shattered to pieces.

Out of pity or embarrassment, they never talked to each other about it, in part because they didn't know what to say, or how to say it, and because discussing such things would have been difficult without mentioning their father. By now, their fanciful childhood tales had run their course, the colorful Suddamerica of Lalla's vivid imagination. The thought of him instead made them realize how fragile the family's bonds were, and think yet again of the harsh, unfair fate their mother had to endure. This especially weighed on Lalla, who felt pushed to the lonely edges of the household, unable to confide in anyone about her recent encounter—so significant.

As always, Lalla's resentment and restlessness were rooted in the fact that Nicola was no longer there to listen and give advice. Enzo, whom she'd warmed up to since the start of winter with the tender hope he might take Nicola's place, was lost before she could win him over. Enzo and Regina seemed keen on each other, according to Milena's indiscreet insinuations, and *keen* meant (Lalla was mature enough to understand) those two must be sleeping together, or soon would. If the rumors were true, it would be the second time Regina came between Lalla and someone dear to her, whom she'd chosen in every way. Lalla didn't hold this against her, but she had to admit that what had happened wasn't at all encouraging, and she'd had to face that risky encounter on her own.

It was a simple thing, at first. She'd gone to a bookshop in the city center, looking for the address of a famous author (a name she'd settled on after much deliberation), and—lo and behold!—there he was in the corner, smoking a Tuscan cigar, chatting with a deferential shop clerk. Lalla fumbled for the words to say why she hoped to meet him and what she wanted: an opinion of her work.

"What, a novel?" the author asked with a suspicious scowl, baring crooked, stained teeth as he shifted the cigar from right to left. The men looked at her with an air of derision, author and clerk. Behind her, snickering, stood the cashier who had just pointed out the author. ("There he is!") The cashier had addressed him informally, barely adding *signor* before his famous name, acting as if they ate lunch together every day! Intimidated, Lalla approached the distinguished figure.

"No, just a story . . . twenty pages or so," she stammered, hoping not to sound overly desperate and that her face hadn't turned too red.

He studied her for a moment with a friendlier look, puffing on the cigar.

"I never read stories, my dear . . . That's the last thing I need!" Suddenly curious, he added, "Pardon me, but how old are you?"

"I'll be fifteen soon," she replied eagerly, as if promising all her future years would come quickly.

"Imagine that!" the author exclaimed to the laughing clerk (that rude idiot), more sarcastic than surprised, without looking in his direction—looking only at Lalla, in fact. "Only fifteen and already writing books . . . Poor us! The war made them grow up fast, that's all there is to it! Oh, when we were fifteen!" He turned to the cashier, who was also laughing. "We got into trouble at the casino, that's what we did. But at least we weren't writing books, for God's sake."

As much as she had expected his words, they petrified her. She wondered whether to hide her frustration behind feigned ignorance or improvise a clever smile. She opted to innocently bat her eyelashes and make it clear she had nothing more to say, though she hadn't said much, leaving it up to the Author to end the conversation. All right! he agreed with a droll look, he'd make an exception and read her story, but she shouldn't expect any flattery—he was harsh, very harsh.

"Writing is serious business, my dear."

It all happened quickly and quite successfully, as Lalla left the bookshop holding tight to a precious piece of paper with an address and telephone number (she was invited to deliver her story the morning after next, around eleven). Only then did she notice several copies of the author's latest novel on display in the shop window. She stood there gazing at the book, entranced: the cover was blue, black, and white, its title intertwined with a background that wasn't clear at first, until, at closer glance, the image of a nude woman appeared, facing a mirror, a bluish, ashen nude whose feminine traits—breasts, hips, sex—were hardly distinguishable, a nakedness made sterile and harmless.

At home that night, Lalla couldn't resist the urge to tell Guido everything. He seemed interested in the encounter, out of curiosity if nothing else, and simply voiced a skeptical comment: Let's see if you chose the right author.

Who else could she have talked to but Guido, in the desert of sadness where she felt lost after Alba's disappearance? And why, when she thought about her sister, did she recall that "casino" meant brothel? She'd often heard or read about certain houses down empty alleys with the shutters always closed, hiding dimly lit, repugnant rooms behind velvet or damask drapes, rooms that smelled of burnt sandalwood and echoed with the immodest sound of running water: women perpetually showering. Lalla was always averse to the thought that Dostoyevsky's sweet Sonia, the faithful beloved of Raskolnikov, was part of that sad legion. Now, another thought pierced her like an arrow: What if Alba had walked down one of those alleys?

Only the baby was cheerful, as always. When she was awake, her lively squeals brightened the gloom in the attic, where they no longer dared complain about the cold and discomfort, the vegetable soups and foul smells, realizing those trivial troubles had easy solutions, whereas what had happened (the look in Camilla's eyes wouldn't let them forget) couldn't be remedied—at least not for the time being.

A sunbeam filtering through the balcony awning was enough to beckon Lalla and Guido outside on that mid-January afternoon: As the sun melted a bit of snow from the edge of the roof, the iridescent drops, along with the baby's squeals, brought an unexpectedly festive mood.

"Don't catch cold, it isn't springtime yet," said Camilla, peeking her head outside the door and smiling at the sight of them crouched atop those old, dusty pillows arranged on the ground along the wall. Perhaps seeing them reminded her of when they used to hide murmuring seashells and shiny pebbles under their pillows at night. Camilla and her faint smile disappeared behind the door. But her voice sounded sweeter than usual, Lalla thought, considering she'd hardly spoken for days now, and the few words she did say were needlessly stern, even when she reminded them to change out of their soaked shoes into a dry pair for the house. Camilla's fleeting smile accompanied the feeble ray of sun that emerged for an instant from underneath the gray blanket of clouds, where the long winter slumbered. Such mysterious echoes existed in nature, Lalla knew: the sun and clouds, water and trees, could speak to an aching heart, like loving traps that spring into action on cue. She knew this, and there were beautiful ways to express such things in writing, it was only a matter of finding the words, which wasn't easy—indeed, it was trying and difficult, but the words existed.

Guido broke the spell. Would she really go see that author? What if he was just leading her on? Would she tell him what the author said about her story?

"Of course, but he'll have to read it first! I can't imagine he'll read it right away—important people never do—especially for someone like me."

The memory of those fleeting, heartfelt moments with her brother, just like when they were kids, as it seemed to Camilla seeing them there together, when they hadn't shared scandalous secrets but playful games to show off their skills and smarts—that memory would stay with Lalla, like a flower floating in clear water. In truth, the dark mud would soon turn the water murky, an inevitable ending Lalla didn't yet realize was coming.

For a while, that morning had been exhilarating. Lalla had gone to school for roll call, but then pretended to feel sick and asked to be sent home. Since she was a diligent, agreeable student, they believed her and let her go. Good thing we don't have a telephone, she thought on her way down the street.

It was another gloomy day, the sky viscous. Cars and motorbikes sped aggressively along the sidewalk, kicking up gusts of icy wind; shop windows glimmered through the sooty fog with their precious, sparkling wares. Lalla walked slowly toward her destination so she would arrive on time. Her heartbeat was steady, but she could feel it in her throat, which never happened except when her emotions ran high, like the nights they'd rushed to take shelter during the war, or, more recently, when she saw her mother cry.

The apartment building near the city center had been severely bombed, to her surprise on entering. Part of the stairwell wall had collapsed, leaving an ominous chasm through which she could see a tranquil old courtyard with bare, motionless trees. A damp drizzle seeped in through the broken skylight with the daylight—they could have at least replaced the glass, Lalla thought. On the upper flights, even the banisters were missing;

a broken chunk of railing hung menacingly overhead. Lalla nervously huddled close to the wall as she climbed the stairs. Luckily the old building had just three floors; she was headed to the top, beneath the dome of shattered glass. Outside, sparrows grazed the glass without hurting themselves—the sweet little sparrows.

She hesitated for a moment outside the door, which had been polished with petroleum—she could tell from the smell. A common Milanese surname was written on the doorplate, not the Author's. Was he renting a room in the apartment, or staying with relatives? The doorbell rang and rang, making Lalla even more anxious. If no one answers, I won't ring again, she thought. Moments later, she heard shuffling, the door opened, and he appeared. It was really him, wearing cloth slippers and a plaid housecoat, without a necktie. He was neither handsome nor ugly, neither young nor old, just an ordinary man, unlike Nicola or Enzo. Not a sound from the other rooms, only the strong scent of coffee. A cat was meowing behind a door.

"Here, kitty, kitty," the Author said affectedly as he opened the door. An ordinary gutter cat scurried out, nuzzled against the man's legs, and meowed insistently, as if it had been kept waiting for too long. Meanwhile, the man invited Lalla in. "Come in, miss . . . I truly forgot you were coming. Good thing you found me. I'll be leaving soon, there's no one home."

A silent, dilapidated house, whose only inhabitant seemed to be that anxious animal. An evil cat, like something out of Edgar Allan Poe, the one atop the murdered woman's head? No, this was just a poor housecat, and she was hardly Poe! Lalla's heart sank; her story was probably worthless, she'd come to hear it from him. How foolish. She stepped inside—what else could she do—but the sudden numbness in her legs wasn't excitement, not at all, but an awful desire to run away.

Camilla was the last to join the others at the table that night. She'd been shut in her room until dinnertime, while Regina and Milena bustled about in the kitchen. When she appeared wrapped in her mother's purple shawl (one of the few things she'd brought back from the country house), no one dared say the color made her look even paler, highlighting the dark circles under her eyes. Nor did they say there was something afoot. Yet Enzo's presence at dinner, though he often came, and the surprising care with which Regina had dressed up and done her hair, compared to her usually shabby look, made her suspect an announcement was imminent. In spite of everything, she'd guessed what the news might be—that Matelda was a clever one!

"What's the matter? You look tired," she said to Lalla, who sat at the other end of the table between Enzo and Milena. Regina was on Enzo's left. Then there was Guido, restless and detached in his own way, next to her. Arrigo sat beside Milena, letting her portion his food for fear she'd later scold him for boorishly overeating. They were seated the same as when Alba was there, Camilla thought, feeling a pang in her heart.

Lalla shook her head, shrugged, and shot a glance at Guido, who winked back. Camilla noticed. It made her happy to see the children joking around.

"Am I mistaken, or do you have something to say?" Camilla asked with mock seriousness, looking around. Even Enzo, who was always a bit scruffy, had slicked back his hair with pomade. "I have a feeling you all have something to tell me."

Everyone laughed in relief. Given the circumstances, they were grateful Camilla hadn't acted oblivious. When they all eyed Enzo and Regina, who laughed along shyly, Camilla added, "I know what's going on. Come here, Regina, give me a kiss."

With flushed cheeks that made her look even prettier, Regina stood and exchanged a sweet embrace before Enzo joined in, giving Camilla an affectionate pat on the shoulder. When they sat down again, amid the hubbub, Camilla gestured to shush them. "The baby!" But the baby was already sleeping peacefully in Enzo's room.

It was all because of that room, Camilla thought; it was bound to happen. Just as she hadn't noticed anything that afternoon—neither that Regina and Milena were cooking for the occasion, nor that they'd moved the baby's bassinet—she also hadn't noticed what had been ripening during those weeks, while she was away. Seated at the head of the table, presiding over an engagement dinner (for that's what it was, despite the unusual setting), wearing that purple shawl, she suddenly felt very old, when in fact she'd taken another lover not long ago. Her eyes stung, not from tears (she had shed enough of those, in vain), but at the sight of the young people around the table, her children and nephew; Alba's empty chair, poorly disguised; and the persistent image of the two graves she felt compelled to conjure, under the circumstances: Nicola's, long since faded, and her mother's, still fresh. It stung to feel torn between being a desirable woman, courted by selfish, greedy men, and the life she was fated to lead, which still weighed her down, all the responsibilities she'd shouldered for years—and for what! No, she wasn't done yet, she told herself, sitting up straight—for it felt like her shoulders really had hunched under the weight of those years and responsibilities—and lowering her shawl.

"Careful, you'll catch cold," said Arrigo, leaning over to cover her shoulders. "It's chilly in here."

Camilla had to perform it well, the role of mother and aunt. "Thank you, dear," she said, resting a hand on his, "but I'm fine." She tried to sound nonchalant, wise and self-assured, despite the constellation of failures that dotted the pathetic sky of her life, then she raised her voice to a more commanding tone to ask Regina if she'd told her parents the news. Regina smiled. Yes, she and Enzo had seen her parents the day before, welcomed with joyful tears and sighs of relief, blessings and promises; they'd even invited her to move back home with the baby right away and settle there after the wedding, if her husband liked.

As she spoke, Camilla noticed Regina's amused sarcasm turn to spite and contempt: Of course she wouldn't go home to her family, the way they treated her! They'd shown her no empathy or generosity, and now their displays of affection were only because everything had gone according to plan—their plan.

"They hardly asked about Enzo. He could be a good-for-nothing, for all they know, but he's a 'husband,' see. That's all they care about."

Regina seemed more embittered now that she felt less hapless, Camilla thought. How could she blame her? Her parents had been wrong; like every parent on earth, in their children's eyes, they were awkward and insensitive, reactionary and unsympathetic. Indefensible. Only Camilla was a mother, too, as everyone seemed to remember in the silence that followed Regina's rant. Their obvious discomfort made Arrigo exclaim, in an uncharacteristically loud, clear voice, "This egg soup really is a treat, instead of the usual vegetables!" as he raised a hearty spoonful.

"Voyons, ne salis pas ta chemise, mets donc ta serviette," Milena said, rushing to tuck a napkin in his collar as everyone laughed. Enzo stood and made the rounds to fill their glasses with a fine red he'd brought for the occasion, along with the cake that awaited them on the sideboard. Their awkwardness subsided. The laughter, cake, and wine weren't just to celebrate an engagement; they also seemed to confirm Camilla wasn't like "those parents," but a beautiful, youthful mother—mortally wounded. That she agreed to join them, smile, talk, pull up her shawl to keep warm, eat spoonfuls of egg soup, even if slowly and half-heartedly—they not only appreciated it, but felt inclined to praise her composure and wistful smiles more than necessary, hoping their affection would truly warm her heart and bring comfort as she fought back tears. (Alba's not here, she's not here. Where could she be at this hour?) The cake shimmered from the sideboard in silence, with its silvery sugared almonds, white and pink candied flowers—oh, it was almost impossible not to cry. But she didn't shed a tear.

Her mother really had been brave, Lalla thought, as they all gathered around the furnace after dinner and talked, just like any other night, same as ever, now that the cake and wine were no longer the center of attention. After a while, Regina went to get the sleeping baby, swaddled in a blanket, as Enzo followed with the bassinet. That was their cue for bedtime, Guido first, then Arrigo and Milena. Camilla tidied up a bit and gave Lalla a peck on the forehead on her way out, suggesting she get ready for bed, since she looked tired. Then she disappeared into the bedroom, shutting the wicker door behind her.

It seemed to Lalla that her mother had simply gone through the motions when all she wanted was just one thing, to shut that door. She'd been brave, yes, but Lalla felt she was still ensconced in a grief that not only kept her isolated, but prevented her from accessing her natural, extraordinary power to transform the world around her, starting with the attic . . . Who else could have done what she did with that miserable, filthy place? In other circumstances, Enzo and Regina's love, for instance (assuming those two really were in love), would have lifted and warmed her spirits so much that their relationship would somehow seem her doing, as almost always happened. That was her mother's power, an abundance of human connection, the power to instantly feel a shared affinity with others. Yet that night's events seemed to wash right over her without making an impression, and her show of concern for any tiredness Lalla might be feeling ultimately seemed a mere formality.

Kneeling on the warm iron floor plate by the furnace, Lalla opened the screen and poked at the smoldering embers beneath the last log. She paused and stared, rapt, then shut the screen again as the flames spread.

Truth is, I'm not sleepy at all, Lalla thought, but I've had a terrible headache all night, the wine didn't help, that's why I must look tired. If I stay here, Mamma will scold. Better shut off the light and make her think I've gone to bed. I'll go out instead, the air will do me good.

It was so dark on the balcony she could hardly see. Bundled in her coat, she wrapped a wool scarf around her head and over her brow, to get some air without catching cold. Little by little, her eyes adjusted. There, overhead, was the outline of the gurgling gutter, the edge of the tiled roof, the white snow; down below, the towering snowbank, frozen in the middle of the courtyard for weeks. Could those bright flashes up above be wandering stars? Could the sky have shed its dark wintry cloak for a moment?

Lalla nervously fidgeted inside her coat pocket with her bare hand—her right—which was to blame for that morning's events, in the silence of that dilapidated building. "Here, kitty, kitty," the author purred to the mewing cat, as he invited Lalla—forced her, really—to admire the photographs strewn across the desk by a window overlooking the grimy, run-down rooftops nearby. The desk sat in a handsome, spacious room, a bedroom perhaps, with a chaise in the corner and an odd-looking chest by the door, piled high with many pairs of dusty old shoes. What did he need all those shoes for? She stood in the doorway, feeling tense and unsettled, wanting only to deliver the neatly typed, rolled-up pages of her story and leave, awaiting his reply. But he insisted she come in, not just inside the foyer where the cat was, but into that room. The cat followed. "Have a look," the author said, pointing to the photographs that caught Lalla's eye. They'd been sent the day before, stills from a film shoot, an adaptation of one of his novels . . . hadn't she heard of it? No, she was ashamed to admit, irritated at her embarrassment. "Here, kitty, kitty," he repeated, but the cat skittered away and paced around frenetically with its tail erect. What could it want? All of a sudden, the man stopped chasing the cat and stood behind her, so close that she would have bumped into him had she moved a muscle. As Lalla leafed through the photographs, uneasy and distracted, he smugly described them one by one: here was the actor so-and-so filming a scene, there was what's-her-name . . . She'd read his famous novel *The Sorceress*, hadn't she? (She could feel his breath on her neck.)

No, she hadn't. Lalla turned around with her back to the desk, unable to take another step. "At home . . .

we don't buy many books, new ones, I mean . . ." she mumbled, sullen and upset. "My family . . . well, we aren't well-off."

"*The Sorceress* is hardly new, my dear, what on earth do you mean? I was barely twenty when it was published—one of my first! Fifteen editions since then!" He suddenly seemed overcome with anger. "My greatest, most formidable success! Don't you know that either? Those critics say I haven't reached such heights again . . . such perfection! Well, those big shots don't know a thing, you ought to learn sooner than later." He looked like a rabid dog with foaming saliva around the corners of his mouth; he couldn't have been more repugnant. "They get attached . . . indeed, attached to those pathetic ideas of theirs, Lord knows when they'll finally manage to break the mold. But us writers, we're quick, we break all the molds, always at the forefront!"

He put his arm around her shoulder and pulled her forcefully toward him, as his fingers wormed their way into her coat and grabbed her chest. "I like you, my dear, so innocent and eager . . ."

Lalla wriggled away and slapped his face with that hand, the same hand that was now fidgeting inside her coat pocket. They stared at each other, steps apart; she couldn't say who looked more shocked. She saw him press a hand against his reddened cheek but left him no time to speak. "You never wanted to read my story! You're disgusting!" she said, grabbing the rolled-up pages from the desk, and she ran out, leaving the door open behind her. The evil cat kept mewing, she heard it all the way down the stairs, staying close to the wall to avoid the collapsed railing. Outside, she dashed across the street toward a deserted avenue, under a row of trees heavy with icy snow—Via Marina, she later noticed. There, slowing her pace beneath those twisted, tattered trees (black and teal, where they weren't covered in white snow), she began to cry, remembering the conversation with her brother the day before. Her joyful, eager hopes, dashed so quickly!

So much for playing hooky, she sighed.

Meanwhile, in the corner of the balcony, a bright glow appeared: Enzo's cigarette. He recognized Lalla right away in the dark. "What are you doing out here? Why aren't you in bed?"

What did he care, the fiancé? "So what if I'm not?" she grumbled. "I'd like to know why all of you want to send me to bed tonight."

"All of us who?"

No answer. He paused, then whispered, "If you stay up late, you'll wake Regina and the baby."

She shrugged. As if Regina would notice, always sleeping like a log, she thought with disdain. Enzo must be so happy tonight, I'd like to ask him, though no one ever says they're happy.

Enzo stepped closer, tossing his cigarette over the railing. "Your mother . . ." he began. He paused. She waited, without saying a word. "She seemed to be feeling better tonight."

"Right. Seemed." The sarcasm was clear. "Maybe she was just being nice. To you and Regina," she added.

"Maybe."

"You deserve it, don't you?" she laughed.

Enzo shook his head in frustration. "Tell me, Lalla . . . Are you mad just because things didn't go your way? That isn't right."

She was speechless. What did he mean?

"You do plenty of foolish things, without asking anyone's advice . . . You should have talked to me, not Guido. Don't you realize it could have gone much worse? And on this of all days . . . your mother's been through enough as it is."

"Guido, that idiot!" she hissed.

"He's no idiot. He should have said something sooner, I'd have gone with you to see that man. A girl your age has no business going to a stranger's house. Just because he's a successful author doesn't make him respectable." Lalla was silent, feeling pathetic and humiliated. "Success built on total smut! You chose the wrong writer. What could someone like that teach you? Even if you'd told me, I wouldn't have brought you there, I'd have suggested someone else." He lowered his voice. "I'm sure Nicola would say the same, if he were here."

Why mention Nicola? What did he have to do with it? Feeling judged, Lalla tried to explain. "It was important to me . . . you all should understand! I thought . . . I mean, I didn't think . . ."

She covered the other half of her face with the rest of the scarf so oddly bundled around her head, sobbing.

"Come now, don't cry," Enzo muttered, clearly

flustered. He hadn't expected her to start crying, and Lalla felt some satisfaction at the thought of him worrying he might have been too harsh, too brusque. Standing there in silence, she could tell he was upset, despite the dark. On his engagement night—it served him right! She wept unconvincingly, sniffling loudly into her scarf. But the tension of that poisoned day was loosening its grip, her bothersome headache was nearly gone, sooner than she'd hoped—what a relief. So talking to someone could help, even when their words sounded unpleasant; tears could wash away the filth one felt. The weakness she'd felt since that morning, when that man's hand grabbed her so shamefully, was ebbing, the usual vigor began running through her veins again. She had the urge to tell Enzo she felt better, buoyed by his curmudgeonly concern. She might even ask that question—"You're happy now, aren't you?"—more kindly than before. But she didn't have the chance. As Lalla wiped her wet cheeks, Enzo said he would have read that story of hers, he was no literary expert, but he could be a careful reader; plus, he knew plenty of people who worked for magazines and newspapers, he'd find the right person to give her advice, without risking another encounter with a lothario like that.

"Would you, Enzo?" Lalla's voice was softer now. She liked everything he said, except the idea of having him read her story. It was as if he'd asked her to undress, right there in front of him—not considering the cold, of course. It really was freezing. She shivered, her teeth chattered. "We'll freeze to death if we stay out here," he said. "Go on to bed, get some rest and don't give it another thought. Everything will be all right."

Nothing will be all right until we hear from Alba, with Mamma in this state, Lalla thought as she nestled under the covers, clutching the hot-water bottle she'd push to the foot of the bed to warm her numb toes. Maybe she'd fall asleep before the chilblains started to itch again. She'd tiptoed into bed without turning the lamp on. Her eyes now adjusted to the darkness.

As she lies there wide awake, old and new ghosts worm their way into her mind: her father, her sister, her grandmother—and Nicola. Dead and disappeared. And Enzo, still tangled in the fanciful thoughts she's been swept up in all this time. She recoils at the thought of him reading her story, as if that would allow him inside her deepest self through a different door—she doesn't want this. Torn between regret and ambition, she remembers that awful day while imagining what's to come. Sorrow and regret are vital to truly expressing oneself, to rendering the world—she knows this well, she's heard it before—but so is yearning for something, delighting in life, holding others close and sharing their warmth, forging ahead together. Everything bears a sign and a message, for sure; recognizing that is what you call growing up. Someday, who knows, she might write a story about what happened in that dilapidated house, with that cursed cat underfoot. Better to bury it deep in her memory for now, to let the sediment settle, like in a good wine.

Nearly asleep, she felt a faint smile ripple across her face, until she lost herself in a final, clever thought, remembering what she meant to ask: Was he truly happy now?

VIII

"Know how you act? Like a bored know-it-all. As if you've lived through so much, for so long . . . But you don't know a thing. Who are you trying to fool?"

He stared as she lay on the terrace, eyes half-closed, lounging in the sun—astonishing, for January, to soak up for a few hours at midday. They'd come all the way to the lake in search of some, though she was under no illusion about the reason why: rather than chase the sunshine, he wanted to spend that weekend trip talking, asking question after question, with the same anxious curiosity he'd shown since their first evening together—that first unfortunate night. They'd talked for weeks now, and his questions were always the same, peppered with the main question he clearly fixated upon, despite repeated attempts at irony or nonchalance. "Why didn't you tell me?" he insisted. "Did you think it wasn't important? These things can intimidate a man, you know.

Quite a commitment to be saddled with. And you never said a thing."

Winter suddenly seemed to loosen its grip by the lake, though majestic snowbanks cloaked the towering mountains from top to bottom. Azure waves lapped and rippled against the rocky shore, a rosy mist enveloped the towns across the water with hardly a wisp of breeze. Still, the innkeeper told them it fell below zero a few days before, you could hear the ice crack at night. It was a tranquil, elegant pensione with central heating (a miracle, in those days). The young man chose the spot because he knew the proprietors, who wouldn't subject them to any uncomfortable questions. Nonetheless, they booked separate rooms, hers with the terrace where they now lay in the sun. Since arriving Friday evening, they hadn't done much but spend most of their time in the room, talking. She was tired.

Alba took off her sunglasses to look him in the eye, smiled distractedly, then put them back on and gazed out at the lake.

"I'd like to know what's boring you . . . Is it me?"

"Of course not, what do you mean?" she replied, concealing her irritation with another half smile. Her fatigue was poorly hidden. "You just refuse to believe that I've told you everything, you can't blame me for having nothing more to say. Can't you tell I don't have a vivid enough imagination to make things up?"

He tossed his cigarette over the railing and sighed, far enough away so she wouldn't hear. Leaning against the stone wall, warm from the sun, he looked down at the nearly empty road bordering the lake that shimmered blue between the trees. It was Sunday. Children played in the street, shouting and chasing each other, but no one else was out. With hardly any guests at the inn, two runaways like them couldn't go unnoticed. Perhaps he was the only one who wanted to lay low, she didn't seem particularly concerned about staying hidden. She had a family, though she hadn't said much about them. The other woman at dinner that night, her friend, had mentioned a father gone missing when he got her talking, while his uncle took an interest in Alba. Not that the friend seemed to know much either—and who'd dare track her down now, after all that happened?

"Careful," his uncle had said, emptying half his wallet and handing him the money to spend on his behalf. "Have fun if you like, but that girl seems out of place here. I know the other one, she's a bit of a lowlife. Don't get into trouble."

When he drove her home that night in the tiny car, Alba had let him kiss her without much fuss but suddenly seemed nervous at the front door when he'd asked to come up for a while. "Want me to?" he whispered, holding her in his arms and brushing his lips against hers. He was about to say he felt lucky for taking his uncle's place, but something stopped him, an unspoken, inexplicable fear of offending her. After a pause, instead of answering, Alba asked an odd question in a soft, meek voice. "You look like a student, what do you study?"

No, he wasn't a student, he was older than he looked, he'd fought in the war since the beginning. (Why had she asked?) "Oh, the war," she sighed. "I don't want to talk about that."

He helped unlock the door as she fumbled around anxiously. They rode the elevator in silence, avoiding eye contact. "I'll show you out later," she mumbled, as if he were coming up to retrieve something and leaving right away.

Really, he was just as nervous as she was, though he didn't let it show—at least that's what he thought, but perhaps it showed all the same. To calm his nerves, he remembered telling himself, It's simple, this rendezvous wasn't planned, I'll spend half the night with this girl I like, pay her, and leave. Yet he could already sense that once he left, he'd be dying to come back. She was so beautiful, with that fresh, flawless skin.

Meanwhile Alba took off her coat and paced from room to room, into the kitchen and bathroom, wearing only the low-cut dress he'd seen at dinner. She must have felt a chill (the heat certainly wasn't on at that hour), for she reappeared in a shawl to offer him a drink. Smoking a cigarette, he sat waiting in an armchair in the living room, where a typewriter sat on the table under a dusty canvas cover. In the next room was a large neatly made bed with a floral duvet. It made him sad to see the place, which felt squalid and provisional; she must not have spent much time there either, like a stranger who didn't know her way around, as he gleaned when she said, "All I have is some tea, if you're cold . . . It's the best I can offer, tonight."

He agreed, because it really was cold, and because he hoped to delay what felt like a forbidden, risky gamble.

As they waited for the water to boil, he saw her rummage around in the wrong places for things she couldn't find, looking hesitant and disoriented when they turned up. She was truly a stranger in there.

Stirred by a sudden rush of excitement, he followed her into the kitchen, where she gave a start at seeing him and asked, "I forgot to lock the door, would you?" The sound of the dead bolt startled her, but he felt a sense of relief, as if he could finally set out at full sail into the sweet confines of those cramped rooms. Rushing back, he embraced her from behind. She stood motionless at the sink with her hands under the rushing faucet that splashed into a basin full of apples and oranges, letting him kiss the nape of her neck. The heat from the boiling kettle on the stove sent golden beads of condensation streaming down the windowpane. "I wanted to give you some fruit, that's all there is to eat," she murmured, holding out her soaked hands, but he brusquely turned off the faucet and the gas flame under the kettle, which had already begun to whistle. "Stop. I don't want any tea, I don't want a thing. Let's go in there . . ."

There were gaps in his memory. He remembered breathlessly saying her name—"Alba, such a beautiful name, I like it, Alba"—and the thrill of those muddled, frantic motions, tangled fabric, the shawl falling to her feet, buttons popping open like peas under his fingers, the soft snap of an elastic band, the sound of a rip (his clothes or hers?), the scent of the firm, uninviting bed, the smell of cold dust, a trace of poorly rinsed bleach on the pillows. Then the bed grows warmer, her scent overwhelms the rest, as he lifts his head and recognizes her face, still visible in the half light (the lamp's on in the next room). In the faint glow cast by a mysterious beam of light on the pillow, perhaps reflected off the mirror, she looks ashen, as if buried in a tomb, her brow veiled with sweat, eyes closed and circled by shadows. His kisses haven't managed to warm her firm, cold lips. If at first he misjudged her coolness as the reaction to an unimportant client come to spend another man's money, now fear and emotion gnaw at his heart. He whispers her name, as if to rescue or revive her, attempting all the while to do the most ancient deed in the world and overcome her resistance. Then a shudder—the most ancient fear in the world—and her nervous voice whispering, Don't hurt me. He pulls back. Finally, he understands; he's sure.

Then she fell silent and lifted her bare arm to cover part of her face and eyes. As he lay beside her, in that bed, under the same sheets, he felt . . . what, really, aside from a ridiculous, baffling embarrassment? Like a pitiful imbecile, not only humiliated but deceived? As he tried to overcome that sense of suffocation (if only his cigarettes had been within reach, he'd have smoked one, but he didn't dare move), frustrated at feeling so ashamed, while she was as cold and motionless as a statue, the heated questions began.

"Why didn't you say something? Did you think I wouldn't notice? How foolish! You're crazy!" In that moment, he couldn't help but think his uncle may have been right to call the other girl a lowlife, but he wouldn't tell Alba, who finally lowered her arm and turned to him with those beautiful glass-like eyes. She pulled him close and pressed the back of his earlobe—her cold hand was gentle and soft—as if finding his most sensitive part. "Forgive me," she sighed. "You're right, I should have told you sooner . . . I wouldn't have been as afraid."

He would never admit it, but he'd fought back tears. Perhaps he fell in love with her right then, and that was why he pitied her. He leaned over and gave her a tender kiss. All through the war, he'd dreamed of a woman like her, so beautiful, he said. Men dream when they suffer, to take heart and find consolation for so much sacrifice, such pain and horror. That was why, having found her after dreaming for so long, he was willing to forgive her situation, the horrible thing she was about to do which he hoped to stop her from, if she'd listen. As his eyes welled up (their faces were so close together, it was impossible not to notice), she asked softly, half smiling, "What's your name?"

The night wore on, a clock tower nearby struck the hours. As the bed grew warmer, something happened.

Those gaps in his memory—what a pathetic hypocrite! he thought, looking sadly out at the lake.

He felt an instinct to protect her, perhaps from the moment they first met around that dinner table, faced with her startling naivete, even as he knew what sordid escapade awaited her. All the same, he'd seized on his good fortune that night, within certain boundaries.

If I claim the right to protect her, he thought, I'll have to take charge somehow.

So he acted like a jealous, possessive lover. When she blushed and turned away after he left the money from his uncle's wallet on the nightstand, he suggested she not take offense but play along instead. From then on, she wouldn't want for anything or see anyone; he'd been blunt and stern, but there was no time to lose. She'd have to obey, or he'd take action, alert her family and the police, launch a search; she must have a family, though she still refused to talk. His words seemed to upset and frighten her—perhaps not the worst thing, given the circumstances, he thought, as he left before dawn. And obey she did, with a submissiveness he could hardly believe. When he returned to the apartment that afternoon, she was lounging in a robe with a book, like a lazy student distractedly reviewing her lessons. She'd slept in and gone out for a bite, she admitted with a laugh, for she couldn't cook a thing! The money was still on the nightstand. As they sat there talking like old pals, exchanging kisses he greedily sought and she generously granted, still somewhat bewildered at her situation, the doorbell rang. He hid in the bedroom as Alba cracked open the door, without unlocking the chain. There was the woman—as if fate had planned it, to his delight and advantage. In she burst, boisterous and all done up. "What's with all these locks, silly? What are you afraid of?" the woman shouted, slamming the door behind her.

• • •

That startling slam still rang in Alba's ears. Seeing the woman at her apartment for the first time, Alba supposed she was eager to find out what happened after dinner the night before—in bed, of course—but before she could ask, the young man emerged from the bedroom. A sly smile formed on the woman's heavily made-up face, quickly giving way to a suspicious glare at the man who stood there menacingly. "Still here at this hour? I suppose you have nothing better to do. Lucky you!" she laughed, satisfied at having enabled what seemed like a successful transaction. As she approached one of the shabby armchairs in the parlor, looking for a place to sit, he blocked her way, brusque and brutal.

"You'd better leave now, sweetheart, or pray I don't throw you down the stairs. I'd hate to make a scene or get this poor girl in trouble," he said with clenched fists, nodding at Alba, who stood motionless in the corner, wrapped in her robe. Looking ashen and tired beneath her rouge, the woman slowly backed away as he paced forward and pushed her toward the door. "And don't you dare come looking for her, here or anywhere else, or I'll report you for aiding and abetting . . . You know what I mean. Make no mistake, you'll go straight to jail, and she'll go back to her family, if I have to take her myself!"

Bewildered, her eyes flashed with such hate that it made Alba shiver and turn away. With her back toward the door, Alba couldn't see the woman but heard the rage in her voice. "So it was a husband you wanted all along! Here's what I get for trying to help a stupid hypocrite like you . . . Go on, get married and knocked up, that's all you're good for!"

He shoved the woman out and shut the door (without a slam, though he did lock the chain), as she kept spewing curses from the landing. Alba covered her face and began to cry, feeling his warm breath as he whispered, "Hear the way those women talk? Is that the life you really want?"

She threw herself on the bed and sobbed in protest. Why had he treated her that way? It wasn't right! The poor woman had nothing to do with it, she was only . . . oh, how cruel he'd been, how insulting, she'd never forgive her . . .

"There's nothing to forgive," he said. "You won't see her again, understood?"

After a long silence, he lay beside her again, stroked her hair, covered her with the rumpled duvet. "Don't cry, now . . . and don't catch cold. You're right, I should pity the woman . . . but the fact that she put a girl like you on a path like this, as if she didn't know any better . . . I couldn't stand it!"

Maybe he really does love me, Alba thought, burying her face in the pillow, remembering she already knew his name. Sandro. His name was Sandro. She always forgot.

The same thoughts surfaced now as she lay there in the sun, eyes closed, listening to the lapping lake. It was still warm enough to be outdoors—Sandro must have been smoking on the terrace with a melancholy air that countered his natural sense of humor, which she'd noticed the night they met, when he looked like a stubbly young student. And later that night, dizzy with champagne, she remembered imagining the slain dragon in a pool of blood, and him, the beaming young knight, returning to her in triumph.

He must really love me, Alba thought, why else would he do all this?

"All this" wasn't just the trip to the lake, a serene locale meant to help clear her head. The biting cold didn't seem as cruel there, but Sandro's constant restless presence hindered the very freedom he goaded her toward, to make a decision. Much more had happened. He'd forced her, for instance, to immediately move out of the apartment where the woman could have tracked her down (without leaving a new address, of course) and rented her a room at another guest house; made her return the typewriter, buy back the gold she'd pawned, and return it to the jeweler; and shrewdly gotten her to admit how the whole ordeal began. She'd lost some money (Matelda's loan, in part), and the rest still wasn't enough (her final wages from the office, and his uncle's money from the nightstand), but he said not to worry and found more.

"How do you manage?" Alba asked uneasily. "Are you rich? If you are, you'd better say so, or I'll really start worrying."

"Pretend I am," he answered with cheerful nonchalance. "Let me help you out of this mess you got yourself into."

"You're always in such a good mood," she marveled. But she bristled at his questions.

"Have you told your family you're coming home, without the job you hoped for?"

"Not yet. I'm not ready. I need to think," she answered, remembering the bitter words she'd written to her mother.

Though Sandro's daytime visits were usually short (surveillance visits, she thought ironically), he picked her up every night after work. If it wasn't snowing, they'd wander the foggy suburbs, despite the threat of crime that still loomed in those days. He'd park the car near a gloomy café or tavern, beneath the bare trees whose towering branches pierced through the fog and disappeared into the darkness, as if keeping vigil. With the heat on, they managed to bear the freezing cold and embraced, performing a make-believe love he could settle for, so he claimed. She submitted quite passively to his outpourings of affection, which seemed erratic and mysterious, wanting only for them to last as little time as possible. She admitted as much while they sipped coffee or mulled wine at one of those taverns. He simply apologized for being unable to give her up completely. As for her coldness, he commented calmly, "I don't mind, you'll warm up eventually. It'll be wonderful, I promise." How naive, Alba thought, acquiescent and vaguely moved, though surprised he hadn't pointed out how her behavior proved she'd have been terrible at the job. Instead, a few nights before, he'd said, "If you're worried the family will turn you away, tell them you didn't find work, you found a fiancé instead. Perhaps that's the best approach, isn't it?" As if to reassure her, he added glumly, "You can always get rid of me, if this isn't what you want. At least I'll have served a purpose."

That made her suspicious. "You're almost too kind. It's starting to get on my nerves! You've already lost at this game, and you want out . . . How?"

"I'm a sucker, right?" he laughed. "I know that's what you think, anyone would agree, but you've got me all wrong. I'm not that generous, I'm neither a saint nor a hero."

They sat inside the tiny car again, invisible behind the foggy windows, as the tall trees kept vigil. With his arm around Alba's shoulder, Sandro looked out. Though nothing was visible, it was as if he could see the whole world and his whole life through the glass, clouded by their breath. Growing serious, he told her about himself for the first time, in detail, as if leafing through a photo album, wanting to show her the different seasons of his life—childhood, youth, adolescence—the happiness, in a word, of those early years that shaped his character, cheerful and optimistic at its core, even as the clouds of catastrophe were already gathering over his family and the nation. He was left an orphan, the uncle Alba met had raised him like his own son. Meanwhile, the war broke out and crushed him as it had every young man his age, horrifying him from the start as the most senseless, shameful injustice to befall a people—a populace that, if not entirely blameless for being thrust into degradation, was in large part exonerated by ignorance and poverty.

Nicola used to say the same, Alba thought as she listened to Sandro. So did Enzo. But what's the use, she thought, why would he care about Nicola, he's long gone, even I knew so little about him. I wouldn't know what to say about Enzo either, I barely know him. I grew up in a house without men, that's why I don't understand them. But I ought to get used to them.

Sandro continued. Willingly or not, he'd fought in the war, even if every part of his soul hoped he wouldn't die there. It would have been rotten luck to lose his life for those crooks who started the whole thing. So he fought, feeling sorry for himself (though he took some satisfaction in passing judgment and criticism, at least) and for everyone else, the masses who could neither reason nor condemn what happened. They simply marched, fought, and died, not knowing for whom or for what. All those poor people had was their miserable existence, and yet they sacrificed it, hardly understanding why . . . those Southerners, for instance, whose only experience of the so-called fatherland was hunger and oppression. It had been a great lesson. In the end, he felt like a tree in February, pruned and bare; the good fruit came later, when he finally joined the other side to fight the necessary, tragic war for Liberation.

He paused and drew closer to her, squinting in the dark. "But you don't want to hear about the war, do you?"

He was right; she didn't. Since the war ended, Alba always thought the best thing to do was forget it—surely, forget all about it. How could they ever be happy again, otherwise?

She sensed him hesitating. Then, in all earnestness—with a hint of kindness, even—he asked if that was why she'd taken the path he found her on: to find happiness again. Before she could deny it (she hadn't yet had a chance at happiness, or the alternative), he continued: This escapade of hers was another consequence of the war, which claimed many victims. A dangerous fall that could have broken her forever, and should at least have shown her that she risked being a victim too—without realizing it, apparently.

"Come on, let's have a warm drink," Alba said, changing the subject as she opened the car door.

She thought back on it, now, at the lake. In those few days, they'd said so much (too much, to her mind) and yet he never seemed satisfied, always wanting to tell her more about his life, hear more about hers. What stopped him was the fear of boring her, like when he'd asked earlier, "I'd like to know what's boring you . . . is it me?"

In fact, he didn't bore her at all; she never tired of him, and regretted that he felt that way, when he should have known her irritable silence was on account of the decision to be made, that very night, a decision he forced upon her. She'd agreed to it the night before, during a heartfelt moment, when he made her promise to call her family and announce her return. Since there was no telephone at home (she admitted), she'd send word through her mother's friend, the one who'd loaned her the money . . . it was about time.

The thought of that conversation (and the sound of Matelda's voice) took Alba back to the attic, as if she'd never left. But instead of the unpleasant odors or the beams creaking ominously under the heavy snow, she saw the soft glow of the lamps filtering through the wicker partitions; heard her siblings' calm breathing as they slept, her mother's footsteps, making the rounds before bed to see that everything was in its place, the furnace off, no imminent danger (indeed, the fire had started while her mother was away). The scent of the baby's bassinet, of rose water and talc, Milena's languid voice, Arrigo's violin . . .

So the desperate courage that drove her to run away was all for nothing. Alba wanted to belong to herself and no one else, free to make her own decisions and choose her own path, forbidden or shameful as it might be, and now that desire came crashing down at her feet—undone, diminished, ridiculous, even—certainly ridiculous! Had he laughed at her? Her turmoil, her crushed plans, it was all thanks to him. He was practically a stranger, who now stood gazing at the sunset behind her, with that hint of a smile on his lips.

(Even so, she knows the poor fellow's suffered enough, he wasn't always smiling. It stung to see his contempt for that woman, a contempt that could have been directed at her, which she couldn't bear to see in his eyes again. And yet this mysterious, nagging feeling—the phone call, obeying his instructions, fearing his disapproval—could it mean she loves him, too? In truth, she wants to love him, but something won't let her—she doesn't know what.)

"I'm cold," she said, standing up from the lounge chair. He went to her.

"Let's go inside. The sun's going down."

Inside, the doors to the adjoining rooms were wide open, lights on, beds made, the tables and chairs cast reflections on the mirrorlike floors. Outside, as the radiant sunset faded, the long night would soon rain down behind the gleaming windowpanes. They'd wait out the rest of that Sunday afternoon and leave after dinner, his decision.

Alba brushed her long, soft auburn waves at the vanity mirror. "What if we went out?" She doesn't want to be stuck in here with me, he thought. I don't blame her.

"Where to?"

"I don't know. Out." She walked over to the bed and stroked the feathery duvet. "It's too warm in here, everything's so soft. If I lie down, I'll fall asleep, and that'll be it! I could sleep all night."

"All right," he answered, "we'll take a walk while it's still light out and have a drink at the Grand Hotel. You'll phone from there."

"Yes," she sighed, "I promise I'll call."

Did they walk along the lakeshore hand in hand, dreaming of the future?

No one could say, no one would ever know. Anyone who saw them on that winter stroll simply saw the shadows of two people in love like so many others, especially on the weekend, for love is also an escape from the everyday. An icy, dense fog rose from the lake to surround them. The gestures they made, the words they exchanged, were stolen and swallowed up by the darkness, erased by the swirling mist. Why should the passersby have paid them more attention than any other Sunday couple? An imminent fate loomed as they walked—he, toward a mysterious pleasure, one he feared yet longed for; she, toward a milestone that might change her life (taking her down a different path, this time) and bring fulfillment. The stroll offered some relief from their struggles.

But they were surely dreaming. The sirens signaling the blind, dangerous journeys of ferryboats across the dark water (lest they crash, in that fog) might have sounded to them like cries of joy. Startled by a barking dog, a backfiring engine, they clung to each other: I'm here with you, you with me. Perhaps they didn't give a thought to what they'd soon do—sit at the warm, lavish bar; sip an aromatic red liqueur from a long-stemmed glass; purchase a token and enter an empty phone booth with bland gray insulation that smelled of cigars—or to the definitive decisions that would follow, as they walked beneath the bare branches warped by winter, near the lapping lake whose color slowly gave way to pure smell. Could the lost souls beneath those dark waters have known? Perhaps they awakened (but no one saw, of course; no one could say whether such things really happen)—pale, shapeless figures that faded into phosphorescence—and screamed without a sound, announcing the irreparable: Hurry, hurry, tell each other everything before it's too late! Perhaps those voices traversing the black sky (which no one heard, much less the two of them) questioned what was about to happen: Why must it all end before beginning? Life's incoherence, shrieked the sirens of the ferries on the lake. The swirling shapes that appeared and quickly vanished on the water (no one saw those either) were perhaps more real, more substantial, than those two shadows walking hand in hand.

PART THREE

I

February began and still the weather hadn't improved. The snow kept falling, the ice-hardened mounds in farmhouse courtyards cruelly refused to melt. Now and then, the caress of a pale, fleeting sun would thaw the dirty snowbanks into muddy rivulets that snaked between the uneven cobblestones caked with wet hay and manure. Then the snow fell again, triumphant, cloaking everything in soft, immaculate white. Women swept the fresh powder to the edges of the snowbanks to clear a path beneath the arched entryways, scaring off the hens and rabbits with their brooms. A freezing draft blew through the porticoes. Though the women were all bundled up, sporting tall boots, they had the impression on glancing up at the sky that the rising and falling breeze already carried the temperament of spring. The days were longer now. When the sun shone, cats lay on the rooftops, licking their fur clean near the warm chimneys, and canaries began chirping cheerfully inside their colorful cages.

Regina had come to help Camilla at the country house. Though she would have happily gone for a stroll on those mild days, Camilla still refused to leave the house, stuck in mournful apathy, and there was no one to look after the baby in any case, if Regina had wanted to go out on her own. She didn't want to ask Camilla, and Martina, the caretaker, who had plenty to do at her own house, only spent a few hours with them.

Regina's desires were fleeting, falling away before they could fully form. She found it impossible to grasp that normal, calmer times could ever follow such horror and strain. Looking forward to Saturdays was her only relief, when she was sure Enzo, Lalla, and Guido would arrive. Some Sunday mornings, if Milena decided to roll out of bed earlier than usual and Arrigo had no commitments, the two of them also came. Then, sometime between Sunday evening and Monday morning, they'd all head back. Week after week, without fail, Camilla begged and sobbed, "Take me home, don't make me stay here!" No, they would say, it's still too soon, better to wait for better weather. "Nonsense! The weather's bad everywhere." She complained to Regina when they were alone. Were Lalla and Guido eating enough, now that Milena the scatterbrain was doing the cooking and cleaning? Were they staying warm and keeping an eye on the furnace, not risking another fire with all that wicker?

"What difference does it make, anyway?" The wry sadness in Camilla's voice broke Regina's heart. "Is this house any less full of memories? Didn't we spend the whole war here? Wasn't she with us? I see her everywhere." Camilla carried on knitting and sewing—"to keep my hands busy, or I'll lose my mind"—and Regina saw the tears stream down her face, not knowing what to say or do. "It isn't fair to you either," Camilla sighed, wiping her eyes. "You ought to be happy, and all I do is upset you." Regina echoed her feeble sigh. "How could any of us be happy these days, Camilla?"

Every conversation was practically the same. My goodness, Regina thought, let's hope Rosso comes over soon. He visited almost every night. Martina would announce his arrival at the door, without Camilla seeing, with arched brows and a nod, as if asking for permission to let him in while implying approval. In fact, Rosso managed to distract Camilla somewhat and she listened along even without joining the conversation. Sometimes, he'd make the baby laugh in her high chair with a tenderness Regina found surprising, and she noticed a smile flashing across Camilla's ashen lips with every sweet gesture or joyful squeal.

She's like a convalescent, Regina thought, I can't forget how she stood by me when I needed her. Now it's my turn.

Thinking back, the way those events unfolded seemed to Regina to have been pulled from a deck of cards shuffled by a devilish hand that drew the worst and wickedest. Faced with such sorrow, it was only natural to wonder whether the game could have been played differently. If only Camilla had searched for her daughter sooner, if they'd learned in time that she hadn't gone to Rome but stayed in Milan, if, found just hours earlier, she'd have avoided that cursed trip to the lake and celebrated an engagement instead . . . the tragedy could have been a romance. But everything fell into turmoil, a sinister mystery that seemed dangerous to even attempt to shed light on. The young man's uncle, for example, so secretive, certainly knew something he wouldn't reveal, and his disconcerting shock in the face of Camilla's despair seemed to warrant an explanation. Enzo must have gotten one, somehow, but when Camilla demanded to know what happened, he replied, "Forget it, what's the use," implying that the wisest, most compassionate thing to do was honor the memory of the poor young woman who'd drawn the deadliest card from the deck.

It seemed an ordinary Sunday at first, though nothing had really been the same since Alba disappeared. They grew alarmed only after Matelda rushed over to report the telephone call she'd received an hour before, announcing Alba's return, repeating over and over what had been said during their brief conversation—brief, but sufficient.

"Where on earth are you calling from? Where are you?" Matelda had shouted. The static kept her from hearing the voice on the other end of the line.

"At the lake," Alba replied, sounding a million miles away. "With my fiancé. Tell Mother I'm coming home to introduce him."

It was too good to be true, Matelda beamed. Alba sounded calm and peaceful, if not cheerful. "I didn't go to Rome. I'll tell you everything. I have your money."

"Don't worry about the money, dear, I told her, and hurry home, everyone's been waiting for you. I'll tell your mother the news right away."

Camilla was beyond happy, practically triumphant.

"I told you she'd come home on her own . . . I was right to not report her missing!" When Matelda finally left, Camilla tidied up and readied the room as if Alba were going to spend that night there with her, Lalla, and the baby. Poor Camilla. Between laying out the nicest sheets, fluffing the pillows, insisting Lalla put on boots and beat the dusty blankets on the freezing balcony, she paused from time to time with a glint in her eye to declare an apt punishment for her daughter. But the punishment had already been dealt: two bodies lay on the asphalt, grimly lit by the headlights of the car that struck theirs in the fog, their faces cold and solemn, Regina imagined with a shudder, as if she'd seen them herself. Death was always a solemn occasion.

The first to hear the bad news the next day was Enzo. When the officers knocked at the door (it was still pitch dark, before seven o'clock on that January morning), the flustered custodian didn't dare alert the poor women but went looking for Enzo, finding him awake. He threw on some clothes and rushed down to speak with the two officers in the entryway, warming their hands over the iron heater and yawning. Was he family? "Almost," he said curtly. "Why?" A body needed identifying, they replied matter-of-factly. Clearly reluctant to follow the officers on his own, Enzo made Arrigo come along ("Sure, call the violinist!" the custodian goaded, with a hint of disdain), since an actual family member needed to be there. On the way, in response to their questions, the officers shared what little they knew: the young woman had spent Sunday at the lake—with a young man, perhaps her fiancé?—and while they were driving on the highway in the middle of the night, because of the fog or a spinout on the slick road, there was a crash. They fared the worst, unfortunately; the other larger car had barely a scratch. Neither Enzo nor Arrigo dared say more. Hadn't they been asked to identify a body? Those words left little room for hope. Both had been hospitalized, said the officers, in serious condition. They tracked down the addresses on their identification papers; the other family had also been notified.

With that, Camilla was snatched away from the happiness that had only just begun to heal the deep wound in her heart, with a violence that nobody wished upon her and she couldn't escape. Death enters a house like a terrible gust of wind that furiously scatters everything in its path, Regina thought. She'd never forget the sound of that cry—that scream. The memory of war was still so fresh, the horror of the bombings and massacres, and so was poor Nicola's death. Perhaps it was because they'd found some measure of normalcy again that Alba's unhappy fate felt so frightening and unfair. The moment she heard Camilla scream, standing by the bed, Regina buried her face in the damp cloth that smelled of baby food as Nicoletta gurgled with delight and tousled her mother's hair with her tiny hands. Regina sat her in the high chair and saw Lalla and Guido in the kitchen, sobbing with Camilla in their arms, convulsed with grief. Always so poised and self-possessed, Camilla had become a fury lashed by the winds of death, even shoving the doctor they'd called to administer a sedative before finally giving in. Milena left with the children, in tears (it seemed impossible to see her cry), while Enzo and Arrigo stayed to look after Camilla. Her spasms, like a wounded animal's, gave way to a daze that lasted nearly all day; the injection had taken effect. Suddenly, late in the afternoon, she leapt out of bed—the same bed she'd made with loving sternness the night before—and asked to be taken to the hospital.

"I want to spend this last night with her, to keep her company one last time," she murmured, barely moving her pale lips, unwilling to let Lalla and Guido come along. "I won't go to the funeral tomorrow," she calmly announced. "You will."

So it went. Later that evening, when the baby finally fell asleep, Milena took over so Regina could go to the hospital. There was no one in the mortuary room but Matelda, crying and praying, Milena said. Camilla sat by the bier where the body lay, gazing at her daughter, whose beauty—she noticed right away—was miraculously intact. A small bruise near her temple was the only clue something had happened to forever cut short her furtive escape toward a new life (but what kind of life?).

She seemed to be waiting for Alba to wake up or wave at her, Regina thought, seeing Camilla frozen in that chair, as if in a trance. No one dared disturb her or say a word. A young nun appeared without making a sound, as though floating across the floor on the hem of her flowing garments; mumbling a prayer, she touched a small crucifix to Camilla's lips, placed it in the clasped hands of the deceased, genuflected, and disappeared. Regina thought she saw a flash of tender irony in Camilla's sad eyes, which now contemplated the course of her life unfolding alongside her daughter's, already extinguished. In those dark moments, as she prepared to say a final goodbye, perhaps Camilla recalled what Regina had taken in earlier: the warm newborn scent of milk and baby food; the smell of tiny hands covered in dirt or sand, of dog-eared pages and ink-stained fingers; the enigmatic fragrance of a blossoming young woman, the same one who now lay there motionless, forever carrying a secret inside. Alas, Alba would soon begin to emit a final, fatal smell, which would cruelly separate her from the living, even from her mother.

Her "fiancé" lay in the room adjacent. ("A handsome fellow, so young!" Milena said when she came home.) Regina later learned that Camilla wanted to see the young man's body while his uncle kept vigil, asking what his name was and caressing his motionless face as she wept. Then Enzo led her away, and she hadn't moved since. During the wake, Regina saw Enzo go for a smoke more than once, pacing up and down the glass corridor with the tall, husky, well-dressed gentleman, who looked like a bon vivant and seemed ill at ease there, in that situation. She remembered the man asking questions, but Enzo wouldn't say what they talked about, denying that he'd asked anything at all. He sent a beautiful wreath of white flowers for Alba's funeral the next day; Camilla was mortified when she found out, having not done the same for the young man. She didn't attend the service; better not to have seen the hearse covered in sodden flowers, lumbering through the aching suburbs of Milan, along the streets and boulevards lined with sad, dirty piles of snow, lost amid the squalid fog.

At the cemetery, Regina noticed a tall, shapely woman, garishly dressed and heavily made-up, standing nearby with a bouquet, as if she were waiting for someone. When they left after the burial, the woman lay the flowers on Alba's freshly dug grave. Regina almost asked Enzo whether he knew her, but he seemed so intent on pretending not to have noticed her that she avoided the question. The others also seemed to have seen but didn't say a word, as if in agreement that any connection to the mysterious world of the dead young woman should never be examined again, filled as it was, now and forever, with shadowy, ephemeral ghosts.

The family's decision to send Camilla to the country for a while caught Regina by surprise, though everyone agreed (as Enzo later said) that she and the baby were the only ones who should join her there. Deep down, she felt reluctant to leave Enzo, wanting to continue their relationship, which had been cut short and upended by the accident, but she knew there was no way to say no. Camilla fought as well, giving in only after they promised to visit on weekends. Regina would go first, to open and warm up the house. Matelda had sent a chauffeured car for them. Luckily, the cellar was full of firewood. Regina managed to clean and heat the rooms with the caretaker's help before Camilla's arrival. By then the baby was weaned, and Regina's scant milk had run dry during those fretful days, so she could leave her in Milan for the night and stay at the country house alone until the others arrived the next day.

"I'll stay if you're scared," Martina offered, but Regina said no, though the quiet, empty house set her on edge when the sun went down. Death had passed through there, too, not long ago. She tried to find comfort in remembering the pleasant sounds of springtime, the chirping crickets and buzzing cicadas, the whispering trees, the rooster crowing. Winter sounds were different, mysterious, more indoor than outdoor. Outside, you might hear a wheel squeak, a dog bark, a bleat from the barn now and then—recognizable noises. But inside the uninhabited house were faint rustles, intermittent creaks and groans that startled her, dull thuds in the attic, and quivering floors, as if someone were walking upstairs or downstairs. Finally, toward dawn, human voices outside interrupted her nightmares and the pale glow of the sunrise against the windowpanes lulled her back to a more peaceful sleep.

Now the days went by, quiet and melancholy, the only way they could with Camilla's silent, ever-present despair. Nonetheless, Regina still sensed in her heart the vague, elusive happiness she found in loving Enzo. Their nascent love would be difficult to sustain, given the circumstances that kept them apart, and this upset her, not for lust, but because she knew how delicate and fragile it was. She and Enzo had endured such bitter defining experiences that words seemed what they needed least, when it would have served them better to carry on with an intimacy made of silent embraces and unspoken joys. Words would help them get to know each other later, along with the tender, dewy-eyed gazes that lovers share when intimacy fortunately lacks any regard for convention. The way things were, they risked stalling at words alone—weak, cold words that served little purpose and might make them feel like strangers again. Yet during those weekly visits, the only double bed was for Milena and Arrigo (Camilla claimed her mother's room); Regina let Lalla stay with her, while Enzo and Guido shared a small room where the boy slept on a cot. Since other arrangements were neither apt nor practical, Regina and Enzo's only intimate moments were shared on walks alone, weather permitting, and if the baby was asleep. Though Regina had no reason to believe Nicoletta was a bother, she kept her out of the way during those few hours, not wanting to subject Enzo to her constant presence. It wasn't easy. She was done nursing (a relief from the inferiority complex she felt lately) but a six-month-old was still quite the responsibility. Sensing those difficulties, Camilla often offered to help.

"I'll watch Nicoletta if she wakes up," she'd say. "Off you go, while there's still a glimmer of sun." But while they were out, Regina felt guilty and wondered if they should ask so much of Camilla, in her state.

"Sure," Enzo replied without hesitation, "so long as we don't wear out her shattered nerves. Of everyone, the baby probably cheers and distracts her the most."

"You know Nicoletta already recognizes her? She reaches out her little arms and Camilla scoops her up, but I see the tears in her eyes."

"Tears aren't the problem. She's shed plenty, and still does when she's alone." He gave her a knowing smile. "It's no accident that we sent you here with her, Regina."

She asked if getting by in the attic was hard on their own. No, they all did their best. The awful shock had actually done Milena well, in a way; she now spent her time helping around the house without grumbling or playing the victim—though that shouldn't have been the reason why. Even Arrigo noticed, half-surprised, half-suspicious, wondering if his wife had been replaced with a device that might explode in his bed at any moment. Enzo and Regina laughed, happy and astonished they still could, as they embraced hidden in the barren woods, where they learned to tell apart the silvery white trunk of a birch from the dark, wrinkled bark of a chestnut or oak. Though the cloak of rust-colored leaves underfoot had turned to a pulp, turgid green buds were starting to sprout among the icy patches ("Lilies—the first to bloom in the woods," she told him), and in late February they brought home a bunch of scentless violet blooms. Camilla placed the cold flowers in a tiny crystal vase on the mantle next to Alba's photograph, where they soon released a delicate fragrance in the warm air.

Rosso never came to visit on the weekends, presumably not wanting to disrupt the family gatherings, but he would reappear a few nights later. As they sat by the fire, Regina was almost always the one to strike up a conversation, since Camilla still made no effort to come out of seclusion and Rosso wasn't especially talkative. Regina sometimes wondered why he bothered coming by to sit there in silence, when he really ought to talk and get Camilla's mind off things. No one in the family dared suggest Rosso was in love, much less joke about it, had they been in the mood to make jokes at all; the children were too respectful and deferential to their mother, and Arrigo wouldn't have noticed a snake if it bit him—as Lalla said. But Regina knew something was afoot. The glimmer she saw in Rosso's eyes from time to time wasn't just the glow of the hearth, but the premonition of a future that would come no matter what, mirrored in the secret, anxious hope he seemed to nurture. So one night, as they sat with Camilla (the others had gone home that morning), Regina mentioned something her "fiancé" Enzo had said earlier, about a change in the train schedule, then quickly interrupted herself, pretending to realize she'd referred to an event Rosso might know nothing about. "Did you know we're engaged?" she asked politely.

Camilla gave a start and shot her a glare, looking surprised and somewhat perturbed. Yes, Regina knew the question would irk her, and felt brazen telling Rosso about the engagement, but she went on. Camilla had to be torn away from contemplating death (she saw it everywhere, Regina knew, even in the thick log that crackled merrily on the fire, sending sparks flying), had to be reminded of the living, with all their hopes. Did she forget she had two young children to care and provide for? Rosso seemed to catch on, perhaps noticing Regina's reddened cheeks and gleaming eyes (she felt flushed). Suddenly chatty, he congratulated her on the happy news, then asked if he might speak frankly. It was a blessing, he said, sounding somewhat uneasy—a godsend for her and the baby—for things to have ended up that way, what with her situation and the trouble that followed, on account of the war, which had scarred them all, of course!

"I'm happy for you, I really am," he said. He already knew about the engagement, Martina had told him the news, but hesitated to say anything without Regina bringing it up. As they chuckled, Camilla pursed her lips and stared stone-faced at the socks she was knitting.

Regina's excitement at having been so bold—talking about her engagement, fishing for congratulations and well-wishes from that man who certainly wasn't there to visit her—clashed with the restless discontent that wrestled inside Camilla, who anxiously smoothed out the knit socks on her lap. Regina leaned over to touch the thick, fleecy yarn. "Who are those for?" she chirped. Camilla looked up, genuinely surprised and embarrassed by her oddly cheerful tone of voice.

"I hope they fit Guido," Camilla replied, as if to justify having knit a pair of wool socks. "He needs a new pair, you know . . . they wear out so fast."

"Sure they'll fit, he'll be thrilled!" Regina turned to Rosso with the same jovial tone, to announce that week would be her and Camilla's last at the country house. Like it or not, the others who left that morning would have to allow them back to the city the following Monday.

"We've made up our minds," she declared in triumph, as if she'd won a battle by announcing the journey that would lead her back to happiness. Silent and lost in thought, Camilla neither confirmed nor denied, pretending not to notice Rosso's disappointment as he awkwardly cleared his throat and stood to toss his cigarette into the fireplace. "Well, I hope you'll all return on the weekends once the weather improves. Won't you?"

Camilla looked up at him, then, and Regina thought she saw a fleeting trace of sympathy in her eyes, or perhaps compassion, which men always appreciate from women. Rosso must have felt moved, though it was just a glimmer. As he left, Camilla let him shake her hand without saying a word about their departure or return, not even turning to say goodbye as Regina saw him out. When she returned, Regina saw Camilla had put down her knitting needles to stare at the fading embers. Her somber, anxious expression was full of regret at having let those things—the knit socks, Rosso's visit, their plans for the future—distract from the memories that should have filled her thoughts, as if her only duty were to accompany and protect her beloved Alba's ghost in the dark realm where she'd vanished, where she would inevitably grow unaccustomed to life. She'd comfort her daughter through this, at least, holding her hand.

Regina sat at the other end of the fireplace, saying nothing.

II

Whenever Lalla thought about the last time she saw her sister, the infamous night of the fire, she felt more shock than heartbreak at the realization that such a thing could happen to a family without warning. The scene played over and over: everyone had been tending to Regina, who sat by the table, shaken and in tears, even the custodian dispensing advice, mop in hand. It was a while later—she couldn't recall exactly when—that Alba said, "I'd rather spend the night somewhere else, if you don't mind." Strange as it was to hear those words on her lips ("If you don't mind!"), they all disapproved, Guido even teased her. Lalla couldn't recall what the others said, but she remembered Alba looking very pale when she added, "I can't stand this burnt smell." As they went on arguing about what to do and where to sleep that night, Alba vanished, and no one saw her leave with the small valise that had fooled them all—there was no way she could have left *forever* with so few things. But it was indeed forever, Lalla now knew, without so much as a crash of lightning, a clap of thunder, a drumroll . . . not a sound to warn anyone that the pale, frightened young woman wasn't really leaving to escape the burnt smell. The invisible vortex that swept her away would soon after hurl her onto the dark pavement on a freezing winter night.

There was that letter to her mother, yes, which brought sorrow and strife into the attic. Meanwhile, Lalla carried on more or less as she always had, despite the pang in her heart. She'd dared to visit the famous author, wasted her time soul-searching, forced herself not to hold a grudge against Enzo and Regina. It all seemed useless now, rather silly and ridiculous, like that author and his cat. She wouldn't dare pick up her pen again or unearth that stack of typed pages, which not long ago still meant something to her, something essential, to be tucked away with delight. Those pages weren't worth a thing now, and neither was the story written on them. Her sister disappeared one night, valise in hand, and they hadn't even said goodbye. Such things could happen, fateful, painful things, Lalla knew, and she might write about them one day, in a "spare, razor-sharp" style, "never pandering," as Nicola suggested years ago, years as long gone and buried as he was. So when Enzo asked to read her story, on the short train ride home from the country one evening, and share it with someone he trusted to give good advice, she refused. In response to his surprised questions ("Why? What happened? What changed?"), she replied that she didn't feel ready. She'd have to start from scratch, probably rewrite the whole thing, after much reflection.

"A lot has changed," Lalla answered with downcast eyes. Enzo understood.

"If you think it needs revising, that's up to you," he said with a sympathetic look. "But don't get discouraged. Life teaches us lessons, you know, it puts our hearts through the wringer. We fade, but our work remains. Remember that."

Lalla took comfort in his invitation to create something that wouldn't die, the way Alba and Nicola had, but endure. That was the fundamental difference: Life is short and senseless (was there any sense in Alba's death?), so we've got to make sense of it, turn what it doesn't teach us into lasting lessons. But did she have the natural talent to do so? She wasn't sure, no one had the answer, for now; indeed, she quickly doubted herself with the last blow fate had dealt. She remembered the night she talked to Enzo on the balcony, after that awful experience with the writer, already feeling that she ought to let the sediment settle like one does with a good wine. Now she imagined her beautiful, wounded heart as a ripe bunch of grapes from which to extract some essence—her dead sister's secret life, for instance. A painful yet fascinating assignment: to make visible what had been plunged into invisibility, without so much as a sign or shriek.

Enzo, who knew what really happened, instead felt suspended in a state of guilt he could never escape unless he said something. But telling the truth felt useless now.

He sensed Regina's suspicion and knew she frowned on the mysterious veil that his silence cast over the conversation with the poor young man's uncle, that night at the hospital. Still, he kept quiet. It wasn't hard to; Regina had stopped asking questions after that first attempt. She was the only one who could have asked, the only one who had seen them walking together down the hospital corridor.

"A tightly knit family, I assume," the gentleman had remarked, apparently shocked at seeing all those people come and go. "And a respectable one. So how could this have happened?"

It was easy for the man to wonder as much, having told Enzo everything: about that dinner, the young woman lured there by her friend, his nephew who fell in love, perhaps for the first time in his life, the poor fellow . . . No wonder he'd fallen head over heels, after so many years of war and sacrifice!

"An escapade like that, see, for a young man who was a hopeless romantic . . . Oh, we were nothing alike, believe me!" the man sighed. "Before that trip to the lake, I didn't object when he said he wanted to bring the girl home to her family, but I warned him: do what you think is best, but be careful, find out who these people are. I knew he wanted to save her, but I didn't want him getting into any trouble—forgive me for saying so. I'd have intervened . . . So it goes." Crestfallen, he furrowed his thick brows. He hadn't admitted the girl had been procured for him by that other woman. But Enzo understood, with dull horror. It was sheer coincidence that saved Alba from the individual who stood in front of him, blowing cigar smoke in his face—he surely wouldn't have treated her with the same tender care as his nephew.

What kind of redemption am I spinning my wheels about? Enzo thought with irritation, rebelling at the thought. Was he honestly trying to weigh the lesser evil—a young woman who was still alive but had lost her way, or this blameless dead body, mourned by her mother?

Enzo chided himself for having such ungenerous thoughts toward that man, who truly seemed distraught in his own way. When he saw the woman holding those flowers at the cemetery, dressed in clothes far too extravagant for the time of day and the occasion, he realized what must have led her to lurk around Alba's funeral: instead of pursuing a fine career, as she had, her unlucky friend had started on the wrong foot and was now being lowered into the tomb where she would lay those flowers, perhaps more irritated than grief-stricken, Enzo thought. A shocking, extreme end, the woman must have told herself, staring brazenly at Alba's family from the wings. (He'd learned from the gentleman, the night before the funeral, that his nephew had rudely thrown the woman out, and begged him not to divulge the details. The man promised without hesitation, since nothing could be done and sympathy forced one to protect a family's illusions, especially a mother's. Not that her mother could nurse such illusions, he added, understandably skeptical, but fully acknowledging her right to demand silence.)

The days returned more or less to normal after Camilla and Regina's sad departure for the country. If anyone asked Enzo what he felt most intensely at the time, he'd have said a nauseating disgust at the snow, exasperation at the cold. He could no longer stand waking up to the sight of the dark world that weighed down on the windows before fading into a pale gloom of mist and fog, which turned out to be the sunrise. He couldn't stand getting out of bed and turning the lamp on at all hours, staring at his reflection in the greenish glare, leaving the house to find the sidewalks choked with icy snow, let alone the silent white flurry that relentlessly cloaked the half-vanished universe, which had lost every plausible shape. If the weather happened to improve as the day wore on, a hazy sun would appear and cast a weak glare onto the windowpanes and metal surfaces, but it was all for show. Soon, everything would dissolve into the leaden gray night that already began to descend in the midafternoon, when the streetlamps came on and shone like pale moons over a submerged world where people wandered like ghosts.

"The winter must take a toll on you, what with you being so used to warmer climes," Arrigo said when they sat by the furnace at night, if loneliness led Enzo to knock on the neighbors' door. The attic was quite a mess despite Milena's best efforts, and the children looked like two caged owls with uncombed hair and wide, bewildered eyes.

Enzo shrugged in irritation, too proud to admit he indeed suffered more than they did. Hadn't he survived more than one winter during his time in Rome, Arrigo asked, and those tough years in Paris before the war?

"Well, it's been nearly a decade!" Enzo said, sounding surprised, as if it had just dawned on him. "1938 or '39 . . . Paris . . . then Munich, and the declaration of war."

Milena scowled. She didn't care for such talk, much less for those references to the past, though she wasn't really a French citizen but an Italian born abroad, just like him. Once, she took offense and scolded him for mentioning the "tragic rot" and "moral unraveling" that wasn't unique to France but common to all of Europe (the ruin of the corrupt, bourgeois Old Continent, which began eating itself alive in a horrid act of cannibalism after spawning the Monster of Munich).

"C'est bien trop facile, maintenant, dites donc! You Italians have a saying, don't you? 'Hindsight fills every grave.' Mais peut-être qu'à ce moment-là on ne pouvait faire mieux! On ne pouvait faire autre chose!"

Milena almost always spoke to Enzo in French, especially when she was in a bad mood. He laughed and teased her, noting that her interpretation of contemporary history was amusing to say the least.

Arrigo worried when he noticed the conversation taking a certain turn. Enzo would have liked to get to know him better, to break the pane of glass that separated them, through which they exchanged friendly smiles. Polite though he was, Arrigo was guarded and reticent, stubbornly shielded inside a musical pantheon where no one could reach him with that kind of talk, which didn't interest him a bit—much less coming from Enzo, whom he answered with silent, stern hostility.

One night, Arrigo interrupted to ask whether Enzo would really send for his parents and bring them to Italy. The question took Enzo by surprise, since he'd discussed the matter only with Regina.

Yes, he would, Enzo answered, it had to be done, and shouldn't the folks meet his future wife? Since he and Regina had decided not to wait too long, he at least owed them the courtesy of not finding him an already married man!

"C'est juste," Milena said, appeased, bobbing her head like a sheep. "Il faut les respecter, les vieux parents."

"So you won't ever go back to Egypt?" Guido asked, sitting on Enzo's lap with an arm around his shoulder.

"Leave Enzo alone," Lalla snapped, glancing up from her book as she lay face down on the shabby rug, as close to the furnace as possible. The long hair that hid her face revealed flushed cheeks and gleaming eyes when she lifted her head.

"Probably not. I've got nothing left there anymore."

But he felt their stares, well-meaning as they were. No one believed him when he pretended not to have regrets or feel homesick—as indeed he did, sometimes. The ghost of the woman engulfed by the river, the image of his broken heart, drifted through his mind for a moment, until someone's words steered the conversation elsewhere.

"So!" Guido continued, with an affectionate pat on his shoulder, "Tell us about the old Jewish families who always welcomed guests to the table, day and night . . ."

"Allons donc!" Milena exclaimed, not believing her ears.

"It's true, he told me so! With the samovar always brewing! Go on!"

Embarrassed, Enzo regretted—too late—having told the boy those stories in a fit of nostalgia, who knows when, certainly long before the recent turn of events. He wanted an excuse to leave right then, but felt guilty, having come over to lift their spirits: it was his job to stay and chase away the gloom that filled the attic whenever silence fell. Lalla's sad eyes seemed to show she was keen to hear the story, curious as ever. Oh, what to say about those days! Enzo had to find the right words, words that wouldn't come across as offensive or disparaging. Even before the war, he had to admit that Europeans almost always lacked the openness that was typical of the "good life" in the Levant for generations. Europe's greed and guardedness never took root there, where abundance and generosity weren't just the prerogative of the rich. Even those who weren't as well-off, on the verge of poverty, followed age-old traditions, Enzo never understood by what miracle. Guido's words reminded him of the old Jewish and Arab families, and others, Russian or Palestinian, who opened their doors to everyone despite their humble means, the samovar always brewing no matter the season. (Lalla's eyes lit up.) The elders sat at the head of the table, sporting long beards and fezzes, calling every guest by name from the moment they arrived. Any friend of their sons or grandsons was welcome, even Christians, invited to share a meal with those gathered around the table, family or guest . . . That bright, generous world was sinking, never to surface again. But didn't he always say, with his historical consciousness, that Levantinism was a crusty growth on the Middle East, one that ought to disappear and make way for modern history, as the population beat against the door of freedom and independence? (This, for instance, was better left unsaid—how could they have understood?) For young people, life was good growing up without prejudice among so many different races and religions and nationalities (this he could say). Even despite the modern outlook of intellectuals like him, well-versed in the avant-gardes of London, Paris, and Vienna (Italy had fallen pitifully behind, abased by its fascist provincialism), that society seemed oddly limited and artificial because it felt rootless, unmoored from history, as colonial or semicolonial lands often are—and thus doomed from the start. Few understood, and no one wanted to hear it, Enzo remembered, but they'd all learn, inevitably: the wheels of history never stop turning, and just as they crushed him, they'd crush anyone who survived and still clung to those half-sunken ruins.

"You shouldn't feel crushed, with all you've done!"

Enzo was amazed at Arrigo's reaction—one that would have made sense, had Nicola spoken those words. He and Nicola might have seen eye to eye, Enzo thought, but the poor fellow had already made his exit, and he'd entered the scene. Nicola was now an epitaph at the cemetery; Enzo, an epitaph walking the streets. Such was life.

"Everything I've done is long forgotten. I've forgotten, too," Enzo mumbled, staring at the fire as Lalla opened the furnace door to poke at the embers. "What's gnawing at me is unhappiness, not nostalgia, if you want to know. The discontent of feeling like a foreigner in your society . . . Italian society, I mean. I can't get my bearings, or fit in. Sometimes I long to leave again, but where to? The trouble's with Europe. The same rot everywhere. And I'd cause my folks a lot of grief, bringing them here, and then taking off. Regina too. I doubt she'd come along."

"Of course not." Lalla shut the furnace and dropped the iron poker, which hit the floor with a clang. "You wouldn't want her wandering the world with Nicoletta still so little . . ." she said, with a look that implied, "just because we all get on your nerves."

Guido sat on the rug by the furnace, eyeing him with the same anxious disapproval.

"So I'm a bad Italian, eh? That's what you're thinking." Enzo stood and gave them a melancholy smile. "A mutt, you might say. You have no idea how I wish I'd wake up one day with a heart full of love for this country and its people!"

"I don't understand you! I feel no love for my fellow citizens," Arrigo said. "All I love is music. And Milena, of course," he added, taking his wife's hand as she listened to Enzo, stunned and bemused. "It's enough that my fellow musicians respect their art and do their duty, to play as well as possible." Arrigo sighed. "Not everyone does, of course, there are plenty of amateurs, but luckily you can't get far in this profession without dedication and hard work." He paused, then added, "One can't betray art for too long."

"Right. You're lucky to live in a world of divine mathematics . . . a world of privilege, where cheats are banned. As for us, on the other hand . . ."

"Us who?"

Enzo didn't say. He sighed, too, feeling as if their sighs had released as much air as they could onto the wicker partitions, which trembled imperceptibly with every puff, every breath. It was time to go now, though he'd disappointed and upset them all. But he couldn't carry on that conversation with Arrigo or Milena, much less the children, who seemed even more innocent and defenseless in grief. Thinking about it later, in bed, he desired Regina for a moment, before his mind drifted back to the kind old anarchist who gazed sardonically upon the universe from his balcony over the East Port (before the war broke out). "You're not cunning enough to be a true Italian," he'd say. "But go on back, if you want, and tell me all about it."

There was nothing to tell; the old man died years ago. Still, Enzo had to admit he'd been right: Italians always had a relatively limited capacity for suffering and sacrifice, hardly ever willing to pay the price for anything. "Then again," the old man said, "what can you expect from a people who have had to stomach centuries of one of the most extraordinary histories on earth, who have seen it all and endured so much . . . How could they let themselves be swallowed up? Believe me, whatever happens, the Italians will always find their way and land on their feet. Their strength lies in this."

And here he was, hoping to wake up one day with a heart full of love! He wouldn't magically find normalcy or trust or affection. Instead, he should tell himself that the same way the enchanted world of his youth had sunk, so the tarnished memory of his useless longings would fade. Reality's already overwhelmed him, with Regina and her daughter. But he can't begin a new life until he stops considering his past useless, his deeds for naught, humanity mostly despicable. Better to try building closer bonds with others, for what it's worth, as he did during the hardest days of battle and danger, war and escape. He knew it wasn't just the ice of that cruel winter he must overcome, but the icy feeling of living in a superficial, intolerant world, filled with greed and injustice. Seeing Regina's fingers caress the wild lilies and their tender green leaves, he knew winter would end soon and he'd leave it behind, along with his dead past.

But that strange season had more adventures in store. While Enzo continued his diligent displays of affection, knocking on the neighbors' door almost every day, the mysterious, invisible wheels of fate kept turning, until one day they suddenly stopped in the sky directly above the courtyard where the snow was still piled high. Enzo was smoking a cigarette in the pale sun that filtered through the awning in the early afternoon, when Guido burst onto the balcony from the stairwell, shouting for his sister. "Lalla! Lalla! Come see! There's a man downstairs asking to come up to our place. A man and a little girl!"

Lalla stepped outside, sweater sleeves rolled up, holding the iron poker in her sooty hands. "The damn furnace isn't working today, it's too low! Who on earth wants to come up here, silly?"

At that moment, as Enzo looked down into the courtyard, he heard a scream, then the sound of the iron poker clanging to the ground. Only then did he turn around.

III

Camilla had begun leaving the house when the sun came out, if it came out at all, but she didn't venture very far. Regina would see her amble under the portico, gaze around aimlessly, then trudge listlessly across the yard through the wooden gate to the garden, and sit on the stone wall behind the row of fruit trees that hid her from view. There was a steep drop on the other side of the wall, which marked the edge of the garden, overlooking the valley below. In the distance, a waterway resembling a canal snaked among the fields and trees and turned deep blue when the sky was clear. Buds appeared on the bare fruit trees (though they'd been forming since the start of winter, right after the leaves fell—Regina learned that too), now bulging and turgid, about to burst; a few more weeks and they might flower. It was a shame Camilla had made up her mind to venture out with so little time before returning to the city, though they'd come back every Saturday, weather permitting. She had no choice, now that her mother wasn't there to look after things.

Camilla knew she'd have to visit often: the spring cleaning had to be done in time, and the caretaker would prune the fruit trees and rose bushes in February (soon, then), and fumigate. The seasonal chores were routine; she'd done them during the war—when Alba was still alive. Back then, Alba and the children would hide from their grandmother and steal fruit from those same trees, though the old woman always noticed and scolded them.

"How does she know?" the children asked, laughing. "Does Nonna count all the fruit on the trees? Does she remember exactly how much there is?"

Camilla sat on the wall and looked down into the valley. Alba was gone, lost to her and everyone. But there was no sense crying. She had to be found again, and Camilla looked for her desperately, day after day, hour after hour, even at night when she couldn't sleep—running through Alba's entire life, from when she a newborn, already such a lovely girl, and through every age and season, cut short too soon. Camilla saw her under the apricot tree (it was barely her height at the time, now tall and verdant), wearing a pink-and-blue linen dress covered in ruffles and bows, she remembered, billowy and graceful . . . it fit her so well, who knows where it went. (To Lalla, perhaps, who must have gotten it all dirty; she always wore Alba's hand-me-downs, and of course they were never the same.) There she was, lifting her soft, plump little arm to pick an apricot nearly as big as a peach, beaming when she noticed the ruby hue on the saffron-yellow fruit, a prized variety her grandmother was proud of and stingy with. During the war, it was Alba who figured out Nonna only ever shared the chestnuts, which tasted bad, since almost every tree in the area was diseased.

"These chestnuts are rotten, Nonna, they stink! Toss them to the hogs."

"Hogs don't eat chestnuts." Offended, Camilla's mother would tap her cane and stare Alba down. Neither of them was sweet at all.

"I can't stand greedy people," Alba said with disdain. There was so much she couldn't stand and wouldn't accept from life. Going to work, living in the attic, all those sacrifices . . . She had wanted a new coat for that freezing winter, and Camilla suggested waiting and saving up every month until the next year. But next winter would never come. Her daughter had been plunged into a season that would never change, having gone down paths that would remain unknown. Camilla clenched her teeth, her heart slowly tied itself in knots. No, she'd never investigate which path led her daughter to that fellow, but she knew she'd thanked the young man with a caress. Better to remember Alba stealing fruit from that tree and arguing with her grandmother . . .

"Good morning," Rosso's voice said behind her. "Here at this hour?"

"I came to check on the trees," Camilla replied after a moment as she turned to him and adjusted her scarf, clearing her throat. She wore a rugged coat and a wool handkerchief over her hair, tied under her chin. I must look like an old hag, she thought, but I couldn't care less . . .

Rosso, however, was happy to find her there, to chat about the trees and the chores to be done; he would supervise the pruning and fumigation while she was away. They'd have to choose a dry day, without rain, he meant, when the time was right.

"But you'll be back, won't you, Signora Camilla?" he asked with a hint of affection.

"Of course," she said, gazing at the water that snaked and gleamed down below.

Rosso had been on his best behavior, she had to admit. Even when they sometimes found themselves alone, he never dared mention that night at the hunting lodge, nor their interactions before and after that walk in the woods. Perhaps she'd only imagined it . . . yet that was when she'd found Alba's letter. She would never forget. He likely remembered as well, but didn't say a word, determined to patiently await the first spark of a new flame. In reality, Camilla felt as if she was sleepwalking—perhaps she might never wake up.

Rosso rested his foot on the wall and looked down at the valley, at the broad patches of icy snow on the tail side of the hills, as the country folk called it, where the sun never hit, and the sparse, dark blotches of evergreen. The leafless trees on the sunlit side instead had a purple hue which turned pink at sunset. But sunset was still far off. At the bottom of the steep hillside, church bells struck a quarter to two as blue-black wisps rose from farmhouse chimneys. For the country folk who ate an early supper, it was already late in the afternoon. And the two of them had nothing to say to each other, Camilla thought. Rosso might not have been in the mood to talk, but something must have stirred between them, for he suddenly grinned—for no reason at all, they hadn't said a word—and she answered with a listless smile. It was then that Camilla heard Regina call her name, startling her (Regina never shouted). Anxious, Camilla stood and gave Rosso a puzzled look. He followed as she rushed through the orchard back to the garden. The dry, frozen grass rustled under their feet.

As they emerged from the row of trees, they saw Regina standing in the bright sun by the portico, but she wasn't alone. Facing her was a tall man with slightly hunched shoulders and silver hair, holding a young girl by the hand. Regina stared, wide-eyed, hands clasped over her lips, as if on the verge of a dangerous decision. Camilla felt a shiver of dread, taking a step past the trees; there, on the other side of the hedge between the orchard and the garden, was Lalla in her brown wool coat and blue hat. "Lalla's here!" she whispered to Rosso, turning pale. "Something must have happened, she should be at school today!"

Rosso stopped a few steps behind and furrowed his brow. Seeing her mother appear, Lalla stretched out her slender arms, ran toward the thorny hedge that separated them, and opened her mouth in exclamation, but the look on Camilla's face stopped the words in her throat. The man talking to Regina turned around. Camilla recognized him.

• • •

As she sat by the fire later—it was already evening—Camilla could hardly control the tremor that had gripped her since that moment. She longed to escape that house, her body, the world—the thoughts that pricked and clawed at her. But her mind kept replaying the scene that unfolded, cruelly, relentlessly, over and over, as if to remember every detail, to make sure nothing was forgotten. And it hadn't lasted long!

From one side of the hedge, dull yet piercing, her voice asked, "Why did you come here?" From the other side, like a statue, the man nervously mumbled, "Why shouldn't I have come, after what happened?"

"What happened doesn't concern you." Like the crack of a whip.

"Oh Camilla."

A few moments—that was all it took for her icy, bitter, vengeful heart to notice he looked older and worn out, as she often pictured him lately. Having lost every hope and illusion, she'd let cold contempt grow inside her, slowly, a lucid, ruthless indifference, perhaps not sensing its intensity until that instant. She felt it now, with the courage to look him straight in the eye. Had she loved that man? (When, my goodness.) Had she trusted him? She'd even waited for him, now she knew. She had been unfaithful. Love was such madness, blind, deceitful madness. She glanced at the little girl holding his hand— a pretty brunette, eight or nine, wearing a red hat and an odd rabbit fur, staring up at her with wide, wary eyes. Despite herself, Camilla's lips formed a question. "The girl . . . who is she?"

Silence. She heard Rosso's footsteps fade into the distance behind her, then disappear. Regina stood there motionless, hands still clasped over her mouth. A winter songbird chirped from the pine tree. Lalla was especially pale, practically shaking. The sullen voice answered, "My daughter."

"Your daughter!" Camilla felt her teeth chatter in her jaw, feeling the same tremor stir each and every fiber of the people standing still in the winter sun under those silent, bare trees.

"Another slap in our face! You'd dare bring her here . . . your daughter!" Her voice grew louder, unintentionally. "Why not her mother, too, while you're at it?" she sneered.

He looked as if he were reading his fate, or looking into the past, and a pall of ash fell on his words. "Her mother's dead."

"So is Alba," Camilla said. He fidgeted with his hat in his free hand, as the girl stared at Camilla, frightened, huddled at her father's side—her father. He still wore a beret, an obsession of his. Who knows whether his clothes still smelled the way she remembered. If he'd stood any closer, she might have recognized it, the familiar scent she knew for years.

Finally, he stammered, "Really . . . can't we talk, Camilla?" There was nothing proud left in him, he was as lifeless as his voice.

"No. Leave. Now." She was nearly shouting. "You

shouldn't have come. Don't ever come back. What happened doesn't concern you. Get out of here."

Regina ran to pull her to the other side of the hedge. Perhaps Camilla had wept, perhaps she'd flailed about . . . she couldn't remember exactly what happened by the portico as Regina held her, but she did remember turning and screaming "Lalla!" as she saw her walk with them down the path toward the front gate. The little girl smiled and held out her hand, Camilla recalled, but Lalla seemed to be crying, her shoulders trembled. Then her father embraced her as they walked together and the girl ran ahead, as if set free.

"Where's Lalla going?" Camilla asked, at a loss.

"Where do you think? Back to the station. She brought them here, didn't she? And she has to go back to school, in the city."

"She was crying."

"She'd been crying for a while, but you ignored her," Regina scolded as she steered Camilla toward the sofa by the fireplace and shut the glass doors. The sun had gone. "Sit here, calm down. You sent them away, what else is there to do?"

Perhaps Regina was frustrated, or appalled, as she took Camilla's coat and scarf. "I'll make some tea," she said, but soon left her alone and ran upstairs to Nicoletta, who'd woken crying from her nap. After a while, she came back and sat by the fire with the baby. Camilla scowled.

"We can't judge what we don't know, Camilla. I was just as shocked to see them, out of nowhere! I can't imagine how you must feel. But ten years is a long time. A lot can happen."

"Right," she said bitterly. "He might have found me with another child, too. But here I am with a dead daughter."

"That's why he came as soon as he heard. He'd been looking for you for a while, he told me. He heard about Nicola, too, about me and everyone. You're upset, we'll talk when you calm down."

"I won't be calm for a while, Regina." Camilla's eyes filled with despair. "Lalla seemed happy, didn't she? That's the thing. She's happy, I can tell, perhaps so is Guido. Their father came back. They'll take his side, see. I'll be the one to blame for everything, not him. He and that girl, the little orphan! He couldn't wait to bring her here and make us feel sorry for her! Lalla fell for it right away, or she wouldn't have come."

After a long, sad silence, Regina sighed. "It won't be easy for any of us, Camilla, that much is clear. It hasn't been for years. First it was me in trouble, then poor Alba. We've been through so much—all the hassles in the attic, the cold, not having enough money, that's the least of it. Enzo's right."

"Alba went searching for luxury, and it killed her," Camilla hissed through clenched teeth. "Shouldn't someone tell her father? He left, not me. I don't feel guilty for not giving her the luxury and comfort she wanted." She hid her face in her hands and wept.

"Oh Camilla, no one could ever blame you! Not even him! Shush, Nicoletta . . ." Regina sat the fussy baby in her high chair and knelt facing Camilla, taking her hands. "You know what? We won't wait for the others to come on Saturday. We'll go back to the city tomorrow, the two of us, and say goodbye to Rosso when he visits tonight."

But Rosso never came. Camilla stayed up late to pack her things. Regina heard soft, restless footsteps pacing in and out of the bedroom for hours.

Good thing we're leaving, Regina thought, this solitude isn't doing her any good. She'll struggle, of course, but she belongs at home. Her husband will return to the fray, as expected . . . He's still handsome, Lalla takes after him. Camilla knows the children will plot a reconciliation, as if that were possible! It might have been, if Alba hadn't . . . I'll see what Enzo thinks, he's always reasonable. Perhaps he'll say it isn't my place to judge a man who had a daughter with another woman . . . But I was just a girl, it's not the same.

Regina's thoughts drifted from Camilla as she dreamed of the marriage that would change her life's course, her thoughts slowly spinning and tangling like a luminous thread into a glowing cocoon suspended in the darkness. Yes, hers were still the dreams of a young woman. She felt glad to marry Enzo, tossing and turning under the smooth warm sheets, feeling a rush of vigor in her veins, a lust she thought lost forever, now reawakened, and an intense youthful longing to set off on a new adventure.

IV

The snow had stopped falling a few days before, and the sky would have shone clean and bright, had the fog not rolled in over the city. Again the attic seemed to drift through a mysterious space, sometimes cloaked in a silence that made it seem as if the house had floated to the surface of a stagnant lagoon or landed on the shores of a sleepy estuary, where the waves of that river of haze flowed from, slowly and imperceptibly. Finally, at sunset, a reassuring glow hinted at the clear sky beyond the fog's shifting edges; suddenly, a gold line gleamed, marking the silhouette of a slanted roof stained with soot.

The weather was milder now. If Camilla had seen Guido and Lalla sitting on the shabby pillows under the awning on that damp day, she wouldn't have scolded them as she had in January—"Don't catch cold, it isn't springtime." In fact, there weren't many days left on the calendar until the spring equinox, and the sun's faint glow now warmed their feet outstretched on the bricks. Nor would their expressions have reminded her of their childhood games, the memory of which, perhaps, no longer held any power over her.

She didn't see them because she was busy tidying up and washing clothes to pack in Lalla's suitcase. With her permission, Lalla would go live with her father for a while. Guido found this strange and stirring, like all the events of the past few weeks: a series of dramatic plot twists that left him stunned but made for a disappointing performance overall. The characters were unconvincing from the start, he felt an odd urge to rewrite their lines and make them more compelling. But it was wrong to see his family that way. They could never be mere characters; they were real, raw and bare, nothing more. In fact, no performance had ever shocked him as much (almost making him nauseous) as that night at the hospital, when he and Lalla had gone to meet their mother, and Alba—his sister—was lying on that bier. He'd left that gloomy room almost immediately and pressed his forehead against the cold glass as he tried to quell the heaving. Enzo appeared and embraced him. "Do you feel sick, Guido? Shall we go home?" Guido managed to compose himself, partly because he felt ashamed in front of the gentleman who had been walking down the hall with Enzo, and rushed back to the mortuary to help his mother say goodbye. She—the Mother—was the only one who possessed some greatness, a noble spirit, and that image helped him forget the times, before and after, he'd seen her agitated and frantic, or frozen in distress, unrecognizable. He was always enamored with his mother's beauty and unconsciously rebelled whenever she transformed into a strange, unsettling figure, stripped of her innate harmony. It had happened again, now that his father had come back.

That was another plot twist, his father's arrival, and Lalla's reaction. Though she recognized him, Guido would have struggled to do the same, relying on photographs of his father as a much younger man, long buried in the family albums . . . Lalla's scream from the balcony, the commotion, their embraces—and the motherless child his father called his.

"So she's our sister?" Lalla exclaimed, as if the girl's sudden entrance into their lives was a beautiful thing. Yet Guido felt hurt and considered the whole situation an inconvenience, to say the least. (He knew that wasn't the right word, but he couldn't think of a better one; plus, Lalla should have said "my sister," not "our"!) He felt torn open and realized he was stuck in childish fancies, swept up in Lalla's unbridled imagination, all those stories about Suddamerica from years ago, stuck in the drama around his father's mysterious absence. Now he saw him for what he was: a tall, thin man of a certain age, with gray hair and tired eyes, a cross between an artist and a scientist. Guido wouldn't hug him right away, though Dario had held out his cold, dry hand and said quietly, "I'm your father, Guido." He hugged him later, half-heartedly. Was he wrong to feel estranged? They hadn't spent much time together, since Lalla had the ridiculous idea go straight to the country to see their mother—no one disagreed; in fact, they all thought Alba's death justified an immediate reunion. Enzo was the only one not to express an opinion. But Lalla seemed sure of doing the right thing, even bringing the girl along, as if she believed (Guido understood right away, he knew her well) that fate had taken away one sister only to reward her with another.

Instead, Lalla came home in tears and wept all night. Milena had her hands full, trying to console her. Mamma and Regina returned unexpectedly the next day. His father stopped coming around, and Guido felt no urge to go looking for him. He'd been too struck by the look on his mother's face, as if she feared finding the attic empty, with all of them gone after "that man," as she called him.

Guido did his best to comfort her, then, and kept her company after school instead of ambling around the city reading the marquees and playbills. He wished she'd shake the anxious feeling that made her jump at every footstep on the balcony, every chime at the door, looking around with tense lips. Even her voice turned into a hiss, viperlike. He hated seeing her that way, wanting to restore the harmony that Alba's death and their father's return seemed to have shattered. Her distraught expression now pained him more than anything else.

Then he noticed how often the grown-ups would gossip (did those fools really consider him just a boy?), and soon heard the latest news: Lalla asked for Mamma's permission to help their father settle into a small semifurnished apartment he'd found by some miracle. As if she could handle such a challenge! He could tell his sister wasn't very resourceful when they'd stayed alone in the attic, even despite Milena's help. She must have felt sorry for her father and the girl, and their mother gave in—right away, in fact. Lalla would leave the next day. She apologized for leaving so soon and promised to visit often.

The sun struggled to pierce through the faint swirls of pale, grimy fog that wafted up from the courtyard. You could hardly see the icy mound starting to melt below; canaries chirped cheerfully in the birdcages that hung on nearly every balcony, just like at the country houses. "Are you really leaving tomorrow?" Guido asked Lalla, knowing theirs was a temporary goodbye. Hesitating, rather than answer, Lalla asked if her mother happened to mention her and the decision they'd made together.

"Of course we talked . . . Well, she talked to everyone else, but I was there. So was Enzo, obviously, he's family now. She said something like . . . you live life as if you were writing a novel . . . or you wish you could live your life like a novel, I can't remember. She said, 'Of my surviving children, one wants to act, the other wants to write, and I let them, of course!' But she didn't seem upset, she was smiling, actually. She wants to move to the country soon, for good. The landlord here would gladly break the lease, he's always wanted to throw us out! Did you know that?"

"I know, she said the same when I asked her permission to help Papà."

She called him Papà right away, Guido noticed. He'd have to get used to it.

"How will you manage in the country?" Lalla asked. "You'll have to take the train back and forth, like during the war. Are you sad?"

"A little," he sighed. "Here, at least I can see a movie or show on Sundays . . . Alba always stood up for me, who knows why she understood . . . She didn't seem to understand the rest of us . . . In the country, no one goes anywhere on Sundays."

"You could stay over sometimes, while the attic's still rented," Lalla echoed his melancholy sigh. "Everyone wants to leave. Milena and Arrigo want to buy a house, Enzo and Regina are getting married . . . so much has happened! I'll miss this place, I always liked it. Until a while ago, everyone seemed almost happy here . . . everyone but Alba. But we didn't know it."

"Maybe Mamma knew."

They were silent for a moment. Then Lalla continued, resentfully, "It's not true that I 'live life like a novel.' I won't write again for a long time, who knows if I ever will. I've learned we're all swimming somewhere, sometimes through storms, but there's no guarantee we'll arrive, someone always drowns and sinks to the bottom. This time, it was Alba."

She's right, Guido thought.

"I understand why Mamma can't see our father now. But I can. I'm his daughter, too. And then there's the girl." She paused. "Maybe Alba could never have been the kind of sister I hope to be to that girl. But I like to think she might have come back to me, one day."

Guido didn't answer. "Why shouldn't I?" she said softly. "No one can stop me or prove me wrong. Who cares if they say I live life like a novel. I know it isn't true."

Who knows how this will end, Guido thought. Everyone playing their part, like the theater . . .

They sat together in silence, listening to the canaries, warming their feet in that sliver of sun.

V

So the attic began taking its last breaths, and no one seemed to notice at first. If Lalla had stayed, she might have sensed the early symptoms of its slow death in the wicker's soft sighs, the hoarse crackle of the fire, the faint creaks and groans of the worn wood, the rusty gutters. But Lalla was gone, and whenever she visited, she was delighted to be there again, to see her family, slamming doors, shouting and making a ruckus. The benevolent fairies she'd summoned long ago with her imagination, insisting they stay, had perhaps already tiptoed away, offended or scared. Then they came back to nestle in the corners and dangle from the lamp wires or the rocking bassinet, and took their revenge by pestering the tenants who stayed behind—all stung by some regret.

Among the many stings, poor Arrigo suffered the worst. After a family meeting, during which Milena didn't dare say a word (though she grumbled afterward and kept her husband up all night, adding to his misery), it was decided that he, the only adult male of the family, would meet with "that man," Dario, to report the details of the sad event—the reason Alba ran away (an assumption, naturally), the trip to the lake, the announcement of her return, the fiancé, the tragedy. No one knew how the conversation really unfolded, since there were no witnesses. All Arrigo said, later, was that he'd spoken exactly as advised, hinting, however, that his explanations seemed to take Dario by surprise, as if he knew he didn't deserve them. So Arrigo had made a useless sacrifice, which caused him to break such a sweat that he'd come home before rehearsal to change his shirt—and not because his uncle's accommodations were especially warm. Normally, he'd put on a clean shirt after rehearsing with the orchestra, Milena recounted with a frown, being the one who did the laundry, so they all realized the meeting had the opposite outcome of what they expected: Arrigo, so uneasy and unhappy looking, had made the other man feel sorry for him. Lalla, who arrived at the end of that family meeting, found the conversation had turned to music, as if no time had passed, nothing had happened. Arrigo wiped the sweat off his brow with a grin of relief.

"Music always offers an escape," he later told his wife, "a realm where people find common ground, no matter what language they speak. I never had much to say to Dario . . . let alone now!"

"Do you think she'll ever forgive him?"

"I don't know." A pall fell over Arrigo whenever he had to face such direct questions that dealt with complicated, often unpleasant feelings. Nonetheless, he added, "She might have, if not for the girl. I doubt she will, now."

"Oh, I can't wait to find a house and get out of here!" Milena sighed. The old roof tiles creaked, as if taking offense, and the fairies began to fret in the dark crevices.

The little girl's story was a sad one, the age-old tale of what can happen to an adventurous man with muddled morals who finds himself wandering the world alone in terribly muddled times. The story wormed its way into the attic little by little, pestering one of them first, then another, eliciting different reactions, almost always dodging Camilla, until she finally learned the few details that left her bitter and upset. Her husband wasn't to be forgiven, that much seemed clear. But those startling, sudden circumstances hit hard, as did the truth, mercilessly exact.

An attractive young woman—Portuguese, alone in the world and apparently quite unhappy—was singing fado in a Parisian tavern. Thus, an encounter that should have been a casual affair ensnared the man instead. The woman got pregnant and had a baby girl, whom they named Paula Raquel, like her mother. Meanwhile, a bigger trap had been set—the war. Since both were foreigners on French soil, and he risked being deported to the camps as an Italian, they soon fled to Brazil (so Lalla was right about Suddamerica!), where the woman would feel at home, if only for the language. Not long afterward, she died there. The man found himself alone, having to raise a little girl who had no one else on earth but him. He continued his dealings from there. As the years wore on, with fading regrets and mounting homesickness, he convinced himself that his money—a whole lot of it—would patch things up with his family when he returned home after the war, no matter how guilty he felt.

If he'd come back sooner, he might have saved Alba, Camilla couldn't help but think, with a resentment that deepened instead of easing. No, she'd never accept Paula Raquel, but she wouldn't stop Lalla and Guido from seeing their father. Since there was some money, finally, she'd file for alimony to contribute to the children's schooling. She discussed it with Enzo after breakfast one day, when he stayed to read the newspaper in the kitchen; her lawyer should intervene, he suggested, so "that man" would be held liable.

"At least you understand me, I hope," Camilla said bitterly, and Enzo remembered their first conversations on the balcony one warm summer, in the moonlight, when Camilla had begun readying the attic for all the people who would soon move in. ("Lots of us," she'd said with a smile.) Those were far different conversations: she still had hope, her memories weren't yet poisoned. As he recalled, she'd even admitted a somewhat romantic fear: perhaps her family didn't care to know whether she still felt any love—the faintest hint—for her devious husband. (More husband than father, back then.) Soon, everything got turned upside down and muddled. Camilla no longer seemed the same to Enzo, and Alba's death wasn't the only reason for her obvious harshness.

In the face of everyone's inexplicable kindness, as she saw it, toward the guilty party, of Lalla's decision and Guido's doubts, Camilla seemed desperate to convince herself she'd been in the right all along, or at least that reason and the law were on her side, no matter what. Yet this brought no comfort. She'd cry out in her sleep, and Regina would leap out of bed to wake her.

Just then, Regina and Milena stepped through the glass doors from Milena's room onto the balcony. Brandishing brooms and carpet beaters, they paced up and down to inspect the items hung outside—sweaters, dresses, coats—then ducked under the clothesline and emerged on the other side, laughing and smoothing their tousled hair. It was premature to stow the winter wardrobe, hoping for warmer weather, but they wanted to make the most of the faint morning sun to air out the damp and dust. Through the closed window, they could see Nicoletta inside fussing and flailing in her high chair, but she started sucking her thumb and stared in amazement with the first swing of the carpet beaters.

Enzo thought better than to answer Camilla's question. Had he said a trite yes, he understood, they all did, and no more, he'd be met with the melancholy resentment that was now part of her demeanor. Instead, he was the one surprised when she spoke again.

"I know what you're thinking . . . I was far less harsh on Regina when I took her in like a daughter and defended her from her parents' angry accusations. Remember? Only it's much easier when things don't concern us, or hardly. We can straighten out other people's lives, but it's harder when it comes to our own." She gazed out at the two young women, perhaps without seeing them, as they laughed and beat the dust, hair disheveled. "Who knows, I might have done the same, had Alba been in Regina's position . . . or Lalla. It would be wrong—unfair, even—but so it is." She gestured to the baby sucking her thumb behind the closed window. "You all must think I act differently around the little one, right? Well, she's also mine, in a way. Through Nicola."

What on earth could I say, Enzo thought, that life's a senseless adventure? His eyes darted about as he tried to compose himself. The place was the same, and yet hardly had anything in common with what it once was. That was how he made sense of the attic's last breaths (without realizing it).

"As for the girl . . ." Camilla sighed. She paused for a moment, then continued without saying her name. "I understand Lalla, you know. I'd be wrong to stand in her way. She shouldn't lionize her father, nor see the two of them as victims . . . victims of mine! Living together will give her some perspective, believe me. Guido doesn't seem as drawn to them yet, but he might be, soon enough." She quickly wiped the tears from her eyes, forcing a smile. "I promised I won't send him to boarding school as long as we stay at the country house, and he promised he'd study hard and finish before pursuing the theater. He's serious about it, he doesn't want to become a guitto, like his grandmother feared . . . Oh Enzo, how different can one family be! I always thought Alba was born all grown up, jaded from the start, always so glum and pouty, even as a kid, snubbing the small joys all children are after. And look where it led—such a violent, romantic end. Lalla, on the other hand, will forever be a girl in search of adventure, never afraid of getting lost in the woods. She has a light inside her. So does Guido, in a different way . . . a spotlight. He thinks I don't understand him, but I can tell he's got his eye on all of us, seeing how well we play our parts."

"You know your children well, Camilla. That's a virtue."

"What's the use? I don't believe children particularly enjoy feeling understood, like their parents 'know' them. They want to be better than us. To feel bigger, more important. To them, we're the ones who were wrong about everything . . . Goodness, what a commotion those two are making! At this rate, they'll beat the clothes to shreds."

Enzo stood and folded the newspaper he hadn't succeeded in reading. It was time to go. Camilla followed and tapped on the glass with a smile, gesturing to the baby, who barely noticed. Then she turned to Enzo.

"I wanted to say goodbye, Enzo," she said, calm and melancholy, "while we're alone. I'm moving to the country soon—maybe not for good, but who knows when we'll have a chance to talk again. So I wanted to say goodbye and wish you well."

"What for?" Enzo asked. "No one ever leaves for good. We'll see each other again, won't we?"

"Of course we will. No one leaves. But things end, Enzo, and we'll never get them back. This attic, for instance." They stared in silence. The ceiling beams answered with a polite creak, the furnace rumbled softly, a glass clinked. "I hope you're happy with Regina and Nicoletta. I'm grateful to you for taking care of them. You'll always be dear to me, Enzo. Just do your best to have some love for the rest of us . . ."

"Camilla!" he said, taken aback. She smiled. "Us Italians, I mean. I know you hope to wake up someday with a heart full of love. It isn't that easy. Great loves don't happen all at once. But you'll get used to us. Sooner or later, you'll realize . . . well, you'll see we're no worse than anyone else. All it takes is some understanding, and some sympathy."

"You sound as if I weren't Italian myself," he mumbled.

"You're rootless . . . There's a rift in you. It's not your fault, it's the life you led, far from your homeland, imagining a homeland that wasn't the way you dreamed it. Maybe it never existed. And it never will." She seemed overcome. "Such a beautiful country! That's another reason I'm leaving the city, not just because of the heartbreak. Nature helps us forgive. We've seen awful things, Enzo, and we'll see more, because we're flawed—just like everyone else. We fall asleep spineless, we wake up brave . . . Goodbye, Enzo." She flung open the window. "Let me help those silly women. Look, Nicoletta's fussing, she's about to cry."

He was glad to see her so energetic, opening that window with a youthful verve that made her resemble the other two. He waved distractedly at Regina, his thoughts tangled but tender as he descended the stairs. Camilla had harsh, honest words for them all, even him. Now he smiled at the thought of her standing tall and youthful, in the middle of a lush meadow, admiring the trees in bloom, finally finding some solace—and perhaps no longer so alone.

VI

She reached the country late in the evening, after the sun went down, without telling anyone. In the cold, empty house, in the warm bed, she slept an undisturbed sleep, worriless and dreamless, and opened her eyes the next morning with the odd feeling of having not been back there for a long time, needing to shake herself awake to remember where she was. When she got up and opened the window, the budding grass was veiled in white. A dusting of snow (the last of it, perhaps?) had fallen overnight, glowing pale on the far end of the orchard, under the pink peach blossoms. It wasn't the first time she'd seen that white and pink together; she remembered seeing it during the war, with the children. As hard as her mother had tried to hide behind her sternness, she loved hearing them squeal with wonder: the snow, the snow on the flowers! Everything was a wonder then—and nothing had changed now. The new buds had the same dazzling hues, pale green and rose, delicate and soft, sharp and rough. Delicate branches swayed in the morning breeze, cascading like garlands, and new leaves sprouted from the ground straight as swords. The rising sun would soon warm the portico, the bricks, the roof tiles. It was finally spring, she thought, with a sudden, unexpected burst of joy, there was no mistaking it—but a familiar icy hand quickly reached out and grabbed her heart in its merciless grip, and she shut the window with a shiver. Naturally, anyone would shiver, standing at an open window in their robe, with snow on the ground . . . Only the dead had stopped shivering. But whoever decided that a young woman should be lowered into a tomb had also decided that Camilla would stay above ground. Would she really have to say *amen*?

No one taught me that, she thought, without resentment or dismay. Just then, Martina walked across the garden with a basket on her arm. She looked tired, the basket must have been heavy. Surprised to see Camilla at the window, she waved excitedly, then lifted the edge of the cloth over the basket: it was full of artichokes, beautiful artichokes, would Signora like some? Yes, Camilla shouted, she could leave some on the kitchen table, the downstairs door was open.

Martina was aghast. Had Signora really spent the night there alone without letting anyone know? With the kitchen door unlocked?

"Of course not," Camilla lied. "I opened it just now when I went down to make some coffee."

She'd forgotten to lock the door, she wouldn't do

that again. Good thing Martina and her husband were there to look after the house, she thought while getting dressed, they were nice people she could trust, despite Rosso's warnings—aside from stealing firewood and vegetables from the garden, as everyone did in those days; she ought to keep her eye on them. She'd be discreet, careful not to bother them by acting suspicious. The bedroom was cold as she dressed. The electric heater was on in the bathroom, and the fireplace downstairs would stay lit all day, but she no longer wanted to light a fire in the bedroom, to persuade herself that spring had really come. She ate breakfast at the kitchen table (Martina's artichokes were fresh and gorgeous, even if it was no longer peak season) pondering all the things she planned to do.

Rosso made her face facts. Even if she repaid the loan her mother had taken out for renovations, a small property like theirs still wouldn't turn much of a profit unless they could farm a prized crop, a risky venture requiring time and expertise. Regardless, she'd sketch out a plan or two, nothing rash—her mind was made up. Meanwhile, she had a house to live in, and no rent to pay, plus the harvest from the vegetable garden and the orchard, the chicken coop, the pig . . . and why not a cow? The stables were still standing, if a bit run-down, they'd make repairs, and she could always ask Matelda for cash to cover any unforeseen expenses . . . (Again, that pang in her heart.) She'd survive, surely, or almost. Her husband would have to provide for the children, she wouldn't ask him for a thing.

We've got nothing in common anymore, Camilla thought, wondering how she could have ever believed they did. The foolish things we do when we're young.

Reluctant to ponder whether her plans were truly reasonable, Camilla quickly rinsed her cup and pot, then milled around the house, upstairs and down, opening the doors and windows to let in the fresh air and sun. As she passed the upstairs bedrooms, she thought to check on the attic, remembering what her mother had said before she died: there was plenty up there, she'd give Arrigo a few things for when he settled into a home of his own, which would happen soon.

Next time he and Milena visit, I'll show them what I've set aside, Camilla thought, pleased with her generosity. After all, no one else knew of her mother's instructions; she could have forgotten or ignored them, but she would have felt guilty.

Camilla felt her way around the dust-covered beams and spiderwebs, careful not to trip over the odds and ends, until she reached one of the attic windows and hoisted herself onto a pile of old, chipped roof tiles to look outside.

How different the view was from up there. The sun was higher now, resting like a sumptuous cloak over the woods and fields where a light haze rose through the cold air. The attic was freezing. The pale sky was turning blue, the little snow left on the ground would finally melt—the last of it, she was sure. It was nearly the end of that cruel winter, from which she'd emerged broken in two, or shattered into pieces, aware at every instant of the destruction it had wrought. An irrepressible sense of life stirred beneath those ruins of herself and began to sprout like the buds she saw earlier, some soft and delicate, others rough and sharp.

At that moment, a car appeared among the trees—she recognized it right away—and stopped along the winding country road where some men stood waiting. Rosso stepped out of the car, wearing his usual corduroy pants and boots, and said a few words to the men, before some of them climbed in and sped off toward town. He must not have heard she'd returned, Camilla thought, but he would surely find out and come looking for her later. They hadn't seen each other since that day—she could still hear his slow, steady footsteps walking away. Who knows if he'd guessed about the man and girl who had come with Lalla . . . Paula Raquel. Her immediate departure, and Martina's gossiping, had likely confirmed what he already suspected. She hadn't sent word since then, but he was used to not hearing from her. Even the first time, after Alba's letter reached the country house in those weeks before the tragedy, she never wrote or called, though he begged her to. Not having a telephone shielded her from his advances, and Rosso, for his part, respected her wishes for silence at the time. Was it his impression (or fear) of a reconciliation with her husband that made him act this way now? She was grateful, in any case, and would tell him so; for years, she'd known him to be fairly reserved, perhaps because he lacked inspiration, or on account of a limited sensitivity, but his discretion and tact ended up stirring her more than the attraction she'd given into once—how distant and unreal it seemed now, their walk in the woods! Her attraction persisted, nonetheless, and not just the desire to maintain some camaraderie between them, with their long conversations about what they had in common (mention the land, the seasons, and Rosso suddenly had a lot to say), or seek his help and advice. The buds sprouting within her signaled something else entirely. She couldn't hide that those nights and days, alone in the old country house, wavered between a temptation and an offering. So the sudden faintness she felt wasn't only from looking down into the void from up there. Camilla reached out to touch the edge of the tiles outside the attic window and felt how warm they were. She would go downstairs, across the meadow, the courtyard, and the garden, and walk upon the soft snow that would melt under her feet.

That was what she did. When she turned from the meadow's edge to look back at the old house, the portico and attic windows, she saw her future, beyond the fleeting, passionate nights that awaited her: a home to love and care for. This irrepressible feeling would join the others to remind her, come what may, that she'd never turn into an icy stone at the bottom of a stagnant pond. Yes, she had cut the cord that tied her to those bitter experiences, but that didn't mean she'd forget the living and the dead. With each slow step in the sunshine—the snowmelt trickled into a cold stream—she sensed Alba and her mother standing behind her, in the distance, and saw the gleam of Lalla's blue hat, half-hidden by the peach trees in bloom. Like it or not, she was part of a ceaseless flow—a ceaselessness that is eternal.

She stopped again. A question rang inside her like the clang of a dull bell: Would she ask to meet Paula Raquel one day? (More than once, she dreamt of the girl's fearful, innocent eyes—"Who are you, what will you do to me?" they seemed to ask, startling her awake.) Would she ever say her husband's name again? (She couldn't bear to now, he'd left her alone during the war. It was unforgivable.) Everything meant to fall had fallen, everything destined to break had broken. Every collapse, every death and rupture, seemed to pulse through the vivid spring air.

Martina was home, elated at having sold her artichokes to the town grocer at a great price (Camilla would also grow things to sell, for sure.) Had she seen the gorgeous trees in bloom? They hadn't been so lush in years, there'd be plenty of fruit unless it went below zero again (that night's snow certainly hadn't done the flowers any good!).

"Come, let's have a look," Martina said, setting out along the garden path. Camilla followed, walking slowly upon the last snow.

FAUSTA CIALENTE (1898–1994) was one of the first self-declared feminist Italian writers. Her early work anticipated modern feminism by decades but was limited by fascist censorship. Contributing to the antifascist movement through her journalism from Egypt, Cialente returned home after the war, and after a long silence, she began publishing again in 1961, eventually winning the prestigious Strega Prize in 1976. Cialente spent the last period of her life in Pangbourne, England, working mainly on translations into Italian from English, including *The Turn of the Screw* by Henry James.

JULIA NELSEN translates between English and Italian. Her work has appeared in journals including *Two Lines*, *Circumference*, *Another Chicago Magazine*, *Chicago Review*, and *Firmament*, and she is a cotranslator of the digital edition of Luigi Pirandello's *Stories for a Year.* A native of San Francisco, she holds a PhD in comparative literature from the University of California, Berkeley, and a Laurea in European languages from the Università Statale di Milano, Italy. *A Very Cold Winter* is her first translated book.

CLAUDIA DURASTANTI is an Italian writer, translator, and cultural critic. *Strangers I Know* was shortlisted for the Strega Prize and translated into twenty-one languages. Her novel *Missitalia* will be published by Summit in the US and Fitzcarraldo in the UK. Her work has appeared in *Granta*, *Apartamento*, *LARB*, and elsewhere. She's the curator of the feminist imprint La Tartaruga.

Transit Books is a nonprofit publisher of international and American literature, based in the San Francisco Bay Area. Founded in 2015, Transit Books is committed to the discovery and promotion of enduring works that carry readers across borders and communities. Visit us online to learn more about our forthcoming titles, events, and opportunities to support our mission.

TRANSITBOOKS.ORG